W9-BZZ-179

MARGARET TRUMAN'S

MURDER ON THE METRO

BY MARGARET TRUMAN

Souvenir

White House Pets

Harry S. Truman

Women of Courage

Letters from Father: The Truman Family's Personal Correspondence

Bess W. Truman

Where the Buck Stops: The Personal and Private Writings of Harry S. Truman

First Ladies

The President's House: A First Daughter Shares the History and Secrets of the World's Most Famous Home

THE CAPITAL CRIMES SERIES

Murder in the White House

Murder on Capitol Hill

Murder in the Supreme Court

Murder in the Smithsonian

Murder on Embassy Row

Murder at the FBI

Murder in Georgetown

Murder in the CIA

Murder at the Kennedy Center

Murder at the National Cathedral

Murder at the Pentagon

Murder on the Potomac

Murder at the National Gallery

Murder in the House

Murder at the Watergate

Murder at the Watergate

Murder in Foggy Bottom

Murder in Havana

Murder at Ford's Theatre

Murder at Union Station

Murder at The Washington Tribune

Murder at the Opera

Murder on K Street

Murder Inside the Beltway

Monument to Murder

Experiment in Murder

Undiplomatic Murder

Internship in Murder

Deadly Medicine

Allied in Danger

MARGARET TRUMAN'S

MURDER ON THE METRO

A CAPITOL CRIMES NOVEL

JON LAND

A TOM DOHERTY ASSOCIATES BOOK • NEW YORK

This is a work of fiction. All of the characters, organizations, and events portrayed in this novel are either products of the author's imagination or are used fictitiously.

MARGARET TRUMAN'S MURDER ON THE METRO

A Forge Book
Published by Tom Doherty Associates
120 Broadway
New York, NY 10271

www.tor-forge.com

Forge® is a registered trademark of Macmillan Publishing Group, LLC.

The Library of Congress Cataloging-in-Publication Data is available upon request.

ISBN 978-1-250-23887-0 (hardcover)
ISBN 978-1-250-23886-3 (ebook)

Our books may be purchased in bulk for promotional, educational, or business use. Please contact your local bookseller or the Macmillan Corporate and Premium Sales Department at 1-800-221-7945, extension 5442, or by email at MacmillanSpecialMarkets@macmillan.com.

First Edition: February 2021

Printed in the United States of America

0 9 8 7 6 5 4 3 2 1

For Margaret Truman, trailblazer

and

Bob Diforio, who helped me walk by her side

Power does not corrupt. Fear corrupts . . . perhaps the fear of a loss of power.

—JOHN STEINBECK

PROLOGUE

CAESAREA, ISRAEL

"I'm not scared, Nana."

Lia Ganz held her three year old granddaughter, Meirav, in her arms in waist-deep water. "You're not?"

"I want to go higher! Make me go higher!"

"You're sure?"

"I'm brave, Nana, just like you."

"All right, then."

Lia tossed Meirav higher into the air and watched her splash down into the warm, crystal-clear waters off Caesarea's Aqueduct Beach. The Israeli schools were currently on spring break, accounting for crowding more typical of the weekend on this weekday, beneath the midday sun amid a piercing blue Mediterranean sky. Never a fan of crowds, Lia cringed as more beachgoers packed in around them, and she resolved to take her leave as soon as this swim was complete, assuming she could coax her granddaughter from the water.

The beach had been named for the ancient structure that adorned the sand, forming a natural barrier between modern civilization and this ancient site. The seacoast grounds of Caesarea, halfway between Tel Aviv and Haifa had been proclaimed a national park. The site had been reconstructed over a long stretch of years to create one of Israel's most attractive and fascinating archaeological locales, featuring an easy mix of the old and the new. The restored Caesarea amphitheater hosted modern-day concerts during the summer months, while the Old City featured a range of boutiques and restaurants. The new town of Caesarea itself, meanwhile, comprised luxurious neighborhoods, dominated by seaside villas, that claimed this beach as their own.

Lia watched her granddaughter bob below the surface and pop right back up, thanks to the arm floaties that her parents insisted she wear at all times if she was anywhere near the water. Lia found herself musing how handy those puffy blue things might have been when she was doing water training for the elite special ops Yamam team she'd joined after serving in the Israeli army as one of the most decorated female soldiers in the country's storied history. For forty years, Yamam commandos had operated under a veil of total secrecy. Only recently had Israel even acknowledged the existence of the country's most elite antiterrorism force, around the time the government had wanted to recognize her in a public ceremony after she had suffered wounds in a bold attack launched on a Hamas stronghold in Gaza. But she had declined, since it was all about being honored as a woman and not a soldier. And she didn't believe in heroes anymore, because all of her heroes were dead.

"One more time, Nana," Meirav pleaded, throwing herself back into Lia's arms.

Reflexively, Lia's gaze scanned the beachfront. Force of habit, she supposed, watching for anything in the scene that stood out, something different from the last time she'd checked. She couldn't say exactly what she was looking for, only that she'd know it when she spotted it.

The Americans had an expression that went "If you see something, say something." The phrase originated sometime after the infamous 9/11 attack, but seeing and saying had been part of the Israeli way of life for a half century prior to that. You learned to live defensively or, sometimes, you didn't live at all.

Today, the unseasonably warm spring temperatures and tepid breezes had brought a flood of people to the golden sand, which was all but invisible beneath all manner of chairs, blankets, towels, and shade cast by the sprawl of beach umbrellas. Lia hated those for how they limited range of vision in the area they covered, either obscuring or obliterating her view. Still, she spotted no more of note on this scan than on the last one or the one before that. The lifeguard chairs were still manned by the same young men and women—one of Lia's prime concerns, given that their height would make them formidable shooting platforms, from which any number of victims could be claimed by a decent marksman before some pistol-toting Israeli zeroed them in their sights.

"Nana?" Meirav said, pulling her grandmother's hair.

"I'm too tired, little one. My arms have nothing left."

And yet, at forty-nine, she felt too young to be a grandmother and was in as good a shape as she'd been on her last day as a field operative with Yamam. After her wounds suffered in the Gaza raid ruled her out of future missions, they'd wanted to put her behind a desk. But Lia found coordinating missions from the group's secretive headquarters in the Ayalon Valley between Tel Aviv and Jerusalem far less fulfilling than leading them, and the process left her with a helpless feeling. The *X*s and *O*s, literal marks on a dry erase board or a chalkboard, represented operatives in harm's way, who could die or be captured if the plan failed in any way. If she missed the slightest sign or signal, or neglected to consider some random factor, some of Israel's best and brightest would pay with their lives. In the field, she missed nothing. Working behind a desk to dispatch others there in her place, though, left her fearing she'd missed *everything*. When her request to return to active duty was summarily denied, Lia announced her retirement to become a full-time grandmother.

"But you're so strong, Nana," Meirav said, snuggling up against Lia's breast and letting her arm stray to the fleshy skin over her shoulder. "I found a hole."

Lia felt her granddaughter's tiny finger pushing and pressing. "It's a scar."

"What's a scar?"

"What's left when a boo-boo heals."

The little girl seemed to ponder that. "I have boo-boos, but I don't have scars."

"Only bad boo-boos leave them, little one."

Lia felt Meirav press deeper into the scar. It felt like a tickle.

"Was this a bad boo-boo, Nana?"

Lia hugged her granddaughter tighter, thinking of that final mission in Gaza. "From a bullet."

Meirav cocked her head backward to meet her grandmother's stare. "You were shot?"

"Yes."

"Did it hurt?"

"It did." Lia nodded.

"I found another," Meirav said, pushing her finger into a depression of ridged, pocked skin above the shoulder blade.

"From the same bullet, little one. Where it came out."

"Eww," Meirav uttered, making a face. "Did it hurt?"

"I don't remember."

More poking and pushing. "Who did it?"

"I don't know. It could have been any number of people."

"Did you hurt them back?"

"Maybe," Lia said, honestly not knowing the answer. "I'm not sure."

She'd suffered the wound in that nighttime Gaza raid on a Hamas stronghold where a meeting of the terrorist group's cadre had been convened. The mission had been ill-timed and hastily prepared, an overly aggressive move undertaken by a government desperate for a major victory against an indefatigable foe. Lia was second-in-command of the ten-person team. Only six made it out alive, and she'd dragged two of the bodies out herself, shot-up shoulder and all.

The democratic world and the West exulted in Israel's many successes in such missions but seldom learned of failures like this. Going back to Entebbe, Mossad had been celebrated for its dramatic strikes and never criticized for those that ended the way that night had in Gaza. That raid had been undertaken by Sayeret Matkal. Yamam was founded shortly after, to undertake missions that required the quick-strike capabilities of rapid deployment. Its superbly trained forces were originally umbrellaed under the Israeli National Police, but of late they were left answerable to Mossad.

Lia had struggled to return fire with her wounded arm, while with the other she dragged one of the downed men from the firefight. Another man fell when the squad was racing back to the extraction point, and she abandoned further fire to drag him along as well. By the time they reached the American stealth chopper, same type of Black Hawk the Navy SEALs had used in their raid on Osama bin Laden's compound, both men were dead.

Her granddaughter scrunched her face up into a scowl. "They must have been bad people."

"They were."

"Somebody should punish them."

Lia couldn't help but smile. Though she was hardly a biblical scholar, she knew her daughter and son-in-law had named their first child after the daughter of King Saul, which seemed quite appropriate for a child who was a bundle of energy forever in motion, given that the word *meirav* also meant "to maximize." Yet, in that moment, she also feared that her granddaughter would follow in her footsteps—too much of the Ganz blood pumping through her veins, which would leave her eventually wanting to spill that of Israel's enemies.

She shelved that thought for the time being and positioned herself to toss her granddaughter into the air yet again. "I'm sure somebody did."

That's when she heard the buzzing sound, something like a lawn mower growing louder as it neared an open window, a soft engine sound that Lia first took for a small motorboat or Jet Ski, until a sweep of her gaze showed nothing of the sort anywhere about.

Then what . . .

Insects, Lia thought, when she first spotted the drones. *They look like giant insects.*

Each was about four feet across, flying in a triangular pattern. The next sound, the staccato burst of gunfire, was accompanied by flashbulb-like spurts of light springing from the barrel of whatever automatic weapons had been rigged to the low-flying murder machines. Lia watched the carnage unfold with her granddaughter clutched tight against her, the sounds of shots and screams reaching her a millisecond after the initial line of bodies fell, drenching the golden sand red. The effect was like watching dominoes fall, the drones closing on the last wave of beachgoers who were trying to flee. A few had the fortune or foresight to rush toward the sea. The rest, who charged off down the open sands toward the ancient aqueduct that had lent this beach its name, did not fare nearly as well.

Lia clutched her granddaughter to her tighter still, ignoring the child's whimpers. The cries of pain and anguish from the beach pierced her eardrums like a thousand needles. A few armed Israelis bravely chased after the drones, their own pistol fire clacking away. One of the dreaded machines went down, then a second, while the third continued its deadly flight, stopping only when its ammunition was expended and it dropped from the sky with the others.

"You're hurting me, Nana, you're hurting me!"

Her granddaughter had felt more like a piece of Lia Ganz than a separate body. She eased her from her breast almost surgically.

"I'm scared, Nana! I'm scared!" Meirav sobbed, fat tears rolling down her cheeks to mix with the salty waters of the sea.

Lia hugged her tight again, both of them shaking, the warm water suddenly feeling like melted ice.

"So am I, little one," Lia said, as soothingly as she could manage. "So am I."

PART ONE

CHAPTER 1

WASHINGTON, DC; ONE WEEK LATER

Shortstop is in for the night," Kendra Rendine said into her wrist-mounted microphone from outside the vice president's bedroom door. "Repeat, Shortstop is buckled in for the night."

As head of the vice president's Secret Service security team, Rendine had personally led the detail that had accompanied Stephanie Davenport, America's first-ever female vice president, from her event that evening back home to 1 Observatory Circle. As procedure dictated, she checked the bedroom where Davenport had slept alone since the death of her husband from cancer, and then moved to the door.

"Good night, ma'am."

"You too, Coach," Davenport had said, with a smile that belied how exhausted she must have been after an exceptionally long day that had seen her up and running from the virtual crack of dawn.

"Will do, Shortstop," Rendine followed, grinning herself.

Davenport's Secret Service code name had come courtesy of a stellar career as a shortstop on Brown University's softball team the year they'd won an Ivy League championship. She'd managed all-Ivy honors, as well as honorable mention All-American. She'd attended Brown as part of the Marine Corps' officer training program before knee and shoulder injuries washed her out. She'd gone to law school and spent the early part of her career defending the poor and indigent, while acquiring a disgust for injustice that knew no bounds and had ultimately drawn her into politics, where she believed she could have the greatest effect as an agent of change.

The rest of Stephanie Davenport's life en route to the vice presidency included stints as both governor and senator, ample proving grounds even before her infectious charisma and fundraising prowess entered into the mix. Rendine had been put in charge of Davenport's Secret Service detail from literally the moment she was officially added to the ticket, meaning that she'd been with Davenport through all moments good and bad, thick and thin, glorious and tragic. The woman unceasingly impressed her, never more so than when she refused to let a recently diagnosed heart condition derail her ambitions or affect her schedule. The vice president considered the whole matter a nonissue, and as of today, only a handful of people in and out of the White House knew the whole truth—how, a month earlier, stents had opened up a trio of nearly totally blocked arteries, after surgery had been ruled out because Davenport also suffered from atrial fibrillation.

Today was one of the few days since the vice president had resumed a full working schedule that Rendine could see the strain on her features after walking even short distances. Rendine found it sad, unfair, that such a magnificent athlete in her youth could be so hobbled in middle age. But it seemed to have been exacerbated in recent days. Rendine had initially passed that off as the lingering effects of the procedure. Earlier today, though, she'd peered into the vice president's eyes and seen something other than fatigue:

Fear.

She'd been around Davenport long enough to trust her instincts, and today those instincts had told her something was bothering the vice president. It would be an unacceptable breach of protocol for Rendine to raise that issue, beyond the mundane utterance, "Is everything all right, Madam Vice President?" And she hadn't bothered with even that, since the query would have provoked nothing more than a smile and a sigh, followed by, "Thanks for asking, Coach," in typically disarming fashion.

The secluded twelve-acre compound that held the vice president's official residence at 1 Observatory Circle sat amid the seventy-two acres of park-like grounds perched on a hilltop in a stately neighborhood about two and a half miles from the White House. Built in 1893, the handsome three-story Queen Anne–style home was surrounded by a forest-like setting, complete with lush greenery, wildlife, and the serene sounds of nature that nursed Davenport to sleep on nights mild enough to leave the windows open. A kind of oasis set just footsteps away from the bustling traffic on Massachusetts Avenue.

Rendine knew the structure up and down, not a single nook or cranny escaping her attention. She'd walked every square foot on multiple occasions, to the point where she could do so blindfolded—not so much folly, since Secret Service agents were well schooled in maintaining their vigil even in the event of a blackout. This wasn't her first detail, only the first she'd ever been in charge of, a duty made all the easier by the genuine high regard and affection in which she held Stephanie Davenport. Though her training had counseled avoiding the kind of relationship that bordered on friendship, Rendine never hid her admiration for the vice president or the genuine pleasure she took in their conversations on long overseas flights and in various green rooms before an event was about to start. She counted herself fortunate to have this be the first detail she'd ever led, typical of everything she'd been taught, with a single exception: Stephanie Davenport's heart condition.

The one compromise the vice president had agreed to make was to wear a watch that monitored her heart rate 24/7, triggering an alarm in the event the slightest anomaly was detected. All Secret Service agents underwent vigorous emergency medical training, but the vice president's detail was further supplemented by having a battle-tested medic manning a shift at all times. There were three of them in the rotation, and Rendine liked them all, especially the fact that all insisted on checking Davenport's pulse, heartbeat, and blood pressure at regular intervals throughout the day. And the vice president had reluctantly agreed to give them final word on whether a trip to the hospital was warranted, on their say-so alone.

When triggered, an alarm would buzz directly in the earpiece of either Rendine or the head of the vice president's detail at the time. For redundancy, the alarm would also be sent to the Secret Service central monitoring station on the Naval Observatory grounds, which used electronic surveillance to watch for intruders or anything else requiring the attention of patrolling or posted agents. That station, too, would respond by dispatching the medic assigned to that particular detail, just in case the detail head's communicator had somehow malfunctioned. Rendine had heard and felt the annoying screech a dozen times during drills but, fortunately, never in a real-time event. Although she was a believer in the mantra that there was a first time for everything, Rendine hoped this case proved to be an exception to that.

With Vice President Davenport tucked away for the night and an agent posted directly outside her door, Rendine made a quick round of the house. She found the rigors and responsibilities of her job to be far easier to bear when she stayed active, kept in motion. Standing still left her contemplating all the things that could go wrong with a protectee, in this case the second most important person in the Secret Service's charge. She found everything buttoned up and secure as it always was, and had just decided to do a check of the exterior perimeter as well, when the familiar screech sounded in her ear.

Even though, Rendine's first thought was that it must be a malfunction, she lit out for the stairs, raising her wrist-mounted mic to her mouth.

"Stellar One," she said to the guard outside Stephanie Davenport's door, who fortuitously also served as this shift's medic, "we have an active medical alarm from Shortstop. Repeat, we have an active medical alarm from Shortstop."

"Breaching now," the guard's voice came back, using the term for entering the vice president's bedroom without pause or announcing himself.

A pause followed, Stellar One's voice returning as Rendine reached the third floor.

"Shortstop is down! Shortstop is down!"

Rendine barked orders into her mic while charging for the open door to Davenport's bedroom herself, calling for an ambulance and ordering her team to set up a secure perimeter, given that the second most powerful person in the world had been incapacitated. Her final order before reaching the bedroom was to activate a protocol whereby security around the current Speaker of the House of Representatives would be tripled immediately, since the Speaker was next in the line of succession after the vice president.

Oh my God . . .

Did Rendine say that or merely think it, when her first look inside the bedroom found the detail's medic feeling for a pulse along Stephanie Davenport's neck? She was seated in a desk chair before her laptop computer. Judging by the reddish bruise on her forehead, the vice president must have fallen forward when she lost consciousness, impact having left its mark amid the ghastly pale visage that made her features look more like a wax figure's.

"No pulse," Stellar One reported. "And she's not breathing."

The agent started to ease Davenport from the chair. Rendine moved in to help Stellar One get her lowered onto the floor, where he began to apply CPR.

"Ambulance?" he asked, when Rendine dropped to the floor on the other side of the vice president.

"Coming. Just a few minutes away."

The agent went back to performing CPR, looking over at Rendine. "A few minutes too many," he said. "We're losing her."

Without needing to be prompted, Rendine rushed to the closet and yanked the portable defibrillator from the shelf. She was well schooled in its operation but preferred to trust the process to a trained professional. And it took Stellar One all of twenty seconds to get the machine charged and paddles readied.

"Clear!"

Rendine lurched back involuntarily, as the detail medic clamped the rubber fittings across the vice president's chest. She heard the eerie whine of the machine get louder, reaching a crescendo before Stellar One pressed them downward with a *thwack!*

After an initial jolt, Stephanie Davenport's frame settled stiffly. Rendine noted her lips were blue and her complexion had turned pasty and pale.

"Charging," said Stellar One. "Clear!"

He shocked her again, drawing an even more pronounced jolt that nonetheless produced no results. The next moment, as Stellar One readied another shock with the defibrillator paddles, Rendine heard the welcome scream of the approaching sirens. That gave her hope that timely treatment might yet save the vice president's life, even though Stellar One's third try with the defibrillator produced the same results as the first two.

The detail medic looked at her grimly from the other side of Stephanie Davenport's stiff, motionless frame, uttering a deep sigh.

"I think she's gone."

CHAPTER 2

WASHINGTON, DC; THE NEXT MORNING

Not again . . .

That was Robert Brixton's first thought when his gaze locked on the woman seated across from him in the Washington Metro car. He was riding into the city amid the press of morning commuters from the apartment in Arlington, Virginia, where he now lived alone, his girlfriend Flo Combes having returned to New York.

Former girlfriend, Brixton corrected in his mind. And Flo's return to New York, where she'd opened her original clothing boutique, looked very much like it was for good this time.

Which brought his attention back to the woman wearing a hijab and bearing a strong resemblance to another Muslim woman who'd been haunting his sleep for five years now, since she'd detonated a suicide bomb inside a crowded DC restaurant, killing Brixton's daughter Janet and eleven other victims that day. He'd seen it coming, *felt* it anyway, as if someone had dragged the head of a pin up his spine. He hadn't been a cop for years at that point, having taken his skills into the private sector, but his instincts remained unchanged, always serving him well and almost always being proven right.

But today he wanted to be wrong, wanted badly to be wrong. Because if his instincts were correct, tragedy was about to repeat itself, with him bearing witness yet again, relocated from a bustling café to a crowded Metro car.

The woman wearing the hijab turned enough to meet his gaze. Brixton was unable to jerk his eyes away in time and forced the kind of smile strangers cast at each other. The woman didn't return it, just turned her focus back forward, her expression empty, as if bled of emotion. In Brixton's experience, she resembled a criminal who found strange solace in the notion of being caught after tiring of the chase. That was the suspicious side of his nature. If not for a long career covering various aspects of law enforcement, including as a private investigator with strong international ties, Brixton likely would have seen her as the other passengers in the Metro car did: a quiet woman with big, soft eyes just hoping to blend in with the scenery and not attract any attention to herself.

Without reading material of any kind, a cell phone in her grasp, or earbuds dangling. Brixton gazed about; as far as he could tell, she was the only passenger in sight, besides him, not otherwise occupied to pass the time. So in striving not to stand out, the young woman had achieved the opposite.

He studied her closer, determining that the woman didn't look tired so much as content. And, beneath her blank features, Brixton sensed something taut and resigned, a spring slowly uncoiling. Something, though, had changed in her expression since the moment their eyes had met. She was fidgeting in her seat now, seeking comfort that clearly eluded her.

Just as another suicide bomber had five years ago

If he didn't know better, he would have fully believed he was back in that DC restaurant again, granted a second chance to save his daughter, after he'd failed so horribly the first time.

FIVE YEARS AGO

What world are you in? Janet had asked a clearly distracted Brixton, then consumed by the nagging feeling dragged up his spine.

Let's go.

Daddy, I haven't finished!

Janet always called him "Daddy." Much had been lost to memory from that day, forcibly put aside, but not that, or the moments that followed. It had been the last time she'd ever called him that, and ever since, Brixton had resolvedly fought to preserve the recording that existed only in his mind. Whenever it faded, he fought to get it back, treating Janet's final address of him like a voice mail machine message from a lost loved one forever saved on his phone.

Come on.

Is something wrong?

We're leaving.

Brixton had headed to the door, believing his daughter was right behind him. He realized she wasn't only when he was through it, turning back toward the table to see Janet facing the Muslim woman wearing the hijab, who was chanting in Arabic.

Janet!

He'd started to storm back inside to get her when the explosion shattered the placid stillness of the day, an ear-splitting blast that hit him like a Category 5 wind gust to the chest and sent him sprawling to the sidewalk. His head ping-ponged off the concrete, threatening his grip on consciousness. Parts of a splintered table came flying in his direction, and he threw his arms over his face to shield it from wooden shards and other debris that caked the air, cataloging them as they soared over him in absurd counterpoint. Plates, glasses, skin, limbs, eyeglasses, knives, forks, beer mugs, chair legs and arms, calamari, boneless ribs, pizza slices, a toy gorilla that had been held by a child two tables removed from where he'd been sitting with Janet, and empty carafes of wine with their contents seeming to trail behind them like vapor trails.

The surreal nature of that moment made Brixton think he might be sleeping, all of this no more than the product of an airy dream that would be lost to memory by the time he awoke. He remembered lying on the sidewalk, willing himself to wake up, to rouse from this nightmare-fueled stupor. The worst moment of his life followed the realization that he wasn't asleep, and an imponderable wave of grief washed over him, stealing his next breath and making him wonder if he even wanted to bother trying for another.

Brixton had stumbled to his feet before what moments earlier had been a bustling café filled with happy people. Now bodies were everywhere, some piled on top of others, blood covering everything and everyone. He touched the side of his face and pulled bloody fingers away from the wound. He looked back into the café in search of his daughter but saw only a tangle of limbs and clothing where they'd been sitting.

"Oh my God," he whispered, his senses sharpening. "Janet!"

Washington's Twenty-Third Street had been crammed with pedestrians at the time of the blast, joined now by people pouring out of office buildings and other restaurants nearby, within view or earshot. Brixton's attempts to get closer to the carnage, holding out hope that Janet might still be alive, were thwarted at every turn by throngs fleeing in panic in an endless wave.

"My daughter! My daughter!" he kept crying out, as if that might make the crowd yield and the chaos recede.

It wasn't until Brixton reached the hospital that he learned that Janet hadn't made it out, had been declared one of the missing. He was serving as an agent for a private security agency outsourced to the State Department at the time, and knew all too well that "missing" meant dead. He had another daughter, Janet's older sister, who'd given him a beautiful grandson he loved dearly, but that was hardly enough to make up for the loss of Janet. And the guilt over not having dragged her out with him when she'd resisted leaving had haunted him to this very moment, when instinct told him that many on this crowded subway car might well be about to join her.

Thanks to another woman wearing a hijab. But it wasn't just that. Brixton had crossed paths with an untold number of Arab women in the five years since Janet's death, and not one before today had ever elicited in him the feeling he had now. She might have been a twin of the bomber who'd taken his daughter from him, about whom Brixton could recall only one thing.

Her eyes.

This woman had the very same shifting look, trying so hard to appear casual that it seemed she was wearing a costume, sticking out to him as much as a kid on Halloween. Brixton spun his gaze back in her direction, prepared to measure off the distance between them and how he might cover it before she could trigger her explosives.

But the young woman was gone.

Brixton looked down the center aisle cluttered with commuters clutching poles or dangling handhold straps. He spotted the young woman in the hijab an instant before she cocked her gaze briefly back in his direction, a spark of clear recognition flashing when their eyes met this time.

She knows I made her, Brixton thought, heavy with fear as he climbed to his feet.

He started after her, heart hammering in his chest, the sensation he was feeling in that dreadful moment all too familiar. He couldn't help but catalog the people he passed in the woman's wake, many of whom were either his late daughter's age or younger. Smiling, gabbing away on their phones, reading a book, or lost between their earbuds without any knowledge of how horribly their lives might very well be about to change. If he needed any further motivation to keep moving and stop the potential suicide bomber through any means necessary, that was it. Doubt vanished, Brixton trusting his instincts in a way he hadn't on that tragic day five years ago when he was still a de facto agent for the U.S. government.

Janet . . .

In Brixton's mind, this was no longer a Metro car but the same restaurant where a suicide bomber had taken a dozen lives and wounded dozens more. And he found himself faced with the chance to do today what he hadn't done five years ago.

Stop!

Had Brixton barked that command out loud, or merely formed the thought in his head? Other passengers were staring at him now, his surge up the aisle disturbing the meager comfort of their morning routine.

Ahead of him, the woman wearing the hijab had picked up her pace. Brixton spotted her dipping a hand beneath a jacket that seemed much too heavy for the unseasonably mild Washington, DC, spring. His experience with the State Department, working for the shadowy Strategic Intelligence Tasking group, or SITQUAL, along with his time as a cop, told him she was likely reaching for the pull cord that would detonate the suicide vest concealed under bulky sweatshirt and jacket.

If you could relive the day of your daughter's death, what would you do?

I'd shoot the bitch before she had the chance to yank that cord, Brixton thought, drawing his SIG Sauer P-226 nine-millimeter pistol. It had survived his tenure with SITQUAL as his weapon of choice, well balanced and deadly accurate.

He could feel the crowd around him recoiling, pulling back, when they saw the pistol steadied in his hand. Several gasped. A woman cried out. A kid dropped his cell phone into Brixton's path, and he accidentally kicked it aside.

"Stop!"

He had shouted out loud for sure this time, the dim echo bouncing off the Metro car's walls as it wound in thunderous fashion through the tube. The young woman in the hijab was almost to the rear door separating this car from the next. Brixton was close enough to hear the *whoosh* as she engaged the door, breaking the rule that prohibited passengers from such car-hopping.

"*Stop!*"

She turned her gaze back toward him as he raised his pistol, ready to take the shot he hadn't taken five years ago. Passengers cried out and shrank from his path. The door hissed closed, the young woman regarding him vacantly through the safety glass as she stretched her hand out blindly to activate the door accessing the next car back.

And that's when she stumbled. Brixton was well aware of the problems with this new 7000 series of Metro railcars, after federal safety officials had raised repeated concerns about a potential safety risk involving the barriers between cars, which were designed to prevent blind and visually impaired people from inadvertently walking off the platform and falling through the gap. The issue initially was raised by disability rights advocates, who argued that the rubber barriers were spaced too far apart, leaving enough room for a small person to slip through.

The young woman wearing the hijab was small. And she started to slip through.

Brixton watched her drop from sight an instant before an all-too-familiar flash created a starburst before him. He felt light, floating, as if there was nothing beneath his feet, because for a moment there wasn't. The piercing blast that buckled the Metro car door blew him backward, the percussion lifting him up and then dropping him back down, still in motion. He was sliding across the floor amid a demolition derby of commuters crashing into each other as the train barreled along. Separated now from its rearmost cars, what remained of the train whipsawed through the tube with enough force to lift this car from the rails and send it alternately slamming up against one side and then the other.

Brixton maintained the presence of mind to realize his back and shoulders had come to rest awkwardly against a seat, even as the squeal of the brakes engaging grew into a deafening wail and his eyes locked on the car door that, to him, looked as if someone had used a can opener to carve a jagged fissure along the center of its buckled seam. The car itself seemed to be swaying—left, right, and back again—but he couldn't be sure if that was real or the product of the concussion he may have suffered from the blast wave or from slamming up against the seat.

Unlike five years ago, Brixton had come to rest sitting up, staring straight ahead at the back door of the Metro car, which was currently held at an awkwardly angled perch, nearly sideways across the tracks. He realized that, through it all, he'd somehow maintained his grasp on his pistol, now steadied at the twisted remnants of the Metro car door, as if he expected the young woman to reappear at any moment.

Janet . . .

A wave of euphoria washed over Brixton as, this time, he thought he'd saved her, making the best of the do-over that fate had somehow granted him. The Metro car floor felt soft and cushiony, leaving him with the dreamlike sense that he was drifting away toward the bright lights shining down from the ceiling.

And then there was only darkness.

CHAPTER 3

WASHINGTON, DC

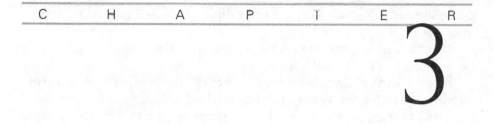

Private detective?" the Washington, DC Metropolitan Police Department detective whose ID read "Rogers" asked Brixton, handing him back his wallet in the makeshift trauma center that had been set up on the Metro platform closest to where the damaged train had ultimately come to a rest.

Fortunately, the station in question was only a few hundred yards from that point, easing the chore of getting the injured treated and of safely evacuating the train's passengers on the backmost three cars, which had been separated by the blast set off by the suicide bomber. The entire Metro system had been shut down as a precaution; DC authorities were very wary that this attack might have been part of a more coordinated, orchestrated effort. Brixton imagined both city and transit officers checking anyone wearing the kind of bulky clothing that might conceal a suicide vest of the type the young woman had triggered when she slipped between the train cars.

Brixton was sitting upon a treatment table set off by itself amid the triage arrangement, which left him as a lower priority, after an initial examination had revealed no more than a possible concussion. He wasn't sure how Detective Rogers had learned of the role he'd played, and Brixton chose not to consider the result if his suspicions had not resulted in his chasing the bomber from the Metro car. Only the fact that she'd triggered her suicide vest between the two cars had kept casualties to a bare minimum, in stark contrast to the attack that had claimed his daughter's life five years before.

"You said you're a private detective," Rogers repeated.

Brixton's decision to open his own private investigation agency in Washington, DC, hadn't been an easy one, given that nothing good ever seemed to have happened to him in the nation's capital. Born in Brooklyn, he'd begun his career in law enforcement in the city, spending four years as a uniformed officer. He'd also met and married his now ex-wife there. The marriage had proven no more successful than his stint as a Washington cop. But it had yielded two wonderful daughters Brixton deeply loved, one of whom was gone.

"Presently," Brixton affirmed. "I used to work as an adjunct for the State Department."

"Adjunct?"

Brixton nodded. "I was attached to a private security arm that served

State's interests, mostly keeping their diplomats safe in overseas deployments."

"Diplomats," Rogers repeated, leaving it there and jotting down something on a memo pad he was holding.

Brixton didn't bother elaborating further on the more clandestine nature of SITQUAL's job description, waiting for the detective to continue instead. He tried to study Rogers closer, but his mind wouldn't focus, to the point that Brixton had to continue looking at the man to remind himself what he looked like. He noticed a tablet of some kind, likely an iPad, protruding from one of the side pockets of Rogers's rumpled sports jacket.

"You mentioned there was something about the woman that made you suspicious, Mr. Brixton."

"What I didn't mention was that this wasn't my first experience with suicide bombers."

"Did the others come while you were deployed overseas?"

Brixton shook his head. "Just a few miles from here, actually. Five years ago."

Recognition flashed in Rogers's expression. "I thought your name sounded familiar."

Brixton looked about the platform, amazed by the rapid response a combination of Washington and federal officials had managed. He knew there were teams from nearby hospitals who acted as a kind of medical SWAT team, prepared to deploy at a moment's notice in an emergency. He imagined that all the equipment in view now—from the portable exam tables to the various medical instruments and supplies—had been prepped and ready, stored on mobile transport units in anticipation, even expectation, of a moment like this.

Fortunately, none of the injuries he witnessed being treated extended beyond bumps, bruises, and wounds that required minimal stitching. By now, anyone more seriously injured would have been transported to local emergency rooms turned trauma centers. Brixton found himself wondering what this scene would have looked like had the bomber detonated her suicide vest inside the car instead of outside it. The mere thought made him shudder.

"We'll be able to pull shots of the bomber off the security footage," Rogers said, as if reading his mind. "My guess is we'll have a name by dinnertime. She's likely to be in the system somewhere. Anyway, I understand now."

"Understand what?"

"What triggered your suspicions," Rogers told him. "Strange, isn't it, how your being on that particular Metro car at that particular time may have saved dozens of lives?"

"I don't know if I'd call it strange. Fated maybe, but not strange."

"Life does have a way of evening things out."

"Sometimes. Not often enough, in my experience, Detective."

"So you acted on impulse."

"More like instinct," Brixton corrected. "I spent twenty years as a cop before I got into the security racket."

"And now you're a cop again, only with your own shingle. Does your work still involve security?"

"Sometimes. I have an office with a DC law firm," Brixton explained, thinking of his best friend, Mackensie Smith. "And I draw much of my business from their caseload. Not exciting, but it pays the bills."

"And gives you license to carry a gun in the city."

"Good thing, as far as this morning goes."

"Still a pretty rare commodity these days."

Something in Rogers's tone irked Brixton more than the substance of his words. "Are you suggesting something, Detective?"

"You don't fancy yourself a hunter, do you, Mr. Brixton?"

"Hunter?"

"Staking out public places to relive the worst moment of your life in the hope of a better ending."

"Was that a question?"

"Do you have an answer?"

"I was on my way to my office, Detective. The only thing I was hunting was work."

"So you had a feeling, like a premonition. Tell me, Mr. Brixton, what would you have done if the bomber hadn't been sufficiently spooked to change cars?"

It was a question Brixton had avoided asking himself. "I don't know."

"Would you have shot her? Made a citizen's arrest?"

"I don't know."

"And you don't work for the government anymore."

"No."

"Or anyone private along a similar track."

"I don't know what that means."

"Were you following the bomber? Did you have reason to suspect something you were following up on behalf of a party or parties unknown?"

"I had reason to believe she was a suicide bomber. I already explained that."

"Who was she working for?"

"ISIS, al-Qaeda . . . Take your pick."

"I'd rather take yours, Mr. Brixton. Was she attached to a cell? Might that cell still be active in the city? Are there more attacks coming?"

"Whoa, slow down, Detective," Brixton said, not bothering to hide the annoyance in his voice.

"Then answer my questions."

"The answer to all of them is a definitive 'I don't know.' I just happened to be there."

"Right place, right time?"

Brixton turned his gaze again on the relatively minor injuries being treated in the makeshift trauma center. "I'd say so. Wouldn't you?"

"That depends."

"On what?"

"The truth."

"Which I've been telling you."

"That fate or coincidence put you on that Metro car five years after another suicide bomber killed your daughter."

"I once read that *coincidence* is another word for *God*."

"So you're God now, Mr. Brixton?"

"No, but maybe he's the one who made sure I was on that train this morning."

Rogers's expression remained flat, empty. "Do you have any reason to suspect the young woman may have had an accomplice?"

"No."

"You didn't see her engage with anyone else, either before or after she boarded the train."

"She didn't speak to anyone on the train. I don't know about before because I wasn't there. She was already on the train when I boarded."

"You're sure of that?"

"I'm sure she was already seated."

"Maybe she got on the train before you. Maybe you followed her on."

"Why don't you check the footage from the security cameras? That will confirm what I'm telling you, that she didn't board the train at the same station I did."

Rogers nodded, not looking at all convinced by Brixton's assertions. "What do you suppose the odds are of the same guy being on the scene of two separate suicide bombings that fit virtually the same M.O.?"

"Pretty high, I imagine. But this one was plenty different from the first."

Rogers flipped his memo pad closed. "How's that, Mr. Brixton?"

"My daughter didn't die this morning, Detective."

CHAPTER 4

WASHINGTON, DC

Shortly after Detective Rogers had finally taken his leave, Brixton was escorted up to street level to be transported to Georgetown University Medical Center to be fully checked out. He boarded the back of an ambulance, joining two other passengers he vaguely recognized from the crowded Metro car, who'd also suffered potential concussions. The street had been shut down to allow the area outside the Metro station to become a way station for emergency vehicles and first responders. There weren't many bystanders or onlookers about; the city was likely undergoing a soft evacuation, given the possibility that the Metro attack presaged a wider, 9/11-like wave of them. So far there had been no further reports, and by the time the ambulance in which Brixton was riding reached the medical center's emergency room, the potential code red had been dimmed to yellow.

Upon arriving at the already chaotic emergency room, Brixton insisted on going to the back of the line to be checked out. Others were clearly in more need, as much for reassurance as for treatment. The injured knew to a man and woman that no matter how shaken they were, they had come very close to being part of an unspeakable tragedy. While they might not have been aware of the specific physics of what the typical deadly contents of a suicide bomb could have done in an enclosed environment like a Metro car, as Brixton was, they certainly understood that the vast majority of them would be nursing far more than minor injuries if the bomb had gone off inside it.

He looked about the jam-packed area where his fellow passengers had been brought and, for the first time really, considered his own actions. What would have happened if his suspicions hadn't provoked the bomber to flee the car? What if he had ignored his instincts and had not studied her in a way that had clearly unnerved her? In that sense, the death of his own daughter may well have saved dozens of lives, at long last lending a measure of sense to that tragedy. He had told Detective Rogers that he'd once read that *coincidence* was another word for *God*. But there was another quote Brixton found even more oddly appropriate to explain his presence on that Metro train this morning, from John Lennon no less: "There's nowhere you can be that isn't where you're meant to be."

And fate had placed him in that Metro car, just as it had placed him in that restaurant with his daughter five years ago. He'd been plagued so much over that period by the question of why Janet had died while he had lived. Perhaps, at long last, this morning had provided the answer.

He continued rotating his gaze about, occasionally encountering a grateful look from someone who recognized him and clearly understood that his actions were what had forced the suicide bomber from the car. He took no special pleasure in being proclaimed a hero, especially since he'd felt like the polar opposite of that after he'd failed to save Janet.

The sound of the automatic doors sliding open turned his gaze in that direction, and he spotted Mackensie Smith barreling in. He hesitated only long enough to spot Brixton before resuming his charge.

"Oh my God, Robert, oh my God . . ."

Brixton rose to greet him and Mac swallowed him in a hug, his trembling making Brixton quiver himself.

"Thank God you called. If you hadn't, when you didn't show up at the office, I might have . . ."

Mac let his remark trail off. No reason to complete the thought, since the rest was understood.

"Thanks for coming down, Mac," Brixton said, squeezing the older man's shoulders.

He'd lived with Mackensie Smith and his wife, Annabel, in their apartment after the media circus had camped outside of his, in the wake of his gunning down of a sitting congressman's son, whom he was certain was complicit in the terrorist bombing five years ago. And it had been Mac who had invited him to set up shop in one of his law firm's offices to both take much of the firm's investigative work while also having a base to find his own. In that moment, Brixton remembered he'd been on that particular train this morning specifically because Mac had asked to see him earlier than he normally came in—something else, in other words, he had to thank his friend for.

A couple who'd occupied the next two chairs over got up to leave, freeing space for Mac when Brixton sat back down. Mac clutched his forearm and showed no signs of letting go.

"I thought you'd be answering questions from the police by now," he said.

"They questioned me at the scene." Brixton laid his free hand atop the one with which Mac was clutching his forearm. "Don't think I'm going to need your guest room this time."

"Offer's always open, Robert. You know that."

Brixton finally slid his arm out from Mac's grasp. "What's wrong, Mac?"

"Are you really asking me that? First, news of the vice president's tragic death, and now this?"

At that, Smith moved his gaze to one of the emergency room's wall-mounted flat-screen televisions, now featuring a split screen of the bombing's aftermath and the tragic news about Vice President Stephanie Davenport, who had died of a heart attack the previous night.

"There's something else," Brixton said.

"That's not enough?"

"What did you want to see me about this morning?"

Smith hedged. "What's the difference? It can wait."

"New case?"

"I said it can wait."

Smith seemed suddenly reluctant to meet Brixton's gaze. "That's what I thought."

"It's nothing."

"Then why are you lying?"

"About what?"

"The fact that it's about nothing. Whenever people say that, it's almost always quite the opposite."

His best friend very much seemed like he desperately wanted to be somewhere else. "How many lives did you save this morning, Robert?"

"I wasn't counting."

"Could have been as many as fifty, if that bomb had gone off inside the car."

"You're changing the subject."

Smith nodded. "Anything to take my mind off the vice president. I knew her, you know. Quite well in fact. Did you ever have the pleasure?"

"You're changing the subject again, Mac."

"I thought you could use the distraction."

"What did you want to see me about this morning?"

"It can wait, Robert."

"You said that already."

"And it's still true." Smith fidgeted, shifting in search of a more comfortable position. "You call Flo?"

"No."

"Why?"

"We're no longer together."

"Something I've never quite understood."

"We grew apart, Mac. What can I say?"

"More than you have already, for starters," Smith scoffed. "You don't think she's worried out of her mind, regardless?"

"She'd have no way to know I was on that train, unless my name's already gotten out. Please tell me it hasn't, Mac."

"Not to my knowledge."

"Because I don't want that kind of attention again."

"Flo called Annabel, you know."

"No, I didn't," Brixton said. "When?"

"Last week, the week before maybe. She was worried about you."

"I'm sure Annabel reassured her."

"As much as she could."

"What's that mean?"

"We've been worried about you, too, Robert."

"Is that what you wanted to see me about this morning, Mac?"

Mackensie Smith's expression changed, his thoughts veering. "You were carrying on the train, I assume."

Brixton tapped his holstered SIG Sauer, giving his friend a pass on not answering his question. "Sure."

"Did you think about shooting the bomber?"

"I followed her up the aisle when my presence made her uncomfortable. I couldn't see her hands, Mac. Figured she might be holding the trigger cord, and I was afraid if I shot her she would have yanked it, even involuntarily, inside the car."

"Makes sense. You'll come out of this one just fine," Smith assured him.

"I already have—relatively, anyway."

"Mr. Brixton. Mr. Robert Brixton. Please come to the reception desk," a voice blared over the emergency room's PA system.

Brixton stood back up, feeling a bit woozy on his feet.

"Easy there," Mackensie Smith said, rising to support him.

"Must be my turn."

Smith accompanied him over to the reception desk, which was nearly blocked by people milling about, waiting to ask about loved ones. Before Brixton could make his way to the front, a pair of men with DC Metro police badges dangling from their necks slid before him.

"Who said you could leave the scene, Mr. Brixton?" asked a detective who looked vaguely familiar to him.

"Excuse me?" Brixton posed, as Mackensie Smith shouldered his way alongside him.

The bigger detective, who had a bald pate, shiny with perspiration, flashed his badge. "Detectives Lanning and Banks, Mr. Brixton. A uniform placed you away from the other passengers in triage and told you to wait for us."

Brixton realized the bald detective, Lanning, had been part of the team that had investigated the suicide bombing five years ago, the local liaison. "Yes, that uniform told me to wait for a detective, who would be questioning me."

"But you left anyway."

Brixton exchanged a glance with Mac Smith. "Only after the detective showed up and questioned me about my actions and what I witnessed on the train."

"After *who* questioned you?" Lanning asked him.

"Detective Rogers."

Now it was Lanning's and Banks's turn to exchange a glance, before Lanning resumed. "I don't know who you spoke with, Mr. Brixton, but there's no Detective Rogers on the force."

CHAPTER 5

TEL AVIV-YAFO, ISRAEL

The location of Mossad headquarters remains one of the world's best kept secrets. Any number of structures have been "positively" identified as the spy agency's home over the decades, but confirmation has always remained muffled. Whether due to subterfuge, distraction, clever disinformation, or a combination of those and more, the upshot has been to shroud the organization's headquarters, along with its very existence, in secrecy. There were even tales of three separate buildings, with personnel regularly shifted from one to the other, to confuse would-be attackers and infiltrators.

Lia Ganz knew this to be the product of myth as much as anything. The one true headquarters of Mossad, where the day-to-day business of protecting the Jewish state took place, was located in the Yafo section of Tel Aviv, in a slate-colored cube of interconnected slabs of buildings that were practically invisible to any form of overhead surveillance. There were just enough neighboring structures to offer camouflage and render the complex utterly innocuous and practically undetectable by drivers cruising past along the nearby roads. In fact, the placement of those buildings was strategic down to the last inch, to create that precise effect. Tens of thousands of Israelis must have looked in the direction of Mossad headquarters every year, taking away no recognition or acknowledgment that anything was there at all.

The meeting she'd requested had finally been granted, a full week after the drone attack that had killed more than fifty Israeli beachgoers at Caesarea and wounded twice that number. Many of the dead and wounded were children, and Lia had woken up every night since in a cold sweat, plagued by visions of her and her granddaughter being on the beach, instead of in the water, at the moment of the attack.

Moshe Baruch, chief of Mossad, was standing by a window that looked out over greater Tel Aviv, hands clasped behind his back, maybe regarding Lia's reflection in the glass and maybe not. Standing behind him skewed the perspective, still leaving her, at five foot nine, clearly taller than one of her true mentors, by three inches. Her eyes fell over her own reflection, making her think for a split second it was someone else's.

When did I get this old?

But it wasn't that so much as a drawn look of fatigue and weariness, visible even in this skewed version of her reflection in window glass. In point of fact, the wan reflection staring back at her now had only taken form after she left Mossad, as opposed to being fostered by so many years of built-up pressure. It was as though losing the purpose that had so long defined her had sapped her strength and left her too much time to ponder the death of her own husband, a captain in the Israeli Defense Forces, during a never-reported enemy incursion into the Golan Heights a decade before.

"We anticipated a drone attack. We planned for it, prepared for it." Baruch finally turned from the window toward her, regarding Lia with the same blank expression he'd worn while looking out into the expanse between here and downtown Tel Aviv. "But not like this. No detectors at such a beach, no advance warning systems or defensive measures. No place to hide."

Baruch's voice was flat and monotone, but laced with an undercurrent of suppressed tension that left Lia thinking he might erupt at any moment.

"Of course, it should have been anticipated. *I* should have anticipated it." He seemed to regard Lia for the first time. "You were there."

"With my granddaughter."

The Mossad chief's eyes flashed. "One of the worst attacks we've ever suffered, and our sources have gone quiet on the possible perpetrator. No actionable intelligence, Colonel," Baruch continued, referring to her by her Israel Defense Forces rank. "Nothing at all."

"Ballistics?"

"Ordinary five point five six load. Available pretty much anywhere in the world. The weapons systems were modified, shaved-down heavy machine guns, internal drum fed, a hundred rounds each."

Lia did the math. The saturation of bodies occupying the beach had made for an easy kill box. Almost literally like shooting fish in a barrel, as the Americans might say. A hundred and fifty dead and wounded in total from three hundred rounds fired. The thought made her shudder. And when the shudder passed, the same series of sensations that had followed the initial sleepless nights since returned: frustration, rage, and the desire for revenge.

It was a combination that Lia Ganz, and all who had fought so passionately to preserve the State of Israel, knew all too well. It was the emotional core that defined their very being, the very basis of their efforts in standing as an eternal David against an equally eternal Goliath. There were some in the political and social arena whose view of that had changed, to the point where Israel had become too much the Goliath over the years and had lost sight of life from the perspective of David.

For those like her, though, the perspective never changed, because it was based wholly on the mission before her at any given time, a transaction to be completed expeditiously and successfully. The evil she had pursued over the course of her long career was no different from that revealed during the War of Independence in the wake of World War II, or the Six-Day War, or the Yom Kippur War, or any of the other wars, named and unnamed, that had followed. It all made for a mind-numbing experience with years, eras, and causes growing indistinguishable from one another, joined together by the singularity of the moment, in which nothing changed but everything was different. The distinction was often lost on those who lacked appreciation for the Israeli mind-set.

"There must have been a targeting system," Lia said, picking up where her thinking had left off.

"Two working in tandem, actually, both motion and heat. The mechanisms were damaged, but not enough to stop us from tracking down their source. Little solace at this point, I'm afraid."

"Only one thing will give us solace at this point," she told the head of Mossad.

They stood facing each other, with the sun's angle through the darkened windows brightening the room. It remained a mystery to Lia how such glass could keep others from seeing in while allowing those inside to see out with crystal clarity. She found that an apt metaphor for how Israel had managed to survive all the bloodshed it has endured.

Baruch's expression tightened. "Is that why the Lioness of Judah has come here today?"

It had been Baruch who'd given Lia that moniker, a play on the national Israeli symbol of the Lion of Judah, named for an ancient tribe formed of the descendants of the fourth son of Jacob and drawn from a blessing Jacob had once made over the favorite of his sons. Baruch had been her shepherd since 2000, when Lia had been chosen to serve in the Caracal Battalion, the first ever in which female soldiers served in combat. It was named Caracal after a small cat whose gender was indistinguishable, and the battalion ultimately was 70 percent women.

She had risen to commander in 2009, when a platoon she was leading responded to a terrorist incursion over the Egyptian border, which resulted in a firefight that climaxed when Lia herself had shot one of the terrorists who was wearing a suicide vest, detonating the explosives. The terrorists who survived fled back over the Egyptian border. That was the first time they'd wanted to give her a medal, but Lia opted instead for a transfer to the elite special operations division Yamam, becoming the first and still the only female to have served in that unit. And only Baruch knew the extent of her exploits, which had finally ended with the wounds she'd suffered in the ill-fated Gaza incursion three years before.

"Because," Baruch continued, "this clearly isn't a social call."

"I need to come back in," Lia told him.

"You *need*," he mimicked.

"What I heard, what I saw, how close I came . . . Whoever was behind this has to pay."

"And you'd like to be the one to make them, even though you're out now."

"*Because* I'm out, and not for that long either. Whoever's behind this has inevitably left cracks too small for even your best active agents to slip through. They won't be expecting an old grandmother to come knocking."

Baruch scoffed at her remark. "You're not old, Colonel."

"No, but I am a grandmother. And my granddaughter was with me on that beach, in the water at the time, which was the only thing that saved our lives."

"An early introduction to the ways of Israel for Meirav."

Lia nodded reflectively, impressed that Moshe Baruch knew her granddaughter's name. "Just before it . . . happened, she'd poked her finger into one of my old scars. This attack, being there to feel those moments, opened up an old one. Scar tissue may not bleed, but the thing I can't get out of my mind was the smell of blood drifting out over the sea. I go to bed smelling it and I wake up smelling it."

"With not much sleep in between, I'm guessing."

"No," Lia affirmed, "not much. Not much at all."

Baruch continued to regard her, his blank expression keeping his thoughts from her while urging her on.

"I think about a lot of things in those hours, but mostly about how I've never felt more helpless. How there would have been nothing I could have done, nothing at all, had one of the drones turned over the water. I never want to feel that way again, and I know only one way to assure that I don't have to."

Moshe Baruch stepped back, so that the fresh shaft of light illuminated only her, leaving him in the shadows. "Last time I checked, Colonel, you were retired."

"No one ever retires from service to Israel."

"Then tell me," Baruch continued, "what does the Lioness of Judah need from me, from Mossad?"

"This twin targeting system interests me."

Baruch flirted with a smile. "I knew it would."

"We find its maker and we find our target."

Baruch nodded a single time and moved for his desk. The clear protective blotter on it was empty save for a laptop computer and a single thumb drive, which Lia hadn't noticed until that moment. Wordlessly, he picked up the drive and brought it to her, squeezing her hand into a fist around it.

"You had this prepared for me," Lia realized.

"Yes."

"You knew I'd be coming, didn't you, Commander?"

This time a slight smile broke over Baruch's expression, the sun between them again splashing up from the thin carpeting. "It's just 'Moshe' now. You're retired, remember? A grandmother, with time now for bedtime stories and fairy tales with happy endings. But be warned, Colonel, not all stories have empty endings."

Lia Ganz held his stare, looking at him with the same determination and gritty assurance as she had in the years she'd been under his command. "This one will."

CHAPTER 6

WASHINGTON, DC

I don't know who you spoke with, Mr. Brixton, but there's no Detective Rogers on the force.

Detective Lanning's statement back at the hospital had thrown Brixton's senses even more out of whack. He had grown increasingly stringent about being able to explain everything around him—the product, he supposed, of being a control freak. Truth be told, though, he knew of no professional in his line of work who wasn't. And getting thrown for a loop in this way left him grasping for answers and explanations about whoever this Detective Rogers might have been.

Of course, it could be that Rogers was new to the department, either promoted or transferred in. Given that there were so many passengers and other witnesses to question, it was even possible he'd been loaned out to DC Metro from the Baltimore PD, even Bethesda, or possibly the Maryland State Police. Brixton recalled the apparent authenticity of the badge dangling by a lanyard from Rogers's neck, but a combination of the Metro platform's murkiness and the lingering effects of what he'd just experienced on the train had conspired to keep him from checking any more about the badge than that. An amateur mistake.

Yup, I'm getting old, all right.

That fact did nothing to mollify him, and nothing would until he figured out, first, who Detective Rogers really was and, second, what he'd been trying to learn from talking to him. The man could have been a journalist, but they were normally easier to spot.

Because of the clutter and lack of available space in the emergency room, Brixton had adjourned with the detectives to a shaded area outside the medical center. They all sat down at a picnic table, where workers likely went to eat their lunch. Mackensie Smith had stayed with him through the detectives' interview. Many of their questions were the same as those that Rogers had posed, some were not, and several were repetitive, phrased in varying ways to provoke a different response from the one Brixton had originally provided.

Detectives Lanning and Banks were clearly suspicious about his presence on the Metro car, seeming to suggest concern over him taking on the role of some vigilante cruising the city in search of lives to save and punishment to dispense. The fact that he'd only drawn his gun but not used it, trailed the bomber up the aisle but not chased her, left Brixton baffled by an assumption they'd come to that wasn't supported at all by the facts.

Having used such an interrogation technique himself on multiple occasions, he knew this to be a means not only to stir new memories and potentially incite fresh thinking but also to trip him up. Brixton didn't blame the detectives for their suspicions at first, though he quickly tired of their repetitive, redundant questions, which clearly indicated that their assessment of him was wrong, to the point of rendering the entire interrogation moot.

"I believe, gentlemen," Mac had said, finally intervening, "that we've accomplished everything we're going to here today. You have my client's contact information, as well as mine, and if you wish to speak with him again, I suggest calling me first to make the arrangements. Are we clear?"

Lanning and Banks had no choice but to acquiesce, their expressions making their displeasure known.

"So I'm your client now," Brixton said to Mac, after they took their leave.

"For five minutes anyway."

"Given that we have privilege between us, care to share with me what you wanted to talk about in the office this morning?"

"Get yourself checked out first, Robert. We'll have plenty of time to talk later."

After Brixton was diagnosed, not surprisingly, with a mild concussion, Smith drove him back to his apartment in Arlington, saying that they could talk then. But those plans were waylaid when an emergency summoned the lawyer back to his office as soon as he dropped Brixton off, leaving Brixton to wonder if Mac might've called himself to put off their discussion further.

Upstairs, he mixed himself a drink, even though the doctor had told him not to consume any alcohol, and switched on the television, even though watching any screen was prohibited as well. So was reading, which Brixton intended to do as soon as *The Washington Post* arrived tomorrow, as was his custom every morning.

He hadn't told the doctor about his previous experience with terrorist bombers, because he knew—or at least feared—what to expect in view of that. And, sure enough, he found himself pacing the floor, unable to sit down and rest, the death of his oldest daughter feeling as if it had happened this morning instead of five years ago. Brixton knew he was suffering from a form of PTSD, in which a traumatic incident stokes intensely powerful memories of a similar event from the past. It was like losing Janet a second time.

The concussion must have been worse than doctors originally diagnosed. They had not ordered a CT scan, with so many of the train's passengers ahead of him, but Brixton found himself having bouts of disorientation through the night, as well as dizzy spells and some minor short-term memory loss. He would decide to do something and forget what it had been while he was moving to prepare whatever needed to be prepared. He kept trying to change the channels on the television, but to no avail, because he'd accidentally put the remote in the wrong mode by pressing a key he thought was a number.

Brixton went through the night like that, but he felt much better the following morning and made some calls to sources to see how the investigation was going and if any further information on the bomber had turned up. By all indications, she was in the United States on a student visa and was enrolled at George Washington University, but she was currently on leave for unspecified reasons. The young woman's fingerprints had drawn a blank with the Automated Fingerprint Identification System, and neither the name she went by—Ursa Raheim—nor her facial likeness received hits from any of the various terrorist watch lists floating around.

He was between such calls when his cell phone rang. He recognized the number but couldn't remember from where.

Maybe I'm not doing better, after all . . .

"Robert Brixton," he greeted.

"Robert, it's Kendra Rendine," said the Secret Service agent with whom he'd coordinated on several occasions while working for SITQUAL.

"I'm so sorry about Vice President Davenport, Kendra. I know the high regard you held her in and how much you liked her."

"I'm sorry, too, Robert, for your finding yourself in the midst of another terrorist attack."

"One with a much happier ending, though."

"Thank God. And it's actually the vice president that I wanted to talk to you about. I need help making sense of something."

"I'm hardly an expert on heart conditions, Kendra."

"That's okay; I'm not looking for one. Because I don't believe a heart condition killed Stephanie Davenport. I think she was murdered."

CHAPTER 7

ARLINGTON, VIRGINIA

Brixton was just getting ready to head out to meet with Kendra Rendine when his intercom buzzed. He'd downloaded an app onto his phone that he'd synched with the building software. Clicking on the app's icon brought up the face of Mackensie Smith standing in plain view of the security camera outside the apartment building's entrance.

"Mac," he greeted.

"Glad I caught you, Robert. Mind if I come up?"

Brixton almost said he was about to leave for a meeting, but he didn't feel like explaining the details. "Sure," he said instead. "I'll buzz you in."

He opened the door and waited for Mac to emerge from the elevator just down the hall. The chime sounded mere moments after Brixton had buzzed him in, and he ushered Mac inside after the man had made the brief walk.

"So, to what do I owe the pleasure of such a surprise visit?" Brixton asked, closing the door behind them.

"I can't get this Detective Rogers thing out of my head, Robert. Why would someone run the risk of impersonating a police detective just to talk to you?"

"With all the chaos, I don't think there was much of a risk. Whoever he is, this man was well versed enough in these things to know he'd be able to steal a few minutes with me."

"Even though you were an eyewitness to what happened?"

"But nothing I did was actionable. I drew my gun but never used it. When you boil things down, all I really did was get up and walk down the aisle."

"Following a woman you suspected to be a suicide bomber."

"I never confronted or even spoke to her. And we can't even be a hundred percent certain that me spooking the young woman is what led her to change cars."

"How about ninety-nine?"

"I'll grant you that, Mac." Brixton smiled.

"Then grant me this, too: I want to put you with a sketch artist, see if we can use the result to get this fake detective identified. You didn't happen to hand him anything, did you? Something he may have touched and then returned, so we'd have his fingerprints?"

Brixton shook his head. "I may have been more out of it than I thought, because of the lingering shock and the concussion, but I can tell you his badge and ID were either authentic or a perfect forgery."

"Did you notice any security cameras on the platform, if any were angled where you were triaged prior to transport to Georgetown?"

"I never thought to look. I had other things on my mind."

"Well, a camera must've caught this guy at some point, if not on the platform then up in the station itself. I think there might be one trained on the spot where the escalator spills onto the platform."

"I've been thinking along those lines, too, Mac, and what I keep coming back to is the timing."

"How's that?"

"Whoever this Rogers was, how did he get there so fast? Even more, how did he learn of my specific involvement? I remember filling in a few uniformed Metro cops on what had happened. But they were too busy getting the passengers from both sections of the train to safety to repeat what I'd told them so quickly."

"So answer your own question, Robert."

"I don't remember it. I've got a concussion, remember?"

"The question was, How did Detective Rogers learn of your involvement?"

"He couldn't. At least, there's no easy way to explain it, save for one."

"What's that?"

"He was already on the platform, Mac, waiting with the other commuters for the train to come in."

Smith weighed that possibility. "Except, if the bomber had been successful—if it wasn't for you, in other words—the train never would've made it to the station."

"Exactly."

"You think he was working with the bomber."

"I do, Mac. In some respect. But if he was involved, it would make no sense for him to be waiting for a bomber whose remains would need to be scraped off the walls."

Smith nodded. "Unless she failed to act, or the suicide vest malfunctioned, and he was there to deal with either of those eventualities."

"There's another possibility," Brixton realized.

"What's that?"

"That he had eyes on that young woman somehow and detonated the bomb himself remotely, when it looked like she was running."

Brixton recalled the tablet sticking out of the pocket of the man's sport jacket. It wasn't too much of a reach to believe he could have hacked into the car's security cameras and was following everything that happened in real time. That would explain how he recognized Brixton, off by himself on the platform, and knew of his involvement.

"As a matter of fact," he started, and proceeded to fill Mackensie Smith in on the conclusions he just reached.

"You're damn good at what you do, Robert," Smith said, behind a hefty sigh.

"Thanks, Mac."

Smith hesitated. "I didn't just come here to discuss Detective Rogers."

"I didn't think you did."

"We need to have the conversation we were supposed to have yesterday."

Brixton nodded. "I'm listening," he managed to say.

Mackensie Smith walked to the window, gazing out it toward the Washington skyline in the distance, visible only from one of the building's higher floors. "This isn't easy for me to say."

"Then just say it, Mac."

"I've decided to downsize the firm, Robert. Being midsize in this town has left us in a very difficult place. Too big to take on smaller clients and not big enough to attract the big companies. We've never made big inroads in lobbying, and all the pro bono work is bleeding us dry. I figure we need to reassess now, while the choice is still ours."

"You mean *yours*, don't you?"

"I told you this was going to be hard . . ."

"Are you firing me, Mac?"

Smith tried for a smile, but failed. "You don't really work for me, do you? I gave you an office, a place for you to meet clients, and sent the firm's work your way. Going forward, I'm not sure how much work there's going to be or if there will even be an office for you wherever what's left of the firm ends up."

Brixton considered Mac Smith's words—insult added to injury, as they say, and quite literally in this case. In the wake of losing his longtime girlfriend and Washington apartment they'd shared and both loved, he was going to be essentially out of work. Although he had clients of his own, he'd relied on the work funneled to him by Smith's law firm for the bulk of his revenue. Without it, there would be no revenue, and he doubted he could afford an office of his own anywhere remotely close to where the action was in DC. So even some of the drier, or at times more sordid, work he'd been getting would dry up too.

"Please say something, Robert," Smith said, making Brixton wonder how long he'd been lost in his own thinking.

"Wow."

"I was hoping for something deeper. That is, if you didn't throw me out the window."

"You thought I'd be angry?"

"Aren't you?"

"I'm feeling a lot of things right now, Mac, but anger at you isn't one of them. After SITQUAL, I only had a career because of you. You gave me an office and talked me up all over town. A bunch of good years, all told."

"Not a good end, though, especially under the circumstances. I was thinking about waiting, Robert, but our lease is up and I couldn't bear you showing up at the office to find everyone and everything gone. I thought you had a right to know, that you'd want to know."

"I feel like a second bomb just went off. How long have you been considering this?"

"The wheels started turning around the time you broke up with Flo."

"You mean, she broke up with me."

Smith let that ago. "I didn't say anything then because I resisted what the numbers were saying. Kept telling myself I could make it work. That firm was my dream. I built it from nothing and I fully expect the last time I walk out the door to be the worst moment of my life."

"I know all about bad moments, Mac."

"And this is a horrible time to burden you with yet another one. If it's any consolation, I've been making calls around the city to talk you up even more, see if anyone's looking for someone with your experience and skill set."

"And?"

Smith frowned. "It's early."

"How about *so far*, then?"

"No takers. A few said they'd get back to me and did. A few others said they would and didn't."

"I'm damaged goods, aren't I?"

"You've got a reputation. Not just for breaking eggs, Robert, but also for mixing the shells in when you scramble them. These lawyers don't like mess and, let's face it, you've made more than your share of them."

"Which defines my experience and skill set," Brixton reminded.

"The town's changed," Mac told him. "Firms aren't looking for former security operatives who are good with a gun so much as investigators who are good with numbers, forensics. Gunfighters are in short demand these days, and when they need one they call a security company and bring on a former Navy SEAL, something like that."

"Someone younger, in other words."

Smith didn't bother denying Brixton's assertion. "There is that, too, for sure. This town is getting younger and younger. Beyond that, throw a stone up in the air and chances are it'll come down on the head of a lobbyist. We had one in your office before I gave it to you."

"I never knew that."

"Because I find the whole business detestable. Thousands of people running around DC believing in nothing and not achieving much more, other than lining the pockets of politicians, to enlist them in their cause."

"And that's new?"

"Not new, Robert, just worse—hyper-exaggerated, you might say, the tail wagging the dog. It's all about fear. Lobbyists used to operate by getting you to believe in what they were pushing. Now they operate by scaring you into wondering what will happen if you don't. Politics has become a job for the weak-minded and thin-skinned among us. The only principles these people know are the ones they're paid to have. Everything's transactional. It's not about what I can do for you anymore; it's about what you can do for me and how can I enlist you to do it. That sound like a world ready to open its doors and welcome you back in with open arms?"

"Not at fifty-six years old, no."

Smith looked like he wanted to stop there, but he made himself continue. "How are you set financially?"

"You already know the answer to that, Mac."

"I was hoping to hear something I didn't. I've included you among those who'll be receiving a severance package, and you'll keep your health care coverage for six months."

"Leaving me only nine years short of Medicare," Brixton said, instantly regretting the comment. "I'm sorry, Mac. You didn't deserve that."

"Yes, I did, Robert. I deserved every bit of it, especially given the timing. This isn't the way friends are supposed to treat each other. I hate to be the one blowing up your world."

It was clear from how low Smith's mouth dropped how much he regretted the inappropriateness of that remark, but Brixton managed a smile.

"No worries, Mac," he said, "given how close I came to getting blown up, period, yesterday."

CHAPTER 8

GEORGETOWN

Brixton suggested Kendra Rendine meet him at Corridor Coffee in Georgetown, a small establishment off the beaten path of the kind of Washington insiders who might recognize either him or her. Washington was the smallest of small towns when it came to who spotted whom with whom, conspiracies of epic levels hatched at every turn about this political race, issue, or otherwise. Corridor Coffee, by contrast, was populated primarily by locals and the Georgetown University community. He often went there alone, secure in the notion that he wouldn't be running into anyone that he knew. They agreed to meet at two p.m. In Brixton's experience, this was the only truly slow time of the day, squeezed between the lunchtime and late-day rushes.

He'd worked alongside Kendra Rendine a number of times while he was attached to SITQUAL, occasions when her Secret Service duties guarding first the president and then the vice president overlapped with his on behalf of the State Department. He didn't know Rendine well, but the pressure of protecting diplomats and dignitaries overseas brought with it a slowing of time and an exaggeration of relationships, both good and bad. He found the time spent in protective service, especially in transit, when not everything could possibly be secured, forged a unique bond between professionals like himself and Kendra Rendine.

I think she was murdered.

Rendine was not the kind of person to voice such an accusation lightly. She was strictly a by-the-book type, never straying outside the prescribed lines and known for paying meticulous attention to detail. She was also exceedingly cautious, trusting her instincts to occasionally divert from a planned route when a sight, sound, or sense disturbed her, especially overseas. And those instincts had produced an exceptional, untarnished record of service to those she was charged with keeping safe and alive.

Rendine was waiting outside Corridor Coffee when he got there, and Brixton made a show of checking his watch.

"You're early."

"So are you, by fifteen minutes."

"How much you beat me by?"

"Fifteen."

"Meaning you were thirty minutes early."

Rendine smiled slightly. "You caught me."

"Old habits die hard, right?"

"*All* habits die hard, Robert."

"Are we talking about any habit in particular?"

Rendine suddenly looked uneasy, standing there on a public street, no matter how far they were from the congested and gossipy center of Washington. "Let's get some coffee and I'll tell you all about it."

Brixton and Rendine both ordered matcha lattes, on her recommendation—large, since they thought they might linger at Corridor Coffee for a while and didn't want to stand out for having nothing to sip. They managed to snag one of the outdoor, umbrellaed tables surrounded by foliage and rimmed by peaked cast iron fencing.

"This is great," Brixton noted, after taking his first sip.

"You doubted me?"

"Not anymore. I just figured, you come to a coffee shop, you order coffee, not some green tea concoction."

She wrinkled her nose at him. "What century are you living in, Robert?"

"Er, the twentieth?"

"That's what I thought."

Being outside, no longer cooped up in his apartment, finally relieved the loneliness he'd felt since returning home from the hospital the day before. In fact, he'd felt that same sense of loneliness ever since Flo Combes had left him to move back to New York. Brixton wanted to believe it was just the natural order of things, that sometimes people grow apart and relationships end. But he suspected it was something more than that, even though Flo had blamed herself for the breakup. He figured she'd done that to let him down easy, keeping the truth of her move back to New York shrouded behind fake smiles and faux explanations. Brixton knew he must have done something to upset her, but he couldn't for the life of him figure out what it was.

Brixton sipped some more of his matcha latte, dabbing his lips with a napkin to wipe away the excess foam. "You also think the vice president was murdered," Brixton said, picking up on what she'd just said and keeping his voice low.

Rendine surveyed the narrow outdoor confines again, not a single crack or crevice in the walls or inlaid brick escaping her attention. It looked very much to Brixton like she was securing the area for herself as she would for a protectee, the most recent of whom had been Stephanie Davenport, until the night before the Metro bombing.

"I'll get to that," she said finally.

"Might make more sense to start with it."

"Not in this case, Robert, because I've got no proof to back up my suspicions."

"Then what do you have, Agent?"

She flinched. "Do you have to call me that?"

"It's what you are."

"So what am I supposed to call you?"

"Old and stupid," Brixton came up with.

"I've got something better to describe you."

"What's that?"

"Heroic."

"I appreciate the compliment, but I didn't do anything, Kendra."

"Is that what you call your actions, saving the lives of dozens of people? I've seen what happens to victims of a suicide attack on a bus." Brixton watched Rendine suppress a shudder. "I imagine that's what you would have been facing, if she'd pulled the cord *on* that Metro car instead of outside it."

"But we're not here to talk about me or what happened on that Metro car, are we, Kendra?"

"I'm not sure I would've called you if I hadn't seen the report on the news."

"In which case you would have pressed *Unidentified Male* in your Contacts."

Rendine flashed him a smirk. "Unidentified male to most, but not to the Secret Service. Can I tell you something you're not going to believe?"

Brixton nodded.

"When I heard the report, I had a feeling it was you. When I looked into the incident, I didn't ask who. I asked if it had been Robert Brixton."

"You're right. I don't believe you."

"It's why I called you, Robert. I may have anyway, but I took that as a sign. I knew I had to go outside the family to see if my suspicions about the vice president are correct. The Metro bombing told me that outsider had to be you."

"Slow down, Kendra. What suspicions?"

"The circumstances surrounding the vice president's death."

"All the reports say a heart attack was the cause."

"Because it was."

"Then what are we doing here? What am *I* doing here?"

Rendine took a deep breath, started to take a sip of her latte, but then, instead, checked the area around them again before lowering her voice. "The vice president had been acting strangely in the weeks leading up to her death."

"Strangely how?"

"Like she was struggling with something, and . . ."

"And what?" Brixton coaxed.

"I think she was waiting for something to happen, Robert. Something bad."

CHAPTER 9

GEORGETOWN

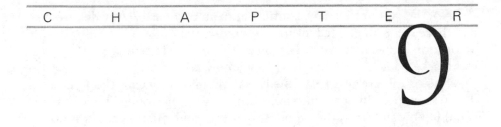

Brixton didn't respond, and instead waited for Kendra Rendine to continue.

"What was your longest protective posting with SITQUAL?"

"Six weeks, I think. A couple months maybe."

"I've been with Davenport since the campaign trail. To do this job on a daily basis at the executive branch level, you can't just follow and watch. You have to be in the president or vice president's head. You have to know what they're thinking as they think it, so you can be ready when they make the move. You know what all of us hate more than anything?"

"Rope lines."

Rendine nodded. "Because they're impossible to secure one hundred percent and place the protectee in a much too vulnerable position. If it was up to me, or any Secret Service detail head, we'd take them off the schedule, especially when they happen spontaneously before we have a chance to check the crowd ourselves."

"That's a far cry from what you're suggesting."

"There's more. What I just said about thinking as our protectee thinks comes down to reading their emotions, knowing when they're upset, angry, or anxious, because that's when they let their guard down and mistakes happen. The vice president was all three of those things."

"Upset, angry, and anxious," Brixton repeated. "She ever tell you why, at least give you a hint?"

"No, and I never asked. It would be a breach of protocol to get involved in business that clearly wasn't in my purview or, potentially, even my security clearance." Rendine hesitated, her stare boring into Brixton. "But that doesn't mean I didn't take note of the where and when."

"So, where and when?"

"The White House, five weeks ago. A meeting with the president. Strictly routine."

"Or maybe not, based on what you're insinuating."

Rendine leaned back. "You don't believe me."

Brixton gave her a long look before responding. "I get the feeling this heart attack didn't come out of nowhere."

"No, the vice president was suffering from coronary artery disease. She had three stents implanted just over a month ago."

Brixton leaned forward. "Hold on a minute. You're telling me the media was blacked out on this, that it was somehow kept secret?"

"The procedure was performed at Walter Reed, where the vice president was supposedly spending the afternoon visiting wounded soldiers. You should know she also suffered bouts of atrial defibrillation and was taking a beta blocker as well as a calcium channel blocker, along with a blood thinner."

"Wow."

"Yeah. And you know what? The vice president insisted on visiting a few wounded soldiers after the procedure was completed. She hated lying to the public."

"How did she feel about lies of omission?"

"If it was up to her, she would have come clean from the start, put the whole procedure up on Facebook maybe, for the public to see. The orders to keep this dark came from the White House."

Brixton's eyebrows flickered at that. Plenty of what Kendra Rendine was telling him here would have passed for routine, but not that. Why would the White House impose a news blackout on what had become a vastly routine procedure?

"You think that's what she discussed with the president the week before the procedure?"

Rendine shrugged. "I already told you I have no idea what she discussed with the president. But whatever it was doesn't explain the White House order to go dark on this."

"Still, that meeting dates back to when you noticed the change in the vice president," Brixton said, calculating the timeline in his head.

"Yes, a week before she had the procedure."

"What was the meeting about, the agenda, Kendra?"

"Routine weekly briefing. The weekly brief with the president was her opportunity to get caught up on what she didn't get in her own briefings. The inside dope directly from POTUS."

"And Davenport met with him the day you remember her whole demeanor changing."

Rendine nodded. "I thought it might be over some information the president shared with her. But when nothing broke in the next couple days, I started to think otherwise."

"Maybe the information deals with something a bit farther off. Or, maybe, a change in policy. Maybe the president told her he was replacing her on the ticket because of that heart condition."

"It was none of those things, Robert," Rendine insisted, shaking her head.

"You can't know that for sure."

"Maybe not. And that's why I need you to find out what it really was."

"I thought you needed me to find out if Stephanie Davenport was murdered."

"For starters."

"Starters? Do I need to remind you that I'm a private citizen absent a portfolio?

"That's why we're having this conversation; because anyone *with* one is inside the system."

"Problem being that the people I need to talk to won't see me, and if they did, they'd never entrust me with anything as serious or dire as you're suggesting this might be."

"I never said it was going to be easy, Robert . . ."

"And that's the rub, isn't it?"

"We're having this conversation because you're the best special operator I've ever worked with. I've seen your skills firsthand and heard plenty about the work you did for SITQUAL that I wasn't around for. Sniffed out quite a few plots and smoked out more than your share of foreign bad guys in the process."

Brixton shrugged. "I had some luck."

"It was skill. And I need that skill now. I need to know what Stephanie Davenport was so riled about, what had her up in arms. You should have seen her, Robert. The calmest, coolest person I've ever known spending her downtime fidgeting, checking her phone over and over again."

"Like she was waiting for something to happen, as you said."

"I suppose. *Expecting* it even."

Brixton studied Kendra Rendine from across the table, through the thin layer of steam still rising from their matcha lattes. He could tell the woman was scared, could tell her suspicions went well beyond the personal or some quest to absolve herself of guilt for being on duty when Stephanie Davenport had been stricken. The annals of Secret Service history were ripe with tales of presidential disease and deaths. But Brixton couldn't name one similar tale passed along about a sitting vice president.

"I'm not sure that, as an outsider without standing, I'll be able to do much with that part of the mystery. Whether it was really a heart attack that killed Stephanie Davenport, though, that I might be able to handle."

Rendine's expression didn't change, but Brixton could sense a weight being lifted off her shoulders, relieving her of the burden she'd been bearing.

"Now," he said, between steamy sips, "tell me everything you remember about the night the vice president died, and don't leave anything out."

PART TWO

CHAPTER 10

AR-RAMLAH, ISRAEL

So what can I do for the Lioness of Judah?" the Arab woman spat at Lia Ganz from the other side of the table, inside the infamous Nitzan prison.

Lia Ganz looked Samir Ibrahim in the eye, ignoring her tone. "I have a message from your parents. And I left a package from them for you with the guards."

The young woman's expression tightened into a scowl. "I never get them."

"I arranged for an exception to be made in this case."

Ibrahim swallowed hard. "And this message?"

"They said 'Abaq gawiaan.'"

Another swallow. "It means 'Stay strong.'"

"I know."

"That's right, you speak fluent Arabic. Better to interrogate us with."

"I have something else to offer you, if you help me today."

"Please don't dangle false promises of an early release before me."

"I was thinking more along the lines of arranging for a visit from your children."

Ibrahim's eyes moistened. "No one receives visitors at Nitzan."

"I know," Lia said, leaving it there.

"I appreciate you looking after them, getting them resettled and all."

"The State of Israel appreciates your cooperation, Samir. We like to help those who help us."

"Only because my suicide vest didn't work," the young Palestinian woman said, with the biting yet sad edge Lia had come to know in her voice.

She was only nineteen, already the mother of two, when her suicide vest had failed to detonate inside a crowded Tel Aviv shopping mall. While Samir had survived, Mossad tracked down and killed the Hamas members who'd trained and equipped her. Although she had refused to give up their names, word was leaked that she had, providing the spy organization with unique leverage over her. With Samir branded a traitor, the only chance her family had to survive was resettlement by Israeli authorities within friendlier confines, under new identities. This had fallen under Lia's domain while she was recovering from the wounds she'd suffered in Gaza and was still contemplating her next steps.

Continuing to look after Samir's young children, though, was not in her purview at all. Nor was retaining an active interest, or even management, of Samir's case after stepping away from her day-to-day duties with Mossad.

Nitzan prison was reserved for the most high-profile prisoners, with scant attention paid to either conditions or, especially, treatment, since the prisoners would never see the outside of those walls again. All that was known of Nitzan came from leaks, some of which had been selectively arranged by Israeli officials themselves to discourage future attacks by advertising what would happen to those who were captured.

Depending on whom and what you believed, that treatment centered on an infamous torture chamber called Cell 9 and may or may not have included prisoners being hung from the ceiling and beaten, wearing a black bag over their heads for days at a time, and being left naked at all times, along with the frequent incursion of both dogs and mice to make anything that passed for rest impossible. All this done during years spent in solitary confinement, during which the only notion of an outside world with sunshine and fresh air was from memory. Prisoners slept on dirty, old, insect-infested mattresses that were as hard as concrete.

Samir once told Lia the story of how she'd seen a tiny cat walking the prison halls outside Cell 9. One day the cat wandered into Samir's particular boxlike chamber and she began sharing her meager portions of food with it, to finally make a friend. Eventually, the cat effectively became hers, spending hours at a time inside her cell, until the guards found out and slit the cat's throat in front of her.

Lia had listened sympathetically to that tale, even though she knew the cat had been a prop that had achieved exactly what it was designed to. When you ain't got nothing, as the song says, you ain't got nothing to lose, so the plan was to give prisoners like Samir something to lose in order to break them further, or to keep them broken.

Lia could see how Samir Ibrahim perked up at the possibility of seeing her children for the first time since her incarceration three years ago. Born a year apart, they had been mere infants when she was sentenced here as a teenage girl. She was a young woman now, still showing a semblance of strong features, though they were virtually obscured by a sallow complexion, limp hair, scaly skin, and teeth chipped and degraded by a combination of torture and denial of hygiene for days and weeks at a time.

"You can really do that?" Samir posed hopefully. "Bring my children here to see me? You're not lying?"

"Have I ever lied to you?" Lia asked, knowing that question to be based on semantics.

"Not about something like that," Samir replied diplomatically. "But what are you after in return? What has brought you here today?"

"There was an attack last week on a beach in Caesarea," Lia told her, knowing that since prisoners had no contact whatsoever with the outside world, it would be the first time Samir was hearing about it.

"I have an alibi," the young woman said, looking around the interrogation room to make her point.

"Drones were used, along with a uniquely sophisticated targeting system. And there were cameras on all three drones—I suspect so the planners could watch as their bullets mowed down innocent civilian beachgoers."

"There are no civilians in this war."

"But there are casualties, and I need to know who was behind them this time."

"And why is this time so important to you? What separates it from all the other attacks?"

"I was there, with my granddaughter." Lia paused to let that part of her point sink in. "The two of us were spared only because we were in the water."

"And now you're here."

The interrogation room was painted the same shade of drab gray as the cells. And the walls were just as plain, the floors just as cold. The overall effect was to make sure there was no respite or relief in being moved to these confines temporarily. Indeed, everything about Nitzan prison was gray, from floor to ceiling, and that included the prisoners themselves, whose complexion had the look of ash refuse from a fire.

"I'm here," Lia picked up, "because throughout your youth you were acquainted with the best technicians Hamas had to offer."

"Thanks to my uncle being one of them."

"The best, from what I understand, and it would take the best to incorporate weapons systems into those drones. How to minimize the weight of the weapons themselves and the ammo so the drones might still fly. How to account for wind and other elements, the flight of the targets, the spread of the fire."

"My uncle is dead."

"I know. I killed him, remember?"

"How could I forget?"

"But his son got away and has avoided capture. He'd be about your age, I believe."

"Older by a few years. Nearly thirty now."

"First name Dar, and he also went by Ibrahim, I believe."

"Ibrahim al-Bis. But you already knew that."

"I know he was the one who built your suicide vest that never detonated. I know he's replaced his father, your uncle, as the preeminent terrorist bomb maker. What I don't know is where to find him."

The young woman seemed to think of something. "You say the drones were equipped with cameras."

"Yes, two of them on each. Six in all. We recovered their remains, along with the remains of the targeting mechanism and transmitter. We assume the cameras were installed so the operator, or operators, could also use them to adjust their aim."

"What do you want from me in return for a visit from my children?" Samir Ibrahim asked Lia, unable to disguise the pleading in her voice.

"Where can I find your cousin, Dar Ibrahim al-Bis, Samir?"

The young woman's perpetually ashen expression softened a bit. "You've seen my son and my daughter?"

"I checked in on them last week."

Samir looked relieved by that. "How old is your granddaughter?"

"Three. Same age your son was when you first got here."

"And if I help you, you'll bring them to me?"

Lia nodded. "Personally."

She could see Samir weighing the prospects of that, looking what passed for dreamy and reflective in a place like this, which was utterly devoid of hope. "You promise not to kill my cousin?"

"I can't make that promise. I can only promise that I'm after information, not trophies."

"There can be no arrest. You need to promise me that."

Lia weighed her options, not finding very many at all. "It will be very difficult to convince my superiors to leave him out there to kill again."

"He does not kill; he designs. My cousin is a technician, a builder."

"Who builds weapons of death so others can kill. I fail to see the distinction, Samir."

The young woman leaned back, suddenly composed, even relaxed. "My terms are final."

"You're not in a position to set them."

"And you're not in a position to walk away from here empty-handed, are you? It could only have been desperation that brought you here to me today."

Lia felt her spine stiffen. "Like the desperation of a young mother who hasn't seen her children in nearly three years?"

Samir Ibrahim nodded in concession. "When will you bring them to me?'

"After you've brought me to Dar Ibrahim al-Bis, Samir."

CHAPTER 11

NEW YORK CITY

"And what game are you here to play with me today, Robert?" the man tending to his pigeons said, barely looking up from his work cleaning their cage on the roof of his apartment building. "What riddle have you to pose to the professor?"

That was how Brixton knew this man. Not a name, a firm background, or even a nationality. He knew there may have been some military experience in the man's background, likely in the blackest of ops. Not as the man carrying out the assignment but as the maker of the device designed to do the deed. How to get at people who were unreachable—that was the professor's specialty, and might still be, for all Brixton knew. He was an enigma, a puzzle, a contradiction, to the point where Brixton had heard the professor being referred to as something else entirely: Dr. Death.

In more recent years, that moniker had been replaced by another culled from a book, or a movie title, Brixton couldn't remember which: the God of War.

There were targets impervious to the efforts of even the Navy SEALs or Delta Force, targets so well hidden or guarded that ordinary commando raids would never succeed. In some cases, the target might be accessible but other determining factors had ruled out a strike, execution, or assassination. Sometimes people had to die with no knowledge or indication left to suggest it had been murder. It needed to look like an accident or natural causes, as may have been the case with Stephanie Davenport. And when that was the case, they came to the professor, aka Dr. Death.

The Russians weren't the only ones to have mastered such dark deeds. In fact, at least some of their most notorious murders, undertaken with poisoned umbrella tips or radioactive isotopes, had been stolen from American lore—although this was never reported, because such operations would have been carried out with far more restraint and alacrity than the Russian examples.

"I heard about that nasty business on the subway," the professor told him.

"Metro. In Washington, it's called the Metro."

"And what do you call the slimy snake pit that is Washington?"

"A slimy snake pit," Brixton said, leaving it there.

He'd taken the eight a.m. Acela out of Washington, hoping to steal some added sleep on the ride, but had found himself barely able to close his eyes. The trauma from his experience on the Metro had left him even more hypervigilant than he normally was, and he spent the entire ride studying each and every passenger in the car, along with those moving up and down the aisle, coming to or from the food service car. In his mind, any of them could be a terrorist, and he nearly suffered a panic attack when one passenger, damp with sweat, likely from running to catch the train, passed by his seat, toting an overstuffed backpack.

"I'll grant you that," the professor said, smiling above the beard that hung over his neck.

It was white with flecks and patches of gray, same color as his wild mane of shoulder-length hair. He'd kept all of it from his youth, didn't seem to have lost a strand, although his craggy face showed the cracks, furrows, and lines of too much unprotected time spent outdoors. Brixton wondered if that might hold some clue as to the man's true past or was nothing more than the product of too many hours spent upon this rooftop with his pigeons.

Do you understand my fascination with these birds? he'd asked Brixton once.

I suspect it has something to do with the fact that they were a subject of interest to the likes of both Charles Darwin and Nikola Tesla. Darwin even included two chapters on them in one of his books.

Good answer but incorrect. As a person who specializes in the technology of war, it was the fact that America had a fleet of two hundred thousand pigeons serving our cause during World War Two. By delivering critical updates, the avians saved thousands of human lives. One racing bird named Cher Ami completed a mission that led to the rescue of a hundred and ninety-four stranded U.S. soldiers in October of 1918, if you can believe that.

I've learned to believe anything you tell me, Professor.

"When you called and said you needed to see me, I assumed it was about the bombing."

"There are some anomalies," Brixton told him.

The professor's eyes perked up. "Like what?"

"There are indications the suicide bomber was being watched the whole time, her actions followed every step of the way by her handlers."

"Any proof?"

"Not yet. It's also possible her suicide vest was detonated remotely, like an insurance policy against the bomber changing her mind or some unexpected element being thrown into the mix."

"Meaning you, in this case, Robert."

He nodded. "I suppose." That provoked a fresh thought. "Would it be possible to detect whether the bomb was triggered manually or remotely?"

"The signal carried would have been along identical receptor lines within the device. So the answer's a qualified yes, only in the event the manual triggering mechanism survived the explosion intact enough to be examined."

"Is that even remotely possible?"

"You'd be surprised how much of a bomb's critical elements are preserved in the explosion," the professor told him. "This is due in large part to the kinetic energy spreading outward from the blast wave, so that unless the triggering mechanism was destroyed in the initial firing, there's a good chance at least a portion of it survived. The question, of course, is whether that surviving portion is sufficient to prove this theory. And there's something else you'll want to have checked, Robert."

"What's that?"

"You mentioned the possibility that the young woman's handlers, as you called them, were watching her in real time."

"A distinct possibility, yes," Brixton said, thinking of the iPad peeking out from the coat pocket of the supposed Detective Rogers.

"Then you should also consider something else," the professor said. "Specifically that the bomber was wearing some kind of camera as well. If it survived the blast—again, a much better possibility than most imagine—it would be among her evidentiary personal effects collected from the scene. I'd look for a pin or brooch, perhaps a hairpin of some sort."

"She was wearing a hijab."

"Offering potential concealment for just such a device. What about her clothes?"

Brixton searched his memory for the proper images. "Bulky, shapeless, too thick for the unseasonably warm spring weather."

"A coat?"

More searching. "Yes, Professor."

"Check the buttons then. They make ideal minicams. I've designed a whole bunch based on that model myself."

Brixton regarded the man who'd spent an entire generation designing weapons of death, handling the pigeon he was holding as if it were a newborn child. He guessed it was the way a man like the professor displaced the ugliness of his work, of designing an instrument intended to kill one human being or scores of them. What it must be like to open the newspaper or turn on the television to news of something he had been party to perpetrating or, at least, made possible. Tending to his pigeons compensated for that, life preserved standing in for lives taken. Surrounding himself with among the oldest of wartime "technologies" served as an object reminder of the enormity of his burden.

"But that's not why you've come here at all, is it?" the professor said to him.

"No, it isn't," Brixton conceded. "I'm here about the death of Vice President Stephanie Davenport."

"A heart attack, I thought," the professor said, looking up from the bird he was currently petting.

"She was suffering from a heart condition, but a source close to the vice president believes the heart attack may have been induced somehow."

"On what basis, Robert?"

"Instinct."

"I'm a scientist. You need to do better than that."

"That's why I'm here, Professor. Because you're a scientist and I *want* to do better than that."

The professor returned the pigeon he was holding to the large cage and eased out another in its place. Brixton wondered if this were a daily ritual for him, wondered if any birds not receiving his affection might be offended.

"Anything turn up in the postmortem?"

"Not so far, according to my source. I suspect an autopsy may be performed, if it hasn't already. But if she was murdered, it would've been through a means sure to be utterly undetectable."

The professor smirked, smiling smugly. "We'll see about that."

CHAPTER 12

The professor said he needed an hour to peek into things, glean what he could before providing Brixton with his thoughts. Actually, it was only forty minutes before he returned to the roof where Brixton had waited.

"You failed to mention that the vice president had stents inserted into a trio of coronary arteries feeding the heart, a month before her death."

"I thought I did."

"Well, you didn't. You wanted to know how the vice president may have been murdered and I just told you."

"Stents?" Brixton posed incredulously.

"Let's back up a bit first. Cardiovascular disease is the top medical reason for deaths worldwide. But that number has been drastically reduced by millions of patients benefitting from angioplasty procedures where stents are placed in clogged arteries to improve blood flow and reduce the risk of heart attack. But there is also a risk associated with stents: plaque can build up, causing arteries to narrow again. You with me so far?"

Brixton thought of his age and lack of exercise these past few years, wondering if he might find himself a candidate for stents before too much longer. "Yes."

"Okay then. Moving on, researchers at the University of British Columbia in Vancouver, Canada, have figured out that stents could do a lot more than just be a dumb tube on the wall of an artery. So they've created a 'smart stent' empowered with sensors that can monitor and provide real-time feedback on blood flow. The feedback can detect renarrowing of stented arteries, known as restenosis, a common complication of stent implantation. The researchers believe in-stent restenosis can reach as high as fifty percent among patients. Follow me?"

Brixton nodded. "In essence, these new generation stents aren't just hardware, they're also software."

"Exactly!" the professor beamed, with genuine enthusiasm. "Call it a technological means to extending life, not just a medical one. The next step beyond pacemakers and internal defibrillators. My first thought, when I hear reporting like this, is 'What took so long?' The smart stents provide an early warning system that the researchers believe is a better way to diagnose restenosis. In-stent restenosis in arteries is currently diagnosed through duplex ultrasound and angiography, usually done when patients complain of heart attack–related symptoms like chest pain, which means more damage may have already been done to the heart muscle itself.

"Stents, in some cases, are coated with slow-release medication to prevent plaque buildup, which can be effective in the short term, but it doesn't protect against a heart attack in the long term. The smart stent detects signs of restenosis and also thrombosis, which is clotting inside a vessel. It has sensing and real-time communication ability via micro-electromechanical systems and antenna functions. The signal sent by the stent is received by an external portable reader that is monitored by computers twenty-four/seven. The point, Robert, is that these smart stents transmit binary signals so it figures—"

"That they could also be used, theoretically, to *accept* signals," Brixton completed, taking his cue.

"See," the professor beamed, "you didn't even need me. You're smarter than you think."

"I'm a fast learner, Professor. And what I'm learning from all this is that it may be possible to transmit a signal to these implanted smart stents, telling them to close the arteries and shut down the blood flow, instead of keeping them open."

The professor flashed the look that many of Brixton's teachers or instructors had given him over the years, after he'd failed at this task or that. "Not *may be* possible; it *is* possible, through technical means I won't bore you with today."

"But simply stated . . ."

"You know I never state anything simply, Robert, but if you're looking for a way the vice president may have been murdered, I believe you've found it."

CHAPTER 13

NEW YORK CITY

Flo Combes hadn't been expecting him, which was just the way Brixton wanted it. He showed up unannounced at her dress shop, loitering uncomfortably until the fashionable boutique's traffic reached a lull.

"See anything you like?" she asked him, smiling.

Brixton made a show of fanning through a rack of dresses with four-figure price tags. "I was looking for something in paisley."

"And what size would that be?"

They finally hugged, Brixton surprised at how tightly and long she held him.

"So," she said, when they finally separated.

"So I happened to be in the neighborhood."

Flo scolded him with her eyes. "Robert Brixton is a lot of things, but he never just *happens* to be anywhere."

Brixton threw his hands in the air dramatically. "Okay, you got me. I'm up here on business."

"Business."

"Well, kind of. You know, looking into something."

"Care to tell me more?"

"Wish I could, but I can't." He held Flo's gaze long enough for discomfort to settle between them. "Can you get out for a coffee?"

She looked around her shop. "No, but I can stay in for one."

They adjourned to her office, Flo closing the door behind them.

"I know Annabel filled you in on what happened," Brixton said, as she moved to the Keurig one-cup coffee machine in a corner.

"And thank God she did. I would've been worried sick otherwise."

"About me? Still?"

Flo forced a smile. "Good thing Annabel told me. I might have thought you made this trip to propose, if she hadn't."

"Really? And how would I have done that?"

Flo fingered her chin dramatically. "Being the hopeless romantic you are, you'd pull up outside in a horse-drawn carriage and ask me to marry you on bended knee."

"I'm not that romantic."

"A girl can dream," Flo said with a smile, all the tension that had characterized their last few months together having slipped away. "Anyway, I would have been worried sick if not for Annabel's call."

"You couldn't possibly have known I was involved."

"Maybe. But as soon as my phone blew up with news flashes, I just had this feeling . . ."

"Well, my reputation does precede me."

"Well earned in all respects."

She came over and hugged him again, while the first cup of coffee began to brew. "I'm sorry, Robert. I'm so sorry."

"For what?"

"Can we start with 'everything'?"

"You can apologize by having an early dinner with me," Brixton proposed, figuring he could still catch the last train back to Washington on Amtrak. "We can celebrate."

"What?"

"The fact that I wasn't blown up two days ago."

She did that thing with her eyes, scolding him again. "That's not funny."

"But it is true."

"Annabel said you were a hero, that you saved a lot of lives on that train."

"The bomber knew I was watching her. When she got up to change cars, I followed her. That's the extent of it."

"And if you hadn't been on that car, what would have happened?"

Brixton shrugged.

The first mug filled, Flo returned to the Keurig machine to brew the second. "An early dinner sounds great," she said, mixing him the first cup just the way he liked it.

"Novita?" he said.

"Even greater."

It was their favorite restaurant in the city, a consistently fashionable establishment that served great food that never disappointed. Flo ordered a martini while Brixton stuck with club soda, in keeping with doctor's orders over the supposedly minor concussion he'd suffered in the blast. They split a crab meat salad, one of the house specialties, and then divided the breaded swordfish and Chilean sea bass between them.

"Did I mess up, Flo?" Brixton finally found the courage to ask her. "Should I have asked you to marry me?"

She looked up from her plate. "How well do you know me, Robert?"

"Oh, I'd say pretty well."

"At least well enough to know I'm not shy about speaking my mind or expressing my feelings. If I'd wanted to get married, you would've known it."

"So you would have turned me down?"

"We had a good thing going. Why mess it up?"

"Because it ended."

"Well, there is that . . ." Flo looked as if she was finished, and Brixton was ready to speak again, when she resumed. "I spoke to Annabel again this morning. She told me about Mac's decision to downsize the firm and what that means for you."

He toasted her with the iced tea he'd moved on to. It was swimming with pieces of fruit, which was another Novita hallmark. "It hasn't been a banner week exactly."

"So what are you going to do?"

"I haven't given it much thought yet."

"Yes, you have. Knowing you as well as I do, Robert, I'd say it's *all* you've been thinking of."

Brixton toasted her again. "Guilty as charged."

"And?"

"And nothing. I'm fifty-six years old with the kind of skills that aren't readily in demand. If I try high-end security work, I'm up against former Navy SEALs. If I go in for private intelligence work, I'm up against computer mavens who can lap me with their keyboards. That doesn't leave me with much."

"Did you come up here on something job-related?"

"Yes and no."

"What's that mean?"

"I guess it could lead to something, but that's not why I came."

Something in her expression changed. "Please don't say it was to see me."

"Would that bother you?"

Flo thought for a moment. "Actually, it wouldn't, not at all. I just don't want you to go home disappointed because . . ."

Her voice tailed off and Brixton didn't bail her out by trying to complete her thought. Instead, he kept his eyes fixed on Flo, urging her to continue.

"I don't want to lose you," she completed finally.

"Didn't you do that already?"

"That's not what I meant," she said, groping for words. "I need to know that whatever this is, it's not final. When I saw you in the shop, the first thing I thought was, 'Oh no, he's going to ask me marry him.' Because I don't know what I would have said and I can't bear the thought of what we had being over for good."

"So we're taking a break, is that it?"

"I don't know what it is, Robert. Maybe we're best not to label it."

"Maybe I should have taken a horse-drawn carriage to your shop."

She cupped the top of his hand in hers, her affection genuine. "What do you want from me, Robert?"

"Truth be told, I don't know."

"Take a guess."

He didn't hesitate. "Reassurance."

"About what?"

"I don't know. Maybe that everything's going to be okay. That I won't have to sell my coin collection to make ends meet."

"You don't have a coin collection."

"My stamp collection, then."

"You don't have one of those, either."

He nodded, frowning. "Then I guess I'm in even more trouble than I thought."

Flo smiled. "I'm glad we did this, Robert."

"So am I."

"And Annabel said Mac was going to find you something."

"She should have said *try* to find me something."

"He won't let you down."

Brixton leaned back in his chair. "Did I let you down, Flo?"

"I couldn't deal with Washington anymore. The lifestyle, the cocktail parties, the expensive dinners, drinking every day."

"You just described plenty of people's dream."

Now it was Flo who pulled back, not as much physically as emotionally. "Does that include you, Robert? Because you seemed to embrace it."

"I thought I was working, that it came with the job."

"And how much work did you get that you wouldn't have gotten anyway?"

"Not much, I suppose," Brixton conceded.

"Exactly. The last six months we were together, you slept past seven a.m. on a workday more times than in the previous six years, and it wasn't even close. You know how many mornings you were still in bed when I left the apartment?"

"Too many?"

"You were soaking up too much of a lifestyle, in contrast to the years I couldn't keep you out past nine o'clock in the evening. I liked the old Robert Brixton better, but I think some good news may have come from all this."

"What's that?"

Flo gave him a long, deep look before responding. "I think he's sitting across from me right now."

CHAPTER 14

JUDEAN HILLS, ISRAEL

Lia Ganz was waiting in a workshop that smelled of rust, grease, and oil when Dar Ibrahim al-Bis stepped through the door carrying a large coupling that dripped oil across the floor.

"Samir sends her regards, Dar," she greeted from the shadows.

Al-Bis almost dropped the coupling from his grasp and looked at Lia blankly. "I believe you have me confused with someone else."

"What kind of man would fashion his cousin's own suicide vest?"

"I wouldn't know."

Satisfied the bomb maker was weaponless, Lia stepped farther into the light. "And what about killing innocent civilians on a crowded beach? Only a coward mows down women, children, and noncombatants. What would you call that, Dar?"

"If I was this man you think I am, I might say I'd call that my duty."

"Then it's a good thing you aren't that man, isn't it?"

Lia gazed about the workshop deliberately, baiting al-Bis to take up some weapon against her and thus end the charade. With his cousin Samir's help, she had traced him to the Kif Tzuba amusement park, located on the grounds of a sprawling kibbutz in the Judean Hills. The park had a number of Israeli Arab workers who dominated the population in this area west of Jerusalem, just off the Jerusalem–Tel Aviv highway, neighboring the village of Abu Ghosh, from which virtually all the Israeli Arabs employed by the park hailed.

Kif Tzuba was cluttered with rides both old and new, the latest being a roller coaster that dipped and darted through the sprawl of the park. The park may have been constructed for kids under ten, but a number of the rides and attractions featured the kind of stomach-churning, dizziness-inducing thrills that left young riders literally screeching with joy. It catered to tourists and locals, including the local Arab population, who were welcomed by the kibbutzniks and park workers with open arms. The park enjoyed a stellar safety record, as Lia recalled, an irony she found striking, since the man in charge of upkeep was an explosives expert and master builder of suicide vests that had claimed hundreds of lives, if not thousands.

"We all look alike to you," the man Lia was more convinced than ever was Dar Ibrahim al-Bis said to her bitterly.

"Actually, you look like your cousin Samir. I can see the resemblance."

"I don't have a cousin named Samir. All my cousins are dead."

"Would you like to know what else I think?"

"I have no interest in anything you think."

"I think that you built your cousin's suicide vest to fail. I think you changed your mind at the last minute and saved her life, although I don't think being in an Israeli prison passes for much of a life. Samir was kind enough to help me find you," Lia said, leaving it there.

Suddenly appearing disinterested in their conversation and in Lia's claims, al-Bis began readying some tools for his next repair job on some piece of Kif Tzuba's equipment out in the park. Lia let his leash extend that much, ready to pounce on him if he flashed a gun.

Al-Bis forced a humorless laugh and shook his head. "You are Mossad?"

"Not anymore. I was on the beach with my granddaughter when the drones attacked."

"Then you should be home giving prayers of thanks to your God."

"I'd rather send the men behind the attack to meet him."

"Then you have come to the wrong place. There was another man who worked here before me, until a few months ago. He must be the one you're seeking, the cousin of this Samir person."

Lia hardened her stare, just enough. "We're going to talk, you and I. We're going to make a deal."

Al-Bis was picking through a metal container of bolts in search of the right size. "Mossad doesn't make deals."

"But I'm not Mossad anymore, remember? I'm free to do as I wish."

"And you came alone."

Lia looked around the workshop. "Is this where you built your cousin's suicide vest? Am I looking at the parts you used to assemble those drones right now? Impressive feat, given the need to retrofit the guns to cut down on weight. I understand a lighter variety of high-velocity round was used."

"I don't know weapons," al-Bis insisted. "Roller coasters and merry-go-rounds, but not guns, Mossad. What did you give this prisoner in exchange for information? Whatever it was, I suggest you go back and see if she knows what became of her cousin after he left here."

Al-Bis seemed to find the size bolt he needed and drew it from the steel box, others of varying sizes tumbling out with it, along with something else: A bullet, the same 5.56 shell, modified with a lighter casing to reduce weight, that was used in Caesarea.

Lia went for her gun. Al-Bis went for the steel box.

She jerked her Jericho 941 nine-millimeter pistol, her favorite sidearm since her days in the army, upward, steady and straight, when al-Bis flung the contents of the box at her, showering the air with steel.

CHAPTER 15

JUDEAN HILLS, ISRAEL

Lia threw her hands up reflexively to guard her face from the shower of bolts and fittings. Impact made her jerk the trigger and a shot exploded into the ceiling. She tried to steady the pistol again, only to realize the impact had also stripped it from her grasp. Her ears, deafened by the bullet's roar, missed the sound of the Jericho clattering to the workshop's concrete floor.

She swung back toward al-Bis to find him lunging toward her with some kind of pneumatic air hammer cutting the air ahead of him. It trembled in his grasp, his face hateful, spittle flying from his mouth as he drove it forward toward her torso.

Lia sidestepped, feeling the heat of the air hammer before it forged a neat, gaping hole in the wall. It wedged there briefly, still long enough for her to hammer the bigger man with a series of blows that produced little effect.

I'm getting old. I'm getting slow. I'm getting weak.

She formed those thoughts at the edge of the same consciousness that recorded that al-Bis was much bigger and stronger than she'd judged, uncoiling his size and strength with the abandonment of his persona. He clamped his hand over her face and drove her head backward, ramming her skull against the shelving at her back.

Tools, machine parts, and containers of lubricant spilled downward, smacking into both of them. Lia's head felt as if it had been split in two, as the same rancid, grimy hand that had closed on her face lowered to clutch her by the throat. She felt him start to squeeze, the air bottlenecking instantly in her throat and making her head feel like it was about to explode.

Lia flailed blindly behind her and to the sides, feeling about the shelves, finally grasping a long-necked plastic container of motor oil used on the churning parts of the amusement rides beyond in the park. The container exploded on impact with al-Bis's face, coating him in thick, dark ooze that he proceeded to cough from his mouth into Lia's face. He was retching now, and his grip slackened enough for Lia to tear free and recover her breath, gasping. She swung back toward al-Bis just as he was coming for her again. Enraged, his eyes, red from being drenched in oil, were now narrowed into anguished slits.

Lia yanked on another of the shelves and drew it downward, collapsing it upon al-Bis as he groped for her. She fully expected it to take him over with it to the floor, but al-Bis managed to somehow right the shelf and jam it hard into Lia, pinning her against the wall. Then he was out the door. Lia jerked the shelf from her, retrieved the Jericho 941, and charged off in pursuit.

Outside the workshop, she twisted left, right, back left again. No sign of al-Bis in any direction, leaving Lia fearing he'd escaped via a long-planned route geared for just this eventuality. She could feel the muscles clench in her stomach from the tension, her ears still feeling as if cotton were stuffed between them.

The workshop was located in a rear corner of the park, leaving its sprawl cluttered with tourists and locals flowing amid the rides and attractions that turned the pathways of Kif Tzuba amusement park into a labyrinth. She glimpsed some kind of disruption directly ahead, bodies shifting awkwardly, with complaints shouted in Hebrew.

"*Hey!*"

"*Watch where you're going!*"

"*Asshole!*"

Lia rushed in that direction, finding an odd rhythm in skirting the crowd in search of gaps, fissures that would put her on Dar Ibrahim al-Bis's trail. And, sure enough, she glimpsed a large male figure plowing through the crowd, pushing, shoving, and practically throwing people from his path.

Lia picked up her pace, Jericho pistol held low by her hip, feeling superheated, thanks to more than just the hot sun and warm temperatures. How many of the tools to wage terror against the State of Israel had been forged on these very grounds by a bomb maker hiding out in the guise of a repairman? Fixing what was broken while breaking untold bodies and lives with the terrible tools of his trade.

She found the irony striking, and it served only to fuel her resolve. She was closing in on al-Bis while remaining careful not to create the kind of ripples in the crowd that might alert him to her presence. She was almost to him as they neared the entrance to the roller-coaster ride that featured an assortment of dips, darts, and stomach-churning steep drops. The interconnected chain of cars had just ground to a halt, one group of passengers exiting beneath raised lap bars so another set could take their place in the same seats.

The attendant was just about to pull back the chain and let the next set of children and their parents board, when al-Bis shoved him out of the way and snatched a small boy from the ground. Lia saw the glint of a knife blade flash in the sun, jammed up against the child's throat. Al-Bis backpedaled along the track paralleling the interconnected cars. Israelis, no stranger to firearms, yanked them out en masse, a staggering number trained on al-Bis by shooters with too much sense and training to risk a shot while he had the boy clutched before him.

"Stay back! Stay back!" al-Bis wailed.

Their eyes finally met when Lia pushed to the front of the line. He pushed the knife closer to the boy's throat.

"Start it! Start the ride!" he ordered the ride attendant he'd just accosted.

The young man balked, remaining frozen.

"Now!" al-Bis roared, drawing a thin line of blood with a prick of his knife against the boy's throat.

Not much of an option, but the only one the bomb maker had. The young attendant finally threw the switch, sending the cars spiraling over much of the park, along its center. Lia figured al-Bis hadn't made his way here randomly or out of desperation. This was part of some escape plan he'd hatched long before, to be invoked when the circumstances required, which was now the case.

She watched the cars edge into motion along the initial straightaway that twisted into the first rise of the coaster. In that moment, her thoughts and action became one, the distinction between them nonexistent. She pushed through the rest of the crowd, past the young attendant, and then found herself running along the track after the cars that were just now picking up speed, with al-Bis riding the front, knife still at the child's throat.

She leaped into the rearmost car when it was almost beyond her and fell into an awkward tumble, her shoulder crashing against the lap bar. She broke her fall with her hands and pushed herself up from the awkward position, starting to rise, when the centrifugal force of the coaster pushed her back down as it banked into the first rise.

Lia held on for dear life as the coaster crested the top and angled into a drop that felt much steeper than it really was. She was back on her feet as soon as it sped into the next curling straightaway and rotated partially onto its side, one of those moments meant to induce shrieks and cackles from its young riders.

She leaped from car to car, fighting gravity, the growing figure of al-Bis watching in shock as she neared him, just a few cars back now.

"Let him go, al-Bis!"

"I'll kill him!" he cried out in a rage, knife tip held just short of the captive boy's jugular vein.

Lia raised her pistol. "Let him go!"

The cars banked into another rise and al-Bis surveyed the grounds around them to get his bearings, perhaps measuring off the point on the ride where he intended to drop off. Lia pictured him tossing the boy off first to create a distraction and draw attention from himself. He'd do that and chance a bullet from her as he vanished into the crowd below yet again. She held fast to the lap bar through the rise, ready with her plan, as the cars zoomed into the next drop.

That's when Lia pushed herself into motion, the move as absurd as it was impossible. It felt like jump school training in a wind tunnel. Air that felt as heavy as mud seemed to hold her up as she launched herself airborne, going against the grain of gravity and daring it to stop her.

She landed in the car immediately behind al-Bis's, as the coaster flattened into the next straightaway. Lia looked up to see the sun blocked by his big shape looming over her, a single ray reflecting off the knife sweeping down toward her.

She twisted and felt the blade scratch at her upper arm, drawing blood while doing no real damage. She found her footing in the next instant, the ride hitting its peak speed as she rose in time to ward off one blow from al-Bis, and then another.

My pistol!

Only in that moment did she realize she'd somehow lost hold of the Jericho in the midst of her leap, and she didn't dare to try to grope for it with the next rise of the roller coaster coming.

"Help!"

She heard the boy's plaintive wail, as she held fast to al-Bis's knife hand. She risked a glance forward and saw the boy clinging to the lap bar to avoid falling out, his tiny legs dangling outside the car. The coaster swept into the rise, the next dip certain to tear the boy's grasp away. Lia hammered al-Bis hard with her free hand, warding off his blows. They were almost to the top of the rise, though, with just moments remaining to act before the child was projected through the air.

She remembered Caesarea, the terror of the attack, with her granddaughter clutched in her arms. Meirav was just a few years younger than this boy.

Lia flung herself forward, airborne in the instant the dip followed the lead car cresting the rise. She banged into the front car, maintaining the presence of mind to flail a hand blindly about, just managing to latch on to the boy before his grip on the lap bar separated. She was holding on to him for dear life to keep his upper body in the car, and then she jerked him all the way inside when the coaster dropped into its next steep descent, twisting from side to side.

It was enough to strip al-Bis's balance away before he could complete the lunging assault to which he'd committed, leading with his knife. He was still coming forward, straining for balance, when Lia joined his motion instead of fighting it. She kept him going forward while lowering her frame, creating a judo-style move that projected him up and over her as the coaster sped into the center of the drop.

Something made her cover the boy's eyes when al-Bis landed just steps ahead of the speeding car, before it rolled over and crushed him. The coaster thumped back down, its front cars separated from the track and skewing wildly to the side as Lia Ganz held on tightly, with the boy pinned beneath her.

CHAPTER 16

WASHINGTON, DC

Brixton had replayed his entire conversation with Flo Combes over their early dinner at Novita the whole train ride home. Funny how different he'd felt when meeting with Kendra Rendine and then the professor—informational sessions as opposed to introspective ones. The scope of his problems didn't hit him until he'd voiced them all out loud to Flo.

Well, maybe not funny so much as obvious. His work had always been all-consuming, often because lives could be lost if he let himself be distracted for even a moment. He had always marveled at the professionalism and dedication of the Secret Service agents assigned to the presidential detail. But they had a virtual army of personnel at their disposal and operated almost exclusively on the friendly turf of the homeland. This was in stark contrast to Brixton's missions for SITQUAL, overseas in foreign lands and often in hostile territory.

Reflecting on that again now left him thinking back to his conversation with Flo earlier in the day, to the reasons she'd decided to leave him and return to New York. He realized that stepping away from SITQUAL hadn't changed anything, that he was merely continuing the descending spiral that had begun with the bombing. It was one thing for a parent to lose a child, but he had borne witness to Janet's death, watched it unfold in real time in abject helplessness. He thought he'd healed, but the blood had only slowed, not stopped. He'd already lost Flo, and he realized how dangerously close he had come to losing himself.

And now he was coming home again, albeit to entirely different circumstances. No job, no income, no girlfriend, no prospects he could point to for the future. Certainly not the kind of life changes any grandfather needed. In fact, he'd long promised his daughter that he would foot the bill for his grandson's education, both secondary and college. He'd made that promise when financial security was a given. Brixton had gotten back off the mat before, but as a much younger man, with more of his life ahead of him than behind. He dreaded going back to his Arlington, Virginia apartment; spending a few fleeting hours with Flo Combes had reminded him of how much he missed her.

But life, in all its vast peculiarities, had given him a chance to reboot. First he'd done on the Metro what he couldn't do five years ago in the restaurant.

And now he was fitting together the pieces of a deadly puzzle that suggested the vice president of the United States might well have been murdered. Beyond that, there was the mystery of Detective Rogers and where he fit into all this. Brixton was struck by the feeling it was leading someplace big and bad.

He'd sat in one of the rearmost cars, and he turned his attention back to what he'd learned from the professor, as he walked the long length of the platform toward the escalator leading up into Union Station. He knew he needed to be extremely cautious about how to bring Kendra Rendine up to speed. If her suspicions about Vice President Stephanie Davenport having been murdered were correct, it figured that whoever was behind the deed would stop at nothing to keep the truth from ever getting out. That could potentially place him and Rendine in grave danger, and they needed to plot their next steps forward with extreme caution, keeping that possibility in mind.

Brixton continued toward the escalator, moving farther into the brighter lights, where passengers were funneling up toward the station. He glanced briefly back at the train as he walked, glimpsing the reflection of a vaguely familiar figure in the window glass, maybe fifteen feet behind him.

Vaguely familiar because the last time Brixton had seen him had been on a murky Metro platform in the wake of the explosion.

It was the man he knew as Detective Rogers.

CHAPTER 17

WASHINGTON, DC

At that point, Brixton had no idea whether the man who'd impersonated a detective had been on board the train or had been waiting for him on the platform. He shrugged off either of those scenarios for now in favor of focusing all his thinking on how to lose this man whose motivations were as nebulous as his true identity.

As casually as possible, Brixton glanced toward the long, nearly unbroken line of train window glass. He didn't spot Rogers again and began to wonder if the initial sighting had been no more than the product of his imagination. But then Rogers's reflection reemerged in Brixton's line of vision, holding the same distance behind him—a classic tailing maneuver when a single man had been tasked with the effort. Rogers had neither lost nor gained ground, was holding still about fifteen feet, three window lengths maybe, back.

Brixton fought against the urge to turn around, feeling safe enough under the circumstances to delay any offensive or countermeasures at this point. Slowing his pace slightly, he weighed his options. His first thought was to report the man to a DC Metro cop he spotted standing vigil on the platform. Smoke Rogers out and see how he reacted. Maybe tell the cop the guy had a gun and that Brixton had heard him engaged in a conversation that could have been interpreted as a threat to the president. Nothing got the wheels of law enforcement turning in this town faster than that, and Brixton would deal with the ramifications of his lie after Rogers was in custody.

He confirmed the fake detective was still there fifteen feet back, and he checked again one last time before angling for the DC Metro cop.

To find Rogers gone.

Or maybe he'd never been there. Maybe Brixton had turned some stranger into the phantom he hadn't been able to cleanse from his mind since Monday's Metro attack. That possibility grew in likelihood when there remained no further sign of Rogers in the reflection off the window glass. Brixton still hadn't turned around to double-check, figuring the best he could do now, under the circumstances, was to take flight from the station and head back home to contemplate his next move.

He was twenty feet from the escalator, standing near the end of a line that stretched upward as far as his eye could see, when something hard pressed against his back through his jacket.

"Keep walking," a voice Brixton recognized as Rogers's ordered, as the man pushed the pistol tighter against him.

"Now," the voice added for emphasis, even though he didn't have to.

Brixton felt himself being pushed past the escalators, hidden from the DC Metro police officer's view by the throngs of disembarking passengers that enclosed them. But the man he knew as Detective Rogers pushed him swiftly beyond the clutter, into the darkness of the tunnel, where the platform narrowed to virtual single file.

"Who are you?" Brixton found enough voice to pose.

He knew the man wouldn't risk shooting him here, not with the echo of the gunshot certain to alert the cop on the platform, who'd be equally certain to alert others.

So where was the man taking him?

"What do you want?" Brixton tried.

"Up there on your right, that door. Open it."

It looked like a fire door of some kind, covered with graffiti. Brixton had glimpsed doors like it from time to time from inside the Metro, always figuring they no longer led anywhere.

It turned out he was wrong.

The door opened onto a set of grated steel stairs descending into a dull haze of light below. Enough to tell Brixton where he was.

Residing beneath Washington, DC, proper was a warren of tunnels laid out like some kind of hive. Some were the product of never-completed sections of the Metro itself, abandoned due to the water table, too much rock to safely blow through, or redundancy. But most of them were the product of the long-discontinued trolley and streetcar system that had been built partially underground.

For nearly a century, a network of streetcars had ferried Washingtonians around the city, originally drawn by horses and later powered by elevated electric cables. The Dupont Circle station, constructed in 1949, was unique in the streetcar system for being the only station that was built underground. It was in operation until the system was shut down and replaced by bus lines in 1962, with plans for building the Metro train system on the horizon.

This tunnel must have been part of an unfinished spur of that underground trolley line from another era. It smelled of rot, mold, and rancid standing water. At the bottom of the grated stairs, the so-called Detective Rogers shoved him forcibly forward, Brixton swinging to find the pistol aimed straight at him.

"Go," the man ordered, gesturing toward a door that matched the one leading onto the steel stairs.

Brixton shouldered his way through this one, too, finding himself on a trolley platform overlooking a nonexistent track bed that had been abandoned before reaching this spur. He heard the rattle of the heavy door closing behind him and felt the man he knew as Rogers shove him forward.

"What did you and the Secret Service agent discuss?"

Brixton turned to face him. "I don't know what you're talking about."

He barely recorded saying that. Whoever this man was working for, they must've been following him. How else could they know about his meeting with Kendra Rendine? And, more to the point, why would that be of interest to someone potentially involved with the would-be suicide bomber?

"Who are you working with?" he challenged, before Rogers could resume. "Who was behind that suicide bomber?"

"Nice try," the man said, his expression tightening. "Now tell me about New York, what you were doing there."

The tunnel shook with a stinging vibration caused by a Metro car thundering along an adjacent tube. The vibration left the man before Brixton a bit unsteady on his feet, a moment of vulnerability that passed as quickly as it had come, pellet-sized debris dropping from the ceiling above and showering the air with dust.

"Seeing my ex-girlfriend," Brixton said, choosing to answer the latter of his two questions at the same time, needing to stall for time.

"You met with someone else prior to going to see her. If you lie again, I'll shoot you in the knee. Lie a third time and it'll be your other knee." He made a show of aiming his pistol low. "Now, what does the Secret Service agent know?"

"About what?"

The man curled his finger around the trigger. "Don't try my patience."

"The Secret Service agent and I are old friends. You already know I worked for a private security contractor called SITQUAL. That's where I met the Secret Service agent," Brixton insisted, not wanting to use Rendine's name, because his captor hadn't. "You also probably know that I'm looking for work right now, and I was hoping my friend might be able to help me find some. Satisfied?"

Brixton still couldn't fathom the man's interest in Rendine. He could hear the distant rumble of another train thundering through the adjacent tube, and he pretended not to hear Rogers's response in order to have an excuse to move another step closer. The train's rumble approached a crescendo, about to pass their position in the adjacent tunnel. Brixton tensed his lower legs, propping himself on the balls of his feet. So when the vibration again left the man a bit wobbly, he was ready.

Brixton had one chance to get this right or he'd be dead, simple as that. He lunged forward, arms outstretched before him to jerk the pistol upward as soon as he impacted the man's hands. A shot rang out, close enough to his skull to make the side of his head and ear feel like they'd been scorched by an open flame.

Brixton and the gunman twisted and twirled atop the long-abandoned trolley platform. It was riddled with debris from the crumbling ceiling overhead, which threatened to trip them up at every turn. The result was a bizarre pirouette, free form as opposed to choreographed, that left both men fighting for control of the weapon while remaining careful to tread lightly amid the precariously placed husks of concrete.

The gunman was as big as Brixton, but stronger, and younger by twenty years or so. Instead of trying to wrest the pistol free of the grappling, he slammed Brixton back against the platform wall, kicking up a cloud of dust that enveloped them like a shroud. Before Brixton could respond, the man had jammed his free hand under Brixton's chin and was pushing it upward, wrenching his neck and stealing his focus from the pistol.

Brixton was losing, and if he lost he was dead.

Jerking his head back had angled Brixton's gaze up toward the patchwork ceiling, with its jagged gaps where the concrete had given up and given way. So maybe, just maybe . . .

Brixton threw all of his attention back on the pistol the gunman still held but that he had neutralized. The barrel was aimed straight up. Instead of continuing to try to tear it from the man's grasp, Brixton closed his finger on the trigger and pulled.

Once, twice, three times . . . Then four, then five, then six and seven . . .

With that, he pulled his hand away, let the man have the pistol, and struck him hard enough to tear free of the hand trying to snap his neck. The gunman had just steadied the pistol's squarish barrel toward him when a rumble turned his gaze upward.

A thick shower of rubble, loosened by the bullets' impact, was cascading downward like mini asteroids falling from the night sky.

Brixton heard the crunch that could only be human bone and skull cracking upon impact. The gunman he'd known as Detective Rogers was left silent and still in the pile of rubble that had virtually entombed him. Brixton didn't need to check for a pulse to see whether the man was dead; the condition of his face and what remained of his skull told him.

You're working with whoever's behind this.

The dead man wasn't alone, which meant others could be coming any moment.

Which meant Brixton had to flee. Now.

CHAPTER 18

JUDEAN HILLS, ISRAEL

Lia Ganz was still on the grounds of Kif Tzuba amusement park when Moshe Baruch arrived, two hours after the roller coaster had crushed Dar Ibrahim al-Bis to death. The head of Mossad was accompanied by a full security and forensics team to take over for the national police, who had secured the scene in the meantime.

"I see the police were wrong," he started, "when they told me a Mossad agent was involved."

"I made clear it was *former*."

"Someone told me recently there was no such thing."

"Close enough," Lia acknowledged.

Baruch frowned. "I seem to have erred in giving you permission to return to the field."

"I don't recall asking for it."

"Close enough," Baruch said, using her own phrase against her. "Once a lion, always a lion. And like a lion you can't stop hunting."

"Lions hunt to live, Commander. I acted so more Israelis don't die."

"What did you have to promise that prisoner to make her give up the name, Colonel?"

"A visit from her two young children."

"Which you knew to be impossible."

"In spite of which, I gave her my word."

"Which you lacked the authority to give."

"I've never broken a promise, Commander."

"There's a first time for everything, including using a roller coaster as a weapon."

"You taught me to use whatever was available."

Baruch shook his head, looking like he'd swallowed something sour. "Too bad you didn't pay as good attention to all of my lessons, like promising something you can't deliver and undertaking a mission without proper authorization or backup. Even the Lioness of Judah can overstep her bounds."

"Why don't we give the man's workshop a closer look and then decide how far I overstepped?"

* * *

After an hour had passed, with Lia pacing nervously outside the old shed al-Bis had appropriated for his repairs and workshop, she had begun to fear that her suspicions had led her astray. More likely it was how close her granddaughter had come to falling victim to the drone attack. Perhaps she hadn't been thinking clearly in her rush to judgment. And now a man was dead—a man who, even if he hadn't designed the deadly flying machines, might have proven an excellent source of information to Mossad.

Then Moshe Baruch emerged alone, his expression dim and blank.

"There's something inside you need to see, Colonel."

She followed him through the fading afternoon light and back inside the dimly lit workshop. It was quiet, no sound of voices or movement. Then again, it had also been quiet in the park itself since the initial national police first responders to the scene had evacuated and closed the park. Lia had noted the noise first ebbing and then vanishing entirely, producing an eerie sense of stillness in her, while she'd waited for Mossad's arrival. It should have made her feel more secure, but instead it had made her feel less so. Lia was left imagining herself taking her granddaughter here, happy and cackling as she rode the roller coaster on which her grandmother had just killed a man to save another child's life.

Inside the late Dar Ibrahim al-Bis's workshop, the dim lighting revealed a rectangular hole in the floor where some shelving had been shoved out of the way. Lia imagined all the seams being covered or camouflaged to keep anyone from noticing the hatch's existence. A ladder that smelled of fresh lumber extended downward into a darkness now broken by several floodlights that had been placed to provide illumination in the dark space. That was enough to tell her that the hidden room must have been some sort of subbasement and that the shed itself likely had been already standing when the rest of the park was constructed, making use of any number of preexisting structures on the sprawling grounds.

Moshe Baruch preceded her down the ladder and then gestured for her to join him. Lia took the rungs agilely, despite the numbness in her now bandaged shoulder, where al-Bis had grazed her with a knife strike. She reached the bottom, which was formed by a flattened gravel floor, and found herself in a space little bigger than a decent-size closet. Except, in place of clothing was an assortment of the tools of Dar Ibrahim al-Bis's true trade: weapons, and the materials required to customize them to the needs of this fighter or that.

Lia's gaze went to a neat array of bullets that she recognized as the very modified 5.56-millimeter ordnance that had been used in the drone attack in Caesarea.

"Colonel," the head of Mossad called out, directing Lia's attention to a wall papered with drawings and schematics.

She took a flashlight from his grasp and studied the drawings closer, fixing on one featuring the very drones he'd designed, and perhaps even constructed, in this very room, following the precise parameters of these blueprints. She realized the stacks of aluminum she'd spotted not far from the modified ammunition must have been used to manufacture the custom housings of the weapons to make them light enough for the drones to carry. All of the walls were papered with such plans, making Lia shudder at the thought of how many lives had been lost as a result of the work performed in this cramped and cluttered house of death.

The flashlight beam held on another drawing, which looked fresher than the others. The paper was still radiant white, without any of the yellowing bubbling from collected moisture, or streaks of grime that marred the plans that had been here longer. Of course, a man of al-Bis's experience and prowess never should have left them here, a kind of shrine to his murderous achievements, but she supposed that was the point, and she imagined him reveling in the sight of them as an art lover might while standing before a Picasso or a van Gogh. Al-Bis likely fancied himself an artist of a different ilk, and since he never got to enjoy for himself the final tapestries drawn in blood, feasting on the sight of his creations was the next best thing. Destroying them would be tantamount to destroying the objects they presaged; it would be sacrilegious in his mind, showing disregard for the glory the acts had brought him. They were the next best thing, in other words, to photographs of the aftermaths of the attacks to which he was party.

"What are these?" Lia asked, beam held on a portion of the drawing's contents: a pair of objects drawn to scale but lacking enough detail to identify.

"We're not sure yet," Baruch replied. "So far, we've found nothing here that matches anything like this."

"We need to find out," Lia told him, "and fast . . ."

With that, she shined her flashlight on the next drawing over, detailed schematics etched upon similarly fresh paper, no more than a month old.

"Because that's a suicide vest," Lia continued, "and someone must be planning to strap it on."

CHAPTER 19

WASHINGTON, DC

"What happened to your face?" Kendra Rendine asked him, as Brixton joined her at the table at Ellē, where they'd made plans to meet for breakfast before he left for New York.

"Welcoming committee when I got back from New York last night," Brixton told her.

Ellē was a combination café, restaurant, and bar that also housed a wholesale bakery called the Paisley Fig on Mount Pleasant Street NW, four blocks from the Columbia Heights Metro station where Brixton had gotten off. It offered counter as opposed to table service, which meant they wouldn't be subjected to any interruptions from a waitstaff. Rendine had chosen a seat in clear view of the window, so she could watch for his approach down the redbrick-colored sidewalk that was actually finished in a gritty, as opposed to stamped, surface that kept the pavement from getting too slick when wet or icy.

"Let's change seats."

"Why?"

Brixton pointed to his face.

"You're worried they're not finished, that maybe they followed you here?" Rendine asked him.

"No, Kendra. I'm worried they followed you."

They switched to a table that had just been cleared, inside a separate, glassed-in seating area away from the storefront and counter display. The table was propped up against a glass partition, and Brixton positioned himself to watch the entrance so he could keep an eye peeled in that direction. They made sure to order, so as not to stand out, and to enjoy the offerings of this relatively off-the-beaten-DC-path establishment, where few government types were known or seen. Rendine ordered granola and coconut yogurt. Brixton was tempted to try the house specialty, salmon on toast, but his stomach felt a bit queasy from an uneasy sleep following last night's attempted kidnapping, which had ended very badly for the kidnapper. He ordered a bagel and a large coffee that was classified as mild.

Brixton hadn't wanted to involve any kind of police the night before. The further attention it would draw to him had to be avoided at all costs, along with his complicity in the death of the man he'd originally known as Detective Rogers, in the aftermath of the Metro bombing. So he called in an anonymous tip to DC Metro police, after bringing up a security app that would block any recognition of his phone or his location at the time.

Brixton told the story from the beginning, his visit to the professor and his pigeons on a New York City rooftop the previous day. He summed up the professor's conclusions as succinctly as possible.

"A weaponized stent?" Rendine posed, not quite sounding like she bought it. "Your friend was speaking hypothetically, right?"

"He's more of an associate than a friend. And something you should know about men like the professor: when they speak 'hypothetically,' it's usually about something they've employed themselves at some point, or have heard of someone else who did. There's not a lot of space between theory and fact, in other words."

"You're saying it's been done."

"I think that's a safe assumption, yes."

"I've gone over Vice President Davenport's autopsy results with a fine-tooth comb. There's no mention of anything amiss or awry with her stents."

"Chances are they weren't checked that closely, but they should still be in secure storage someplace, maybe even under Secret Service auspices. That means we could do a deeper dive and analysis into them."

Brixton could see Rendine making a mental note of that.

"But we'll want it done by someone you're certain you can trust," he resumed. "We need to keep the circle on this as tight as we possibly can."

She looked at his face again. "Because it's already widened too much?"

"I was getting to that. The man who assaulted me was the same fake cop who interrogated me on the Metro platform after the bombing. But we didn't pick up on that discussion. He wanted to know about you: what you knew, what you'd shared with me, what I'd learned in New York."

Rendine returned her spoon to her bowl of yogurt. "Wait a minute . . ."

Brixton let her fit the pieces together for herself.

"This man was on the platform in the immediate aftermath of the bombing."

He nodded. "That's right."

"But last night he was asking about *me*—what I knew about the vice president's death, presumably."

"Also right. And you know what that means, Agent."

Rendine leaned forward, elbows straddling her bowl of granola and coconut yogurt. "There has to be a connection between the Metro bombing and the potential murder of Vice President Davenport."

"Bingo," said Brixton.

CHAPTER 20

WASHINGTON, DC

Rendine leaned back, and Brixton gave her all the time she needed to process the same conclusion he'd reached himself the night before, losing hours of sleep.

In the ensuing moments, he found himself thinking about his grandson and how pitifully little time he'd been spending with the boy. He was almost thirteen years old now, playing Little League baseball after a season of Pop Warner football in the fall and church league basketball through the winter. His surviving daughter and son-in-law didn't live in the Washington, DC, area, but he'd made unconscionably little effort to take time out of his schedule, something he never would have imagined happening, after Janet's tragic death five years ago. He always seemed to be too busy, always on this case or that, and loath to let any client down, especially those who were referred to him by Mackensie Smith or someone else in the firm.

What had he been thinking?

Brixton watched Rendine narrow her gaze on him. "You really *shot out* the ceiling?"

He nodded. "Six, maybe seven bullets."

"Unconventional."

"Hey, it worked, didn't it?"

"Your attacker didn't say anything else that might help us?"

He shook his head. "Like I said, his interest lay in what you were up to, what we'd discussed."

"The man used those words?"

"I don't remember his exact words. He wanted to know what you knew, what you had told me, along with who I'd met with in New York."

"So he knew you'd been there."

"He was waiting for me on the platform in Union Station when I got back."

"Are you sure about that, Robert?" Rendine asked him.

"What do you mean?"

"Maybe he was on the train. Maybe he was following you all day."

Brixton felt a cold chill at that potential reality. He needed to warn the professor to be on his guard. Maybe he should warn Flo Combes as well.

"Either way," Rendine picked up, "they're monitoring your movements.

That means they could be listening in on your phone calls, might have even wired your apartment. Can you have it swept?"

"I know some people," Brixton told her, leaving it there.

"Because I can't be of any direct help. We've got to keep our connection as dark as we can."

"That's why I suggested we change tables."

Rendine sighed, used a spoon to further mix in her granola with her yogurt. "This kind of thing isn't supposed to happen for real. You're talking to someone who still believes that Lee Harvey Oswald acted alone."

"We've both got our work cut out for us, Kendra. Can you put together a list of all medical personnel at Walter Reed who were part of the team who installed the stents in the vice president?"

"I ran detailed backgrounds on them in advance, and I'm sure I still have those."

"Can you follow up with them? Subtly."

"I can follow up with them. I'm not sure how subtle I can be."

"How many are we talking about?"

"I was in the room myself, Robert, in full scrubs. I remember the interventional cardiologist who performed the actual procedure assisted by a pair of catheterization lab nurses, a video technician, and an anesthesiologist."

"The vice president was under?"

"Not entirely. It was IV sedation, a small combined drug cocktail of fentanyl and valium. Normally a tech can perform that part of the process, but since it was the vice president, we had an actual anesthesiologist. But not all of them would have come into contact with the stents themselves. Following that chain will involve several more people not present in the operating room."

Brixton weighed what Rendine was saying. "Who actually prepped and delivered the stents?"

"Another tech, a woman. As I recall, the stents were packaged, to keep them completely sterile until opened. Each of the three was packaged separately."

"They must have been inspected prior to being implanted, right?"

"By who, Robert? For what?" Rendine asked, an edge of frustration creeping into her voice.

"I wasn't criticizing you, Kendra."

"You don't have to. *I* was criticizing me, just like I've been doing since the night Stephanie Davenport died. You've just given me more reason to."

"So if the professor's theory on the means of the vice president's murder is correct, it figures the stents were tampered with prior to being packaged and delivered to the operating room, by parties currently unknown."

Rendine nodded. "It couldn't have been done by any of the surgical staff present. I was watching every motion they made, and there's also a recording of the entire procedure I intend to watch in slow motion to see if I might have missed something."

"I'm sure you didn't," Brixton told her. "We should also make up a list of everyone who knew the vice president was going in for this procedure."

"Makes sense," Rendine said, nodding again, "since whoever set all this in motion had to know the when and where of the procedure's scheduling."

"And how about a detailed itinerary of what Davenport had been doing in the hours or days after you came to believe something was wrong?"

"You mean, after her meeting with the president, which would take us back over five weeks now. I can have that itinerary broken down by hours."

"Were you there with her at the White House?"

"I accompanied her, yes, but wasn't present for the meeting itself. It was their normal working Wednesday lunch. Nothing out of the ordinary at all, except for the fact they hadn't had one in a while."

"Until the vice president emerged from it."

"That's right."

"And you have no idea what was discussed?"

Rendine shook her head. "None, whatsoever. But I do know someone from the White House had called to try and cancel the lunch, but the message was never relayed to the vice president."

"Any idea who?"

"I never asked. I'm wondering now if Davenport did get the message about the cancellation but ignored it and showed up anyway. And she emerged from the meeting shaken, and not just because lunch was never served."

"She didn't mention anything?"

"She didn't volunteer anything, and you've been at this long enough to know the drill, Robert. We never ask such questions of the persons we're protecting."

"But you're sure she emerged from the meeting unsettled, something clearly bothering her."

Rendine nodded. "I picked it up from her mannerisms and general sense of anxiety. Spend enough time with a person in this kind of relationship, where you're responsible for their very lives, and you learn to read them better than a CT scan. I wouldn't have paid nearly as much attention if it hadn't persisted, even worsened, over the next month, right up to her death."

"Is it possible Davenport told someone else what was bothering her?"

"Without me knowing?"

"Without you knowing," Brixton confirmed.

"Of course, Robert. The vice president doesn't need to keep the Secret Service in the loop on all her communications, only the in-person meetings."

"Was there any follow-up communication between her and the president in those weeks that followed?"

"Not that I'm aware of, no, at least not in person. I can't speak as to phone calls."

"Then I guess we both have our homework laid out," Brixton said, remembering the bagel he'd slathered cream cheese on but hadn't taken a bite of yet. Nor had he managed even a sip of his coffee.

Neither had Rendine, though she continued to play with her granola and yogurt, poking at it with a spoon. "Mine's obvious, but what's yours?"

"Finding out who the man on that trolley platform last night really is and who he was working for."

CHAPTER 21

WASHINGTON, DC

Sorry for the disruption, Robert," Mackensie Smith said, rising from behind his desk and skirting boxes to greet Brixton after Smith's assistant had sent him in.

"It's me who's sorry, Mac, for disrupting your day further by showing up without an appointment." Brixton said, laying a garment bag he'd carried in with him over the back of the same chair he plopped himself into.

Smith scoffed at him. "Since when do you need an appointment?"

"Since I no longer work here."

"Neither will I in less than a week," Smith said, sweeping his gaze about the boxes scattered through the office for a moving process that had only just begun. "As you can see."

The disruption he'd spoken of moments before was rooted in the fact that most of the other lawyers and office personnel, on this floor of the firm's offices anyway, were packing up their offices as well. Brixton heard phones ringing unanswered and dodged several people toting boxes of either personal items or work product of the firm Mackensie Smith had founded and was in the process of dissolving. He imagined that the partners would reap a sizable payout from the firm's profit-sharing agreement, something Mac had decided to forego in favor of dividing up his share to provide generous severance packages for the firm's clerical personnel and first- and second-year associates, who otherwise wouldn't have qualified for one.

Which, Brixton thought, includes me.

It felt like a handout, which made him feel guilty. Worse, he felt embarrassed by the fact that he wasn't in a position to turn it down.

"Do you mind if I shut the door, Mac?" Brixton asked the man who'd been his employer and remained his best friend.

"Not at all," Smith replied, although it didn't sound that way, given that he'd long made it a practice never to close his door and encouraged the lawyers of the firm to do the same.

Brixton had to move some boxes to get the door closed.

"What's wrong, Robert?" Smith asked him. "You've got that look."

"In this case, it's the look of someone who was attacked last night."

"Which explains that nasty bruise on your face. I thought you were going to tell me you walked into a door."

"I might have, under normal circumstances."

"Being mugged hardly qualifies there."

"Are you my lawyer?" Brixton asked him.

"I'm your friend."

"That's not what I asked."

Smith finally realized where Brixton was going with this. "Do you have a dollar on you?"

"I think so."

"Then let's make this official."

Brixton found a five in his pocket and handed it to over.

"I owe you four dollars in change," Mac told him.

"Our next drink's on you."

"And now that we have established confidentiality . . ."

"I wasn't mugged, Mac, I was *attacked*. By the same man who called himself Detective Rogers."

Mackensie Smith rose and came out from behind his desk, angling the chair next to Brixton's closer to him. "Since you're sitting here, I assume he got the worst of it."

"Oh," Brixton said, "most definitely."

Smith listened to the story without interruption, Brixton sparing him for now the real reason why he'd gone to New York, instead just saying it was to see Flo Combes.

"What can I do, Robert?" Mac said, leaning even closer to him, once he'd finished the tale about the man who'd taken him captive being crushed to death.

"For starters, I'd like to know who he really was. I imagine the police would have that information in hand by now."

"I didn't even know that trolley line ever extended that far underground."

"Apparently, there were stations built that were never linked together. Taking down your shingle hasn't robbed you of your police contacts, I trust."

"Not at all," Smith said, easing his cell phone from his jacket pocket.

Brixton watched him press a number from his saved contacts, then listened to Mac's side of a terse conversation that was no more than a request for information. Judging by the speed of the call and the lack of response or argument from whomever Mac had called, Brixton guessed it was an officer or detective Smith had worked with over the years, who may or may not have owed him a favor.

"He'll get back to me as soon as he's got something to say," he said, pocketing the phone again. "Now, I'd like to hear what you've been leaving out up until this point."

"You know me too well, Mac."

"I get the feeling this is bad, Robert."

"Worse," Brixton elaborated.

* * *

Brixton laid it all out for him, every bit, starting with the suspicions Kendra Rendine had raised with him about Vice President Stephanie Davenport's death and proceeding to what he'd learned from the professor. He finished with the conclusion he and Rendine had reached about the Metro bombing and the possible murder of the vice president of the United States being somehow connected through the man they knew as Detective Rogers, whom he'd left dead on the old trolley platform the night before.

"Connected *how*?" Smith wanted to know, having again remained quiet through the whole of the tale.

"I have no idea, Mac. Neither does Kendra."

Smith leaned back in his chair and took a deep breath. "I don't know what your Secret Service friend expects to find, Robert, but I wouldn't hold my breath. If the vice president was murdered, especially this way, whoever was behind it would never have left any clues behind."

"That's what I'm afraid of."

"Rendine knows how to be discreet, I assume."

"I hope so."

"Because if she reveals her intentions in any way and the wrong people find out . . ." Smith let his thought dangle there, no reason to complete it. "What else can I do, Robert?"

"Nothing for now, at least not until we find out who this Detective Rogers really is."

As if on cue, Smith's cell phone rang and he drew it from his pocket. He checked the number and nodded toward Brixton, their eyes locking through a brief conversation with the person on the other end.

"Say that again?" Mac requested . . . "And you're sure?" . . . "No, don't bother with that for now. I'll get back to you."

He ended the call but kept the phone clutched in his hand this time, looking both mystified and befuddled.

"The police responded last night immediately after receiving your call, Robert, though they had a hell of a time actually finding the platform."

"I can see why."

"What they didn't see was a body. The remains of this Detective Rogers, whoever he really is, weren't there."

CHAPTER 22

WASHINGTON, DC

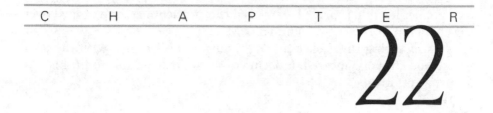

"Who just told you that?" Brixton heard himself ask Mac Smith, as if it were someone else posing the question.

"A source at the Washington PD, a trusted source, who didn't bother asking any questions he knew I couldn't answer."

"I shouldn't be surprised, Mac. It was abundantly clear that whoever this Detective Rogers was, he was waiting for someone else to show up—maybe multiple someones."

"So when he, or they, did and saw what happened, they removed the body from the scene."

"What about blood?" Brixton persisted. "Did they find any blood?"

"They didn't say and I didn't ask, as you heard for yourself."

"Okay. Did this source say anything about security cameras?"

"That trolley tunnel was built before they were even a thought in anybody's mind."

Smith's point was fair, and given that they were toting a body from the scene, it was a safe bet that whomever Rogers had been working with wouldn't have dared to resurface through the same access point in Union Station above. In fact . . .

"Can you ask them, Mac?" Brixton blurted out, before he had a chance to fully complete his thought.

"The police? Ask them what?"

"To check the platform again, a wider circle. How did they get the body out? What if it was only one or two men? Maybe they hid it someplace, figuring they could come back to retrieve it later."

"Makes sense," Smith conceded. "Might have to provide more information explaining the basis of my suspicions, though."

"Maybe not a good idea."

"That was my thought, Robert. But let me see what I can come up with, some half-baked cover story that's just enough to make them move on this."

"They'll have to move fast, Mac. Whoever's pulling the strings here wouldn't want that body down there for any longer than absolutely necessary."

Smith nodded. "Anything else I can do for you?"

Brixton figured his friend was doing this out of guilt over needing to let him go, but he didn't care. He retrieved the garment bag he'd draped over the chair and held it between him and Mac.

"I was wearing this jacket last night during my struggle with the man whose body has disappeared. It occurs to me we may be able to lift his fingerprints off it."

"We?"

Brixton forced a smile. "Do you still have those kind of contacts?"

Smith grinned. "I'm downsizing, Robert, not dying."

Brixton's expression wrinkled. "Let's hope so."

CHAPTER 23

TEL AVIV-YAFO, ISRAEL

As a civilian, Lia Ganz came to Mossad headquarters when she was called. In this case, she was summoned back there the day after Dar Ibrahim al-Bis's underground workshop at Kif Tzuba amusement park had been uncovered. She'd expected to find Moshe Baruch waiting for her in his office alone but instead was ushered into a conference room in which all the chairs were occupied, most by men and women she recognized, only a few by people she didn't.

The room was silent and subdued, tension riding the air like smoke and raising the temperature by several degrees compared to that of the hallway. The men and women gathered around the table followed Lia's entry into the room without truly acknowledging her presence. All knew of the exploits of the Lioness of Judah, and it was clear from their expressions they'd already been briefed on the reason for her presence.

"Sit down, Colonel," Baruch ordered, indicating a chair adjacent to his at the end of the table. "Things have turned rather complicated, and they've turned that way fast."

As she sat down, Lia was struck by the feeling that she'd done something wrong, the tension in the room rooted in the reprisal and punishment that were coming. That said, whatever misstep she was about to be called out for didn't require such an impressive gathering of high-ranking security and government officials.

Baruch touched a button on a notebook computer and a screen mounted to the wall at the front of the room filled with one of the drawings from the wall of al-Bis's workshop. The next shot isolated drawings of two different devices laid side by side. The third shot showed either models or finished versions of those devices.

"You are looking, Colonel, at the transmitter and camera that were salvaged from the remains of the drones recovered at the site of the attack in Caesarea."

Lia nodded, still trying to make sense of why she'd been called to what was clearly a vital planning session with operatives from both the intelligence and operations sections of Mossad, along with the kind of government officials capable of blessing major operations. The fact that Baruch had addressed her as "Colonel" in front of them suggested that she was present on an official basis, as if she weren't retired at all.

"Which confirms the part al-Bis played in the attack," she concluded, thinking again of his cousin, serving life in prison and so desperate to see her children that she'd given him up.

"That's not why we called you here today, Colonel," Baruch said, as if to confirm her assumption.

He held his gaze upon her as he touched the space bar again. This time the screen filled with the mangled and burned remnants of two similarly sized but virtually unrecognizable versions of that same transmitter and camera. Identical in all respects, as far as Lia Ganz could tell.

"I don't understand," she said.

"Neither did we initially, because at first glance what you're looking at makes no sense."

"What *am* I looking at, Commander?"

"You're aware of the terrorist attack in the Washington Metro three days ago?"

Lia nodded. "*Failed* terrorist attack."

Baruch seemed annoyed at her use of a qualifier, since in Israel a terrorist attack was defined by its intent and not its upshot, justice dispensed with equal fury in either case, given that the entire process was aimed, as much as anything, at preventing the next operation.

The head of Mossad gestured toward the screen behind him. "Those are remains recovered from the scene of that *failed* terrorist attack, side-by-side with virtually identical remains recovered from Caesarea. I hope you've kept your passport up to date, Colonel, because you're headed to Washington."

PART THREE

CHAPTER 24

ALBUQUERQUE, NEW MEXICO

The president took the podium after the eulogies had been completed and the muffled sobs and sniffles had abated somewhat. He stood between two pictures of the teenage victim of a school shooting, which had left the boy dead after he had heroically saved the lives of enough classmates to fill a classroom. One was an action shot taken on the football field, beautifully framed by the sun and crowd, the boy flashing a smile from within his helmet as he charged unmolested toward the end zone. The other was a prom picture, capturing him with his date in full formal regalia, holding the corsage he'd yet to pin in place.

President Corbin Talmidge gazed from one picture to the other prior to commencing his speech. He cut an impressive figure, having retained the stature and build that had won him All-American Honorable Mention as a football player himself while he was in the air force, before he'd gone on to a career as a fighter pilot and then astronaut and then into politics. His hair had gone mostly gray, his gait was a bit slowed by deterioration in his hips and knees, but his blue eyes were those of a younger man, still radiant with hope and the kind of positive nature that was rare for a politician and even rarer for a president.

"We all face the devil at some point in our lives," he began, speaking from memory rather than using a teleprompter or paper speech, "and often, how we handle that confrontation defines who we are and what we will be. Most of us turn away, or run, and there's no shame in that. Once in a while, though, a true hero rises up to confront the devil head-on. A hero who, faced with his own death, seeks to prevent evil from claiming others. A hero who embodies everything that is great in us and achieves his greatest potential in the last moments of his own life."

From the darkened shadows off to the side of the church, First Lady Merle Talmidge stood reciting the words from memory in cadence with her husband. The habit relieved her of the stress over a potential flub of the speech the president had rehearsed the night before, his capacity for that kind of recall having remained intact. She needed to be prepared to join him behind the podium, should that flub or stumble devolve into a moment where the world froze up around him to the point that he was aware of only himself, amid a church packed standing room only, in a ceremony being broadcast live across all the news stations.

Merle Talmidge hadn't approved this, of course—would never have approved it, under any circumstances. And normally she would have overridden whatever aide had arranged for the president to speak in front of millions. But in this case, before she could intervene, the president had accepted the invitation to speak at the funeral of seventeen-year-old Joseph Hobbs, who'd rushed a fellow classmate turned school shooter as bullets from an AR-15 tore into him. The boy had been pronounced dead at the scene, but among his classmates, only five others suffered gunshot wounds at all, and none of these were deemed to be life-threatening, meaning Hobbs had saved dozens of his classmates from the fate he'd suffered himself.

So far, so good, the first lady thought, continuing to mouth the words that were coming from her husband's mouth. And then it happened, something entirely unpredictable, off script.

President Corbin Talmidge began to cry.

He stopped his words long enough to swipe a sleeve across his eyes. The first lady of the United States heard sniffles and quiet sobs beginning to spread among the mourners squeezed into the church. She looked back at her husband to see dollops of tears running down his face, making it seem like he'd been caught in the rain. The moment she'd feared above all else was upon her, and there was nothing she could do. Approach to comfort her husband and the president would look weak, a big strong man who needed a woman to support him, instead of the rugged American hero with the right stuff the country had fallen in love with. Then it got worse still.

He started to speak again, pushing the words through his sobbing, hopelessly off script now. He was lost in a fugue of his own making, the memorized words no more than a jumble of letters in his mind.

"My son was a good boy! He didn't deserve this—no child deserves this! Those kids he saved were all my children, too, all our children, and we let them down. *I* let them down. I let my own boy down. I wasn't there when I should have been, didn't realize how precious the time I had with him was, because I always figured there'd be more. Until one day there wasn't and he was gone and the call came and my life changed forever."

First Lady Merle Talmidge felt her heart skip a beat when her husband's face turned blank, his wide-eyed gaze making her wonder if he'd suddenly lost track of where he was and what he was doing there. Then he resumed, his words bathed in incoherence to an audience that desperately wanted to believe in what he was saying.

"When was it?" he asked, as if expecting someone to give him the answer. "Was it yesterday? Last week? Last month? Last year? When did this happen?"

He squeezed the sill of the podium with his big hands, hard enough to force the blood from them. He cocked a gaze behind him, looking at the twin pictures of Joseph Hobbs, football and prom, a befuddled look falling over his expression.

"What's his name?" President Corbin Talmidge posed to no one in particular, a forlorn look of fear spreading over his features. "Why can't I remember his name? My own son and I can't remember his name!"

His voice quickens in cadence, in panic. Merle Talmidge watched the president of the United States falling apart before her, unable to recognize a boy he'd taken for his son just moments before. But the mourners squeezed into the pews saw something else. They saw a man uniquely in touch with exactly what they were feeling. The sense of loss, hopelessness, desperation, helplessness. This could have been any of their sons too, and in that dreaded realization they grasped the point of the president's feigned confusion because their confusion was real. He spoke to them in a way that struck them like a gut punch, moving the most hard-hearted among them to tears and sobs.

President Corbin Talmidge, crying over a lost son whose name he couldn't remember.

Except that their son was quite alive, a happily married thirty-year-old lawyer who, along with his similarly successful husband, had promised to give them grandchildren through adoption or a surrogate.

The moment destined to become legend in the annals of American political history deepened even more when, in front of the crowd that had been utterly silenced, save for those sobs and sniffles, the president moved to the football picture and touched it in loving fashion with a trembling hand. He turned back to the mourners hanging on his every word, his every action.

"It's me," he said, his face squeezed in confusion. "That picture is of me. That's my helmet, my uniform. I must have scored a touchdown that day. Why can't I remember? I need to remember. Please help me remember."

The first lady knew the break had been made, no choice left now. She strode across the church dais purposefully, not too fast and not too slow. Her husband, the president, spotted her coming and flashed an instant of recognition before she embraced him. She felt his tears soaking into the jacket of her dark designer suit, which she'd selected specifically for this day.

"Our boy," Corbin Talmidge moaned. "Our boy . . ."

"I know," the first lady comforted. "I know. But it's going to be all right. Everything's going to be all right."

It would indeed, in a way only a handful of people in the entire country understood, because they alone were willing to do whatever it took to save the United States of America. To set it on the right track once and for all, with her husband steering the ship he no longer grasped he was riding. She had to hold it together just a bit longer, hold *him* together just a bit longer.

That's all it would take. Just a few days left to go now.

And the countdown was on.

CHAPTER 25

BETHESDA, MARYLAND

How can I help you, Agent?" the Secret Service liaison asked Kendra Rendine, after closing the door to her office in the south wing of Building 1, along the same hall as the office of Walter Reed's inspector general.

"The vice president's death requires some routine follow-up, given the proximity of her passing to the procedure recently performed here."

The woman, a hospital administrator named Sheila Wigg, nodded, her expression genuinely mournful. "Such a tragic loss for the country, for this hospital, for everyone. She was a wonderful woman."

Rendine could only nod. Prior to coming to the Walter Reed offices, she'd made a quick stop at the hospital to pick up the autopsy records on Vice President Stephanie Davenport. She cursorily checked the report's contents—sad, dry, and virtually all boilerplate—before briefly studying photographs of the three stents that had been removed during the procedure. They'd been thoroughly cleaned and Rendine had no real idea of what she looking at.

"As you may recall, we met the day of her procedure. She didn't know my name, of course. But she promised to remember it the next time she came by to visit the troops."

"And she would have," Rendine said, because it was the truth, something else that she had admired in the woman she had no doubt had been murdered.

Located in Bethesda, Maryland, the Walter Reed National Military Medical Center was a military medical facility serving the region's army, navy, and air force personnel. It was also commonly referred to as the Bethesda Naval Hospital and had previously been called the National Naval Medical Center. Walter Reed provided care for service members and their families as well as the president, vice president, members of Congress, justices of the Supreme Court, and, on occasion, foreign military and embassy personnel. The massive facility was staffed by more than 8,500 personnel from all three services and was situated on 243 acres, which included the National Intrepid Center of Excellence, built to support the care and rehabilitation of the wounded warriors whom Stephanie Davenport had visited every single week she'd been in office.

"How can I help with this follow-up?" Sheila Wigg asked.

"I need to interview the medical personnel and staff members who participated in the procedure. Just routine, but I need to go over the details and talk with them in order to rule out any connection with her death."

Given Rendine's suggestion, Administrator Wigg could have gotten defensive, but she showed no signs of being anything but cooperative. "I understand. You've reviewed all the camera footage, I assume."

Rendine nodded. "Multiple times. Nothing struck me, nor the outside medical personnel the Secret Service consults with on such matters, as anything but routine and professional. In fact, they were extremely complimentary."

Wigg looked pleased by that. "I'll pass the news along. Do you have the names in question?" she asked, positioning herself closer to her computer. "I could look it up, but if you have them handy, it would save some time."

Rendine produced the list and handed it across the desk to Wigg, who regarded it, after donning her reading glasses. "Seven personnel on the roster, when the norm for this procedure is four."

"As you'll recall, we had a surgeon present just in case something went wrong. His chosen OR nurse as well, along with anesthesiologist, in addition to the tech."

Wigg laid the list of names down in easy view. "Let's go alphabetically, if you don't mind."

"Whatever's easiest for you. And I'll need all the contact information you have on file for them."

"Of course," Wigg said, working the first name on the list—one of the techs, Rendine recalled. "Hmm . . ."

"What?"

"That's odd. I don't seem to be able to find that name. Are you certain it's spelled right?"

"I pulled it from the detailed background check we did on all the names your office furnished us."

Wigg frowned, not seeming to like the prospects of that at all. "Let me try again."

As she did, Rendine was able to tell from her expression that this search, too, had come up blank.

"It could be a glitch in the system," Wigg offered, as an explanation.

"Try another name."

"The operating room nurse is next alphabetically."

"That's fine."

"Oh," Wigg uttered, when the results came up on her screen.

Rendine waited for her to continue.

"She was transferred to the Center for the Intrepid on the grounds of Brooke Army Medical Center, outside San Antonio."

"When?"

Wigg squinted slightly, even though she was wearing reading glasses. "Five days after the vice president's procedure. I don't have a forwarding address, but I do have a phone number," Wigg said, jotting it down.

"Is that unusual?" Rendine asked her.

"The transfer? Not necessarily. Normally, such things are requested, though it's possible the transfer was mandated by a staffing shortage at that facility. I can look into it further, if you like."

"I would, but not now. Let's continue down the list."

"Next name, then," Wigg said, going back to the keyboard.

She looked up moments later, staring at Rendine across the desk, her expression speaking even before she did.

"I don't know what to make of this, Agent," was all she could say. "Two of these names aren't even in our system anymore, a nurse and another of the techs."

"How can that be?"

"A glitch, temporary or otherwise, would be the most likely explanation. The system may have misidentified them somehow and performed a purge."

"A nurse and a tech who both just *happened* to be part of the surgical team involved with Vice President Davenport's procedure?" Rendine asked, not bothering to disguise the skepticism in her voice.

"I know it sounds odd." Wigg regarded her screen again, working the keyboard. "But I can print out the contact info for the other four people who were in the room that day—five if you include the technician, who wasn't actually part of the team."

"I don't recall an eighth person in the room."

"She wouldn't have been there very long, necessarily, and it was a *she*, which probably explains why. Her role was to make sure all instruments were properly sterilized and to be entrusted with custody of, in the vice president's case, the stents that were to be implanted during the procedure."

"Custody?" Rendine posed.

"She would be responsible for filling the surgeon's order, confirming all the requisition codes were correct, and to double-check the condition of the stents prior to passing them on to the cardiologist performing the procedure."

"What about him, the cardiologist?"

Wigg nodded. "Dr. Safron, one of the best anywhere. Let me check."

Her fingers danced across the keyboard, stopped, and then danced some more.

"Hmm . . ."

Again, Rendine thought.

"Apparently," Wigg picked up, "Dr. Safron is on leave."

"Effective when?"

"The beginning of the week that followed the vice president's procedure."

"Any way to tell if the leave was planned prior to that?"

"No, I'm afraid not. I can give you both the doctor's home and cell numbers, though. After all, you are the Secret Service, and this does pertain to the death of a sitting vice president."

"Right on both counts. And this operating room tech?"

Wigg clicked back to the previous screen. "Patricia Trahan."

"Where can I find her?"

"The second floor of Arrowhead Building, that's building number nine, where the cardiology department is housed."

"Might she be there now?"

"If she's on duty. Want me to check?"

"Don't bother." Rendine did some math in her head. "So, of the other six people in that operating room, Dr. Safron is on leave, a nurse was transferred to San Antonio, and two technicians have somehow been purged from the system, which leaves the anesthesiologist and cardio surgeon present in case of emergency."

"I was going to check those."

Rendine watched Administrator Wigg do just that, and then repeat the process from the beginning. "Hmm," she uttered again. "Good news and bad news."

"What's the bad news?"

"The anesthesiologist, Dr. Invantino, has left the hospital. But the good news is that the surgeon, Dr. Callasanti, is operating today, starting at eleven o'clock." She checked the time on her cell phone. "If you hurry, Agent, you might be able to catch him."

CHAPTER 26

BETHESDA, MARYLAND

Rendine went straight to the Arrowhead Building, where the hospital's cardiology wing was housed. She sped through the security stations, thanks to her Secret Service ID. She was told that Dr. Matthew Callasanti was in the surgical prep room, trading his civilian clothes for scrubs, and she was waiting for him when a man emerged through the door.

"Dr. Callasanti?" she asked the large figure with hands like meat hooks, hardly looking like those of such an eminent surgeon.

"That would be me," a voice said from the doorway, belonging to a smaller, mustached man who'd just emerged through the same door. "That's Vincent from Facilities Management."

Vincent had already taken his leave, disappearing into a nearby supply closet.

Rendine flashed her ID for Callasanti. "Do you have a few minutes, Doctor?"

He regarded her badge with something between annoyance and disdain. "Not really."

"I'm doing some routine follow-up on the death of Vice President Stephanie Davenport."

Callasanti scratched at the thick head of hair tucked awkwardly inside his surgical cap. "If it's routine," he said briskly, "it can wait."

"Not really, because one of the things I'm specifically looking into is any potential connection between the vice president's death and the angioplasty procedure performed on her approximately five weeks prior."

"Then let me save you the trouble: there isn't one. No connection."

"How can you be sure?"

Callasanti walked off briskly, the same way he did everything, Rendine imagined, and she sped up her pace to match his.

"I watched everything from the observation room, Agent Rendine," he said, even though he'd barely regarded her ID case, "which provides a much better view than floor level to observe something going wrong."

"And did anything go wrong, Doctor?"

"No, not a thing. It was textbook from beginning to end. I might as well have been out playing golf."

"Nothing stands out?"

"The procedure was being done on the vice president of the United States, Agent. *Everything* stood out, but nothing awry." Callasanti cocked his head back, as if to look at Rendine at a different angle. "I thought you looked familiar. You worked Vice President Davenport's detail. You were in the operating room, right?"

Rendine nodded, instead of elaborating.

"Stephanie Davenport was a wonderful woman," the doctor said. "I don't think I've ever met anyone from either party or political persuasion who didn't like her."

There must have been someone, Rendine almost told him.

The sprawling Walter Reed campus maintained a Secret Service hub in a converted break room to serve as a de facto command post when foreign or domestic dignitaries were being treated or hospitalized for an extended stay. The post was seldom occupied, and this was the case when Rendine accessed it with her key card and took a seat at one of the desks. There were phones, computers, and security monitors everywhere; even Rendine was unable to explain the redundancy.

This was as good a place as any to work and plan her next moves in the wake of her meeting with Hospital Administrator Wigg, which had proven both confounding and unsettling, adding to her unease.

The anesthesiologist, Dr. Invantino, had moved on from Walter Reed, and the cardiologist, Dr. Safron, who'd performed the actual procedure, had gone an extended leave shortly after performing the vice president's procedure. From her seat, Rendine tried them both, at home and on their cells, and got no response on either. That left four more hospital personnel who'd been present in the operating room during Stephanie Davenport's procedure. The operating room nurse had been transferred to the Center for the Intrepid in San Antonio, and the two surgical techs present had somehow been purged from the hospital's computer system. That left Patricia Trahan, the operating room tech responsible for the surgical instruments and stents themselves, who Rendine had learned wasn't on duty today.

When calls to the operating room nurse's cell phone failed to go through for some reason, Rendine phoned the Center for the Intrepid, where the nurse had been transferred, to see if she could be put through directly.

"What did you same the name was again?"

Rendine provided it.

"Could you spell that, please?"

Rendine did.

"I'm sorry, we have no one by that name employed here at present. Is there someone else you'd like me to check for you?"

She absently declined the offer and tried the cell phone numbers of the two surgical techs next, only to find both numbers had been disconnected. Rendine pressed out each of the numbers again for good measure, with the same result. She was starting to see confirmation of what had begun to dawn on her, what she'd started to fear, up in Administrator Wigg's office. She made a mental note to check the precise dates on which those numbers had been disconnected, wondering whether it might have been on the same day.

That left Patricia Trahan, the operating room technician, who fortunately answered her phone on the first ring.

"I'm looking for Patricia Trahan," Rendine said.

"Well, you found her. Unless you want to sell me something, in which case I'm not buying unless it's free."

"I'm not selling anything, Ms. Trahan, don't worry. This is Special Agent Kendra Rendine, head of Vice President Stephanie Davenport's security detail," she said by way of introduction, wondering if saying *former* head might have been more appropriate under the circumstances.

"What a terrible thing. Such a wonderful woman."

"She was a pleasure to work with, Ms. Trahan, and all of us miss her terribly."

"So what can I do for you?"

"You were a member of the surgical team during the vice president's procedure at Walter Reed last month, is that correct?"

A pause followed, long enough to make Rendine wonder if the call had been dropped. She was preparing to hit Redial when the woman's voice returned.

"Is this about the report I filed?" Trahan asked her.

Rendine felt something scratch at her spine. "What report?"

"We're supposed to take note of such things. I didn't think much about it really, but when I heard about the vice president's death . . ."

The woman's voice tailed off. Rendine was unsure what she might have been about to say next. "You filed the report after you heard the news?"

"No, in the aftermath of the procedure itself. That would've been over a month ago now."

"What was in this report?"

"Can I call you back?" Trahan asked her, instead of responding. "There's someone at the door."

Rendine felt that same scratch up her spine again. "Don't answer it!"

"What?"

"And don't answer the phone, either. Is your address still the same? I have one in Gaithersburg."

"Yes, I'm still there."

"I'm on my way, Ms. Trahan," Rendine said, bouncing up out of her chair. "Don't do anything; don't talk to anyone else until I get there."

"They're ringing the buzzer again. Can't I—"

"No! I want you to sit down where you can't be seen from outside and wait for me."

"You're scaring me, Agent."

Rendine was already on her feet and heading for the door.

"I know the feeling, Ms. Trahan. I'm on my way."

CHAPTER 27

GEORGETOWN

"MAC" lit up in Brixton's caller ID a mere two hours after he'd handed over the garment bag containing the coat he hoped bore the fingerprints of his attacker from the night before.

"That was fast," he greeted.

"We need to meet, Mr. Brixton."

Not Mac's voice.

"Who is this?"

"That doesn't matter."

"Where's Mackensie Smith? What are you doing with his phone?"

"I didn't take his phone, just borrowed his number to make sure you'd answer."

Brixton didn't bother considering the ramifications of that, technical and otherwise. "And now that I have?"

"We need to meet. Do you know Georgetown Waterfront Park?"

"Sure."

"I'll be sitting on a bench beneath the pergola directly before the river front steps."

"How will I know you?" Brixton asked.

"You won't," the man said, leaving it there.

"Then maybe we need to do this a different way."

"This is the way we'll be doing it, Mr. Brixton, and you've got no one to blame for that but yourself."

"I'm not the one who 'borrowed' somebody else's phone number."

"No, you're the one who inquired about a certain set of fingerprints. If you want to know who they belong to, I suggest you show up."

Brixton knew he had no choice at that point. If he failed to show up, the mysterious voice on the other end of the line would find him under considerably more adversarial conditions. He was used to the wheels of Washington turning slowly, the exceptionally vital commodity of information often needing to make its way through various levels before finally reaching its destination. The fact that a hit had come back this quickly on the fingerprints lifted from his coat, and that he'd been "ordered" to a meeting under such clandestine circumstances, testified either to the dead man's identity or to his apparent involvement in a terrorist bombing.

Maybe both.

Georgetown Waterfront Park, the site for the meeting, stretched along the banks of the Potomac River from Thirty-First Street NW to the Key Bridge. The park was beloved by many, due to notable design elements such as a labyrinth, a majestic fountain, and charming rain gardens. Visitors came to enjoy the sun and quiet or to take advantage of the open space and walkways. Cyclists, skaters, and pedestrians alike could enjoy being outdoors with no cars about and a view of the Washington waterfront.

There were also the river steps, comprising five levels of tiered seating originally created as viewing grounds for rowing regattas. The steps made for a popular year-round place to take a picnic lunch. More seating, meanwhile, could be found beneath the tall steel and cable pergola, designed as a testament to the waterfront's more industrial past as a once dynamic center of commerce and trade.

Brixton entered the park on foot, at the point where Wisconsin Avenue NW and K Street met, allowing him to stroll past the fountain that had been a favorite spot of his ever since he'd moved to the Washington area. He walked to the river steps and meandered his way along the row of benches and tables set beneath the pergola, waiting for some sign or signal from someone seated there. When none came, he repeated the process and, having failed to establish any contact, sat down on a stray bench set farther down in the shade.

"That was clumsy," a man suddenly seated by his side told him. "You stood out, made yourself obvious."

Brixton collected his thoughts, still trying to determine how this man had managed to take a seat right next to him on the bench without him noticing. The man was the very definition of nondescript, his features no more memorable or distinctive than those of a department store mannequin. He seemed more a projection than actual flesh and blood, his gray shirt and slacks a nearly perfect match for his ashen complexion and Panama hat, which shaded his face from the sun while shading his features from anyone who looked his way.

Brixton thought that if he stared at the man long enough, he might be able to see right through him, as if he were translucent.

"I expected better," the man resumed, "given the duties you performed so admirably for SITQUAL."

"You seem to know an awful lot about me, while I know nothing about you," Brixton said, instantly regretting the lameness of his remark.

"And that's the way it's going to stay. I go by lots of names, so feel free to pick one that suits your fancy."

"Somebody knew how to find you," Brixton said, not about to mention

Mackensie Smith's name, even though this man almost certainly knew of Mac's connection to all this through him.

"Because of what I do, not who I am."

"And what's that?"

"I make connections, determine where information should be routed. With all the various three-letter organizations and others staking out their own territories, somebody needs to know which is best suited to handle what."

"'Somebody' meaning you."

"That's right, Brixton. I imagine this doesn't come as a shock to you, given that you did a stretch with the private security arm of the State Department."

Brixton briefly considered some of the internecine conflicts and jurisdictional squabbles he'd been party to, wondering where the man in the Panama hat had been when he'd needed him.

"Your expression tells me you know I'm right, so we can skip the remaining pleasantries and cut to the chase, as they say."

"The *chase*," Brixton interjected, before the man could continue, "being the identity of the man whose body disappeared from that old trolley platform."

"Your assumption that it was hidden, instead of removed, was spot on. I got word that it was recovered while I was watching you pace back and forth."

Brixton waited for the man to continue.

"Of course, by then we'd already IDed him—those fingerprints lifted off your jacket did the trick, and sent red flags flashing everywhere."

"Who was he?"

"His real name doesn't matter. You've got a reputation for stepping in shit, Brixton, but this time you landed up to your neck in it."

CHAPTER 28

GEORGETOWN

The man waited tautly for a trio of walkers to pass before them, a bit too close for comfort. The man's hand was there, and then it was inside his jacket, before Brixton could blink.

"I'm going to assume," he resumed, "that the subway bomber you spotted was personal for you."

"You know about my daughter."

"I know a lot more than that," the man said, leaving it there. "But that'll suffice for today. It explains how you recognized the woman for what she was and chased her from the car."

"I didn't chase her. I *followed* her."

"Same thing. Did anyone tell you about the camera?"

"I heard the bomber was wearing one, probably disguised as a button on the coat that concealed her suicide vest."

"Means when she was looking at you, so was whoever put her on that train to murder an innocent bunch of commuters. That means they blame you for their operation going to shit."

"There was also mention in the report about the remains of a transmitter being found."

"Not all that unusual, really, although in this case it was actually a receiver. See, that bomber didn't blow herself up at all. Her suicide vest was detonated by remote control.

"They must've thought she was fleeing, giving up the mission," the man in the Panama hat continued, before Brixton could get a word in edgewise. "They blew her up, fucked their op, to make sure she wasn't captured. Classic zero-sum-game shit, my friend."

"I didn't know we were friends."

"We move in the same circles," the man said, eyeing Brixton a bit differently.

"And what circles did the man whose body you recovered on the trolley platform move in? The wet kind, I imagine."

The man's expression crinkled. "That's not an expression we actually use, you know."

"What *do* you use?"

"Nothing in particular for men like the one you met in the bombing's aftermath, the one you knew as Detective Rogers. Our assumption is he was running the op, meaning he was the one who triggered the blast when things went south, thanks to you."

Brixton recalled how agitated the man had been in the midst of his questioning on the subway platform. Now he understood why.

"You're a lucky man, Brixton. He must've figured you knew more than you were saying, might have been working for somebody else, or he probably would've killed you. He must have believed you were on that train because somebody put you there, somebody wise to the op he was running."

"Op he was running for *who*? Who does this guy work for? He was a goddamn American, or have I got that wrong, too?"

"Nope. You're right as rain, Brixton, which explains how we turned this around so fast and why you and I are having this meeting. This man's the ultimate hired hand, the kind whose contact info we've all got encrypted on our phones. String any three letters together and chances are he's worked for that organization at some point. A dark history in black ops, to say the least, but one that has never included foreign employment unless it was ordered through the proper channels."

"Wait," Brixton interjected. "You're suggesting that the suicide bomber was part of an *American* operation."

"Was that a question?"

"No."

"Because if it had been, Brixton, the answer would be yes. I'm not an easy man to scare, but I'm scared right now. That's why I'm here without backup, why we needed to put this meeting together so fast."

"I'm guessing you already know everything I do. It's all in the police report."

"Now amended for accuracy."

"So why are we having this conversation?" Brixton wondered, wishing he had a name for the man in the Panama hat.

"Because we need to keep the circle tight and that circle already includes you. You passed what amounted to a background check without issue, and you've already worked for us a few times without knowing."

"SITQUAL?"

The man didn't bother to nod. "Your mission was to protect State Department personnel, and especially diplomats, who weren't always diplomats."

"Yours?"

He almost smiled. "From time to time. You were never aware of their real missions or your part in them."

Brixton shuddered slightly at that revelation. "And now here I am."

"Here *we* are," the man continued. "Nobody gains anything much from a bombing on a subway train. That, and the involvement of the man you knew as Rogers, tells us it was part of something bigger."

“I’d call any terrorist bombing big enough in its own right.”

The man lifted the tip of his Panama hat enough for Brixton to get his first clear look at his hooded eyes, which looked as flat and emotionless as glass.

“I’m sorry about your daughter, but everything’s relative, Brixton. Killing a couple dozen people in a subway car, or restaurant, is as awful as it gets, until something bigger comes along.”

“World Trade Center big?”

“Our assumption is bigger than that, a lot bigger. It’s all hands on deck, the problem being we’re not sure which hands are hiding a joy buzzer.”

Brixton flashed his. “Mine are empty.”

“That’s why you’re here. You’re already connected, with a background that can be exploited.” The man paused, giving Brixton a look that cut right through him. “You’re also out of work and pretty much broke. You should know that working for us is not a volunteer effort.”

“I’d do it for nothing.”

“Another reason why we’re having this conversation.”

“So what happens next?”

“You and I are going for a ride, Brixton,” the man in the Panama hat told him. “Just before I joined you on this bench, we came up with a lead, a big one.”

CHAPTER 29

LANGLEY, VIRGINIA

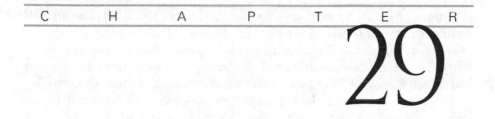

Upon arriving at CIA headquarters in Langley, Virginia, Lia Ganz was escorted to an empty conference room and ushered to a chair to the immediate right of the head of the table. Following protocol, she had bypassed the main entrance, instead using a secret underground tunnel known only to fellow intelligence operatives. The dangers of leaks and social media had mandated such a process, to avoid prying eyes and prevent inquisitive minds from wondering, in this case, what had brought a former Mossad operative known as the Lioness of Judah to Langley. Even then, the tunnel was used only in the most sensitive and clandestine of cases, which might further explain why Mossad had dispatched her instead of a still active agent with an ongoing relationship to the organization's American counterpart.

Lia had heard rumors of the tunnel's existence, but nothing had mentioned its elaborate construction or warned her that the agents who picked her up at Dulles Airport would blindfold her before accessing the tunnel. Other foreign intelligence operatives might have found such precautions to be a bit much, but she'd endured similar ones for a lifetime.

A pair of bulky escorts were waiting for her when the car reached its debarkation point and her blindfold was finally removed.

"Sorry for the inconvenience, Colonel," her driver said, the fact that he'd addressed her by her rank indicating that he'd been briefed on who she was and where she'd come from.

"I've subjected others back home to far more inconvenient practices than this," she told him. "Perhaps someday I can return the favor."

The man shared a smile with her. "Perhaps."

At that point, the man who'd picked her up at Dulles turned her over to a pair of escorts, who took up posts on either side of the single door of the windowless conference room, lit only by recessed fixtures built into the ceiling. They would remain there, Lia knew, until whoever was coming to meet her appeared.

Those are remains recovered from the scene of that failed terrorist attack.

Clearly, there was a connection between the deadly drone attack in Caesarea and the suicide bombing on the Washington Metro, which had claimed only the life of the bomber. Since it had been a search of Dar

Ibrahim al-Bis's secret workshop on the grounds of the Kif Tzuba amusement park that had sparked her visit, Lia knew that's where the connection must have originated. She'd been ruminating the whole trip on the possibility that the suicide bomber might be part of the same terrorist cell that had struck Caesarea. But Hamas had quickly claimed credit for that strike, and al-Bis was reputed to be that organization's top bomb maker, with no links to either al-Qaeda or ISIS that Mossad could find. This made no sense to her, since Hamas had never attempted a strike inside the United States.

You are looking, Colonel, at the transmitter and camera that were salvaged from the remains of the drones recovered at the site of the attack in Caesarea.

She was replaying Mossad chief Moshe Baruch's words in her head when the door opened and an older man with wispy white hair entered. He was dressed casually, a rumpled sports jacket worn over slacks and a shirt without a tie, his appearance more in keeping with the less formal Israeli approach to things, and Lia had the feeling he was the kind of operative who moved among the ranks and operations without ever having his name or identity revealed. Back home, such men were called "lifers." They might step away from day-to-day operations, but they never really retired. She'd also heard of former New York police detectives called "tin badges" being enlisted at times to run lead on cases they were better equipped to take on than any of those who still carried a badge. The United States and Israel, it seemed, were of one mind in respecting experience and institutional memory, both of which were irreplaceable when it came to fighting an enemy who never retired.

The white-haired man waited for Lia's two escorts to exit and then closed the door behind them, smiling at her as if they were old friends.

"It's been a long time, Colonel."

"We've met before?"

He smiled again. "Never formally. Let's just say we've been in the same room on a few occasions, and on the same video conference on others. We were never introduced, and you not recognizing me is understandable in that I tend to stick to the shadows."

"You too?" Lia posed, matching his smile with her own.

"You shortchange yourself. The Lioness of Judah was never known for keeping a low profile."

"I haven't been that person in a long time."

"And yet here you are."

Lia nodded. "Here I am."

"My name is Winters and I'm here to brief you on the circumstances that have brought you halfway across the world." His expression tightened, soured. "My condolences for the loss of so many to that drone attack."

"Thank you."

"I understand you were on the beach at the time."

Lia nodded. "In the water, which is the only reason why I was spared."

"Along with your granddaughter." Winters's expression tightened even further. "I've been at this a long time, since the days of Black September, and I've never understood the penchant of terrorist organizations to target children."

"It goes to the low regard in which they hold human life in general," Lia told him.

"But it sets their cause back, robs them of the hearts and minds they need to succeed."

"And yet the ruthlessness helps replenish their coffers. They are nothing without money, Mr. Winters, and their backers feast on the spilling of blood, the younger the better, because of the anguish it breeds."

The man finally took a seat at the head of the table and laid a manila folder on the wooden surface before him. "It's not 'mister.' Just 'Winters,' Colonel. And I assume you know what you're doing here."

"I know it involves a connection between the drone attack in Caesarea and the failed bombing on your Washington Metro that occurred one week later."

"Indeed, it does," Winters said, opening the manila folder and extracting a photograph, which he eased in front of her. "These objects are familiar to you, yes?"

Lia responded while keeping her eyes locked on a pair of objects pictured. "The camera and transmitter each of the drones contained."

Winters extracted a second standard-size photograph. "And this?" he posed, sliding it in front of her as well.

Lia regarded the twisted pieces of metal recovered and reassembled as much as possible after being shredded in the blast that had claimed only the bomber's life. "Remnants of the suicide vest the bomber was wearing, I assume."

"Nothing more?"

"The remains are too mangled to make much out of."

Winters smiled tightly, as if Lia had made his unspoken point for him. "Then try this," he said, handing her a fresh glossy printout. "The computer digitally reassembled the remains. Tell me what you see."

Lia gave the enhanced photo a long look, then compared it side by side with the transmitter and camera Mossad had recovered from Dar Ibrahim al-Bis's workshop.

"They're the same," she said, of the conclusion that Mossad had reached as well. "It's why I'm here."

"Not the only reason," Winters told her.

"You think the Washington Metro bombing was the start of a wave?"

"I believe, Colonel, it's the precursor to something much bigger, yes. I think somebody wants to bring this country to its knees."

CHAPTER 30

RESTON, VIRGINIA

"You mind riding the Metro again?" the man asked Brixton, while they were still seated on a bench beneath the pergola at Georgetown Waterfront Park.

"Why would I, Panama?"

"Panama?"

Brixton pointed toward the man's head. "I like your hat. You told me I could make up any name for you I wanted, and since you haven't given me a name . . ."

"Then Panama it is."

"And why would I mind taking the Metro to wherever we're going?"

"What happened three days ago, of course."

"Worried we might come across another suicide bomber?"

"No," the man said, stone-faced as ever. "But I'm afraid *you* would be."

"Once is more than enough for one lifetime."

"Twice," Panama corrected.

"The first time was at a restaurant, and I haven't stopped eating out either."

"So where are we headed?" Brixton asked Panama, after they'd set out on foot for the nearest Metro station, at K Street and Wisconsin Avenue.

"Reston, Virginia."

"I'm surprised a man like you doesn't have a driver."

"If a man like me had a driver, Brixton, he wouldn't be a man like me."

"Good point," Brixton acknowledged, as they continued their stroll.

"You haven't mentioned your trip to New York," Panama said suddenly.

"You didn't ask me about it."

"You paid a visit to a man affectionately known in our circles as the professor."

"You were watching me?" Brixton said, feeling his shoulders tense.

"We were watching *him*, actually. Picking you up at that point was a matter of routine. Your former girlfriend is quite the attractive woman, by the way."

Brixton felt surprisingly at ease with the knowledge that his movements had been tracked the day before in New York City. "Maybe that explains why it's *former*."

"What was the name of the restaurant you enjoyed an early dinner at?"

"Novita. You should try it sometime."

"I'll keep that in mind. I'm going to assume your visit to the professor wasn't a social call. Care to enlighten me on what the two of you discussed?"

"You don't know already? Since you're watching him, I'm surprised you don't have his rooftop wired."

"We did," Panama told him. "Several times. The professor found and destroyed the transmitters within hours on each occasion, so we gave up. He's strictly hands-off these days. Too many names in his digital Rolodex, too many operations he can bring out of the darkness into the light. So I'll have to rely on you to enlighten us."

"Maybe it was a social call."

"No such thing when it comes to the professor—or when it comes to you, for that matter, Brixton."

"I'm not sure how to take that."

"I meant it as a compliment." Panama moved slightly in front of him and slowed his pace before stopping altogether and then backing up into the shade. "I'm going to make an assumption: there's something else going on here that you don't want to talk about because you're not sure you can trust me yet. Perfectly understandable, given that you've already proven yourself to me but I've done nothing to prove myself to you."

"Not to mention that we've known each other for all of thirty minutes," Brixton reminded him.

"But I'm here now because you made a phone call."

"A friend of mine did."

"At your behest, which makes it the same thing. Another safe assumption I can make is that how quickly this all developed, and we responded, is testament to the gravity of what you find yourself involved in."

Brixton noted Panama's ever so slight emphasis on the word *we*, as he continued.

"Given that, if what you're *not* telling me carries a comparable, equal, or even connected gravity, I suggest you come clean, no matter any doubts you may have about my identity or position. I don't have a rank, a badge, a position, a portfolio—nothing like that."

"Or even a name," Brixton reminded him.

"Well, truth be told, I kind of like 'Panama.' In my work, I've learned not to trust a lot of people, especially strangers. I'm going to make an exception in your case."

"And how exactly are you going to do that?"

"By bringing you inside, by making you a party to what we're about to learn, in real time, by making you part of my world." Something changed in Panama's expression. "But beware, Brixton."

"Of what?"

"That once you step through that door, you can never step out again."

* * *

But the next door Brixton stepped through was to a UPS Store in Reston, Virginia, located in a strip mall on South Lakes Drive, between a Safeway and a CVS drugstore. Just a run-of-the-mill storefront, its interior laid out like every other UPS Store that he'd ever seen.

He and Panama had taken the Metro to the Wiehle-Reston East station, then a taxi to a local community college branch, before an Uber driver took them the rest of the way.

"I never go anywhere directly," Panama explained.

"And you don't drive a car because they're too easy to paint."

"*Paint*," Panama repeated. "An intelligence term. I'm almost impressed. You're a quick study."

"I learned the whole spy lexicon when I was with SITQUAL, since that's who I was often charged with protecting, as it turns out."

The UPS Store had been shut down and closed off, any number of harsh-looking men in dark suits watching over the place, both inside and out, when Panama arrived. They yielded to him, parting in deferential fashion to clear a path for him to enter the store, where another pair of suited figures stood before a single mailbox, which was propped open.

"Your friend Detective Rogers was going by the name of Brian Kirkland these days," Panama told Brixton. "That's who the mailbox is registered to."

"So how did you find it?"

"We didn't find *it*; we found *him*. We pulled a still shot off security cameras down on that Metro platform, where the triage was set up after the bombing, and red-flagged it in our facial recognition software. Remember that door I mentioned walking through? Beyond it you'll find the fact that NSA computers are now capable of scanning an individual face across multiple platforms in milliseconds."

"*Platforms* meaning security cameras and systems, I assume."

Panama nodded. "Care to take a guess as to how many that is?"

"Thousands? Tens of thousands?"

Panama came close to smiling. "The ones people know about, anyway. Then there are those cameras nobody knows about. The ones that watch you when you fill up at a gas station or pass under a tolling gantry on some highway or walk down any major city street. NSA's computers have access to all of them and stores the feeds in real time."

"So you're NSA."

"Did I say that?"

"You just mentioned—"

"That we used information cobbled off the NSA's computers to find the so-called Brian Kirkland."

Brixton held Panama's stare for a moment. "But not in the past two hours."

"Like I thought I'd said, he was on our radar, which means we were doing a digital tail on him to see if we could determine patterns in his movements, what he was up to and who he might've been working with. We pinged the most visits to any single location to this particular venue."

Brixton considered the timeline. "You work fast, Panama."

"One of the advantages of being accountable to no one."

"Everyone's accountable to *someone*."

Panama remained silent, letting his last remark stand on its own. His blank expression cracked briefly into the semblance of a smirk before dissolving into nothingness again.

Brixton turned his attention to the two men, who might have been twins, standing on either side of the open mailbox. Two more, who might have made them quadruplets, stood farther back in the store, near the counter, upon which he spotted something lying.

"You're telling me something important, vital even, got mailed to him here?"

Panama scoffed at the comment. "I doubt anyone even had the address. Nothing but junk mail delivered since he rented the box three months ago."

Brixton wondered if that spoke to the timeline of whatever it was they were facing, three months back marking the start.

"Who knew, Brixton," Panama continued, "that the internet would carry more security risks than ordinary paper? It's become ridiculously easy to track a person's digital footprint, so operatives like our friend Brian Kirkland have gone old school. No digital footprints left behind when all you have is paper."

"He was using that mailbox as a storage drop," Brixton realized.

"Beats the hell out of a safety deposit box. You know how many mailboxes are available for rent in the United States?"

"Haven't got a clue."

"Neither have I, but I'm sure it's a staggering number. And nobody would think twice about somebody renting a box who happens to be more interested in deposits than withdrawals."

Brixton looked toward the open mailbox again. "And I'm guessing you found several of those when your people opened the box."

Panama's expression remained empty. "Follow me, Brixton. I've got something to show you."

CHAPTER 31

LANGLEY, VIRGINIA

There's only one possible explanation for how the devices could be identical," Lia Ganz said to the man who called himself Winters. "But it makes no sense."

"You mean the fact that the bomb maker you killed, this Dar Ibrahim al-Bis, was responsible for the munitions in both attacks?"

Lia nodded. "There's nothing in his background to suggest he fancied himself as anything but a patriot. He wasn't a terrorist for hire."

"And what does that suggest to you?"

"Somebody wanted us to find this connection. Somebody knew that we'd find it."

"Explain that rationale to me."

"Whoever's behind this wants us to believe that the Metro bombing was the work of Islamic terrorists."

"Suggesting it was the work of someone else entirely."

"Is Mossad aware of this?"

Winters looked as if he were going to nod, then didn't. "Why do you think you're here, Colonel?"

"They didn't really need al-Bis, either, just his signature design for assembling the elements of the bomber's suicide vest. It's on record with every intelligence organization in the world."

"Thus assuring we'd know exactly who to point the finger at. Same way we pointed it at the Saudis after nine eleven."

"Only that was legitimate," Lia reminded the American spymaster.

"Was it really? Are you sure? Or did we *fall* for that, just like we're falling for this?"

"We're not falling for this."

"But we could have, Colonel, by all rights *should* have. We'd be running around chasing our tails, following ghosts, while they prepped the next attack."

In that moment, for the first time in longer than she cared to remember, Lia Ganz felt like the Lioness of Judah again. Gone was the fear and anger stoked by the drone attack that would likely have left her granddaughter dead if they hadn't been in the water. In its place was the cold, calculated reason of the professional warrior, a human missile who only needed to be pointed in the proper direction.

"How can I help?" Lia said to Winters. "Tell me what you need."

After a pause, Winters said, "I need you to believe me when I tell you that we don't know how deep this stretches."

"I don't understand."

Winters leaned closer to her. "Do you understand why we're meeting in this room?" He continued, answering his own question before Lia had a chance to, "Because it's got active jamming measures and is still swept for listening devices every hour."

"You don't want anything I might say to leave this room."

"No, I don't want anything *I* might say to leave this room. We have strong reason to suspect whatever's coming is coming from the inside."

"Your own people?"

"But, like I said, we don't know how deep it goes."

"You mean high up, not deep."

"Semantics."

"Not where I come from," Lia told him. "I'm here because you can't trust your own people."

"I trust them to a point, Colonel, but none of the ones I trust possess your unique skill set, not even close."

"Which I haven't used in a long time."

"You survived the attack in Caesarea."

"I happened to be in the water at the time."

Winters ignored her statement. "You didn't just *happen* to become the Lioness of Judah, though, did you?"

"That was different."

"Why?"

"Because Israel was at war. Israel is always at war."

"And now America is following suit."

"From the inside," Lia said, her gaze boring into Winters.

"We have our share of crazies, too, Colonel."

"And laws to protect them, which we don't."

"I think you're getting the point."

Lia looked him in the eye. "You need an assassin . . . So I'm on my own. That's what you're telling me," Lia said to him.

"Not quite, Colonel."

CHAPTER 32

RESTON, VIRGINIA

We found a single item in Kirkland's mailbox," Panama said, as he led Brixton toward the counter, where an oversize document that covered much of the space between a pair of cash registers had been laid out. "Our best guess is that it's been there for just about a month, based on what we've been able to string together from his visits."

"He's been here since then, right?"

"Several times. We're assuming in some cases to tuck something away and in others to take something out. But what I'm about to show you has, by all accounts, stayed right where it was."

They reached the counter upon which rested the document, still showing the many folds that had allowed it to be stored in a UPS Store mailbox.

"Any idea what you're looking at?"

Brixton studied the contours of a scale drawing of some kind, noticing two or three additional pages peeking out from behind it. "Looks like blueprints or structural schematics of some kind." He turned back toward Panama. "Of what?"

"We're good, Brixton, but only God can work that fast. It's obviously a building of some kind, a secure installation that's been potentially targeted, but we don't have a clue yet as to what or where."

Brixton looked back at the drawing. "Could be architectural plans."

"Could be a lot of things, including nothing at all. Operatives like Kirkland have been known to leave red herrings in their wake to throw us off the track. So the plans you're looking at might be utterly meaningless, a distraction to keep us from seeing something more important that's right before our eyes. Like this," Panama said, pointing to a series of numbers scrawled in handwriting in the bottom right-hand corner of the page: 66543076.

"Those numbers mean anything to you?" Panama wondered.

"Eight of them," Brixton said, counting.

"I didn't need you to tell me that."

"Social Security numbers contain nine figures and phone numbers ten. I was just trying to figure out what utilizes an eight-number sequence."

"Anything come to mind?"

"I would've told you if it had."

"Like you told me what really led you to visit the professor in New York?"

Brixton wasn't about to break Kendra Rendine's trust. It was her call when to inform others up the food chain of her suspicions regarding the death of Vice President Stephanie Davenport. The problem with that was that Brian Kirkland, whoever he really was, might have also been implicated somehow in Davenport's murder, suggesting a clear connection among that, the Metro bombing, and wherever the plans laid out before him led. That connection seemed to trump all else when it came to telling Panama the truth, but Brixton still felt he owed it to Rendine to discuss the latest revelations with her first. And once she approved, it might even be best to bring her in to meet Panama so he could hear the story directly from her.

"You wouldn't have brought me here if you didn't trust me, Panama."

"My trust extends only so far."

"Then it needs to extend a bit farther," Brixton said, leaving his intentions there.

Panama came close to a smile again, eyeing Brixton as if seeing him for the first time. "Maybe I can find a place for you with us, now that you're looking for work."

It came as no surprise, of course, that Panama knew that about him, since he seemed to know everything else.

"I'm not sure I'm cut out for your kind of work, Panama."

"Maybe you're not giving yourself enough credit."

"Maybe I'm giving you too much."

"The pay's really good on my team, Brixton. You should think about it."

"Sure, it's good, since I'm sure plenty of your people don't live long enough to enjoy their golden years."

"Longevity is overrated."

"Saves you on pension costs, I suppose."

Panama moved up to the counter, seeming to photograph the structural schematics with his eyes. "Assume the woman on the Metro car was working with or for Kirkland. Assume this," he said, pointing, "is the next target."

"You haven't mentioned anything about that young woman—where exactly she was radicalized and what group she was part of."

"Because we can't seem to find any evidence of either. As near as we can tell, your suicide bomber was an ordinary Lebanese exchange student on scholarship at George Washington University. Nothing in either her or her family's background to suggest any terrorist activity whatsoever."

"That makes no sense."

"Precisely why we're pursuing a theory along different lines."

"What's that?"

"A new twist on a false flag operation, in this case relating to national security professionals like myself wanting to test the vulnerabilities of certain high-value targets."

"Like the Washington Metro . . ."

"You know how we do that, Brixton? We keep it under the radar by recruiting civilians and paying them extraordinarily well to let us use them as bait. Big bucks in exchange for the risk they're taking."

"Wait a minute," Brixton said, incredulous over what Panama had just told him. "You're telling me the bomber was working for *you*?"

"Not me, Brixton. Your friend Rogers."

"You mean Brian Kirkland."

"What's the difference? They're both names and nothing more. Fakes, just like your bomber was a fake."

"There to gauge vulnerabilities, find holes in the security."

"Makes sense, don't you think, since now we know that a suicide bomber could walk right onto a Metro car and blow themselves up."

"One problem with all this," Brixton said. "If this was one of these false flag operations, why was the bomb live?"

"How else could we determine whether our detection systems could read the signature?"

"There are detection systems on the Washington Metro?"

"I'm speaking theoretically here."

"Oh."

"Of course, there wasn't supposed to be a trigger, detonator, or fusing, and there was a host of safety measures to make sure those explosives couldn't go off."

"And yet they did. You think Kirkland set this woman up."

Panama's expression remained noncommittal. "A desperate foreign student studying in the States on scholarship . . . You do the math."

"Don't tell me, Kirkland threatened to have her scholarship revoked, have her deported."

"That's the way the conversation likely started, Brixton, yes. Kirkland would have provided assurances, made sure the woman was paid half the fee in advance."

"If she was a plant, one of these false flags of yours, why'd she run when she realized I was watching her?"

"Instinct maybe, or fear you were going to mess up what she'd been instructed to do. Maybe she thought that was what she was supposed to do."

"Sit there, until they blew her up remotely. So why not trigger the blast when she got spooked?"

"My guess is they were waiting for the train to hit the station. Add some additional casualties on the platform, not to mention horrific footage that would rival the Twin Towers coming down. They only blew her up when they realized their patsy had become a liability. In the time it took her to walk up the aisle, they also might have managed to identify you: a security professional who's had some direct experience with suicide bombers.

I imagine your presence made them panic. You saved a lot of lives on that train, Brixton, but you got the woman blown up in the process."

"That's on whatever Kirkland's a part of, Panama, not me."

Panama looked almost hurt. "I meant it as a compliment."

"Sorry I didn't take it as one. Too busy considering the obvious."

"That the Metro bombing was only the start, step one."

Brixton tapped the plans laid out on the UPS Store counter. "And this is step two."

"And you're sure you have no idea what these numbers mean," Panama said, pointing toward the "66543076" in the lower right corner.

"No," Brixton said, holding back what he'd figured out. "Not at all. What's next?" he followed, hoping to change the subject as quickly as possible.

Panama glanced back down at the schematics laid atop the counter. "I give these to our tech people and hold my breath while awaiting what these plans are for. And I give you a phone number."

"One of yours, I assume."

"If it's not answered or you receive a disconnect message . . ."

Brixton waited for Panama to continue, not bothering to prod him.

"It means the operation's been canceled."

"Meaning I'm on my own, hung out to dry."

"Comes with the job, Brixton. You know that as well as I do."

"What about you, Panama?"

"What about me?"

"If the operation gets canceled. If I call that number and nobody answers."

"In a word," Panama said, not hesitating at all, "we're both fucked."

CHAPTER 33

GAITHERSBURG, MARYLAND

Patricia Trahan lived in a small, modest home nestled in the middle-class enclave of Gaithersburg, in the city's older eastern section, on Fields Road just off Interstate 270. No one on the street had much of a yard to speak of; the houses were built close to each other, with little more then five feet separating one from another.

Kendra Rendine parked just short of the woman's narrow driveway, trying to ascertain whether anyone was watching the house. Given that all of the surgical team involved with Vice President Davenport's procedure were missing or unresponsive, it was a fair bet that Trahan was at risk of suffering the same fate. Then again, Rendine found herself wondering whether Trahan had managed to escape detection by whoever was behind the disappearances of the others directly involved in the angioplasty procedure performed on Stephanie Davenport. Dr. Callasanti hadn't vanished into the ether, almost surely because he hadn't actually been in the room, having viewed the procedure from a gallery that afforded a better view of what he needed to see. Trahan had found herself in a similar situation. Her role had been confined to delivering the surgical instruments and stents to the operating room and getting one of the surgical techs to sign off on receiving them, once confirming that the inventory control numbers matched.

Trahan's driveway was barely wide enough to accommodate Rendine's compact car. She parked and called Trahan to let the woman know it was her in the driveway. Rendine climbed out and angled her approach straight across the lawn, then up the two steps onto a small porch. She rang the buzzer, waited, and then rang it again.

Patricia Trahan answered as the second ring was still sounding. "Agent Rendine?"

"Thanks for listening to me, Mrs. Trahan."

"Call me Patty. I like to be on a first-name basis with everyone who scares the hell out of me."

"In that case, please call me Kendra."

"Kendra."

"Nice to officially meet you, Patty. Now, tell me about this report you wrote."

* * *

The house was simple, modest, and well kept, which pretty much described Patty Trahan herself. She had the look of a woman who didn't go overboard on her appearance anymore, from her flat, limp hair to clothes that had clearly seen better days.

Well, haven't we all, Rendine thought. *Especially lately.*

They sat at the kitchen table. Rendine had favored the living room only because the windows there gave an unobstructed view of the street, but the kitchen came complete with a back door in case they needed to get out of the house fast.

"I've done more coronary procedures than any other operating room tech at Walter Reed," Trahan told her, the pride evident in her voice.

Rendine was about to say something, but decided to let the woman continue instead.

"I think it might be some kind of record."

"So you know your way around an operating room and the kind of procedure performed on the vice president."

"Simple angioplasty with stent implementation? I've probably done a thousand of them, and I mean literally. Vice President Davenport's procedure was more complicated because three stents were required to open her coronary arteries. How much do you know about stents and the procedure itself?"

"Only what I learned in order to prep for those two hours spent in the operating room."

"I don't remember seeing you there," Trahan said, suddenly sounding suspicious.

"I get that a lot. Blending in with the scenery is a big part of the job the Secret Service does. 'Never stand out' is one of our commandments."

"Do you have ten, too?"

"I never counted, Patty."

"What about the stenting process?"

"Assume nothing," Rendine said, leaving it there.

"Then let me give you a bit of background. The vice president had a minimally invasive procedure utilizing three stents, expandable mesh tubes made of medical-grade stainless steel, one for each blocked artery. Each stent was mounted onto a tiny balloon that was then opened inside of a coronary artery to push back plaque and to restore blood flow. After the plaque was compressed against the arterial wall, the stents were fully expanded into position, acting as miniature scaffolding for each artery. The balloons were then deflated and removed, the stent left behind in the patient's coronary artery to help keep the blood vessel open. Once the stent is implanted, it remains there permanently."

"Have you ever heard of a smart stent?" Rendine asked her.

She watched Patty Trahan stiffen, suddenly anxious. "Why do you ask? Have you seen my report?"

"It wasn't present in any of the hospital files I was able to access, at least digitally."

"Don't bother looking elsewhere. You won't find it. You won't find it, because it was buried."

Rendine felt a slight chill course through her and leaned forward. "By who?"

"I don't know."

"What did the report contain, Patty?"

The woman started fidgeting, her knees bouncing and fingers flexing atop her knees. "I shouldn't have done it."

"Written the report?"

"No, let the procedure continue after I'd confirmed the requisition number on the three stents to be used for the vice president's procedure. I went by the book, everything I was supposed to do, and that includes confirming that the serial numbers on the stents themselves matched the labels on the packaging."

"Go on," Rendine urged, when Trahan lapsed into silence.

Trahan swallowed hard. "I figured I must be seeing things wrong. And my job was to confirm the numbers. I wasn't supposed to go beyond that, but I knew what I was looking at."

"You're talking about the stents."

Trahan took a deep breath and let it out slowly. "They were smart stents, the kind we just discussed. But that's not what was ordered. I confirmed as much when I ordered them and when a clerk from requisitions delivered them to me the morning of the procedure. I double-checked the requisition numbers, Kendra, believe me I did, to make sure these were the traditional stents ordered for the vice president's procedure. And they were correct. But I know what I was looking at when I removed the three of them from their foil seals didn't match the stents I had ordered."

Rendine tried to get a grasp on what she was hearing, to focus on the facts. The operating room technician responsible for all surgical equipment to be used in Vice President Davenport's procedure had opened the packages containing the stents and found them to be different from what they were supposed to be, because someone had made a switch.

"You want to know why I didn't say anything then and there," Trahan resumed. "You want to know why I stayed quiet, why I didn't say a word, unless you count the report I added to the surgical record."

Rendine's expression urged her on.

"This was a procedure being performed on the Vice President of the United States by the top cardiologist at Walter Reed. Who was I to interrupt things? Who was I to say something wasn't right? What if I turned out to be wrong? Every minute of delay would have cost thousands of dollars."

"You were scared."

Trahan nodded.

"Completely understandable, and something I can relate to. Like me, you were balancing your knowledge and instincts against the greater good. I remember you entering the operating room in your scrubs and surgical mask. I remember you removing the stents from their wrapping. I remember you double-checking the inventory number in two different logs to confirm you had delivered the right ones. At that point the vice president had already been sedated, since going any further would likely have necessitated a general anesthesia, which carries far more risk to someone in the vice president's condition."

"Yes! Yes, that entered my mind, and I didn't want to be the person responsible for that. Do you think I made a mistake?"

"I think you made a judgment call that was neither wright nor wrong, just the best available option. It's what we do at the Secret Service every day."

"I hope you're hiring, since I may be looking for a job soon."

"Because of this report you filed."

"I wasn't accusing anyone," Trahan said defensively. "I was only noting what I observed. I filled out a form. It's not like I wanted to become a whistleblower or anything like that. Who would I have been blowing the whistle on?"

"What about the requisitions clerk who delivered the stents to you? Did you know him?"

"Not this one, no. I'd never seen him before. But Walter Reed is a mammoth hospital, and sometimes orderlies make the deliveries, even though they're not supposed to."

"So this man could have been an orderly?"

"I suppose, yes. Like I said, I'd never seen him before."

With that, Rendine finally eased from her shoulder bag the autopsy report on Stephanie Davenport that she'd picked up at Bethesda Naval Hospital. She'd already placed at the front a single piece of photo-grade paper showing sharp images of each of the three stents that had been inserted into the vice president's arteries a month before. She slid it from the folder and handed it to Patty Trahan.

"This is a picture of the three stents removed from the vice president during her autopsy, Are you able to confirm they are, in fact, the same stents you delivered to the operating room?"

Rendine watched Trahan's eyes widen and then narrow, as she studied all three photos.

"No," she said, still holding the paper.

"No *what*?"

"No, I can't confirm they're the same stents I delivered to the operating room," Trahan told her. "Because they're not."

CHAPTER 34

WASHINGTON, DC

First Lady Merle Talmidge stood behind her husband's shoulder in the Oval Office as he signed the stack of letters before him, just beginning to make a dent in the pile. The president stopped suddenly, his expression taking on the blank, quizzical look she'd come to know all too well and had seen exhibited with increasing frequency as of late.

"It was a wonderful funeral, wasn't it?" Corbin Talmidge asked her, sighing deeply.

"Whose funeral?"

"Our son's."

"He wasn't our son. That was just part of your speech."

"I gave a speech?"

"You spoke beautifully, from the heart," the first lady assured him.

"Then why can't I remember what I said?"

"It was an emotional afternoon."

"I should think so, the funeral of our own son."

"It wasn't our son," Merle Talmidge repeated.

"Then why I was there? I remember crying. Why would I cry if it wasn't our son?"

"Because it was someone else's son. And you were there to offer comfort and support and make the greater point that we cannot tolerate violence in our schools."

"How did I do?"

"You were wonderful," the first lady said, meaning it.

"Then why can't I remember what I said? Were you there?"

"I joined you on stage."

"When?"

"Near the end of your remarks."

"What remarks?"

Merle Talmidge didn't respond right away, having learned that sometimes it was better to let things go and allow her husband's failing mind to move elsewhere on its own. And, in this case, "elsewhere" turned out to be the formidable stack of letters still before him.

He'd been diagnosed with something called Creutzfeldt-Jakob disease, which occurs when prion protein, found throughout the human body, folds into an abnormal three-dimensional shape. Ultimately, the prion protein mutation in the brain causes a type of dementia that worsens much faster than even the most rapid of all Alzheimer's cases. Through a process that continues to baffle experts, misfolded prion protein lays waste to brain cells, the damage leading to a rapid decline in thinking, reasoning, and cognitive capacity in general. The symptoms vary by the patient, but one thing that doesn't is the utter lack of medical treatments to slow the progression even slightly.

Watching her husband's steady and rapid decline had been the worst and most painful experience of Merle Talmidge's life, and the lack of hope for anything but a steady decline was the most agonizing part of all. But at the same time it had hardened her to other realities, including political. She came to see the fragility of human life as no different from the fragility of the country in general. She found herself only able to relieve the agony of her husband's condition by contemplating a fitting legacy for him, one he would want for himself if he could so choose. He wouldn't accept defeat and go quietly into obscurity. He wouldn't want his achievements squandered. He knew the country wouldn't survive the opposing party rising back to power in the chaos of the next election, staged without him as a candidate. He'd want to do anything and everything to see his vision for America come true.

"You mean the remarks I need to give at the vice president's funeral?" Corbin Talmidge resumed suddenly.

"They're being prepared now. We can go over them for the first time tonight."

Fortunately, perhaps anomalously, her husband could still give a prepared speech. It had proven the one saving grace, but it no longer satisfied the press's demands that he make himself more available. There were rumblings of something afoot with his health, rumors the White House Press Office had managed to deflect and define up until this point.

And they only needed to continue doing that for three more days now. Three more days until America was changed forever.

"She was a good person," the president said.

"Yes, she was," the first lady agreed.

"I just saw her, didn't I? Was it yesterday?"

"No, dear."

"Last week?"

"Last month," the first lady said.

"Oh," the president said, looking confused.

Stephanie Davenport had been ushered into the Oval Office just over a month ago for a lunch her husband's chief of staff had canceled too late, though Merle Talmidge suspected an increasingly suspicious vice president had gotten the message and had shown up anyway. The first lady been dealing with something else at the time, and the Secret Service agent who'd passed the vice president through was new to the detail. By the time Merle Talmidge got there, the damage had already been done; she could see the concern, fear, and befuddlement on the vice president's face, could see that it had taken her all of five minutes alone with Corbin Talmidge to realize his deteriorating condition.

FIVE WEEKS EARLIER . . .

"What's going on?" Stephanie Davenport demanded, in the private office off the Oval that was normally utilized as a waiting room for guests.

"I don't think I know what you—"

"Yes, you do. Is it dementia, Alzheimer's, a stroke?"

"It's not a stroke," Merle Talmidge managed to assure her.

"I guess that answers my question."

The first lady had grasped the vice president's arm tenderly, a show of friendship. "Please, Stephanie."

"Shouldn't it be 'Vice President Davenport,' under the circumstances?"

"We're going to deal with this appropriately. We just need a little more time."

"How much time?"

"A month. I promise. That's all."

"And it's too much, with the election so close."

"Do you want to take my husband's place that badly, *Vice President Davenport?*"

Davenport's eyes looked as sharp as daggers. "Do *you?*"

Merle Talmidge had known in that moment that the vice president was a threat, but one she believed could be mitigated, stalled at least for a brief period. The timetable for the operation had been moved up as much as possible. Even then, though, Davenport's concerns quickly escalated to the point that she had insisted on a clandestine independent review of the president's condition. It had been around that time that she'd scheduled her own angioplasty procedure at Walter Reed, providing the first lady the opportunity to have the problem remedied in a wholly different fashion by placing a time bomb in the vice president's chest. She had pushed Davenport as far as she could, put her off for as long as she could. But when the threat she posed became too great and it became obvious she intended to force the issue, that bomb had to be detonated.

The vice president's funeral had been scheduled for the very day that would change America forever, with the unfolding of a plot that she and others had hatched to maintain the administration's hold on power in the face of the president's otherwise inevitable decline. And once that plot came to fruition, the election that was just six months away would be utterly forgotten. Americans would be left with far too much on their minds to worry about voting.

"Why do I have to do this?" the president asked her suddenly, looking up from the stack of letters.

In counterpoint to his deteriorating mental condition, Corbin Talmidge still looked strong and vital, not all that much different from when they'd met, more than thirty years before. He had the same build, the same hair, the same smile, and the same eyes, though those eyes had lost their certainty and luster in a gaze that had grown increasingly tentative and unsure. It was like living with someone who was forever waking from a nightmare in the middle of the night in abject disorientation. But there were still enough moments where those eyes took on a youthful innocence and vibrancy, the look that had made her fall in love with him from the first time they'd met, though these days their view was considerably narrowed.

"To offer comfort and support, just like at that boy's funeral."

"Our son's . . ."

"No, dear, someone else's son, remember?"

"Oh. If you say so."

"And congratulations in some cases, as well," the first lady picked up. "And thanking them for their service."

"Thanking who?"

"The people those letters are addressed to."

"Why do I have to sign them?" the president asked, his gaze shifting back to the pile before him.

"Because you want to."

"I do?"

Merle Talmidge nodded. "You've always had a gift for seeing the good in people and wanting to see them rewarded for that. Those letters provide that opportunity."

"Oh."

His interest renewed, the president slid the next letter from the top of the stack and readied his pen. "I forgot how to write my name."

"Want me to help you?"

He nodded, looking more like a child than the president of the United States. "And my hand hurts."

The first lady eased an armchair behind the big Resolute desk, presented to President Rutherford B. Hayes by Queen Victoria in 1880, built from English oak timbers salvaged from the British exploration ship HMS *Resolute*, and mostly a fixture in the Oval Office ever since. She had practiced signing her husband's name so much over these past few months that her elbow ached. Corbin Talmidge had actually gotten through more of the letters than she'd expected, a nominal improvement over the process last week. A small victory, since the big ones were in the past now, salvageable only in memory.

With one exception, that exception being the biggest victory of all—a victory for her husband's administration and for all of the United States, though at a cost that would change the country forever.

Of course, Corbin Talmidge never would have conceived, much less approved, of such a plan. He had too big a heart, too much genuine fondness for those like the boy buried earlier in the day. As a result, he'd become the most popular president in a generation. Corbin Talmidge had won the presidency as the antipolitician. The country had fallen in love with him, and the affair continued to this day.

And now it would be prolonged. Indefinitely. At least long enough to secure the vision of America the first lady now held in her husband's place. First and foremost, the team of like minds she had assembled needed to go about selecting the right candidate for vice president.

But who? And, under the circumstances, what if no such person existed?

The first lady slid the stack of letters before her and began signing them robotically as her husband looked on with a distant expression that seemed whimsical.

"Can I watch television?"

"Later."

"Can you turn it on for me?"

"Of course."

The first lady signed ten more letters before he spoke again.

"What was his name?"

"Who, dear?" she asked her husband.

"The boy whose funeral it was."

"I'm afraid I don't remember."

"I should know his name. My own son and I can't remember his name."

Merle Talmidge let that go, knowing the president's attention would be diverted soon enough.

"Shouldn't I be signing those letters?" he asked suddenly.

"You need to rest."

"I'm not tired."

"You have a lot of work ahead of you."

"Can I watch television now?"

"I wonder what you'd say if you knew the truth," the first lady said, as she continued scrawling her husband's name in the proper place. "Would you tell me to stop? Would you tell me I'd gone too far?"

The president just looked at her.

"This was the only way to keep you from embarrassment and pity. You don't deserve that. You're much too good a man. So I'm really doing this for you. I'm committed because I know in my heart you would approve of the ends, despite the means."

"I'm not mean," Corbin Talmidge insisted.

"No, you're good, and what we're doing is good for the country. The country needs you, and the people will need you to comfort them in the wake of the greatest tragedy the United States has ever faced, one that will leave scars for generations. But it's a tragedy to be celebrated, my love."

"Like a birthday party?" the president asked her.

"Pretty much, yes, as a matter of fact."

"I'd like a birthday party. When's my birthday?"

"Two months ago."

He looked down, then up again. "Did I have a party?"

"A big one," the first lady lied.

"What about presents?"

"Lots of them."

The president beamed. "How many?"

Merle Talmidge tapped the top of the stack of letters. "This many. These are the thank-you notes."

"Then I want to sign them! Let me sign them!"

"I thought you wanted to watch television."

"After I sign them," Corbin Talmidge said, sliding them back before him and centering himself in his chair again. "Will you watch with me?"

"Sure, I will."

"But I get to choose the show."

"Of course you do."

"And not the news. I hate the news. Boring."

Not for long, the First Lady of the United States almost said out loud. *Not for long . . .*

"I don't know what I'd do without you," her husband was saying.

Merle Talmidge looked at him with a start, a crystallizing thought striking her like a lightning bolt. So clear and vivid, she couldn't fathom how she hadn't considered it before.

Of course!

"I'd like to discuss something with you," she said to her husband.

Before he could respond, though, Merle Talmidge heard a knock and watched the entry door to the Oval Office open and then close behind her chief of staff, Alan Moorehouse. She saw the look on his face and had a sense of what he was going to say even before he spoke.

"We've got a problem, ma'am."

CHAPTER 35

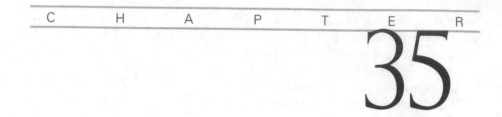

WASHINGTON, DC

Not the same stents?" Brixton asked.

Kendra Rendine nodded. "Looks like we've both had interesting days, Robert."

"That's one way of putting it."

"What's the other."

"Scary."

Brixton had met Kendra Rendine for dinner at the Mansion on O Street, a magnificently renovated classical residence on a quiet, historic, tree-lined street in Dupont Circle, within walking distance of the White House and Embassy Row. Originally built in the late nineteenth and early twentieth centuries, the Mansion retained many period details, including original Tiffany stained glass windows. But the room in which Brixton and Rendine were dining boasted no windows. It was one of the little-known, and little-used, private interior rooms, among the Mansion's total inventory of more than a hundred, accessible through one of the more than seventy secret doors that were among the worst-kept secrets in Washington.

A far-better-kept secret was that a number of federal organizations had laid claim to their own private rooms that could be utilized on short notice toward virtually any purpose. Being a haven for heads of state, foreign dignitaries, and business leaders, along with leaders of the entertainment industry, made it easy for less noticeable Mansion patrons to come and go as they pleased, hiding in plain sight, where press and media seldom, if ever, paid attention to their presence.

Brixton had no idea what the Secret Service utilized this particular room for, wondering if it had been chosen for the letters of Abraham Lincoln that adorned the walls, along with a beautiful portrait of Lincoln that dominated the decor. Combined with the leather-bound books adorning a series of shelves, the overall effect was to create a chamber boasting true elegance, no bigger in size than an ordinary conference room. And tonight, with only a single table occupying that space, it actually seemed absurdly large for their purpose.

On Rendine's instruction, he had used a side door marked "Emergency Exit Only" to gain admittance, plugging in the code she'd provided. Rendine was already waiting when he was escorted to the room by a plainclothes security guard posted just inside that secretive entrance. To avoid interruptions, they used iPad-like devices to order their meals, specifying when the first course should be served, along with the intervals for the succeeding ones.

"Scary how?" Rendine asked Brixton.

"You go first. Back to this bit about the stents."

He listened to her explain what she'd learned from Patricia Trahan, before she transitioned to the fact that all those who had participated in the procedure performed on Vice President Stephanie Davenport were currently unreachable, or perhaps worse, with the exception of the cardiologist who'd been viewing everything from above.

"Incredible," was all Brixton could say.

"Incredible that somebody would murder the vice president, yes. That they subsequently made the people who participated in the procedure disappear, not so much. They couldn't risk leaving anyone out there who might remember something that could hurt them."

"Except for this Patty Trahan."

"She wasn't listed as a participant. Her only role was to deliver the instruments and the stents that were used in the procedure."

"Which were different from what Trahan remembers."

"She was certain that the stents she delivered to the operating room were the so-called smart kind."

"While the autopsy photos show that the stents removed postmortem were the ordinary variety that had been originally ordered for the vice president," Brixton completed.

Rendine held his stare. "Looks like this friend of yours in New York was spot on."

"So a switch was made," Brixton said, picking things up from there. "Someone substituted the stents that ultimately killed Stephanie Davenport for the ones that were supposed to be implanted during the procedure."

"There should be security camera footage I can review," Rendine said, nodding as her voice drifted off.

"But . . ."

"But whoever's behind this would never leave that kind of trail. Whoever made the switch would never leave any fingerprints behind, either real or figurative. And that person isn't who we're after anyway."

"We're after whoever gave the order," Brixton reasoned. "And I think I may be able to shed some light on that."

Brixton proceeded to tell Rendine about his meeting with Panama, after the prints on the jacket he'd been wearing the night before had been identified as belonging to the man known as Brian Kirkland. She listened without interruption, although it was clear from her expression that she had numerous questions to go with a palpable sense of unease. When Brixton was finished, she jumped in right at the point where he'd left off.

"So we're going on the assumption that the schematics recovered from that UPS Store mailbox are directly connected to the bombing on the Metro."

"That's right."

"And connected as well to the apparent murder of the vice president."

"I don't think we need to use the word *apparent* anymore," Brixton told her, "but the answer's yes—through this man Brian Kirkland. Don't bother writing that down, because he's got a dozen names, and that particular one won't lead anywhere at all. He thought for a moment. "You mentioned a period around the time of her procedure, when you noticed a change in the vice president."

Rendine nodded. "It was just before the procedure, by a week or so, but it continued afterward."

"And you also mentioned that it started after a meeting with the president in the Oval Office."

"That's right."

"Did you ask the vice president about that?"

"Strictly against protocol—I mentioned that too."

Brixton weighed the impact of that timeline. "So Stephanie Davenport leaves that meeting with the president distressed over something, and a week or so later those smart stents were implanted during her angioplasty procedure."

Rendine nodded. "It was seven days. I checked."

"And she was dead a month after that."

Another nod. "I've run the minute-by-minute diary reports from all protective shifts for that entire period."

"And?"

"No gun, smoking or otherwise. In the time I can account for, everything was strictly routine."

"No meetings or phone calls which raised any flags?"

"Not according to the detailed logs and reports generated by agents in the field."

"You think the president shared something that unsettled Davenport during that meeting a week before her procedure. And whatever it was, it might well be somehow connected to the Metro bombing and, now, to whatever's coming next," Brixton said, thinking again of those structural plans recovered from the so-called Brian Kirkland's UPS Store mailbox. "They knew I went to New York," he added, after a pause. "They knew I met with the professor and my ex-girlfriend."

"But they don't know what you discussed."

"With Flo?" Brixton asked wryly.

"I was thinking more like this professor friend of yours."

Brixton shook his head. "No. I wasn't about to reveal any of that without consulting you first."

"So what now?"

"You tell me, Agent."

Rendine took a deep breath. "If we're on the right track here, whoever switched those stents at Walter Reed did so with killing the vice president in mind. That means the key to all this is whatever happened when Stephanie Davenport met with Corbin Talmidge the week before her procedure. I need to find out what they discussed, what the vice president learned." She paused and took a deep breath. "What about you?"

"I'm going to ask you for a favor," Brixton told her. "Six six five four three zero seven six."

"What's that?"

"The numerical sequence that was jotted down on those schematics at the UPS Store. I told Panama I didn't recognize them. I lied."

"Because you do recognize them."

"I think the eight-number sequence is a federal prisoner ID designation. I need you to find out who it belongs to, Kendra."

CHAPTER 36

BROOKLYN, NEW YORK

"Why's the book called that, *Catcher in the Rye*?" the inmate in the third row asked Sister Mary Alice Rose.

"It's a metaphor," Sister Mary Alice, who'd celebrated her eighty-fifth birthday the preceding week, told him.

"What's a metaphor?"

"Saying something other than what you mean, to make your point."

"That's more fucked up than a black man trying to ice skate, woman."

"That's a metaphor, too," Sister Mary Alice followed, drawing a ripple of laughter from the classroom. "But in the case of the book we've been reading, the title comes from a poem by Robert Burns called 'Comin' Thro' the Rye,' which is about preserving the innocence of childhood."

"This Holden dude," commented another inmate, "he don't seem so innocent to me. That boy knows how to sling the shit, and he don't take no shit from nobody."

"The dude's cold, man," a third voice chimed in. "Like this place was when the power went dead last winter."

That drew a smattering of chuckles from the inmates squeezed into school desks too small to accommodate their bulk, aligned in neat rows before Sister Mary Alice. They were neat because she'd straightened them out herself prior to the beginning of class.

The Metropolitan Detention Center was located on Twenty-Ninth Street in Brooklyn, a ten-story processed slab of a building housing prisoners who had pending cases in the United States District Court for the Eastern District of New York. MDC Brooklyn was also a potential stop for prisoners serving brief sentences. Only within the past few years had it begun housing prisoners interned for longer stretches, many for drug-related crimes, violent and otherwise.

A nun for some sixty years now, Sister Mary Alice had no idea what crimes the inmates seated before her had committed or how long their respective sentences ran. She knew the bulk of them only by the eight-digit ID numbers displayed on their khaki prison jumpsuits, the only exception being those inmates she saw regularly for tutoring sessions.

"It's drugs that fucked him up," a new voice, attached to a face and ID number Sister Mary Alice had never seen before, chimed in. "His parents loading him up on this shit and that. Fucked him up good."

"He grows up, I can sell him the good shit," an inmate who invariably sat in the back row said, high-fiving the men on either side of him.

"I don't get where he's going," the inmate who'd started the conversation put forth. "Dude's running away, but where's he running *to*, exactly?"

"Maybe that's the point," Sister Mary Alice said, aiming her words in his direction.

"Everybody's running from something," a new voice agreed from somewhere in the middle of the makeshift classroom.

"Mostly the cops," said the same inmate who'd drawn chuckles a few moments before, drawing all-out laughs this time.

Sister Mary Alice joined in.

"So what you running from, Sister?" a man in the front row asked her. "How is it you come to be here with a bunch of lowlifes like us?"

"You think you're a lowlife?"

"I'm here, ain't I?"

"Which would make me a lowlife, too, wouldn't it?" Sister Mary Alice challenged him. "But I don't consider myself that any more than I do you, any of you. I think you're all victims."

"Hey," came the booming voice of an inmate standing in the back because the school desks couldn't accommodate his vast bulk. "Don't lay any of that societal bullshit at my doorstep."

Sister Mary Alice held her gaze on him. "You know who you sound like?"

"Not off the top of my head."

"You sound like Holden," she continued, holding up her tattered paperback copy of J. D. Salinger's *The Catcher in the Rye*. "He thought society was bullshit too. Maybe that's what he was running away from, not his school or his parents."

"Dude got no friends, no homies," said the same inmate who'd referred to Holden Caulfield as "cold" before. "What's up with that? You ask me, he ain't running from nobody but himself, 'cause the dude ain't got no clue. You know what happens in the sequel? He end up with us, in a place like this."

"Was there a sequel?" a voice wondered.

"Second's never as good as the first," from another.

"Oh yeah? You check out *The Godfather* lately?"

"I was thinking more along the lines of *Jaws* and *Jaws* shit *Two*."

"Hey, don't forget *Aliens*," the inmate in the back noted, "you wanna talk about how good a second film can be."

"Hey, Sister," came a fresh voice, the inmate waving his own paperback copy. "They ever make this book into a film?"

"No. The author wouldn't allow it."

"He nuts or something?"

"He didn't believe a director or studio was capable of doing it justice," Sister Mary Alice told him. "And that includes filmmakers like Elia Kazan and Billy Wilder, who both tried their utmost to acquire the rights."

"Elia . . . what kind of name is that?"

"I'll bet that Wilder was a wild dude. Can't have a name like that without living up to it."

"Hey, Sis," boomed the big man standing in the back, who looked as wide as he was tall. "What we gonna be reading next?"

Sister Mary Alice held up an equally dog-eared copy of *The Adventures of Huckleberry Finn*. "Huck Finn."

"Who's that?"

"Not another kid."

"Hey, check out the cover—that's a kid, all right."

"This boy Huck must be running from something, too, Sister, like all the rest of us," said the big man in the back. "But you still haven't told us what *you're* running from, why you wearing the same jumpsuit we got for a wardrobe."

"That blue color they give the broads beats the shit out of khaki."

"That's because it's *powder* blue," another inmate elaborated.

"Let her answer the question, will ya?" snapped the big man, accompanying the statement with a stare that could melt ice.

"I'm here because there was something I couldn't live with, couldn't accept."

"What's that exactly?"

Before Sister Mary Alice Rose could answer, a bell sounded, signaling the end of class and the time to file straight out to dinner. The two federal prison guards, who'd made themselves as unobtrusive as possible in the room's back corners, started to move forward to escort the prisoners to the cafeteria.

"Until next week, then," Sister Mary Alice said to all of them. "Don't forget to pick up your copy of *Huckleberry Finn* on the way out."

"Just tell us one thing, Sis," a familiar voice rang out, amid the inmates rising from their desks. "Does this dude ever get where he's going?"

"I'm not sure any of us ever gets where we're going," Sister Mary Alice told him.

"Well, one way or another, we all ended up here, right? Whether it be for slinging drugs, doing dope, or some combination thereof. 'Cept for you, of course."

"No," interjected an inmate, as he filed past Sister Mary Alice in the front of the room. "She inside for fighting injustice."

"I heard she blew up a building."

That froze all the inmates in place.

"That true, Sis?" someone asked.

"You really blow up that building?" from another.

"Not exactly," Sister Mary Alice told him. "But maybe I should have."

"Hey," started an inmate who was fighting against the determined efforts of the guards to herd them from the room. "You one cold bitch, Sis."

"Amen to that," said Sister Mary Alice.

PART FOUR

CHAPTER 37

ARLINGTON, VIRGINIA

As was his custom, Brixton walked the six blocks from the Metro stop to the Arlington, Virginia, apartment he could no longer afford. Real estate values and apartment rental costs hinged on many things, not the least of which was distance from the nearest Metro station. Inside a block was the benchmark, while more than five threatened to render you irrelevant. Nobody who was anybody had to walk that far.

Brixton normally enjoyed the walk for the time it left him alone with his thoughts. He made it a habit not to check email or texts and even avoided conversations—so as not to distract himself from his surroundings, as much as anything. Too many people these days ruined a leg on a broken sidewalk or, worse, walked into moving traffic while looking down. So Brixton always looked up to better focus his thinking, to let his mind wander toward where he needed it to end up.

Right now he was waiting for a call from Kendra Rendine on the identity of federal prisoner number 66–543076, adding the dash in his mind. Normally, this would have been a simple-enough process. But the connection to whoever was behind what was rapidly taking on the shape of a conspiracy that might well have led to the murder of the vice president of the United States meant she didn't dare leave even a hint of a cyber trail. If Brixton were running the check himself, he'd exercise deep discretion by jobbing the task out to someone whose digital footprint would not attract any undue attention. A bureaucrat or administrator running a simple check—that's what it had to look like, to avoid any bounce back on Rendine. They could take nothing for granted at this point. Nothing. This was too big, and getting bigger all the time.

Brixton's one-bedroom at Exo Apartments was just over a half mile from the station, and he'd learned how to make the best use of side streets to cover that distance in the shortest possible walk. His gleaming apartment tower featured an array of amenities he never took advantage of—like the yoga lawn, pool and grill area, rooftop deck, and community garden—but it was still a better deal than the DC apartment he'd shared with Flo Combes. The building had just come into view at the next block as Brixton cut through a narrow side street used mostly for deliveries, servicing the rear entrances of buildings on both sides of it.

The two men must have burst out from the cover of one of those. But Brixton wasn't thinking that when the punches began to land, before he could adequately defend himself.

I'm being mugged.

A fate he'd managed to escape for all these years living in cities had finally caught up with him. He hesitated before going for his gun, reluctant to use deadly force, and the hesitation cost him, as his attackers continued to show no interest in his pockets, only in pummeling him instead. He managed to unleash a flurry of blows that knocked one of the men off to the side. He turned toward the second in time to see a knife flash forward in his hand, angled on an upward slant toward his thorax in the kind of practiced thrust a mere mugger would never try.

Which meant this was man was no mugger; he was a pro, someone well schooled in such things, who'd stuck blade in flesh before.

Brixton tried to twist aside to retaliate, but a pair of powerful hands belonging to the attacker he'd thought he'd neutralized—another pro, clearly—grasped him from behind, pinning him in place, with the knife close enough that Brixton could smell the lubricant oil.

And that's when the blur appeared, shape more than substance. A whirling dervish of blows wielded with a dexterity that seemed almost like a dance, hands and feet working in unison. One attacker down and then the other, before Brixton could form his next thought. The knife ended up by his feet, and he stamped on it for no real reason.

He didn't remember looking down, but he must have, because when he looked up, a woman almost as tall as he was stood before him, her breathing even. The knife Brixton thought he'd clamped his foot on was somehow in her grasp, now dripping blood.

"Let's get out of here," she said, taking him by the arm.

CHAPTER 38

ARLINGTON, VIRGINIA

Brixton pulled his arm from her grasp as they moved fast toward the head of the side street.

"You killed them," he heard himself say, as if someone else had uttered the statement.

"No choice," the woman said, eyes shifting about.

"They could've been muggers."

"They weren't muggers. And I couldn't risk leaving them alive so they might identify me. *We* couldn't risk it."

"So you killed them to protect both of us."

"After I saved your life."

They reached the head of the street, and Brixton stopped in his tracks. "Who are you?"

"Time for that later. Right now we need to get to your apartment. There could be more of them."

"You know where I live. You were following me . . ."

"Lucky for you, Robert, since you'd be dead otherwise. Can I call you Robert?"

"You just saved my life. You can call me anything you want."

Brixton's right hand had swelled up badly around the knuckles. The woman was filling a ziplock bag with crushed ice from the automatic dispenser built into his refrigerator.

"Do you have something I can strap this on with?"

He pulled his belt from his pants loops and handed it to her. "I need to make a tighter fist. What you did . . ."

"It's called Krav Maga, a martial art I've been practicing for, oh, forty years maybe."

"Israeli," Brixton realized.

"I suppose the accent would've given me away soon enough."

The woman placed the ice pack atop the swollen back of his hand and then fastened his belt tightly around it. She stepped away to inspect her handiwork.

"I once watched a bullet being removed from one of our commandos in the field."

"I'm glad you didn't have to go that far tonight."

"Lia Ganz," the woman said, extending her left hand toward Brixton so he wouldn't have to use his right.

"Name rings a bell."

"You were with SITQUAL for a stretch, meaning it's quite possible that our paths crossed at one time or another."

Brixton eased his hand away. "I guess I don't have to introduce myself. You must have picked me up outside the Metro station."

She nodded again. "To make sure nobody else was doing the same."

"I'm feeling really stupid right now."

"Don't. Those men were pros."

"And since you were following me . . ."

Lia didn't nod this time. "We need to have a talk."

She went first, laying out in detail what had brought her to Washington. She told the tale chronologically, starting with Caesarea and moving on to her visit to the young woman in the Israeli prison, and then the Kif Tzuba amusement park in the Judean Heights, where Dar Ibrahim al-Bis had built a terrorist workshop beneath an old storage shed. She stressed the evidence of the link between the transmitter and camera recovered from that workshop and the ones worn by the suicide bomber in the Metro.

The bomber who, if Panama was to be believed, hadn't been a terrorist at all but a stooge of the man who had rented a UPS Store mailbox under the name Brian Kirkland. Brixton laid all that out for her in similarly meticulous fashion, one professional to another, although the physical prowess of Lia Ganz far exceeded his own—and that of pretty much everyone else he'd ever worked with.

The Israeli mind-set and penchant for training their warriors, it seemed, hadn't changed since 1948.

The more Brixton dove into the events that had begun that morning three days ago on the Metro, the more he realized how much his knowledge paralleled hers. He finished with meeting Panama at Georgetown Waterfront Park and then moved on to the UPS Store in Reston, Virginia.

"You want to give me a hint about what you're leaving out?" Lia Ganz asked him, once he'd finished.

"What makes you think I left anything out?"

"Take a guess at how many Islamic terrorists I've interrogated—no, don't bother. Suffice it to say I've learned how to tell when a man is lying."

"I'm not lying."

"No, only omitting. Same thing, in my book. By the way, remind me to tell you what I once did with a book to an especially vile enemy operator."

"I'm hoping the same fate doesn't await me."

"That depends."

"On what?"

"On you, Robert. Whether you want to come clean about what you're not telling me. One grandparent to another."

Brixton tried not to look surprised or unnerved by Lia Ganz's knowledge of his personal history. He had no doubt she was also aware of the suicide bombing that had claimed his daughter's life while he watched. Israelis were no stranger to misery, either.

"How many do you have?" he asked her.

"One."

"Me too."

"I know. And I'm sorry about your daughter."

"My next question," Brixton started.

"What am I doing here, why was I following you . . ."

"That's two questions."

"Let's start with the latter," Lia Ganz said. "I was following you for my own good as well as yours."

"To make sure it was safe for you to approach me."

"They couldn't be allowed to learn we're working together, Robert."

"*I* didn't know we were working together."

"We started when I saved your life."

"You're here because of the Metro bombing," Brixton said, taking a step back. "Although by all accounts, that woman was no suicide bomber."

He could tell from Lia Ganz's expression she was hearing that for the first time.

"A setup?"

Brixton explained it to her the way Panama had explained it to him, stressing the false flag designation.

"Makes sense," Lia Ganz said matter-of-factly when he had finished.

"What doesn't make sense is why they've tried to kill me twice now."

"They must think you're on to them, that your random presence on the Metro car might not have been so random at all. You're a threat, Robert. This is how men like that deal with threats."

"What about *women*?"

"What about us?"

"You killed those two men without your pulse rate even going up."

"It had to be done. I explained that."

"This isn't Israel, Lia."

"Really, Robert? Tell that to your fellow Metro car passengers."

CHAPTER 39

ARLINGTON, VIRGINIA

"How's your hand?" she asked him, after removing the ice.

Brixton flexed his fingers through the swelling, found he could close them into the semblance of a fist without effort or pain. "Not broken."

"That's something."

Brixton couldn't say why he was starting to trust this woman, a stranger until barely an hour ago, so much. It wasn't their common experience, given that hers undoubtedly made his look bloodless and boring by comparison. He figured the fact that they both were grandparents had something to do with it, how she'd almost lost her granddaughter in a similar fashion to how he'd lost his daughter. Such bonds tended to be indelible.

He laid out what he'd learned about Vice President Stephanie Davenport's death, without mentioning Kendra Rendine by name, stressing the fact that the murder was connected to the Metro bombing through a now deceased special operator who'd been using the name Brian Kirkland. Brixton didn't elaborate on the means of his death.

"Smart stents," Lia Ganz repeated, after he'd finished his tale. "I never would have imagined."

"Especially them being employed as the instruments of murder."

"Not according to that postmortem report, from what you've told me. Someone must be covering their tracks, somebody very good at what they do—and very determined, Robert. In my experience, that makes for a dangerous combination. And you're in touch with this Secret Service agent?"

"Who said anything about a Secret Service agent?"

"How else would you have come by such information?"

"The answer's yes, Lia. We're still in touch."

"And you trust him?"

"It's a *her*, but the answer's yes again. Definitively."

Lia Ganz weighed that briefly. "She's in danger too."

"She knows that."

"But not from whom."

"That's what she's trying to find out, just like us." Brixton thought for a moment. "The men who attacked me . . ."

"They wouldn't have been carrying any identification. Their fingerprints would have led nowhere, and there'd be no record of their DNA on file anywhere."

"Ghosts, in other words."

"Our world is teeming with them, Robert."

"Your world, Lia, not mine."

"Really? They're keeping the circle tight on this," Lia continued, "both here and back in Israel. When men like Winters and your friend Panama get involved, we're nearing the top of the food chain."

"He's not my friend."

"Yes he is, and for good reason."

"What's that?"

"He didn't kill you."

Brixton's phone rang, "NO CALLER ID" lighting up.

"Yes?" he answered.

"It's Kendra, Robert. I've found that federal prison inmate, but . . ."

"But what?" Brixton asked, eyeing Lia Ganz.

"She's not what I was expecting."

"*She?*"

CHAPTER 40

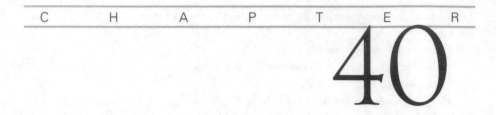

WASHINGTON, DC

"You want to tell me what's wrong or finish your drink first?" Teddy Von Eck asked Kendra Rendine.

Rendine swirled her glass before her, the ice cubes crackling against each other. She'd headed over to meet Von Eck as soon as she'd passed on the identity of the woman attached to the federal prisoner designation Brixton had given her.

"How about both, Teddy? You did teach me how to multitask, after all."

"And you definitely mastered walking and chewing gum at the same time before I retired."

"I need your wisdom, Yoda."

Kendra Rendine sipped her drink: scotch and soda, with lots of soda and lots of ice. She'd chosen a table with clear view of the entrance to the Showtime Lounge, a small bar known almost exclusively to locals on Rhode Island Avenue. She'd long used it as an after-work meeting spot and was fond of observing the ever-growing murals of local musicians' album covers that adorned the walls. The bar also featured a free old-fashioned jukebox that piped nostalgic music through the wall-mounted speakers whenever a band wasn't playing. Oldies, mostly, like the Fleetwood Mac song "Don't Stop," which was currently into its chorus.

Right now, Rendine was thinking about today, specifically about how to handle the quickly evolving conspiracy she believed she'd uncovered, with Robert Brixton's help, which suggested not only the assassination of the sitting vice president of the United States but also something much worse in the offing. Toward that end, she'd put in a call to Teddy Von Eck, a retired Secret Service agent who'd been her first field supervisor and had headed the presidential detail she had worked before she was promoted to detail head for the vice president herself, on Teddy's recommendation. Everybody needed a "rabbi," and he was hers.

"Can I order a drink first?" Von Eck quipped, looking for a server.

He was a tall, rangy man with a close-cropped haircut that hadn't changed in the twelve years she'd known him. In fact, Teddy hadn't changed in those twelve years. His build was the same, complexion was the same, grin was the same, even his suits were the same, despite no longer showing the telltale bulge of a concealed weapon, now that he was retired. Rendine wondered if the continuity in appearance might have been due to the old urban legend about Nixon firing an agent after he'd gained an appreciable amount of weight, or Bill Clinton having one reassigned for smiling too much on the job.

"You're going to need it, Teddy," Rendine told him.

"In that case, I better go to the bar."

He came back with a beer and a shot of something dark—bourbon, Rendine guessed.

"Which one should I start with?" he asked her.

"The shot."

"That bad?"

"Worse."

Von Eck took the shot in a single gulp, a wince stretching into a brief grimace that vanished when he chased the bourbon with a swallow of beer, sifting through the foam. "Okay, I'm ready."

Rendine took a sip of her own. "I believe Vice President Davenport was murdered."

He looked at her, dumbfounded. "I think I need another shot."

He came back to the table with two more, instead of one.

"Two, Teddy?"

"Only because I didn't want to carry three. The hands, you know," he said, holding both of them up.

Rendine did know. Von Eck had left the Secret Service on a disability pension after being diagnosed with Parkinson's disease. It hadn't been his choice; he believed he could continue to do detail supervisory work while on medication. But the agency wouldn't bend their policies on his behalf, and Von Eck had finished out his career behind a desk at headquarters on H Street.

"I'm not seeing any tremors," Rendine said to him, hopefully.

"Any shaking you see will be the result of what you're about to tell me."

She didn't see any shaking as she laid it all out for him in blow-by-blow fashion, chronologically, with her visit to Patty Trahan forming the climax.

Von Eck looked about the bar before responding, to satisfy himself no one was sitting within earshot. "Somebody switched the stents, that's what you're saying."

Rendine nodded. "Replaced the standard variety that had been ordered with the smart variety that can transmit signals."

"And apparently receive them as well, if your theory is correct."

"It's not my theory."

"Whose then?"

"An expert."

"In stents?"

"In killing."

Von Eck thought about that for a moment. "Not someone who'd normally travel in the same circles as you."

"No, not me."

"You're working with somebody else on this," Von Eck concluded, the concern giving a nervous edge to his voice.

"I am."

"Secret Service?"

"A professional."

"But not Secret Service."

Rendine shook her head. "State Department," she said, taking a bit of a liberty, since SITQUAL was actually a private contractor. "And he's following this up along a different line entirely."

"And what line is that?"

"He was on the Metro car with the suicide bomber on Monday. His actions saved dozens of lives."

"Okay, Kendra, so this man's a pro. But what has he—what has the bombing—got to do with why I'm about to have another shot of Jack Daniel's?"

This one seemed to go down even faster than the first, and Kendra waited for the wince to abate before she resumed.

"We think the same people behind the subway bombing were behind the assassination of the vice president."

"And I'm sitting here with you getting drunk because you don't think they're finished yet."

"There's more," Kendra confirmed.

CHAPTER 41

WASHINGTON, DC

"You're saying the entire surgical team was compromised," Von Eck said, after Rendine had laid out what had transpired in the four weeks since Vice President Stephanie Davenport's procedure, finishing with the fact that different stents altogether had been removed from the vice president's chest during her autopsy.

"That's a mild way of putting it."

"You know what I mean."

"I do, Teddy, and the answer's yes. They're all off the grid, some permanently."

Von Eck glanced down at his third shot of bourbon but didn't reach for it. "Except for this Patty Trahan. Under the circumstances, I'm going to assume you didn't leave her in place."

"She's staying at a motel on my dime."

Something changed in Von Eck's expression. "So you haven't reported on this, on *any* of it."

Rendine shook her head. Slowly.

Von Eck drank his third shot. "The woman know the drill? Not to answer her room door or phone, all the usual?"

Rendine nodded. "And I got her a burner phone to use."

"But not with her family."

"I know the drill, Teddy. You taught me well."

Von Eck moved to his beer. "Not well enough, apparently, unless one of the lessons was on going rogue."

"I haven't gone rogue."

"What exactly do you call not reporting your suspicions up the ladder?"

"Precautionary."

"Against what?"

"Against the service reporting to someone who's involved."

Von Eck guzzled the rest of his beer. "We need to bring this inside. We need to bring *you* inside."

"You think I have enough evidence to convince somebody who matters up that ladder?"

"The anomaly with the stents is more than enough there," Von Eck told her, shaking his head. "To think: without your efforts, that would've gone undiscovered . . ."

Someone had cued up a new song on the jukebox, Simon and Garfunkel's "Sound of Silence" replacing "California Dreamin'" by the Mamas and the Papas. Rendine found the lyrics, about nobody talking amid the darkness, oddly appropriate.

"That's why I called my rabbi. I can't take this in off the street on field level. I need to get through a bigger door, the door to someone they can't get to."

"*They*," Von Eck repeated.

"I thought I'd drawn you a clear enough picture."

"You have. It's just that my buzz is starting to kick in."

Rendine noticed that his right hand, the one more affected by the Parkinson's tremors, was quivering now. She felt her insides tighten, wondering if she'd made the right move in involving Teddy Von Eck, potentially placing him in danger too.

"You didn't tell anyone you were meeting me, did you?" she asked him.

"You think because I'm retired, all of a sudden I was born yesterday? Of course I didn't. And who would I tell, anyway? My wife stopped paying attention to anything I told her years ago."

"For once, I'm glad."

Von Eck clutched his empty beer glass as if wishing it contained more than the suds riding the sides. "Okay, we need to get you inside, to someone big. I'm thinking the director himself."

"You trust him?"

"He's a lifer, like me." He paused, just long enough. "Like you." Von Eck held up his glass to a server to signal for a refill of his beer, not shots. "Tell me more about your source from the State Department."

"He's more than a source."

"What is he?"

"Personally involved," Rendine told him.

"Care to elaborate?"

"Not right now. I've gone as far as I can."

"As far as you can?" Von Eck said, his speech starting to slur. "You know the one thing I never felt when I was in the field, Kendra?"

Rendine shook her head.

"Fear. Worry—sure. Concern—absolutely. But I was never scared, because I knew that so long as I did my job right, I'd have no reason to be scared. Follow procedure, follow the rules, play it by the book, and always assume there may be a base you've left uncovered so you're ready when something bad happens." Rendine watched Von Eck tighten his gaze on her. "My point is that everything we do is designed to stop threats from the outside. You're describing one that's clearly coming from the *inside*."

Rendine swallowed hard, trying to keep her emotions at bay. "I think

Vice President Davenport caught wind of what was happening. I think she tried to stop it, and that's why they killed her."

A server set a frosty, fresh glass of beer down in front of Von Eck, but he made no move to reach for or even acknowledge it. "Okay, I'm going to make some calls, maybe just one. In the meantime, get yourself a burner phone too. I'll give you a number so you can text me yours."

"You always keep a burner handy, Teddy?"

He smiled thinly. "Just a phone nobody knows about. I'll contact you as soon as I've got something to say, either that a meeting with the appropriate parties has been set . . ."

"Or," Rendine prodded, having never seen Von Eck flash so grave an expression.

"Or it's time to run for the hills."

CHAPTER 42

BROOKLYN, NEW YORK

Brixton took the seven a.m. Amtrak Acela train from Union Station, which got him into New York just before ten o'clock. He ordered an Uber to take him to MDC Brooklyn, where prisoner number 66–543076 was being housed.

It's Kendra, Robert. I've found that federal prison inmate, but . . .

But what?

She's not what I was expecting.

She?

The prisoner's gender was only the beginning of a nearly impossible story that Brixton wouldn't have believed if his research hadn't confirmed it to be the truth.

Beyond the fact that the Metropolitan Detention Center was located in the South Slope neighborhood, all he knew was that it had far exceeded its capacity, in large part because it had begun housing prisoners for longer stretches instead of serving purely as a way station for those awaiting trial. He had been there once before as part of SITQUAL, in an attempt to get a recently incarcerated prisoner to flip on the overseas drug dealers he was working with, and he remembered the complex as vaguely resembling an inner-city self-storage building. It was a drab ten-story structure that at any time maintained a prisoner population of between 1,600 and 1,800, which was several hundred above its stated capacity. There were practically no windows in evidence anywhere, but there also was no barbwire, just a high steel fence enclosing a portion of the building's perimeter.

Brixton hadn't called ahead to alert prison officials of his coming or the nature of his visit, since there was too much he couldn't say and too many questions he'd be unable to answer. He'd opted for this strategy because it would give him less to explain and a more receptive audience to explain it to. The problem, of course, was that he had no active credentials or portfolio that would allow him to meet with a federal prisoner without prior notification. Instead, he was just a run-of-the-mill private citizen attempting to access a federal prison that, like all such facilities, was notoriously difficult for anyone not directly involved in a particular case to access.

Not surprisingly, he met resistance at the main entrance. After initially being turned away, he identified himself, falsely, as a State Department operative and produced his SITQUAL ID to establish his credibility. Of course, if the guards ran anything beyond the most cursory of checks, they'd find he was *ex*-SITQUAL and he could be arrested then and there for impersonating a federal officer.

Brixton breathed easier when it became clear the guard behind the thick glass fronting the caged entrance he'd just been passed through had no intention of contacting anyone, accepting both his ID and his intentions at face value. Brixton could feel his heart rate slow back down, as a result, and was escorted to the security station by one of the guards behind the glass.

"Who are you here to see, sir?"

"Sister Mary Alice Rose," Brixton said, without hesitation.

This was the point where things promised to get dicey, given that the old nun was under no obligation to talk to him or to any other federal officer, apparent or otherwise, who simply showed up. He'd learned over his years of working as a quasi federal law enforcement agent that the last thing inmates wanted was to speak to an official like him in a traditional interview setting like a meeting room. Word would get out that the prisoner was talking, giving someone up to get their sentence reduced, and they would be summarily ostracized, or much worse, by the prison population. While Brixton expected nothing of the kind when it came to an eighty-five-year-old nun, he knew the possibility existed that he'd be placing her in some jeopardy, if the proper precautions weren't taken.

The guard behind the desk consulted his computer. "You sure you have the name right, sir?"

"Maybe I've got the spelling wrong."

"Not a lot of ways to spell Mary Alice Rose," the guard noted.

"Is there a problem?"

"There's a mistake, because we don't have a prisoner at this facility by that name."

"The Bureau of Prisons says otherwise," a flummoxed Brixton told him, not bothering to add that his source was a Secret Service agent.

Or maybe that explained things a bit, since Kendra Rendine would have access to databases that ordinary officials might not.

"I'm here on behalf of the State Department," he added, flashing his SITQUAL credentials yet again. "This is a matter of national security."

"It doesn't matter what kind of matter it is, sir. She's not here."

Brixton recalled some of the domestic cases he'd worked on behalf of SITQUAL. His prisoners in the federal penal system had occasionally "disappeared" from visible records, kept off the books in order to bury them from the outside world through the duration of their sentence, which could then be extended indefinitely, in wholly arbitrary fashion, since for all intents and purposes they'd ceased to exist anymore.

Such treatment was normally reserved for political prisoners, mostly terrorists, who didn't qualify for the rigors of Guantanamo but needed, effectively, to drop off the grid. At the age of eighty-five, Sister Mary Alice Rose didn't fit that description.

"Do I have to come back here with a warrant or judge's order?" Brixton asked him, not even sure either was possible.

"You can come back with anything you want, sir. You can have the president phone down here personally. I can't produce someone who's not an inmate of this facility."

While exasperating, this was all starting to make a degree of sense to Brixton. All he'd been able to learn about Sister Mary Alice Rose was that she was eight-five years old, had been a nun for sixty of them, and had spent the last two years at this facility after being arrested on federal trespassing charges.

That was the whole of it. No matter how deeply Brixton probed or how much he Googled, he could find no further details on just how a woman long past retirement age had ended up incarcerated in a federal penal institution for more than two years, nor could he locate anything more about the charge—no trial, plea agreement, nothing. It was almost as if she was a Josef K–type figure from the Franz Kafka novel *The Trial*, where a man finds himself on trial for an undisclosed charge.

Again, not entirely unusual or unprecedented, but a fate reserved for federal prisoners the government believed it had good reason to keep off the books, which clearly was not a policy to be employed lightly.

"Check under 'Jane Doe,'" Brixton suggested, recalling the protocol he'd witnessed a few times while with SITQUAL.

The guard behind the desk did, or least seemed to. "We've got a few Janes but no Does."

The frustration over what should have been a simple procedure began to nag at Brixton. Then again, this woman's federal prisoner number had been in the possession of a reputed black ops specialist, the reason for which likely explained Sister Mary Alice Rose's being disappeared from the system.

"Tell you what," he said to the guard, realizing he was getting nowhere, "I'm going to come back with some higher authorization."

"You can get it from God himself and she still won't be here."

CHAPTER 43

BROOKLYN, NEW YORK

Brixton walked to a nearby Dunkin' Donuts to collect his thoughts and plan his next move, if there was one. He took one of three weather-beaten outdoor tables, using some napkins to clean off the chair before sitting down with a large regular.

Halfway through his coffee, with no other option, he called the number for the man he'd come to know as Panama.

"Brixton," the man said, by way of greeting.

"How'd you know it was me?"

"Because I don't recognize this number. You're using a burner."

"I am."

"And you're in New York—Brooklyn, it looks like."

Brixton didn't bother asking Panama how he knew that. "Know what the weather's like up here?"

"Give me a second . . ."

"Don't bother. Give me an update on those schematics instead."

"I would if I could. But so far we're drawing a blank."

"What happened to that unlimited access to everything you told me you had?"

"Meaningless. The one thing I can tell you is that they've been tampered with, just enough to keep us from identifying what we're looking at. So far, we're looking at around a thousand possibilities."

"You haven't been able to narrow it down?"

"We started at fifty thousand. Whoever altered those plans knew exactly what they were doing. Next best thing to spontaneous combustion, in the event the wrong person opened that mailbox. To say we're in the dark would be putting it mildly."

Brixton shouldn't have been surprised. "Then allow me to shed some light. That number scrawled at the bottom of those schematics you found in Brian Kirkland's mailbox was a federal prisoner ID."

Panama didn't respond right away.

"Nearest facility to your location," Panama said finally, "would be the Metropolitan Detention Center."

"That's where she is. Sister Mary Alice Rose."

"Did you say *Sister*?"

"She's a nun."

"Never heard of her."

"Convicted, or pled guilty, to federal trespassing charges."

"How'd you come by this information?" Panama asked sharply.

"I do have a source or two."

"And you decided to pursue this on your own, without alerting me?"

"I'm alerting you now," Brixton told him.

"A while after you learned something you should have made me aware of immediately."

"I'm still trying to figure out if I can trust you."

"Likewise, Brixton, and this doesn't represent a positive step in that direction."

"Why would Kirkland have the federal prison ID number for a nun?" Brixton asked Panama.

"The better question is what she's doing in federal prison in the first place."

"She's eighty-five, incarcerated for two years already on that trespassing beef."

"Give me a second."

Brixton did, and it stretched into a minute.

"She's not in my system," Panama said, when he came back on.

"Maybe you spelled her name wrong."

"I'm not talking about the federal inmate database, I'm talking about *my* system, one accessible by a select few, listing persons of interest."

"Because they're dangerous?"

"Because they're persons of interest, Brixton, for one reason or another. Persons we've got eyes on, have wired, or are on our radar for one reason or another. Come on, you're supposed to be a pro. Figure it out."

Brixton felt a layer of sweat beginning to work its way through his shirt, making him wonder if he should have opted for iced coffee instead of hot. But it was more than just the temperature of the coffee that had suddenly left him unsettled.

"You've got your own people. What do you need me for?"

"Because you *are* one of my people. Now. And you were motivated, already wound up when we met on the waterfront. All I had to do was point you in the right direction."

Being more of a "fixer" than a spymaster, Panama wouldn't have troops of his own to call upon. Instead, he would rely on the likes of Brixton to do his dirty work, because Brixton was professional while being disposable at the same time.

"Do your job, Brixton," he finished.

"My job?"

"You've been waiting for this opportunity for five years, since your daughter died in that suicide bombing. Your greatest misfortune was not meeting me sooner. So focus. I'm going to make a call. Go back to the facility in one hour and ask for Captain Donovan."

"Captain Donovan," Brixton repeated, committing the name to memory.

"He's my guy there. This isn't the first time I've needed to arrange an ex parte meeting with a prisoner, just the first nun. Donovan will make the proper arrangements. If she's there, he'll make sure you get your meeting."

"She's there, all right. The question is why they would make Sister Mary Alice disappear within the system."

"So she wouldn't be in a position to speak to somebody like you. Or me. Which means there's something they don't want her telling anyone."

"Aren't you one of the 'they'?" Brixton asked Panama.

"If I was, we wouldn't be talking right now, would we? Stay in the system too long and it rots you to the core. Just ask Brian Kirkland."

"A difficult task, under the circumstances."

"That was my point, Brixton. And here's another one: I don't have to tell you what it means to be on the radar of a man like the late Mr. Kirkland."

"Speaking of which, can you text me his picture to this number."

"Why?"

"I'm playing a hunch," Brixton said, not elaborating further.

"Doesn't matter anyway, because there aren't photos of men like Kirkland on file. He's a ghost, remember?"

"A dead ghost, remember? You told me his body had been recovered. So you'll be able to get me his photo after all."

CHAPTER 44

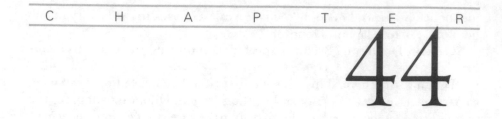

WASHINGTON, DC

The Watergate Hotel's Kingbird Restaurant had been a fixture in the city long before the Nixon years made the whole sprawling site infamous, a popular haunt for politicos and diplomats.

Ali Shadid, cultural attaché to the Saudi ambassador to the United States, dined there frequently, always alone and always at the same table, nestled in the shadows, out of sight of anyone who might be peering through the glass wall that looked out into a courtyard on the restaurant's southern side. Shadid's server had just set his dessert, the house specialty of lavender-infused crème brûlée, before him, when a woman took the chair on the other side of the table.

"Excellent choice," Lia Ganz said, everything in her demeanor suggesting she'd been expected, a ruse she intended to continue. "Although I've always favored the chocolate tart."

"I had that yesterday," Shadid managed, forcing a smile.

"I hope it was as good as I remember, General," Lia followed, addressing Shadid by his former rank in the Saudi military. Now he was a high-ranking officer with the General Intelligence Presidency, that country's equivalent of the CIA, also known as al Mukhabarat al 'Amma al Mamlaka al Arabyah Saudihya.

"That depends on when you were last in Washington, Colonel."

"It has been a while."

"I thought it would likely be forever, given your retirement."

"Circumstances forced me to rethink my plans."

"So I heard," Shadid said, ignoring his dessert and the espresso that had been placed alongside it. "I trust you're not here to blame my country for that drone attack."

"Not at all, General. Quite the opposite, in fact. I'm here to give you the opportunity to help me prevent a potentially much greater attack."

"Since when did Israel's problems become my problems?"

"Since this particular attack looks to be aimed at the United States."

Shadid's deep-set eyes, laden with heavy bags beneath them, flashed. "The problems of the United States are not my problems either."

"This one will be. And I'm giving you the opportunity to be either the country that helps save the day or the country that will suffer the bulk of recriminations if this attack isn't stopped."

"So why am I talking to an ex–Israeli intelligence officer instead of an active American one?"

"Because I was on that beach in Caesarea, Ali, and I tracked down the bomb maker behind those drones. Perhaps you've heard of him: Dar Ibrahim al-Bis."

"I've heard of him. Hamas."

"But he was born in Saudi Arabia. Turns out he's also been implicated in the Metro bombing and, by connection, the bigger attack yet to come. How do you think the Americans will respond to a national of yours being party to something like that?"

Shadid's expression curled into the semblance of a snarl. "Al-Bis hasn't been to Saudi Arabia since he was four years old."

"The newspapers are likely to leave that out of their headlines, especially after Mossad offers proof of Saudi collaboration in that major attack."

"Lies!" Shadid said, loud enough to draw the attention of diners from nearby tables.

"Lies are dangerous things, Ali," Lia told him. "You know what's even more dangerous? Well-funded terrorist operations. Saudi Arabia managed to survive the recriminations that followed nine eleven. You won't survive this time."

Shadid softened his expression and spooned out a small bite of his dessert. "This is the way you treat a friend?"

"We were never friends, just colleagues. This is the way I treat colleagues, and friends, when lives are at stake."

Shadid leaned back in his chair, espresso and crème brûlée forgotten for now. "What do you want from me, Colonel?"

"We've fought many battles, General. Some on the same side and some against each other. This is a battle you can't afford to see lost."

"Even though it isn't our fight."

"It's yours as much as it is mine. Mine because of Caesarea. Yours because your country will be the first America targets in her crosshairs, if indications about the magnitude of the attack are proven true. Your future king can kill all the journalists he wants, but he won't be able to kill that particular truth. And there will be no future in Saudi Arabia for him to preside over."

"I ask again, Colonel, what do you want of me?"

"Everything, General, points to the fact that whoever's behind the Metro bombing and whatever's to come is going to make Islamic terrorists the fall guy. I don't know whether they want a rationale to start a war, to invade the Middle East, or if something even more nefarious may be afoot."

"You don't consider starting a war or invading a region to be nefarious enough?"

"Everything's relative," Lia told him. "I don't have to tell you that."

"No, you don't."

"Something else I shouldn't have to tell you. I have meetings already set up with the Turks, the Egyptians, the Syrians, and the Iranians. The message I intend to pass to all of them is the very same one I've given you. I came to you first, out of courtesy and respect for those times in which we've fought on the same side. Make no mistake, though—I will go elsewhere, should you disappoint me."

Shadid leaned forward, lowering his voice ever so slightly. "And what do I need to do to avoid disappointing you?"

Lia let him see her smile. "Glad you asked, General. Glad you asked . . ."

CHAPTER 45

WASHINGTON, DC

Thank you for seeing me, sir," Kendra Rendine greeted the director of the Secret Service, after he'd closed the door to his private office behind him.

Clayton McGrath escorted her to a sitting area set off to the right of his desk, by the window overlooking H Street, his expression looking as compassionate as it was concerned. "When are you going to start calling me Clayton, Kendra?"

"Maybe when I take your place, sir."

"Sooner rather than later, I fully expect," McGrath said to her, forcing a smile.

It was the "forced" part that concerned Rendine, something off just enough to be cause for concern. In the wake of their meeting the night before, Teddy Von Eck had secured a meeting for her with the director of the Secret Service himself, in his office at headquarters, located on the top floor of the stately nine-story postmodern low-rise on H Street NW. Even though the agency's origins dated back to the Civil War, when it was founded to combat the then-widespread counterfeiting of U.S. currency, it didn't get a dedicated home of its own until the Memorial Headquarters building opened in 1999, marking the first time all Secret Service personnel had actually been housed under a single roof. The service had previously rented space throughout Washington, DC, as far back as the 1901 assassination of President William McKinley, after which its agents had assumed full-time responsibility for presidential protection.

"Again, I'm sorry about Vice President Davenport, Kendra," the director said, expressing his condolences in person after doing so on the phone the morning after Davenport's death. "A very impressive woman, and a terrible loss for this country to bear." He studied her briefly, before resuming. "And a terrible loss for you personally, as well."

Rendine nodded, responding with her eyes while waiting for McGrath to continue.

"I've never lost a protectee, to natural causes or anything else, while working a detail, so I'm not going to say something as stupid as I know what you're going through. But I do know the pressures presidential and vice presidential details are under and the emotional blowback losing a protectee has on the psyche."

"I wish I'd done more," Rendine said, honestly. "I wish there'd been something more I could have done."

"When I took this job, I personally interviewed the few Secret Service agents still alive who'd been with Kennedy in Dallas. I wanted to understand the toll it took on their careers and their lives. I wanted to better educate myself so I'd be able to better manage the worst-case scenarios of being an agent. You know the common denominator that emerged? None of them felt effective as agents anymore. They started looking for anything and everything, stopped trusting their instincts, after those instincts had so badly let them down in their own minds. Some continued to work details, others wrote books down the road, but all said the effects never wore off or even mitigated. For the rest of their lives and careers, they'd be known as the detail agents who lost a president."

Rendine remained silent, again waiting for Director McGrath to continue. She found it strange that he'd started along these lines instead of plunging straight into her suspicions, which were the basis of this meeting Teddy Von Eck had arranged.

McGrath leaned forward, empathy widening his eyes even farther. "How would you feel about moving into a more administrative role here at headquarters, Kendra, at least for a time?"

Something scratched at Rendine's spine. "Sir?"

"I'm not necessarily talking about anything permanent. Let's just wait for the dust to settle and then go through the usual psychological protocols to see if the field's still calling your name."

"I'm not sure I know . . ."

McGrath nodded as if *he* did, picking up on Rendine's thought after her voice drifted off. "I can make it an order, but I'd rather not have to. I want this to be your choice, you doing what's best for yourself, above all else."

Rendine fidgeted in her chair, her thoughts a jumble. Teddy Von Eck had called her to say he'd set the meeting after running all the numbers for Director McGrath. He assured her it would be just the two of them, as she had insisted, since the situation was so dire and her conclusions so potentially catastrophic to the country that she didn't dare share her suspicions or evidence with anyone else.

"Teddy said you wanted to see me right away," she told the director, searching lamely for a bridge to reach what she'd really come here to discuss.

"He insisted that I see you right away, sharing the same concerns I've expressed. You have a lot of friends in the service, Kendra . . . something to take solace in right now."

Rendine clawed through the confusion slowly enveloping her. "Teddy didn't raise any of my suspicions with you?"

"Suspicions?" McGrath repeated blankly.

"From our discussion last night."

"He was concerned, Kendra, and with good reason, since Vice President Davenport is the first executive-level protectee to die on our watch in almost sixty years."

"What about the issues I raised with Ted pertaining to her death?" Rendine asked, trying to couch her words as carefully as she could.

McGrath didn't respond, not directly anyway. "Very few of us know what you're feeling right now. Especially as head of a detail losing a protectee, even due to natural causes. That's a lot of baggage, a lot of emotional weight to bear . . ."

McGrath kept talking, but a single phrase stuck in Rendine's mind.

Even due to natural causes.

Hadn't Teddy Von Eck voiced her suspicions to the director? Had he lied to her? Or had McGrath ignored his assertions?

Rendine felt suddenly disconnected from reality, the director's voice droning on in her head without any of his words registering in her mind. She was looking at him but not really seeing him, her thoughts lost behind her intentions. This conversation was going in an entirely different direction than she'd been expecting, one that left her discomfited and her neck and shoulders stiffened enough to send throbbing pangs, akin to a migraine headache, through her skull.

"I'm sure you'd agree this is best for all concerned," she heard McGrath say, finally registering his words again.

Since Rendine hadn't been listening, she had no idea what "this" was, though she suspected it was a lengthened version of his original point.

How would you feel about moving into a more administrative role here at headquarters, Kendra, at least for a time?

That hadn't been a suggestion, though, as much as an already determined intention, not so much for her own good as to get her out of the way. Had McGrath chosen to disregard what she'd shared with Teddy Von Eck the night before? Had Teddy failed to follow through on his promise to bring the director up to speed in the process of setting up this meeting?

Someone was to blame. Someone didn't want the truth coming out.

Someone was involved in whatever had gotten the vice president of the United States murdered.

The director? Von Eck?

Had the Secret Service itself been compromised?

"I think you're right," Rendine heard herself say, forcing herself to play along, in full awareness that there was no sense in persisting.

McGrath rose, a clear sign it was time for her to take her leave. "We'll get this sorted out, Kendra. Everything will be fine."

"I know, sir."

"Clay," he corrected again. "Please."

"Clay," Rendine said, obliging him.

The director smiled, the gesture looking wholly genuine. He led Rendine toward the door. This was the time when he might have thrown a comforting arm around her shoulders, before such contact became tacitly forbidden by all the new protocols. She was glad for those protocols in that moment, which kept McGrath from feeling the tension that had swept through her. Her legs felt heavy, the office door seeming to get farther away instead of closer.

"Take a few weeks for your head to clear," he said, opening that door when they finally reached it. "Then we'll see about finding you a proper position to settle your thoughts and chart a new path forward."

Whatever that meant, Rendine thought, as she nodded.

"I'd like you to see one of our counselors as well, Kendra," McGrath told her, as she moved past him. "Someone you can share anything and everything about this with."

Just like I did with Teddy Von Eck, and look where that got me.

Rendine was still trembling slightly when she emerged from the building. She'd set her phone to silent but could feel it vibrating inside her shoulder bag, so she plucked it out.

"I just texted you a photo from this number," Brixton told her.

Rendine checked her phone. "Yup, here it is. Not very flattering."

"Death tends to have that effect."

"This is the man from the tunnel," she realized.

"That's right. I thought you might want to show it to Patricia Trahan, see if he looks familiar."

"I'll reach out to her."

"You sound . . . shaken," Brixton said to her, after a pause.

"I just met with the director of the Secret Service."

"How'd that go?"

"Let me get back to you on that, Robert, after I figure it out for myself."

CHAPTER 46

WASHINGTON, DC

"Madam First Lady, I'm sure you understand our concern," the attorney general of the United States said to Merle Talmidge. "We're only seeking your assurance that the situation has been contained."

She was seated on her husband's immediate right, the president occupying the head of the conference table that dominated the White House Situation Room. "It has been contained."

"We've heard that assurance before, with all due respect, when it came to Vice President Davenport."

"And it was correct."

"Yet now we're faced with this matter of the head of the vice president's security detail. Can we be certain Davenport shared nothing with her?"

"From what we've been able to gather, yes. All she has to go on is supposition, assumptions as to my husband's condition, and a few holes we failed to adequately fill that are no longer an issue."

"So we should accept your assurances at face value?"

"Assurances about what?" Corbin Talmidge asked his wife, turning toward her suddenly and freezing the breath of those seated around the table.

The president seldom commented during these meetings—less and less as his condition continued to worsen over the past few weeks. And when he did speak, it was usually to offer some off-kilter comment on the topic they were discussing, or some irrelevant non sequitur. But today he seemed more engaged, which often led to increased levels of anxiety and left the other participants in the meeting waiting for the first lady to respond.

"What we discussed yesterday," she told her husband calmly, patting his forearm.

"We did?" he asked, his gaze bearing the look of a driver who just realized he was lost.

"Yes," the first lady nodded. "And you agreed the steps we were about to take were necessary, mandated. That the future of the country needed to be secured and the only way to assure that was to take the kind of drastic measures that would keep you in power long enough to finish your work."

"My work is very important," the president agreed.

"Yes, it is."

"I'm president of the United States."

"Yes, you are."

That seemed to reassure Corbin Talmidge. "Are we going out today?"

"Where would you like to go?"

"To give another speech, like the one I gave the other day."

For a moment, the first lady thought her husband might have been caught in a moment of clarity, the once brilliant mind that faded in and out with increasing frequency sharpening for at least that moment. Then his expression faded, the emptiness returning, the brief control of his train of thought lost.

"The one where everyone was cheering and it snowed inside."

He was talking about the speech he'd given after accepting his party's nomination, when he was running for his first term, the "snow" in question being confetti that had dropped from the ceiling as he stood on the stage, triumphantly holding Merle Talmidge's hand overhead, clasped in his own. In that moment, anything and everything seemed possible.

Nearly four years had passed since that glorious time. Corbin Talmidge now faced the end of his term, with no hope whatsoever for reelection, given that the rigors of the campaign trail would be sure to expose the deteriorating mental condition that had dominated the last year of his first term, with the November election just five months away. No way he could ever endure the campaign trial, of course. But in a mere two days such concerns would be the last thing on any American's mind, the entire election rendered an afterthought.

SIX MONTHS EARLIER . . .

The president had wanted to step down upon receiving the initial diagnosis of his condition and had told his wife of his intentions to do just that, sharing them with no one else.

"Let's think about it," she'd said.

"What's there to think about?"

"The country."

"That's exactly what I'm doing. I need to speak with the vice president and begin planning for an orderly transition."

"Let's take some time here," Merle Talmidge had urged. "Let's not rush into things."

"Not rush? I don't know how much longer I'll be able to string together coherent sentences. We need to make the announcement that I won't be running for reelection, before it becomes obvious why. Do that, and I can preserve my dignity, while giving Vice President Davenport time to get her own campaign up and running."

The first lady's expression wrinkled in derision at the mere consideration of such a possibility. "What about preserving the country?"

* * *

It was in that moment that the first lady had conceived the basis of the plan they'd gathered in the Situation Room to discuss the final preparation for today. Merle Talmidge had managed to delay her husband's resignation long enough for his condition to deteriorate enough to leave his intentions in her hands. She also succeeded in getting him to replace cabinet officials with individuals she knew would be sympathetic and supportive of her intentions, because she'd vetted them before feeding their names to her husband. She needed the cabinet on her side to enact her plan, and she had managed to build an inner White House circle that was convinced of the necessity of the actions to which she was committed. If her husband's legacy couldn't be one thing, it would be another: of being the man who presided over the greatest attack the United States had ever weathered, an attack that would change America forever under his stout leadership, which was no more than him repeating the lines that she fed to him.

Merle Talmidge could read all the cards clearly because she had stacked the deck.

"Why are all these people here?" the president asked her, as if suddenly realizing they weren't alone.

"They're helping us," Merle Talmidge told her husband, as the five men and two women gathered before them remained stiff and silent.

"Helping us *what?*"

"Save the country."

"Is it in danger?"

"You know it is, dear."

"From what?"

"Itself. The country has strayed outside the lines and we need to bring it back between them," the first lady said, as much to the group assembled before her as to her husband, lest any of them be harboring doubts about what was to take place in just two days' time.

"What lines?" Corbin Talmidge asked her, an edge of agitation starting to creep into his voice. "I don't know what you mean by *lines.*"

"To act outside the interests of what's best for the United States."

"Then why didn't you just say that?" He leaned closer to her and lowered his voice. "I don't know who any of these people are."

"They want to help you make the country strong again, save it from itself."

"I can't do that alone."

"That's why they're here."

The president glanced across the table at those seated around it and smiled. To a man and woman, they smiled back.

Merle Talmidge elected to direct her next remarks toward her husband, even though they were meant for the seven officials before her. If the operation went bad, they would be labeled coconspirators. The press and opposition party would claim a coup had been staged. Recriminations would mount with all the congressional hearings. But they weren't going to get that chance.

"Madam First Lady," said the secretary of state, "we need to get back to the matter at hand, specifically these potential setbacks to our operation."

"We must consider postponing," interjected the secretary of defense, "until we are certain of containment."

Merle Talmidge forced herself to remain calm, not about to reveal how roiled such comments left her. "Postponement means failure."

"And not postponing risks recriminations."

"You miss my point, Madam Secretary," the first lady said to the Homeland Security secretary. "If we postpone now, we invite our adversaries, traitors to this nation all, to dig deeper. In this city, digging a hole is an end in itself, even where there's nothing to be found. Proceeding as scheduled is the surest way to avoid the very recriminations you so fear and to force them to drop their shovels."

"No one here doubts the urgency of this operation," said the national security adviser. "But we're only going to get one shot, and we must assure ourselves the conditions are right."

"They will never be more right than they are right now—or more necessary. We already went over this when we discussed the threat posed by the vice president."

"You mean the fact that she picked up the president's deteriorating condition so easily," said the director of the FBI. "I don't need to remind you, Madam First Lady, that condition is only going to worsen, further complicating our task."

"No," Merle Talmidge said softly, gazing at her husband, "you don't have to remind me."

"And no potential candidate for vice president is going to sign on with reservations even approaching those," added the president's chief of staff.

"Unless the candidate came from inside this room."

"Do you have someone in mind, Madam First Lady?"

"Yes. Me."

Heads immediately hung downward, expressions suddenly reluctant to meet Merle Talmidge's, at this announcement, which had struck her all at once a few days earlier. It was natural. It was obvious. She was the perfect person for the job—in point of fact, the *only* person for the job. Her husband had agreed, even excited about the possibility, in a moment that had already faded from his memory.

"The announcement would be made in the immediate aftermath of the attack, stressing that it would only be temporary, until the country is fully up and running again," the first lady added defensively.

"Of course," said the national security adviser, "it would also position you to take your husband's place on the ticket, should the election go forward."

"There is that, too, yes," the first lady agreed. "If we wait until after the attack to make the announcement, we'll be looking at an entirely different playing field, where the American people will have plenty more commanding their attention. Speaking of which, I'd like to move on to a discussion of the potential casualties we're going to be facing two days from now. . . ."

CHAPTER 47

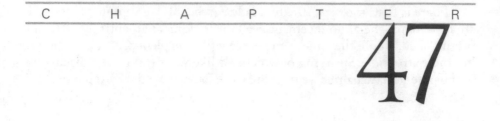

BROOKLYN, NEW YORK

His call with Kendra Rendine complete, Brixton returned to the Metropolitan Detention Center after exactly one hour. This time he asked for Captain Donovan, as Panama had directed. The same guard behind the glass partition told him to wait, and that wait stretched to ten minutes before Donovan appeared, looking every bit the part of the tough Irish cop he had likely once been.

"Right this way," Donovan said, holding the door open for him. "Follow me."

Brixton stored his weapon and phone in a box-size locker and had to go through the metal detector three different times before the buzzer finally stopping sounding, thanks to his watch, then his belt, then the meager change in his pocket. Brixton fell into step behind Captain Donovan and they approached an elevator. Donovan used an old-fashioned slot key to activate the cab and pressed the six. After exiting on that floor, he led Brixton past a row of windowless rooms with arrays of chairs arranged in a classroom style. Donovan opened the last door before a break in the hallway and bade Brixton to enter, closing the door as soon as he did so.

Brixton found Sister Mary Alice Rose standing at a blackboard, working a chunk of yellow chalk across the surface.

"Thought I'd take advantage of the opportunity to get a head start on my lessons for this afternoon," she said without turning.

"Lessons?"

Sister Mary Alice finally looked his way. The white hair, glasses, and dark liver spots on the backs of her hands attested to Mary Alice Rose's age, but her slate-blue eyes looked youthful, full of hope, despite her residing for the past two years in a federal detention facility instead of a retirement home. They were the kind of eyes that missed nothing and spoke as clearly as words.

"I teach writing and literature to the other inmates," she told him.

"Making the best of your time, no doubt," Brixton noted.

Sister Mary Alice's blue eyes narrowed on him. "I may be old, but I'm not so old that I can't remember a face. And I don't remember yours at all, my boy."

Brixton cracked a smile at being referred to as "my boy" for the first time in twenty years.

"Robert Brixton, Sister," he said, extending his hand.

Mary Alice Rose took it in a surprisingly strong grasp. Brixton's hand came away with a coating of yellow from the chalk.

"You seem to have the advantage on me, Robert. I thought you must've come from the lawyers. But you don't look like a lawyer—certainly not one of mine—and you're not dressed like one, either."

"I'm not a lawyer."

"And yet here we are. I haven't had a visitor, besides my lawyers, since I've called this place home."

"There's no record of you even being incarcerated here, Sister."

"To keep the media and other prying eyes and ears away, in all probability. Speaking of which, Robert, who are you exactly? Since you managed to get through the wall around me, you must be someone very important."

"Not really. But I am here about some*thing* important."

"What does that make you exactly?" Sister Mary Alice asked him, taking a seat at one of the desks, which reminded Brixton of his high school days.

Brixton took the desk immediately across from hers in the next row, adjusting it to better face her. "I used to be a cop. These days, I call myself a private investigator."

"I'm afraid if you've come looking for dirt in a divorce matter—"

"Not that kind of private investigator."

"Then what kind might you be?"

"I handle international issues, to a great extent, and more delicate, sensitive matters involving Washington types."

"I'm not a Washington type," Sister Mary Alice told him, "and last time I checked I had no delicate, sensitive matters that required investigation."

"Besides what you're doing here—other than teaching, that is."

The nun smiled, looking as comfortable within these prison walls as she was in her own skin. "Even my lawyers have trouble seeing me. I'm told I've been placed on some list."

"Reserved for federal prisoners deemed to still pose a significant risk. They're made to disappear inside the system."

Sister Mary Alice nodded. "Makes sense. One of the guards slipped me a letter from a fellow sister who was told I was no longer here and there was no updated record of where I was."

"Gone and forgotten," Brixton said.

"Something like that, at least the *forgotten* part. But I haven't *gone* anywhere. And what risk could I possibly pose to anyone?"

"You're considered a national security risk."

"Me?" She stifled a laugh but let herself chuckle. "What do you make of that, a simple sister of the Order of Immaculate Conception?"

"Apparently not so simple," Brixton offered.

Sister Mary Alice took a deep breath. "What are you doing here, Robert?"

"I think you're in danger, Sister."

"In here?" she asked him, sounding almost playful. "Where nobody knows where I even am anymore?"

"Somebody knows," Brixton said, leaving it there.

She took his hands in hers. "You sound concerned."

"With good reason, I believe."

"So you've come here, what, to rescue me?"

"The somebody in question is out of the picture."

Sister Mary Alice studied him closer. "Why do I get the feeling that you were responsible for that?"

"Because I am. He's dead. And if he wasn't, I would be."

Sister Mary Alice's big, bright eyes flashed behind her bifocal lenses. "And me, too, by connection. Gives us something in common, I suppose. But why would a man like that care about an old nun?"

"I know your imprisonment here involves a federal trespassing charge. To answer that question, I'll need to know the details."

"Ah," the nun said, a realization striking her. "You mean, as in where I was arrested."

"Exactly."

Sister Mary Alice nodded before responding. "The Y-Twelve nuclear facility in Oak Ridge, Tennessee."

CHAPTER 48

BALTIMORE, MARYLAND

"Can you spare some change?"

Lia Ganz gave the homeless man a dollar to avoid drawing any attention to herself. She stood in downtown Baltimore, down the street from the Masjid Us Salaam mosque, a stately building that had once housed a nightclub, of all things, and then a bank, before it was bought and converted into a mosque in the early 2000s.

It still looked like a bank, in her mind, thanks to its ornate construction and the raised "Provident Savings Bank" chiseled out of the marble finish of its façade, over the door. The color scheme combined rose, ivory, and a touch of mauve over a redbrick sidewalk leading to a majestic, heavy double-door entrance that looked more fit for an armory or bunker.

Ali Shadid had called her from the Saudi embassy two hours after she'd sat down at his lunch table. She took the call in the fifth hotel room she'd checked into since arriving in Washington, each under different identities. The need for the fifth had surfaced last night; she feared her actions in saving Robert Brixton's life might have compromised her.

"I'm going to assume whatever mission your presence in Washington involves is approved at the highest levels of your government, Colonel."

"That isn't relevant to our conversation."

"But the assurances I require are."

"Meaning?"

"That you assure me that, however this ends, you will make it plain to your government that we cooperated to the fullest extent of our abilities."

"Which, of course, remains to be seen."

"It is important they know that," Shadid persisted. "Vital."

That could only mean the Saudi intelligence operative had uncovered information that suggested something very big indeed was in the offing, something with which the Saudis wanted no association.

"In that case, you have my word," Lia assured him.

"In that case, Colonel, be advised that there are indications that a major terrorist cell is operating right here in Washington. Toward what end, no one seems to know. With whose backing, everyone claims ignorance on. As to which organization is to blame, the intelligence officials with whom

I spoke waffled from one to another and back again. They are chasing ghosts."

"If it were only ghosts, we wouldn't be having this conversation."

"We *aren't* having this conversation," Shadid reminded her. "This conversation never happened."

"Until it comes time to assure my government of your cooperation."

"I'm glad we understand each other. The inklings are out there, but nothing firm or actionable. All I was able to learn for sure is that the Americans have a number of mosques under surveillance across the region, which they suspect of offering aid and comfort to these jihadis that have melted into their midst."

"I could've gotten that information myself from the internet," Lia Ganz told him.

"But not this," Shadid assured her.

He proceeded to tell her that his own underground Arab sources indicated that Masjid Us Salaam mosque had attracted the most attention, from a surveillance standpoint. Without going into specifics, the Saudi intelligence officer said that information he'd gleaned from his sources indicated that recent acquisitions suggested anomalies that had drawn the attention of Saudi intelligence. Air mattresses, for one thing; an inexplicable uptick in food and beverage orders, for another. And a subtle rise in electricity usage.

All three of those, along with several other clues, indicated the mosque was hiding something, along with some*ones*. It was the kind of information the Americans, left to their own devices, would never have been able to attain. A single piece, perhaps, but not the entire string, collated in a fashion that suggested that whatever operation was in the offing had been based just down the street from where she was standing now.

The homeless man, meanwhile, had moved on, leaving Lia Ganz to further tighten her focus on the mosque, as worshippers began to trickle in for afternoon prayers. None of them stood out or sparked any sense of recognition at first glance, nor was there any discernible pattern associated with what she witnessed.

A call back home to Mossad had produced intelligence on the mosque's imam, a nationalized American named Haussam Zimaar Alaf who had spent his youth in Lebanese refugee camps. He and his mosque enjoyed a stellar reputation in the Baltimore area, going as far as to invite Jews to use Masjid Us Salaam for their own services after a nearby synagogue was vandalized. There wasn't the slightest hint in his profile suggesting any association with radical Islamists or jihadis; in fact, he had publicly denounced such movements on multiple occasions.

If Shadid's intelligence was correct, Imam Alaf must have gone to great lengths to establish the kind of cover that would keep him off the radar when the Americans were poking about. Lia Ganz had seen that process play out before, far too often, with the equally common refrain of "If only we had known" or "There had been previous association" inevitably arising during the attack's aftermath.

Lia had dressed for the occasion in the garb typical of an Arab woman, a disguise she'd donned often enough over the years that it felt like a second skin. She fastened the hijab over her hair and looped it tight, the final element of a disguise bolstered by a shapeless dress that more resembled a smock. Then she ambled slowly down the street, picking up her pace only to follow a group of women through a single open door, where the group broke right, toward the women's area.

But Lia stopped short of following them into the worship room reserved for women, instead continuing down the hall. Checking doors, appearing lost. It took a few minutes, but soon a burly guard wearing a black suit and flashing a smile that looked painted on his face approached her warily.

"You are not permitted down here, woman," he said in Arabic.

"I'm new. Just looking for the restroom. But I don't want to miss the start of prayers. I'll return to the chapel."

The man grasped her arm when she attempted to slip past him. "The imam wishes to see you."

"But—"

"He enjoys greeting all of those new to our halls."

"What of my prayer?"

"There will be time for that. The imam will see you when his service concludes," the man said, still holding fast to her arm. "You can pray on your own while you wait. My advice would be to ask Allah for mercy."

CHAPTER 49

WASHINGTON, DC

After receiving the autopsy face shot of the man Brixton now called Brian Kirkland, Kendra Rendine had tried the number for the burner phone she'd given to Patty Trahan, four times in the past hour. She didn't want to just text the photo of a dead man to her without alerting her to the fact that it was coming. No sense in spooking her any more than she was already. All four times the calls had gone straight to voice mail.

Which meant . . .

Cold fear tightened its grip on Rendine's insides when her phone rang, the burner number lighting up in her Caller ID.

"Patty!" she answered excitedly.

"I saw your missed calls, Agent. I'm so sorry. I plugged my phone in to recharge it and I must have accidentally—"

"I'm going to text you a picture," Rendine interrupted. "I want you to tell me if this man looks familiar to you. Be warned, the photo doesn't show his good side."

She hit Send. Waited.

"Oh my," she heard Patty Trahan utter.

"I'm sorry. It's an autopsy photo."

"It's not that, Agent. I've seen this man before, I'm sure of it."

"When?" Rendine asked her, an edge of excitement replacing the cold fear that had been flooding her.

"He was the man who delivered the stents to me the morning of the vice president's procedure."

Trahan said more, but Rendine was too distracted to recall any of her words. She needed to tell Brixton, needed to call him now.

Brian Kirkland.

He was the link between the murder of Stephanie Davenport and the terrorist attack on the Metro that Brixton had foiled. Considering that made her reflect on what was coming, whatever all this was building toward. And Patty Trahan wasn't the only person to have gone dark on her. Her calls to the cell number Teddy Von Eck had texted to her burner phone drew nothing but silence—no ring, no voice mail, no message of any kind. Just dead air.

Either Von Eck was somehow involved in whatever was happening or someone he'd contacted, close to the director, maybe even the director himself, had been compromised. It was testament to the scope of whatever it was she and Robert Brixton had uncovered.

Focus! Rendine willed herself, knowing there was no point in fixating on the terrifying ramifications before her.

She had, for all intents and purposes, been removed from active duty as a Secret Service agent, her credibility and means of access to what she needed cut off. Beyond that, the fact that she couldn't reach Teddy Von Eck suggested she might well be a target herself, compromised just as he must have been.

Focus!

This had all started with the vice president, specifically with that fateful visit she'd made to the White House. When Rendine had begun looking deeper into Stephanie Davenport's death, that was as far back as she'd gone, just short of six weeks ago. She'd neglected to consider the fact that something else within that time frame might prove useful, even enlightening. Something on the vice president's schedule she'd failed to follow up.

Though she was now technically on leave, she still had access to Vice President Davenport's Secret Service logbook, which basically spelled out her every waking moment in diary form—where she went, with whom she met, how long it took to get there and back. Once written out in meticulous detail, the log was now archived online for easy access.

Rendine started her review with the days when she wasn't heading up the vice president's security detail, since those were the days about which she'd be least informed of the minutiae of Davenport's schedule. All detail heads regularly reviewed the action reports and logs for the shifts immediately preceding theirs, but even she tended to gloss over the mundane and routine as not particularly relevant. So she started her review of the log by focusing on what she might have missed in her initial cursory review. She also focused on the days immediately after the vice president's meeting at the White House that had left her so unsettled, to see if there was anything Stephanie Davenport might have done in its aftermath.

Rendine was able to pinpoint five log entries of interest for the week after that fateful visit. Four of these seemed easily explainable, once she did a slightly deeper dive, nothing more than a visit to one of the bookstores the vice president enjoyed frequenting, a last-minute radio interview, and a pair of off-the-books meetings that were more political in nature.

That left an address where Stephanie Davenport spent just over a half hour, having met there with someone alone, no member of her detail present in the room. Rendine found this odd, in large part because it represented a break in protocol. She wondered if the vice president had purposely scheduled it for a period when she wasn't on duty, as if trying to keep it from her primary detail head. Something, in other words, she hadn't wanted Rendine to know about.

The address in question, she learned next by running a search, housed the office of a psychiatrist named Elinor Marks, of all things. It made Rendine wonder whether a deeper check of the vice president's log would reveal more such visits, but that wasn't foremost in her thinking right now.

She called Dr. Marks's office, but it went straight to voice mail.

"Dr. Marks," she started, "this is Kendra Rendine, head of Vice President Stephanie Davenport's security detail, and I have a few questions pertaining to a routine investigation I'm following. If you could please call me at . . ."

As soon as she hung up, Rendine thought about heading over to Marks's office in Georgetown, but her latest burner phone ringing with the very number she'd just dialed saved her that bother.

"Agent Rendine, this is Elinor Marks. I got your message."

"Thanks for such a quick response, Doctor. I was wondering if I could steal a few minutes of your time."

"I'm between appointments right now, if that's convenient for you."

Rendine had hoped to meet with the doctor in person, but this would suit her just as well. "According to the logs, the vice president met with you just over a month ago."

"She did, for the first time in several years. I treated her for a time, well before she became vice president, around the time of her husband's death. As a matter of fact, before she was added to the ticket, I was interviewed as part of the vetting process."

Rendine let that remark hang in the air. "A delicate question next, Doctor: Did she come to you seeking treatment of any kind again?"

Rendine waited for Dr. Marks to respond, continuing when she didn't.

"Since Vice President Davenport died of a serious health issue, we want to make sure we didn't miss—*I* didn't miss—any health-related issues."

"I can definitely say you didn't in this case, Agent," Dr. Marks told her. "The vice president didn't come to me seeking treatment, at least not for herself."

"Who, then?"

"Her mother, just past eighty now, with her health rapidly declining."

Rendine was glad they were speaking over the phone so Elinor Marks wouldn't be able to see her reaction to what she'd just heard.

"Mental health, I'm assuming, then," she managed to respond.

"I'm afraid so, yes. Her questions were specifically related to symptoms of dementia and Alzheimer's disease, but they weren't all related to her mother's condition. She was interested in the genetic prevalence of mental deterioration."

"So the vice president could gauge whether she was a candidate as well."

"She mentioned her father, too, Agent, specifically that he had begun displaying symptoms at a much earlier age. Late fifties, I believe, but I might be able to pin that down further if I check my notes."

"No need," Rendine said, through the heaviness that had settled in her chest, making her feel short of breath. "I'm just filling in some general holes here."

"The vice president was most interested in the specific symptoms of early-onset dementia and how the disease generally progresses. I told her it doesn't 'generally' progress, that everyone is different and the only thing all patients have in common is it never ends well, although the mental deterioration can be slowed, sometimes significantly, by medication and mental exercises aimed at retraining the mind for its new reality."

New reality indeed, Rendine thought, that phrase frozen in her mind.

"Is there anything else I can do for you, Agent?" Dr. Elinor Marks resumed, when Rendine failed to respond.

"Sorry, Doctor, I was just making some notes," she lied. "No, I think I've got everything I need. Thank you for your time."

"A pleasure. Stephanie Davenport's death is a terrible blow for this country."

"I do have one last question."

"What's that?"

"Did anyone else contact you about your meeting with the vice president, either from the Secret Service or another agency, even an individual?"

"No," Marks told her. "The conversation was so mundane, if it had been held with anyone else, I would probably have forgotten it by now. But since this was the vice president . . ."

"I understand, Doctor."

"Well, if there's anything else I can do . . ."

"Thank you. Of course."

Rendine ended the call without realizing she'd done so. She was still staring at her now darkened burner phone, a layer of cold sweat starting to slip through her shirt.

Stephanie Davenport's Green Beret father had been killed in the latter days of the Vietnam War, when she was a child, having never made it to his thirtieth birthday. And her mother was still alive, a spry eighty-three-year-old. The vice president had lied to Elinor Marks, after making an off-the-books visit to her office to inquire about a problem that didn't exist, just three days after her fateful meeting with the president.

Because there was a problem, all right, and if the suspicions that had left Rendine trembling were correct, it was bigger than she or anyone else could have possibly imagined.

Far bigger.

CHAPTER 50

BROOKLYN, NEW YORK

Ever heard of it?" Sister Mary Alice asked Brixton, after a pause that seemed longer than it was.

"This Y-Twelve facility? At some point. Nothing that sticks, though."

The nun folded her arms atop the school desk in which she was seated across from him. "Don't feel bad, Robert. Most people haven't, even though it's a nuclear facility."

"Did you say *nuclear*?" Brixton said, knowing he was about to learn the nun's connection to all this.

"The largest nuclear storage facility anywhere in the world," Mary Alice Rose elaborated. "Specifically, radioactive fuel for the country's nuclear weapons stockpile."

Brixton thought back to the blueprints that had been spread out on the counter of the Reston, Virginia, UPS Store when he and Panama had entered, how Sister Mary Alice Rose's federal prison ID number had been scrawled beneath plans for something Panama had yet to identify.

Largest nuclear storage facility anywhere in the world.

So the man calling himself Brian Kirkland, who'd orchestrated a suicide bombing in the Washington Metro, might well have been in possession of blueprints that provided everything he needed to know about the Y-12 facility from a structural standpoint.

"And that's where you were arrested?" he asked, the unimaginable nature of that conclusion still numbing his thought process.

Sister Mary Alice lifted her arms from the table and leaned back, crossing them before her. "Are you in a rush, Robert?'

"Not at all."

"Good, because I have a story to tell you . . ."

Sister Mary Alice Rose started closer to the end than the beginning, with the fact that she had been charged with sabotage, trespassing, and destroying government property as part of what she called a peaceful protest not so much against the Oak Ridge, Tennessee, facility in question as against the entire U.S. nuclear arsenal.

"Why this particular facility?" Brixton asked, interrupting her.

"Because Y-Twelve stores hundreds of thousands of pounds of radioactive fuel, meaning highly enriched uranium, for the country's aging nuclear weapons stockpile."

Brixton felt the same chill go up his spine at mention of that. "Did you say *hundreds of thousands*?"

She scolded him with her eyes. "I'm the one who's eighty-five, Robert. I think you heard me just fine."

"And, just so I'm clear, we're talking about *weapons-grade* uranium here."

"Hundreds of thousands of pounds of it," Sister Mary Alice reiterated. "Shocks you to the core, doesn't it?"

She went on to explain that she had gained entry to the facility armed with only paint, candles, a hammer, and a Bible. Once inside the perimeter, she wrote passages from Scripture on the side of the facility and chipped at its white concrete walls with her hammer. When security guards finally closed on her position, they found her singing "Take Me to the Mountain," and she proceeded to offer the officers Communion bread.

In response, they handcuffed the then eighty-three-year-old nun and left her sitting on the ground for hours, under watch by a bevy of security guards wearing body armor and brandishing assault rifles. When Sister Mary Alice was arraigned the next day, she was ushered into court in shackles. Federal prosecutors charged her with intent to injure, interfere with, or obstruct the national defense of the United States, along with the more serious charge of sabotage. Sister Mary Alice was sentenced to ten years in prison and fined tens of thousands of dollars, which she was unable to pay, thanks to her vow of poverty rendering her basically penniless.

"Okay," Brixton said at that point. "Why?"

"Why what?"

"Why risk your freedom?"

Sister Mary Alice's expression turned reflective. "My father fought in World War Two. He was in Nagasaki six weeks after the bomb. The stories he told when I was a young girl . . . Let's just say those words never left me. He made me feel like I was there, witnessing the devastation firsthand. You know the biggest problem with time, Robert?"

"It passes," Brixton tried.

"Exactly. And with the passage of time, as I grew older, the world forgot the horror a nuclear world can unleash. Even Chernobyl didn't make enough of a dent in the world's psyche."

"And you thought breaking into a secure government installation with a hammer and some song lyrics could change that?"

"I think I had to try. Words, op-eds and the like, were all meaningless. Somebody had to make a difference."

"You."

"Me."

"And did you make that difference? Was it worth it?"

"No, to the first question," Sister Mary Alice told Brixton. "Yes, to the second, because it drew attention to the fact that over the years hundreds of millions of dollars have been slashed from nuclear nonproliferation programs. That money has been funneled into maintaining stores of bomb-ready enriched uranium and plutonium. Y-Twelve, for example, is operating with three hundred less private security contractors than were employed when they were storing half the fissionable material they are now."

"Wait, did you say *private* contractors?"

The old nun nodded. "The Y-Twelve National Security Complex may be umbrellaed under the Department of Energy, but it's actually managed by a private concern, and I couldn't even hazard a guess as to the level of training their security personnel receive."

"Not enough, compared to the pros, it's safe to say." Brixton paused to stare into Sister Mary Alice's crystal-blue eyes. "And that's why you staged this one-person protest, to draw attention to all this."

"Do you know how many times over those hundreds of thousands of pounds of fuel could destroy the world, Robert?"

"No."

"Just short of three hundred, conservatively."

"Not a figure you drew out of a hat."

Sister Mary Alice smiled at that. "I did a master's thesis on future nuclear proliferation and studied nuclear isotopes under some of the best minds in the world."

"All because of your father."

"The horrors of Hiroshima and Nagasaki can never be repeated, Robert. But if we don't do something about it, they surely will. It's inevitable. The Y-Twelve facility isn't the only one that stores enriched uranium, just the largest. And there's no way to even estimate how much more of the stuff there might be out there these days, what with Israel, North Korea, India, and Pakistan not exactly being up-front about the size and scope of their nuclear arsenals. How long do you think it will be before an ISIS or al-Qaeda get their hands on enough bomb-grade material to kill millions? And, unlike the nations long stopped from using nuclear weapons by the old mutually assured destruction mandate, you can't bomb a cause the same way you can a country."

Brixton smiled. The nun was right at home, playing the role of teacher here in her prison classroom. "So you also broke into Y-Twelve to demonstrate how easy it was."

Sister Mary Alice nodded. "Now it's my turn, Robert," she said, before he could further press that issue. "You said you had reason to believe my life was in danger."

"*Strong* reason, Sister."

"Why?"

"I was hoping you could tell me."

"And have I?"

"Maybe," Brixton said, thinking again of those structural schematics pulled from Brian Kirkland's UPS Store mailbox. "I'm not sure."

The old nun eyed him like an old-fashioned Catholic school teacher ready to take a wooden ruler to his knuckles. "What really brought you here, Robert?"

"I told you."

Her eyes scolded him again, even harsher. "I haven't had a visitor other than my lawyers in over two years. I don't receive any mail. I'm not allowed to send any mail. You think I'm going to believe that a simple private investigator was able to get in here to see me?"

"I'm not working alone," Brixton said, leaving it there.

"I suspected as much."

"And I think this Y-Twelve facility may be part of something much bigger."

"What?"

"I'm not sure."

"Okay, then tell me what else has happened that brought you here. Was there another break-in? Was some of that bomb-grade material found missing?"

Brixton could have told her about the connection between the murder of the vice president and the Metro bombing. How whoever was behind both of those was, by all indications, in possession of the plans for the largest nuclear storage facility in the United States and had clearly taken an interest in an eighty-five-year-old nun who'd managed to penetrate its security to gain entry. The forces behind Brian Kirkland clearly wanted Sister Mary Alice Rose out of the way so she couldn't pass on what she knew to anyone else.

"Robert?" Sister Mary Alice prodded. "You haven't answered my question. Was there another break-in at the facility that calls itself the Fort Knox of uranium?"

"No," Brixton said, struck by the irony of her statement. "But I'm afraid one might be coming."

CHAPTER 51

BALTIMORE, MARYLAND

They kept Lia Ganz waiting for well over an hour. It was approaching three o'clock by the time a key rattled in the lock. The sky had darkened beyond the single grated window centered behind a large wooden desk kept meticulously neat, not even a telephone or computer atop it. The room was rustic, the walls wood-paneled, the bare wood floors stained dark. She imagined this to be the office of one of the former bank's executives. There were slightly discolored rectangular patches of paneling where wall hangings had clearly been removed. Even the ornate bookshelves built into a portion of a side wall were virtually empty, save for a small selection of books with Arabic writing down their spines.

Lia had, of course, set this course for herself purposely, wanting to arouse the kind of suspicion in the men guarding the mosque that would ensure she was brought to the imam for questioning. She'd learned over the years that those who believed they had the upper hand gave away much more in their conversations.

The door opened and the man who'd originally accosted her entered first, his back against the open door as the imam of Masjid Us Salaam, Haussam Zimaar Alaf, entered. He was a bit portlier than the picture Mossad had texted her had showed, indicating it must have been an older shot, likely "borrowed" from the American FBI, since Mossad databases themselves would never have been that outdated. He had soft, warm eyes that bled compassion, his very stride reverent as he moved past the guard, who closed the door to leave the two of them alone.

"My man tells me there may be a problem," the imam began.

"Not with me, I assure you."

Alaf seemed to be studying her words carefully. "My man told me your Arabic was far too precise for an American, and yet your appearance clearly indicates a convert."

"From Judaism," Lia confessed, doing her best to sound ashamed.

That caught the imam's interest.

"A mistake of birth that will forever be the source of embarrassment," she continued, her voice humble and her eyes held downward.

"You are Israeli, then?"

Lia nodded reluctantly. "I married a man of Arab descent. We could not have children, but our love more than compensated for that . . . until the Jews came and took him away. To prison, where he died, where they killed him."

"You have my deepest regrets."

"And I thank you for them," Lia said, amazed at how easily her mastery of Arabic had returned. "I'm new to this area and looking to make it home, starting with finding a place to worship."

"You understand we must be sure of all this before you can be welcomed."

"Of course."

"You understand your story must be checked out."

Lia nodded.

The imam hesitated before resuming, his soft gaze hardening as his vision narrowed. "You understand that you speak our language exactly as Israeli spies and killers are trained to."

"No, I don't, actually."

"You are not Mossad?"

"No."

"You weren't sent by the Americans on a fool's errand?"

"I was not, Your Holiness," Lia said, just enough reverence in her voice.

"You would claim not to be part of any setup, nothing like that, then."

Something scratched at Lia's spine. "I know nothing of any of that," she said.

"It is difficult sometimes to tell our friends from our enemies."

"This I know all too well."

"The Americans seem to suspect we are harboring radicals within our walls."

"How terrible. How wrong."

"They did not send you?"

"No one sent me, Your Holiness."

"And what if we resorted to more persuasive techniques to make sure you were telling the truth?"

"I would invite you to do just that," Lia told him. "I would volunteer to be questioned by any means and under as much duress as you wish. Anything to prove my faith to the Prophet."

The imam's expression grew stoic and flat. "In that case—"

Alaf's words were interrupted by screams coming from the floor below, an instant before the gunfire rang out.

Lia detected brief bursts of silenced staccato gunfire, followed by more desperate screaming.

"You did this!" the imam wailed at her. "You brought them, brought death to these walls!"

"No! No! I'm telling you that—"

The heavy door burst open and the guard rushed in, brandishing a Glock handgun.

"Shoot her! Shoot her!"

But Lia had pounced on the guard before the imam's order could be completed. The gun was in his hand and then it was in hers. Taking him by surprise allowed her to subdue him effortlessly, choking the man unconscious with one hand while the other held the gun on the imam.

"Don't move!" Lia ordered, as the guard's limp frame slid to the floor.

"Kill me if you wish," Alaf said, sinking to the floor in a position of prayer. "I have made my peace with Allah."

"Listen to me! I'm not the one here to kill you!"

More gunfire echoed below, now followed by shrieking, the screams of male and female worshippers intermingling, telling her the gunmen downstairs had come at this time to maximize casualties. A raid launched on a mosque identified by Ali Shadid's Saudi Arabian sources as having been a front for terrorists about to launch a strike on the United States.

Lia wondered how he'd come by the information, where exactly it had been manufactured and who had managed to so effectively plant it. This was very likely the next phase in the crazed plot that had begun with the suicide bombing on the Washington Metro.

"Stop them!" the imam screeched at her. "Call them off, I beg you, before more innocents are lost!"

"Stay here," she ordered him, readying the Glock as she headed for the door.

Lia encountered the first two shooters in the stairwell. They were masked, gloved, and dressed entirely in black—coming for Imam Alaf, no doubt. They twisted their sound-suppressed, shaved-down assault rifles on her, leaving her no choice. She aimed high, head shots only, to avoid their body armor. Four bullets, two for each, did the trick. Instinct took over, even as she recognized the distinct design and shape of a version of the M4 used exclusively by American special operators.

Operators who had come to Masjid Us Salaam, the mosque identified by Ali Shadid as the launch site of radicals planning a major strike against America.

Except that they weren't, not here anyway. Lia could read a man's words better than any lie detector machine. She knew Alaf had been telling the truth, just as she was certain that the evidence that this mosque was implicated in a looming terrorist strike had been fabricated.

Alerted by her gunshots, two more of the operators had just spun onto the stairs as she neared the bottom. Lia took both of them in the legs this time, both legs, kicking the world out from under them and stripping their weapons from their grasp in one fluid motion. She discarded the Glock in favor of the commando version of the M4, barreling on amid the crush of bodies pouring from both halls of worship, men's and women's, chased out by gunfire. Orders and signals were being barked in English as the masked special operators continued their sweep, firing indiscriminately, to a constant cacophony of screams.

Lia neared the main entrance, positioning herself to herd those fleeing through it. Each time a commando surfaced, she chased him back behind cover with a three-shot burst from her M4. She was still garbed as an Arab woman in a shapeless dress and hijab, the commandos no doubt seeing her as some wild-eyed radical Wonder Woman. They had stormed this mosque in search of something that wasn't here, their actions somehow connected to all that Brixton and his Secret Service friend had managed to uncover so far. Whatever that was, it was clearly bigger than they could possibly have imagined, the facade of the subway bombing representing only the start.

Lia joined the last of the fleeing worshippers and then disappeared amid them in a desperate rush down the street, into the approaching wail of sirens coming from both directions.

CHAPTER 52

WASHINGTON, DC

Rendine started walking, phone tucked in a pocket. She had no destination in mind, just needed to be in motion. She had lived off the high of the Secret Service's protective division for so long that she didn't know what it was like to not face constant pressure. The details, the minutiae, the danger, the risks, the threats—all ingrained in her life, not just as a part but providing its very definition. It was a fix not unlike a drug, which she had been forced to relinquish cold turkey. She no longer doubted that the "leave" the director had placed her on wouldn't be short-lived at all, or that the decision was connected to the threat the country was now facing, which the vice president might well have uncovered, leading to her assassination.

But why the visit to psychiatrist Elinor Marks? Why all the questions about Alzheimer's disease and dementia, just days after Davenport's visit to the White House? It made no sense.

Unless . . .

Rendine felt her stomach seem to dive toward her feet. She needed to call Brixton, needed to share with him the notion that had just occurred to her, which was as terrifying as it was impossible.

"Keep walking," a voice whispered from just behind her, before she could pull out her phone. "Whatever you do, don't turn around."

Teddy Von Eck.

Rendine kept her gaze fixed forward, fighting the urge to look toward him to comply with his instructions.

"There's no time, Kendra. You have to listen. No questions. I need a phone number for the burner you're using."

Rendine recited the digits, keeping her voice low. Aimed forward, she wondered if he'd even heard her.

"Got it," Von Eck said. "I'm going to send you an MP3 recorded inside the White House Situation Room this morning."

Still in motion, Rendine started to crane her neck around. "Hold on, did you say the White House Sit—"

"No! Don't look at me! They're on my tail. I can feel them."

"Who, Teddy?"

"Doesn't matter. You scared the hell out of me last night, Kendra, scared me so much I made some calls to an agent I trust, who's part of the president's Secret Service detail. An agent who owes me, who understands the code."

"Code?"

"We serve the country, not just the man. I briefed him on our suspicions, and he mentioned that agents have had virtually no direct contact with the president, going back several weeks. He mentioned POTUS almost never leaves the White House anymore. He's part of the advance security team, and during a check of the Situation Room before the meeting, he hid a cell phone, and then retrieved it after the meeting was finished."

"How is that even possible?" Rendine asked, reminding herself to keep walking.

"We're the Secret Service. It's our job to sweep the room for such things," Von Eck said, by way of explanation. "But none of that matters. What matters is what's on the recording. I'm sending it now. Go someplace where it's safe to listen. Don't go home. They'll be there."

"Who, Teddy?"

"That doesn't matter either, not right now. They're on to me, which means they're on to you. But they haven't picked you up yet. I'd know it if they had."

"This recording . . ."

"You need to hear it for yourself, Kendra. Everything you need to know is on it. I can't tell you what to do, can't tell you who to trust, can't tell you how to stop it."

"Stop *what*?"

Teddy ignored her question again. "Walk faster. We need to put distance between us before anyone notices. I'll fall back, take the next side street."

"How can I reach you?"

"You can't," he said flatly, the resignation clear in his voice. "Just do what I say and then nail the sons of bitches. There's nothing more I can do. You'll hear everything else you need to on that tape."

Teddy's voice was getting softer as the distance between them widened. It took every bit of her willpower to keep from turning around. She looked toward a storefront window on her right to see if he was still visible behind her, but there was nothing.

Rendine continued on, careful not to rush, doing nothing that might draw undue attention to herself. Still facing forward. She was not about to let herself turn.

Until she heard the screech of brakes and a crunching sound of impact. She stopped and swung with everyone else around her to check out the source of the collision. The street was full of rubbernecking pedestrians.

A block behind her, a delivery truck had struck someone in the crosswalk. She didn't need binoculars to spot a man wearing a ball cap and sunglasses sprinting away from the truck, or to recognize the broken frame of Teddy Von Eck lying on the street. The condition of the truck's front end was enough to tell her it had been a direct blow. People were swarming toward the body, but there was nothing anyone could do for him at this point.

He had known what was coming. His one final, desperate mission was to deliver the recording that a trusted Secret Service associate had made in the White House Situation Room that morning. She felt the burner phone buzz in her pocket—Teddy's text message containing the MP3 arriving. Rendine resisted the temptation to listen here and now; that could wait until she got somewhere more secure than the street where someone had just plowed into Teddy Von Eck and killed him.

But not before he managed to pass the recording onto her. Whatever had led to the assassination of Vice President Stephanie Davenport was now tucked away in her pocket.

CHAPTER 53

WASHINGTON, DC

Brixton was waiting at Penn Station for his train back to Washington, preparing to contact Panama with all he'd learned from Sister Mary Alice Rose, when his phone rang, the number for Kendra Rendine's burner lighting up in the Caller ID. He took a seat in the Acela area reserved for passengers needing redcaps, because it was reasonably confined and easy to spot anyone suspicious approaching, since they wouldn't have bothered to bring any luggage with them.

"Kendra?"

"Robert! Oh my God, Robert, oh my God," Rendine hissed, panic driving her voice.

"What's wrong? Are you all right?"

"No, I'm not, not even close. Everything's clear now, clear as a bell, and that bell's about to strike midnight."

"You're not making any sense."

"Because there's no sense to make of this, none of it. First off, Patty Trahan identified Brian Kirkland as the hospital clerk who delivered the stents to her the day Stephanie Davenport was operated on."

Brixton should have felt a sense of satisfaction over that confirmation, but something held him back. "What else, Kendra?"

He heard her take a deep breath on the other end of the line. "I think the president is mentally incapacitated. I think someone else is running the country. I think Stephanie Davenport must have found out and that's why they killed her."

"Slow down," Brixton urged her. "Take another deep breath and slow down," he added, over his own pounding heart.

"I can't. There's no time to slow down. I need to play you something. You need to hear this. It explains *everything*. You've got to hear it."

"Hear what?"

"A meeting in the White House Situation Room this morning. I've cued up a section. I got it from a friend, an associate, just before they killed him."

"*Killed* him? Who? *When?*"

Brixton could hear Rendine choking up. "You need to listen to the whole thing, but I want you to start with this, while I'm still on the line. I need to hear your reaction. I need to know I'm not crazy. Tell me when you're ready."

Brixton pressed the phone tighter to his ear. "I'm ready."

"The first voice you're going to hear belongs to the director of the FBI. You'll recognize the others as the secretaries of State, Defense, and Homeland Security. Those are the ones that matter. Oh, and the first lady, of course."

"Why do you say 'of course,' Kendra?"

"Because she's running the show, standing in for her husband, who, from what I could tell from the recording, doesn't know the color of the White House. And there's more. She's arranging to be named vice president. We're witnessing a coup taking place right before our eyes." She stopped. "Ready, Robert?"

"Ready."

Brixton could hear a brief wisp of dead recording air before the voice of the director of the FBI began.

"Speaking of which, I'd like to move on to a discussion of the potential casualties we're going to be facing two days from now."

Next came the voice of the first lady of the United States.

"I believe the number will be between three and five million over time, enough time to ensure that the crisis will persist for years, allowing us to mold the country into the shape we desire."

"That's a terrible price to pay," a voice he didn't recognized interjected. *"The earlier estimates were considerably lower."*

Again the first lady spoke, and her words explained the panic and desperation he had heard in Kendra Rendine's voice.

"All great movements require sacrifice, and this is no different. How many more lives will be lost a decade down the road, two decades, if we lose power?"

Someone mumbled something unintelligible. Then the second voice came back, now loud enough to be recognizable as that of President Corbin Talmidge.

"Generators."

Silence followed his comment.

"We have generators, don't we? The White House has generators. So if we lose power, we'll use generators. Nothing to worry about there. Why does everyone seem so worried? We've weathered big storms before."

The striking irony of his statement produced more silence, followed by the muffled voice of the first lady saying something to her husband. Then she resumed for all to hear.

"Getting back to the subject at hand, we need to have all emergency response systems ready to go. Madam Secretary, the floor is yours."

Brixton recognized the next voice as that of the secretary of Homeland Security.

"I've scheduled an emergency response, first responder drill for the following day. That way, our preparedness will be maximized, everything in place to assure we're ready to roll for immediate deployment to the hardest hit areas."

"*Generators*," the president's voice returned. "*We need to order more generators.*"

"Still there?" Kendra Rendine broke in, ending the playback there.

"Still here. And you're right about the president. You could hear it in his voice."

"I'm scared, Robert."

"So am I."

Between three and five million over time.

"We don't know the how or the where," Rendine continued, as if thinking along the identical lines. "I listened to the entire recording twice and there's no mention of specifics."

"I think I can provide some."

He told her about his meeting with Sister Mary Alice Rose, an eighty-five-year-old nun made to "disappear" into the federal prison system after being arrested for trespassing and vandalism on the Y-12 nuclear repository facility in Oak Ridge, Tennessee. He stressed the hundreds of thousands of pounds of bomb-ready radioactive fuel stored there.

"They're going to blow it up," Rendine managed. "Somehow, they're going to blow up those hundreds of thousands of pounds of highly enriched uranium."

"The whole thing is nuts, crazy."

"Crazy like a fox, Robert. You heard what the first lady said about sacrifices."

"Right, three to five million sacrificed to maintain their hold on power. She knows—*they* know—the president would otherwise have to resign. Never mind seeking reelection, given his condition, so they think a disaster of this magnitude will allow them to win the election or to suspend it altogether. Declare martial law, if they have to."

"They'll never get away with it."

"Really? Remember, Kendra, it's three to five million *over time*—that's what Merle Talmidge said, the exact wording. That means we're looking at an ongoing disaster as the radioactivity spreads. They'll get away with it all right, because the people will be more worried about staying alive than about Election Day. And by the time the president can no longer continue even a semblance of this ruse, their hold on power will be too tight to remove, with the first lady sitting in the Oval Office."

"Oh my God . . ."

"What is it? What's wrong?" Brixton asked, so tense he could feel his hand holding the phone cramping.

"It's all over the news. Haven't you heard?"

Brixton realized he'd been basically out of pocket since his interview with Sister Mary Alice Rose at the Metropolitan Detention Center. "No. What?"

"The FBI's Hostage and Rescue Team staged a raid this afternoon on a mosque in Baltimore. There was a gunfight, during which the terrorists they were hunting apparently escaped. That can't be a coincidence."

"Of course it can't, because there weren't any terrorists, just a cover. Just like the suicide bomber on the Metro," Brixton realized, putting it together. "We're going to war after Y-Twelve blows, Kendra."

"We can't stop them alone," Rendine insisted, her voice quivering now.

"We're not alone," Brixton said, thinking of the Israelis and Lia Ganz.

"You don't understand. No one who knows anything about this is safe. They're covering their tracks, Robert, filling in the holes with bodies inside."

Brixton recalled the fate suffered by of the members of the surgical team who'd performed the procedure on Vice President Stephanie Davenport. The attack on him last night, which Lia Ganz had thwarted, saving his life, now made perfect sense, fitting into a far larger pattern supported by the administration's plans to murder between three and five million Americans to solidify its hold on power. Led by the first lady, they'd concocted an elaborate scheme to cast blame on Islamic radicals, starting by linking a known Hamas bomb maker to the attack on the Washington Metro. Now a raid had been launched on a mosque the country would be made to believe had been harboring terrorists, who would subsequently be blamed for the attack on the Y-12 facility.

"You need to get somewhere safe, Kendra," he told Rendine. "You need to get somewhere safe now."

"I don't think there is such a place anymore. Not even close."

CHAPTER 54

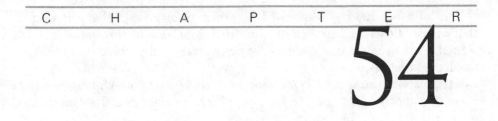

WASHINGTON, DC

"You promised you wouldn't make trouble for us with our American friends, Colonel," Moshe Baruch said to Lia Ganz, after she'd completed her report.

Lia Ganz might have smiled, if the head of Mossad wasn't watching her through the secure video line. "Did I? I must've forgotten."

She'd been waiting in a secure room inside the Israeli embassy on International Drive NW, in the Cleveland Park neighborhood of the city, seated in front of a computer monitor, when the screen glowed to life and Baruch's face appeared before her. The desktop offered no keyboard or other controls, just that monitor directly before her at eye level.

Taking at least temporary refuge at the embassy in the aftermath of the gunfight was in keeping with the cover story concocted to explain her presence in the United States, specifically that she was to conduct a review of the embassy's security protocols and make recommendations for improvements in the fenced-in, cream-colored compound that was modest in scope compared to some of its contemporaries. Her intelligence and operational background more than qualified her for such a task, though anyone hearing of that would greet the claim with a wink and a nod. Such cover stories were orchestrated all the time to disguise an operative's real reason for being in country. Since she was retired, though, Lia hadn't been concerned that anyone would give her presence in Washington a second thought.

Until now, in the aftermath of a gunfight that had seen her kill two men who could only have been American operators. Instinct had driven her actions; she'd had no time to think before they would have killed her instead, and then Imam Alaf.

"You did not have our okay to carry a firearm out of country," Baruch said, continuing to chastise her.

"I took it off one of the imam's guards."

"You were seen wielding an assault rifle as well. You took that off one of the American operators, I assume."

"I only wounded the others, Commander. Four of them, by my count. Have the Americans managed to identify me?"

"Not yet, Colonel, but it's only a matter of time. What would you suggest we offer as an explanation?"

Out of habit, Lia had positioned herself in clear view of the only door that accessed the secure room on the third floor, one of three rooms designed for the same purpose. She kept her eyes on it the whole time, ready in case it burst open.

"How about the fact," Lia started, "that this may be much worse than we originally thought, that indications point to the fact that the American government is spinning out of control?"

"I'm sure they'll love to hear that."

"Did you ever meet the American vice president, Commander?"

"Indeed, I did. A very impressive woman. If I didn't know better, I'd say she was one of us. Her death was a terrible tragedy."

"It turns out she was murdered, assassinated."

Silence on the other end of the secure line followed Lia's statement.

"I'm not going to ask you how you came by this information," Baruch said finally. "Because it's coming from you, neither will I challenge that information's veracity. I'd ask only how this pertains to your original mandate."

"It's very much connected to that original mandate."

"Chasing down terrorists."

"Who were supposedly staging an operation out of that mosque."

"Supposedly," Baruch repeated. "I'm going to assume that a source pointed you in this direction."

"But there were no terrorists, no cell based in the Masjid Us Salaam mosque."

"What reason did this source have to lie?"

"None. Because he didn't lie. He was misled. He only reported to me what he believed to be the truth, because that's part of the ruse the Americans have concocted."

More silence, a bit shorter in length this time, before the head of Mossad's voice returned.

"You're describing an extremely elaborate operation, Colonel."

"I'm well aware of that, Commander."

"And putting us in a difficult position, given that our American friends would appear to be creating some kind of rationale for further action."

"They killed the vice president because she must have uncovered their plans."

"Plans that included a suicide bomber on the Metro, blamed on a terrorist cell that doesn't exist."

"As near as I can tell," Lia said, nodding toward the computer's tiny, built-in camera. "Because something much bigger is coming."

"Our American friends are normally not clever enough to be so devious," Baruch said, almost admiringly, before uttering a deep sigh. "You're certain about the murder of the vice president?"

"I have extremely high confidence, yes."

"Most unfortunate."

"Why?"

"Because our contact there has requested your immediate censure and recall."

Lia knew Baruch must be talking about the man she'd met at CIA headquarters who called himself Winters.

He continued, "You made a mess, Colonel, and left it for our friends to clean up."

"They're not our friends, Commander. And the mess is theirs. I was the one doing the cleaning."

"You're missing the point. Our relations with our American friends are not what they once were, Colonel," Baruch resumed. "They don't have patience for us conducting operations on their soil."

"They were conducting their own operation at that mosque. Perhaps we need to save them from themselves."

"But what you're suggesting . . ."

Lia waited for Moshe Baruch to continue.

"This could only have originated at the highest levels of power, Colonel, the absolute highest. As in, the executive branch. Would I be correct in that assumption?"

Lia's cell phone began to vibrate on the desktop before her, the number Robert Brixton had provided for his latest burner lighting up in the Caller ID. "Give me a few minutes, Commander. I may be able to answer that soon."

"Forget the answer. This isn't our problem, and we must respect the wishes of the Americans, friends or not. I want you on the next plane back home. I'm having an El Al flight held at Dulles so you can catch it. Is that clear, Colonel? Is that—"

Lia Ganz reached out toward the monitor and pressed a button to end the call.

CHAPTER 55

NEW YORK CITY

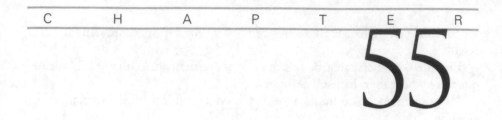

"Where are you?" Brixton greeted Lia Ganz.

"The Israeli embassy."

"Not to seek refuge, I hope."

"Far from it."

"What happened, Lia?"

"Long story. You go first."

"I think I know what this is all about, where it's all heading, thanks to Sister Mary Alice Rose."

"Did you say *sister*?"

"As in nun, a nun who might just spend the rest of her life in federal prison."

"Someone take offense to her prayers?"

"She broke into a federal nuclear repository facility."

"A *nun*?"

"She was trying to make a point, ended up making her bed at the Metropolitan Detention Center for the last two years. That nuclear facility must be the target, Lia. That's what all this is building toward."

When she remained silent, Brixton prodded, "Lia?"

"I think you're going to find my day interesting too, Robert."

"That was *you*?" Brixton managed, before Lia Ganz had finished her story.

"You're not going to believe this, but I had a feeling it was."

After his call with Kendra Rendine had ended anxiously, he'd busied himself reading as much as he could find on his phone about the raid launched on that Baltimore mosque, on the pretext it was harboring an Islamic terrorist cell. Details were sketchy and the data stream on his disposable phone moved agonizingly slow, but several reports mentioned casualties from friendly fire. These assertions were refuted by on-scene witnesses who claimed that an unidentified woman had returned the commandos' fire while shepherding innocent worshippers from the building. By all accounts, depending on which report proved valid, she'd killed two and wounded six.

An unidentified woman.

Lia Ganz.

There was no way Brixton could be certain of that, and yet he was. He scoured the news reporting, focusing on the most recent time stamps, in search of more information to confirm his hunch, but there was nothing. Just conflicting eyewitness testimony and no firm evidence yet of anything, other than claims that the raid had been staged on firm intelligence about a terrorist cell that must have fled earlier in the day. The upshot being to concoct a scenario that would culminate in an attack on the Y-12 facility in Oak Ridge, Tennessee.

And now Lia Ganz had all but confirmed his supposition. She'd followed a trail that nobody was supposed to find, everything planted carefully to achieve a desired effect that she'd almost literally blown up by being on the premises when the raid was staged.

"My people have ordered me home," Ganz said, while Brixton continued to ponder the ramifications of her tale. "For going too far at the mosque. If I'm caught, I'm on my own."

"They tell you that?"

"They didn't have to."

"Plane ticket waiting for you at Dulles?"

"How'd you guess?"

"I've had more than my share left for me over the years. Something else we have in common."

"Along with being grandparents, you mean."

"This won't be an easy world to grow up in, for either of our grandchildren, if this plot succeeds."

"But exactly whose plot is it?" she asked him.

"I was getting to that."

He told her about the recording made in the Situation Room, the suggestion of what was coming. Actually, he didn't get much beyond the three million to five million casualties that had been mentioned. He didn't have to.

"I see what you mean about our grandchildren, Robert. And all this is about politics. Your president's declining mental health is the whole reason for the plot being hatched in the first place."

"I'm not sure it's the whole reason," Brixton told her. "Maybe it's something this cabal led by the first lady genuinely believes in."

"In my experience, politicians believe in nothing, and their conviction changes with the polls."

"That's been my experience, too. In this case, they need to do something drastic, catastrophic, to not just maintain their hold on power but expand it."

"Sounds like the governments my country has been dealing with for generations."

"I think I can stop it, Lia, stop it all. But I'm going to need your help."

"Help with what?" Lia Ganz asked him.

"Breaking an eighty-five-year-old nun out of federal prison."

CHAPTER 56

NEW YORK CITY

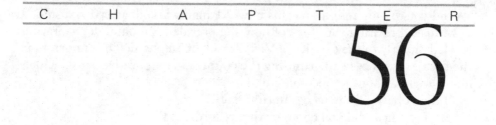

It was their only chance, Brixton thought, after he'd run out of minutes on his burner phone, just as his call with Lia Ganz was ending. His visit to the Metropolitan Detention Center and Sister Mary Alice Rose had undoubtedly attracted the wrong kind of attention, and by later today, tomorrow at the latest, she'd be gone. Disappeared deeper into the federal penal system, or just murdered.

Brixton was guessing the latter of those two was more likely, based on what Rendine had told him. The old nun clearly had been incarcerated for reasons beyond making an example of her. Her infiltration of a facility that should have put security at an ultimate premium meant she knew something that Merle Talmidge and others behind this plot couldn't let out. Brixton had no idea what that might be, only that it might enable the proper parties to stop it—"proper parties" including the man he called Panama.

He replaced that disposable phone with another purchased at a Duane Reade drugstore inside Penn Station and dialed the number Panama had provided.

"It's worse than we thought," Brixton said, as soon as Panama answered. "As bad as it gets. Check those plans from the UPS Store against the schematics for the Y-Twelve facility in Oak Ridge, Tennessee. I assume you've heard of it."

"I've heard of it, Brixton," Panama affirmed. "Now tell me why you brought the place up."

"Are you sitting down, Panama?"

Brixton laid it out for him in blow-by-blow fashion, everything he'd learned from Sister Mary Alice, along with what he'd learned from Lia Ganz.

"Do I have to connect the dots for you?" he asked when he was finished.

"You think they're going to attack Y-Twelve. You think they're going to make the world think that radical Islamic terrorists killed millions of Americans."

"It's not what I *think*, Panama. It's what everything adds up to."

"Except one thing: Why?"

"I was getting to that," Brixton told him.

* * *

And you're only telling me this now?" Panama asked, after Brixton had finished relating the story of how the president's mental deterioration had led directly to the murder of Vice President Stephanie Davenport, how the first lady was basically running the country in a figurative sense, which might well be about to become literal.

"I didn't have all the pieces until today."

"And just how did you come by that recording, Brixton?"

"That doesn't matter."

"Wouldn't have come to you by way of a certain Secret Service agent, now, would it?"

"Like I said, doesn't matter."

"Too bad, since we could protect her."

"What makes you think you can protect anyone from this, Panama? It doesn't just go all the way to the White House; it started there."

"Maybe you've forgotten that I don't answer to any of these clowns. They come and go, while the people I represent don't go anywhere. Trust me on that one."

"Wish I could."

Another pause.

"Okay, I need to check some of this out before I get the wheels turning. Those wheels carry steamrollers, Brixton, that will obliterate this plot and everyone behind it. The country can weather the collateral damage of that. I'm not sure it would be able to weather five million deaths to an apparent terrorist attack. I want you to call me back in one hour—that's sixty minutes on the dot. Meanwhile, I'm going to send the cavalry to Y-Twelve. That place is about to become the most well-secured facility in the world."

"I'll be using a different phone," Brixton told him.

"I don't care if you're calling me on the Batphone. I'll have more to say then. I can tell you what you're telling me makes all the sense in the world in the wake of the mosque raid in Baltimore this afternoon. That didn't go through any channels I can find, like it sprang out of nowhere."

"They're going to kill five million people, Panama," Brixton told him. "I don't think channels mean very much to the people behind this."

"One hour, Brixton. On the dot."

He called Panama back as instructed, one hour later to the second. The call didn't go through at first, and Brixton thought he may not have initialized the new phone properly. He repeated the process detailed in the instructions and dialed Panama again. Brixton heard a *click* this time, and was waiting for Panama to answer, when an entirely different voice greeted him.

"The number you have reached is not in service at this time. Please check the number and dial again."

PART FIVE

CHAPTER 57

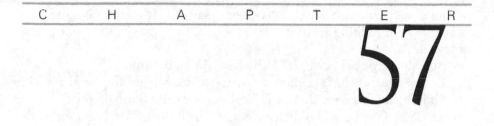

WASHINGTON, DC

In conclusion, ma'am, initial reports indicate there is significant cause for concern."

Merle Talmidge accepted the report from the director of the FBI in silence in her private study in the White House residence. Her husband had enjoyed an early dinner without her, after which some special seasoning she'd added to the meal, in the form of ground-up Ambien pills, left him drifting off in front of a television tuned to ESPN.

He'd stopped watching the news several weeks back, thanks to a combination of having lost interest in the events unfolding around him and his inability to retain information for very long at all. He was in the next room, which they'd converted into a media suite for viewing movies and sporting events, the door open so she could keep a watchful eye and ear upon him.

"How did this happen?" the first lady asked the director, not bothering to disguise the exasperation in her voice. "How did things go so wrong? You said we lost two agents on a raid where the team wasn't supposed to encounter any resistance. Did I hear you right?"

"You did, I'm afraid. Two dead and six more wounded, some seriously."

"At the hands of this—Who was it exactly?"

The FBI director pointed to the photograph captured by surveillance cameras trained on the Baltimore mosque entrance. It showed two different shots of the woman in question, first entering the building, and then fleeing amid a throng of worshippers. The second photo had spot-shadowed her face.

"We've identified her as Lia Ganz, an Israeli operative, most recently for Mossad, where she was part of the country's most elite squad of commandos. She's a true legend over there, the most decorated woman to ever serve in the Israeli military, where she earned the nickname the 'Lioness of Judah.'"

Merle Talmidge managed a chuckle. "That sounds like a cartoon character."

"Lia Ganz is as far from that as it gets, I assure you."

"And have we contacted the Israelis to see what they have to say on the matter?"

"The State Department has already utilized the proper channels. The upshot of such conversations is never made plain, but it's safe to assume she's been recalled. Judging from her file, though, my guess is she's not going anywhere."

"But what brought her here? Why now? Why Baltimore?"

"Let me answer the last question first: because we did too good a job of planting the intelligence about a radical Islamic cell taking up residence in that mosque. Ganz could only have gotten the information from someone who got it from us, just as we planned."

"This is no time to be patting yourself on the back, Director."

"I was only stating a fact, ma'am."

"What about the other facts?"

The director of the FBI laid it all out for the first lady, step by step, starting with the fact that Lia Ganz had been on the beach in Caesarea when the worst terrorist attack Israel had suffered in years took place. That led her to uncovering the link between the drones used in that attack and the suicide vest worn by the bomber in the Washington Metro. The director elaborated on all that and finished by stressing the fact that the Israelis had provided no indication they were sending one of their own to join the investigation.

"Isn't that against protocol?"

"The Israelis respect only their own protocol."

Merle Talmidge was still trying to make sense of all she'd just been told. "So we have bad luck to blame for this mess—that's what you're saying, isn't it? If Lia Ganz wasn't on the beach with her granddaughter . . ."

The director of the FBI could do nothing but nod, swallowing hard.

"I'm afraid there's more, Madam First Lady."

CHAPTER 58

NEW YORK CITY

Brixton walked out of Penn Station via the nearest exit, careful to keep his face down to avoid security cameras.

"The number you have reached is not in service at this time. Please check the number and dial again."

Panama was clearly out of commission, and with him the operation he was coordinating, leaving Brixton out in the cold during one of the warmest springs on record. Clearly, he'd gotten too close to the truth, and, just as clearly, that truth must have stretched to levels of power beyond what he'd anticipated. The man whose job it was to clean up other people's messes had finally made one of his own, a big one—big enough to shut down either his operation, or him, or both.

Brixton didn't see much of a distinction among the three. He wondered if he'd made a mistake by informing Panama of all he'd learned from Kendra Rendine, including the truth she had uncovered about the state of the president's mental condition. Because the suspicions that had gotten Vice President Stephanie Davenport killed now seemed directly related to an attack to be launched against the Y-12 facility in Tennessee and made to look like an Islamic terrorist strike. The pieces were all falling into place, and the finished puzzle was terrifying, Sister Mary Alice Rose having supplied the biggest piece of all.

Kendra Rendine wasn't answering her phone. The last time they'd spoken had been that phone call when she'd played a portion of the recording from a meeting held that very morning in the White House Situation Room. Brixton resisted the temptation to leave a message warning her to go to ground, to drop off the grid until they could figure out their next step. He kept calling the number he had for her, futilely, since she could no longer reach him on the burner phone he'd discarded.

Whoever had pulled the plug on Panama's operation would be coming for her, too, tying up all the loose ends, which also included him and Sister Mary Alice. The nature of her crime shouldn't have led to a federal prison sentence at all, much less a now open-ended one in which she had effectively dropped off the face of the earth. Their conversation hadn't yielded the reason behind that, specifically, and Brixton figured she'd be spirited to another facility to vanish anew before he could follow up.

Unless they just killed her, these same people behind the murder of the vice president for learning of the president's mental incapacity. Other forces were running the country in his place, led by First Lady Merle Talmidge, and those forces must be the ones pulling all the strings, from the Metro bombing to Brian Kirkland to calling off Panama's operation to the attempt on Brixton's life, which Lia Ganz had thwarted last night.

One grandparent saving another, she'd said, or some version of that. What was it Mark Twain had said about age? Something like "*Age is an issue of mind over matter*," Brixton recalled. "*If you don't mind, it doesn't matter.*"

It mattered now, though not as much as the fact that, right now, they were alone, with no one inside the government they could reasonably trust to help them prevent the looming deaths of five million Americans.

Brixton tried Kendra Rendine again. Nothing. Then, out of frustration—or desperation maybe—he hit Redial.

Same result.

All he could do now was wait for Lia Ganz to reach New York.

CHAPTER 59

WASHINGTON, DC

Who is he?" Merle Talmidge asked, studying the picture the FBI director had just handed her.

"Robert Brixton, former State Department contractor. This was shot by a security camera inside the Metropolitan Detention Center, where Brixton met for just an under an hour with Sister Mary Alice Rose."

"A nun in federal prison?"

"Not just any nun, ma'am," the director said, and proceeded to explain.

"So why did we make an aging nun vanish without a trace into the federal penal system, even on a trespassing and sabotage charge on a secure facility?"

"I'm not privy to all the operational details, and I haven't been able to track them down yet. But somebody must've had their reasons."

"You need to find this 'somebody,' Director."

"As I said, I'm working on it, but such things are buried purposefully so they can't be found. Our people are very good at such things."

"How comforting to hear," the first lady chided, regarding the picture of Robert Brixton again.

"You said he's with State?"

"*Was*, and only in an adjunct capacity, working for a contractor known as SITQUAL. You recall the suicide bombing right here in Washington five years ago?"

"Of course."

"His daughter was killed in the attack. The repercussions of what followed led him out of government service and into the private sector as a rather high-end investigator specializing in international matters."

"And now he's chasing down incarcerated nuns."

"Just one nun, ma'am," the director reminded her, hedging a bit before continuing, "There's more. He was also the man on the Metro who foiled the suicide bombing. That's what set him down this path, by all indications."

"A thorn in our side, in other words. Do we have eyes on him, Director?"

"Not at present, not since he departed the Metropolitan Detention Center. But we're watching his residence and have eyes out in Union Station and both airports. So far he hasn't returned to the city."

"Meaning he's still in New York."

"Or somewhere else we don't have eyes. And it's possible he got off a train or plane at some intermediate point and drove the rest of the way to throw us off."

"I'm sure you're taking a close look at traffic cameras."

"Of course, but their effectiveness is minimal on highways and we have no idea what vehicle Brixton may be driving."

The first lady laid the picture atop the one of Lia Ganz. "We need him found, Director. If he paid a visit to this nun who managed to infiltrate the Y-Twelve facility . . ."

She let her thought drift there, no reason to complete it.

"There's also some additional news to report, ma'am, pertaining to the Secret Service agent who headed up the vice president's detail."

"That would be the problem you briefed me on earlier?"

The director nodded. "It's about to be solved."

CHAPTER 60

Kendra Rendine listened to the recording a third time, and then a fourth. By the time she'd completed the fifth, she could recite the content verbatim from memory and had also managed to identify all the speakers present in the White House Situation Room at the time.

That content was beyond chilling, and not just the parts that pertained directly to her.

"Yet now we're faced with this matter of the head of the vice president's security detail. Can we be certain Davenport shared nothing with her?"

That was the attorney general.

"From what we've been able to gather, yes. All she has to go on is supposition, assumptions as to my husband's condition, and a few holes we failed to adequately fill that are no longer an issue."

The first lady.

Those words made Rendine's chest contract so tightly, she thought she might be having a heart attack. She composed herself with several deep breaths, feeling suddenly claustrophobic inside the crowded Starbucks on Pennsylvania Avenue Northwest near the White House. Afraid to go back anywhere near her apartment, she'd taken refuge here, safe among the crowd, to collect her thoughts and plan out her next move. Brixton had the recording, too, meaning he knew everything she did. Insurance against something happening to her once she left this Starbucks or the next place where she sought refuge. Rendine didn't dare enlist anyone else's help, not in the wake of the fate suffered by Teddy Von Eck. She couldn't bear the guilt of getting anyone else killed.

No longer an issue.

Clearly that phrase pertained to the medical personnel involved in the vice president's procedure, who were either unreachable or had downright disappeared. But even that chilling reality paled in comparison to the president himself, who, with each word, revealed more and more what Vice President Stephanie Davenport must have concluded about his condition, which had led directly to her murder.

"So we should accept your assurances at face value?" The attorney general.

"Assurances about what?" The president.

"The issue we discussed yesterday." The first lady.

"We did?"

"Yes. And you agreed the steps we were about to take were necessary, mandated.

That the future of the country needed to be secured and the only way to assure that was to take the kind of drastic measures that would keep you in power long enough to finish your work."

"My work is very important."

"Yes, it is."

"I'm president of the United States."

"Yes, you are."

"Are we going out today?"

Suspecting what Stephanie Davenport had uncovered about President Corbin Talmidge was nothing compared to bearing witness to the president's condition playing out in real time, at least on tape.

"Why are all these people here?" The president again.

"They're helping us." The first lady again.

"Helping us what?"

"Save the country."

"Is it in danger?"

"You know it is, dear."

"From what?"

Later, the president had said, "I don't know who any of these people are," even though they were all either members of his cabinet or officials he'd personally appointed.

Everything was clear now, and in that clarity was madness, an unspeakable tragedy about to be visited upon the country purely for political gain, so that power would be secured through the next election and for who knew how long after that.

"We must consider postponing, until we are certain of containment." The secretary of defense.

"If we postpone now, we invite our adversaries, traitors to this nation all, to dig deeper. In this city, digging a hole is an end in itself, even where there's nothing to be found. Proceeding as scheduled is the surest way to avoid the very recriminations you so fear and to force them to drop their shovels." The first lady.

"No one here doubts the urgency of this operation. But we're only going to get one shot, and we must assure ourselves the conditions are right." The national security adviser.

"They will never be more right than they are right now—or more necessary. We already went over this when we discussed the threat posed by the vice president."

Kendra Rendine had choked up every time she'd heard those words spoken by the first lady or replayed them in her mind. But she found the next exchange the most terrifying of all, for vastly different reasons.

"Unless the candidate came from inside this room."

"Do you have someone in mind, Madam First Lady?"

"Yes. Me."

"Of course, it would also position you to take your husband's place on the ticket, should the election go forward."

"There is that, too, yes."

All indications pointed to the fact that the first lady was positioning herself to actually replace her husband as president. Outlandish at first thought, but not so much at second. In this highly polarized political climate, Corbin Talmidge enjoyed over a 60 percent approval rating, while his wife was even more popular, clocking in closer to 70 percent. There wasn't much you couldn't do with a 70 percent approval rating, especially after presiding over the devastation that was to come.

In two days, the first lady had gone on to say. The day after tomorrow.

"Sally," a server called out from the coffee bar, using the name on the cup that had been refilled with a fresh latte. "Sally."

Rendine rose to retrieve it from the counter, a bit wobbly on her feet and needing to briefly grasp the chair back to steady herself. At the counter, a man was grasping the latte with her name stenciled on it.

"Excuse me, but that's mine."

The man smiled apologetically. "Is it, now?" he said in an English accent. "A thousand pardons. Won't happen again."

Kendra Rendine was too distracted to notice that he left the Starbucks without any cup at all.

CHAPTER 61

WASHINGTON, DC

Lia Ganz knew her actions earlier in the day at the mosque had drastically limited her options for travel. Her picture was sure to be circulating among security personnel at both Washington area airports, as well as at Union Station and the various bus terminals serviced by Greyhound.

That left rental car outlets, and in her experience the security at these was far laxer, especially at locations other than an airport. She chose an Enterprise location downtown on Vermont Avenue, timing her arrival for just a few minutes short of the six p.m. closing time—it was also her experience that the closer it got to closing time, the less clerks focused on anything other than getting home, the timing itself providing the ultimate distraction.

The downtown Enterprise outlet had a surprisingly sparse collection of vehicles to choose from, and Lia chose the most innocuous vehicle left on the lot, a Chevy Cruze that was functional and likely to attract no attention whatsoever once she was headed north to New York City. She'd meet up there with Brixton, with the express purpose of—how had he put it?—breaking an eighty-five-year-old nun out of prison.

She hadn't called Moshe Baruch back and had taken none of the calls to her secure phone, which had started coming in as soon as she failed to show up for the flight back to Israel that he'd held for her at Dulles Airport. She had broken rules, misbehaved, become an embarrassment. Not the way she'd expected to enjoy her retirement.

She'd spent too much time away from her own children over the years, resolving at some point in each mission that it would be her last. That never stuck; it became a promise to herself that was repeatedly broken. She was a stranger to her own family, who as often as not was raised by relatives and friends, with her husband gone and her inability to pull back on the missions that defined her. Becoming a grandparent was supposed to change that, and it had, for a stretch long enough to delude Lia with the notion it would last forever. She knew otherwise in her heart, though, knew that sooner or later something would draw her back in, though she never expected it would be an attack that had come so close to taking her granddaughter's life. The two defining elements of her life, family and duty, had clashed in that horrible moment, the former ultimately leading her back to the latter.

The navigation app on her phone put the drive at just over four hours if current traffic conditions held, getting her into New York City not long after ten o'clock. She had left it up to Brixton to determine a meeting spot, and she guessed it would be someplace close to the federal penitentiary where Sister Mary Alice Rose was incarcerated. A woman after her own heart, by all accounts, who had managed to somehow infiltrate a secure government facility with spray paint, rosary beads, and a Bible—different weapons than Lia would have chosen, for sure.

Lia hadn't had much time to probe deeper into the Y-12 facility in Oak Ridge, Tennessee, but the pictures were enough to tell her that breaking into the facility should have been impossible for someone like Sister Mary Alice. From what she'd been able to glean, that means of access had been one of the primary things the federal authorities had wanted out of her, but by all accounts the nun had never told them a thing. She had never put up much of a defense at what passed for a trial, and she hadn't given her lawyers much to work with, given that she'd been arrested on the Y-12 grounds while singing hymns.

Lia was almost to Philadelphia, the virtual halfway point of the drive, when she saw the flashing lights appear in her rearview mirror. The thought of gunning the engine and trying to outrun them never entered her mind, not in a Chevy Cruze. So Lia pulled over into the breakdown lane on I-95 and punched on her flashers as the police car pulled up a discreet distance behind her.

It looked like a Pennsylvania State Police car. She knew it had been stolen as soon as the figures emerged from inside. Civilian clothes in the style of dark tactical wear, instead of uniforms. Not seeing a reason to extend the ruse.

Lia rolled down both the driver side and passenger side windows as the two men approached. She'd already tucked her gun under her right leg but, for now anyway, left both hands on the wheel.

The men might have been twins, impossible to tell apart in the darkness, as they came up on either side of the car with sidearms in plain view. The man on the driver's side laid his hands on the sill of the open window and leaned forward, close enough for Lia to catch the greasy stench of fast food from a recent stop the two men must have made.

"You need to come with us, Colonel," the one closest to her said, his Israeli accent entirely undetectable.

"To the airport or the morgue?"

The speaker glanced through the car cabin toward the man on the passenger side. "We're on the same side here."

"Then we should be working toward the same ends," Lia told him. "In this case, that means preventing an unspeakable tragedy from taking place on American soil."

"That isn't our problem."

"Ours or Israel's?"

The man lifted his arms from the driver side window and backed slightly away. "We have our orders, Colonel."

"I'm sure you do."

"Please step out of the car. Don't make us resort to force."

Lia nodded, hands still glued to the wheel to keep the men calm. "Since you know my rank, I'm going to assume you know who I am, that you've been properly briefed."

The man closest to her nodded. Lia thought the other man might have, too.

"Then you also know that I'm not getting out of this car."

Lia could feel the men on either side of the car tense.

"I may die in what follows, but both of you definitely will. If you've been briefed appropriately on my reputation, you know that to be a virtual certainty."

She paused, just long enough to let them consider that for a moment.

"My hands will remain right here in place, where you can see them, until you make a move. It then becomes a matter of whether you trust your skills are better than mine. So let me ask you a question, both of you," Lia added, choosing that moment to glance toward the passenger side of the car. "When was the last time either of you saw action? When was the last time you smelled blood?"

Neither man responded.

"For me it was two weeks ago, on the beach in Caesarea."

She could tell from the closer man's expression that he knew exactly what she was referring to.

"I'm here, in America, after the people behind that attack. The men who gave you this assignment didn't include that part in their briefing, did they?"

Lia could smell dank sweat rising off the closer man now, swallowing the scent of fast food.

"I could use your help instead," she continued, "but I know that's too much to ask. So I'll only ask you to return to your car and let me go on my way. You could report that you were unable to find me, or you could tell your superiors the truth. They'll understand. They'll know you did the right thing. They might even have hoped you would do just that. Why else would they have sent only the two of you when they knew that wouldn't be enough? Think about it."

It was clear from the sudden flutter in the closer man's eyes that he was doing just that. Weighing his chances, the odds, whether this was truly worth it.

"It will happen like this," Lia told him. "Your friend on the passenger side will go for his gun first, but he'll hesitate before firing, which will give me a chance to kill him."

As she said that, she glanced ever so subtly out the passenger side window, where that man's hand had indeed strayed to his holstered nine-millimeter pistol.

"You will have drawn yours in the meantime. You may get a shot off, might wound me, perhaps even mortally. But you'll be dead before you can get a second shot off. That's the choice before you, the decision you have to make. There's no middle ground here, no need for further discussion. You have a job to do, but I can't let you do it."

Lia paused again.

"I'm going to drive on now, slowly, with both hands remaining on the wheel. I'm going to continue my mission to stop what's coming, which will be very bad for America and almost as bad for Israel. You don't have to believe that I'm right. You only have to trust me and make the choice that will see you safely back to your families. This isn't what you signed up for, and once my efforts prove successful, you will be hailed for your judgment instead of having your families sobbing at your grave sites."

In deliberate fashion, Lia eased her hand to the rental's keys and turned the engine back on.

"So," Lia resumed, "what will it be?"

CHAPTER 62

NORTHERN NEW JERSEY

How was the drive?" Brixton asked Lia Ganz, after answering her knock on the Westview Motel's door.

"I ran into some old friends," she said, leaving it there as she filed past him. "And you didn't check the peephole."

"Oops."

"What am I going to do with you, Robert?" she asked, as he closed the door behind them.

He double-locked it and eased the swing bolt over for good measure. "Happy?"

"I won't be happy until all this is over and we've won."

Brixton watched Lia Ganz scrutinizing the room, paying special attention to the window and the sight lines beyond.

"I asked for a room facing the back," he told her. "This was the best they could do."

"This place is off the beaten path. You chose well."

"They also take cash and don't ask any questions. A struggling family operation."

She finished her once-over. "Sounds like Israel."

Brixton filled her in on all the details of his conversation with Sister Mary Alice Rose, focusing on the Y-12 National Security Complex and its vast stores of bomb-ready radioactive fuel in the form of highly enriched uranium.

"They're going to blow it up," he finished. "That's got to be the plan. Once the vice president got wise to the president's condition, they might have tried to draw her into the circle, then killed her when she refused to go along."

"She must not have wanted to become an accessory to five million murders."

Lia sat down on one of the beds, Brixton facing her from the other. "What's your level of experience with this kind of threat?"

"Nuclear? Not much, Robert, beyond playing the scenarios out. And most of those scenarios involved a nuclear bomb itself, a suitcase-type model, specifically, as opposed to what we're facing here, a dirty bomb."

"I'm not sure that's the actual term in this case, but we're talking about hundreds of thousands of pounds here, anyway, not just a single car or truck. I can't even begin to calculate the effects of that."

"I can't either. It wasn't one of the scenarios we played out."

"And I don't know how we can stop this scenario from playing out, not cut off and hunted by the very forces we should be going to for help."

"What happened to your contact, the man who approached you after your friend interceded?"

Mac, Brixton remembered. He hadn't thought of him since, and was now struck by the fear that Mackensie Smith may have followed Panama into oblivion.

"I called him Panama because of the hat he wore. Beyond that, the only thing I knew about him was the phone number he provided."

"Don't tell me . . . it's been disconnected."

"They're tightening the circle, Lia. If you're not in, you're out. And we're as out as it gets."

"How do we get in?"

"Sister Mary Alice Rose," Brixton told her.

"You mentioned a jailbreak," Lia Ganz said.

Brixton nodded.

"From a secure federal prison in the middle of Brooklyn."

Brixton nodded again, only once this time.

"Going in, guns blazing, loaded for bear."

"Unless you've got a better idea, Colonel Ganz."

"As a matter of fact, I do."

"Let's hear it," Brixton prodded.

"They won't kill her, at least not within the confines of the facility itself."

"So they pick her up for a nonexistent transfer to parts unknown?"

Ganz nodded. "Those 'parts unknown' being heaven, in this case."

Brixton frowned. "Close enough, I suppose. Could be we're already too late. We could go in tomorrow with guns blazing to find Sister Mary Alice's cell empty."

"You ever hear of a federal prison transfer happening at night?"

He had to think about that. "Now that you mention it . . ."

"Exactly. And chances are the personnel at the Metropolitan Detention Center have never heard of a transfer happening after hours either, because they don't happen at night, especially in this case, since the last thing this cabal led by the first lady would dare do is risk drawing attention to themselves by doing something that stands out. No, Robert, it'll be tomorrow morning, likely first thing."

"And how does that help us, exactly?"

Lia Ganz smiled. "Glad you asked."

CHAPTER 63

BROOKLYN, NEW YORK

The woman pushing the man in the wheelchair down the sidewalk approaching the Metropolitan Detention Center attracted no attention from the pedestrians emerging from a nearby subway stop. They politely moved aside, sacrificing those few moments from their day so that the wheelchair wouldn't have to alter its speed or path.

The sidewalk had been closed off in the area immediately before a fenced-in parking area where prisoner transfers, either coming or going, took place at the rear of the building. A massive black SUV rode the curb tightly, and four men wearing Windbreakers that identified them as U.S. Marshals flanked the open gate to steer pedestrians off the sidewalk for a brief detour onto the street. They made an exception for the wheelchair-bound man, sending him on while diverting the others, just as two more marshals escorted an older woman with white hair and shapeless clothes toward the gate.

Lia Ganz squeezed Brixton's shoulder before returning that hand to the chair's holds.

"Here we go," she whispered.

Eight a.m.," Brixton had said the night before, after Ganz had laid out the initial plan. "That's when the prison opens for business."

"This nun's escorts will be waiting," Lia told him. "How long before she's processed for the apparent prisoner transfer?"

"Between fifteen and eighteen minutes, assuming all their paperwork is in order."

"That's very specific."

"I've been involved in a few of these myself over the years."

"Under different circumstances than what we'll be facing, I trust."

"Entirely," Brixton affirmed.

Lia Ganz had paid cash for the wheelchair at HomePro Medical Supplies, not far from the prison, which opened at seven. They'd loaded the wheelchair into the trunk of a cab, which dropped them a few blocks away, out of the sight line from the federal facility. At that point, Brixton had plopped down in the chair, craned his shoulders, and slouched appropriately to let Lia do the driving from there.

"Anything we need to go over again?" she asked him, when the building came within view.

"Just be careful when you dump me."

Here we go."

In that moment, Lia Ganz rocked the wheelchair forward, pretending to have hit a crack in the sidewalk. Brixton barely needed to add any of his momentum as he was thrust forward, up and out of the wheelchair. He hit the sidewalk hard, just as the two federal marshals with Sister Mary Alice Rose between them emerged fully through the gate.

Instinctively, two of the marshals standing guard rushed to the fallen man, kneeling to provide assistance, and Ganz shoved the wheelchair into the nearest man, hard enough to strip his legs out from under him. Brixton grabbed hold of the other kneeling marshal's shirt in what looked like desperation instead of calculation, the man hesitating long enough for Lia to launch herself on the other two guards, who came at her in tandem, coming to grips with what was happening. They were standing when they reached her.

Then they weren't. In what seemed little longer than a heartbeat, Brixton recorded a flash of motion, the two men suddenly reduced to a blur at the center of a shape whirling around them. Sweeping their legs out, the upper half of their frames seemed to be separated from the lower. They landed with crunching impacts, facedown on the sidewalk, not moving.

The marshal Brixton was clutching tried to pull free of his grasp. Brixton hammered the man hard in the groin and used the next moment to jerk him down, face-first into the sidewalk, adding his second hand to the top of the marshal's head. That man's face seemed to compress on impact, his legs twitching as he passed out.

Brixton swung around, lurching to his feet while keeping his eyes on the marshals on either side of Sister Mary Alice. Both of them were going for their guns when Lia Ganz engulfed the one nearest her in a twisting flurry of blows. Brixton launched himself toward the other, but his gun was out and steady by then, which meant Brixton was too late and the distance between them too far for him to act fast enough.

So Sister Mary Alice acted, grasping the man's gun hand with both of hers and pinning it against his body long enough for Brixton to get there and unleash his own strikes, which toppled the gunman. He was still conscious when Brixton leaned over to kick aside the pistol he'd shed. Then he turned to see the nun herself climbing back to her feet, her own efforts having led to a fall that had torn the material over both knees, revealing nasty scrapes where she'd landed.

"Let's go!" Lia Ganz implored, rushing for the giant SUV after fastening plastic flex cuffs on the wrists of all the downed federal marshals.

Its engine was still on, purring, when she leaped behind the wheel. That left Brixton to help Sister Mary Alice into the back seat and then to tumble inside after her.

"Nice to see you again, Mr. Brixton," she said to him calmly.

CHAPTER 64

BROOKLYN, NEW YORK

Good morning to you, too, Sister."

"Don't believe I've had the pleasure," Sister Mary Alice said to Lia Ganz, not missing a beat when the big SUV screeched away from the curb, tearing into traffic amid the horn-honking protests of impatient drivers.

"Lia Ganz," Lia greeted from behind the wheel.

"Your accent . . ."

"Israeli."

"Oh, my. What have I done now?"

Brixton ignored the joke. "When did you learn you were being transferred?"

"This morning, when they woke me up in the pod I share with three other women. Told me to get dressed while they waited. Then they brought me downstairs. Wouldn't even allow me to brush my teeth." She glanced toward Lia in the driver's seat, then back toward Brixton. "Were those men really federal marshals?"

"Yes," Lia answered, before Brixton had a chance. "But this was no ordinary transfer."

"Apparently not," the nun said, managing a smile.

"We need your help, Sister," Brixton said to her.

"You made that plain yesterday, Mr. Brixton."

"There's going to be an attack on Y-Twelve," Lia Ganz picked up. "A big one."

"Oh, my," Sister Mary Alice repeated. "Not by federal marshals, I trust."

"No, by some of the people they work for."

"Oh, my, indeed."

Brixton explained it all as well as he could while Ganz careened the big SUV through the congested streets. Even the summary was terrifying as he told it. How a shadowy government cabal led by First Lady Merle Talmidge had chosen to strike, both to secure indefinitely a mentally ailing president's hold on power and to pursue a world-changing agenda that was to begin with a staged terrorist attack against the homeland.

"And I was the one who ended up in prison," Sister Mary Alice said at the end, as Ganz squeezed the SUV into a no parking zone directly across the street from a parking garage, a block over from the Barclays Center. "So you're saying that there are no terrorists."

"The cabal behind this made them up. A straw man for what's to come."

"Come on!" Ganz ordered, lunging out of the SUV.

Brixton led Sister Mary Alice across the street in her wake, the three of them taking the nearest garage stairs to the fourth level, where they'd left Ganz's rented Chevy Cruze, now complete with pilfered plates in case anyone was looking for the car. That would do for now, although Lia suspected they'd need another vehicle to complete the drive south.

"We're headed to Y-Twelve, aren't we?" Sister Mary Alice asked them both.

"Eventually," confirmed Lia Ganz, as they reached the Chevy.

"We need to make a stop in these parts first," said Brixton.

He gave Lia the address and explained where they were headed.

"You trust this man?" she asked him.

"I trust that he can provide the answers we need."

"Like what?"

"Exactly how blowing up Y-Twelve is going to kill five million people. That's what the professor will be able to tell us."

Sister Mary Alice looked across the seat at him. "The professor?"

CHAPTER 65

NEW YORK CITY

They found him, again with his pigeons on the roof.

"You're late, Brixton," he said, looking up from tending to one of their cages.

"You were expecting me?"

"Ever since our last meeting ended. Definitely seemed we were at the start of something that would require my expertise again before we reached the end." He regarded Lia Ganz, then Sister Mary Alice. "You've got company today, I see."

Brixton introduced them both to him.

"A nun and a Mossad agent?"

"Retired," Lia Ganz elaborated.

"*I'm* not," Sister Mary Alice chirped.

"Makes for strange bedfellows, doesn't it?" the professor said to Brixton. "So what can I do for you today?"

It was drizzling, but none of them was dressed for the weather, even the professor, who lived in the building. In fact, Brixton noted, he seemed to be wearing the same clothes he had been the other day.

"I want to give you a hypothetical," Brixton told him.

"Hypothetical," the professor repeated, getting the point. "I'm all ears."

"Say you're storing more than a hundred thousand pounds of highly enriched uranium in a secure facility. Say somebody, terrorists, want to blow it up. What happens?"

"Not very much, compared to what most would expect." The professor finally turned away from the cage he was cleaning, careful not to disturb the pigeons currently roosting inside. "You're thinking, *How can that be,* right? That much of the prime ingredient behind nuclear weapons goes *boom* and the survival rate is somewhere around a hundred percent? *Come on*, you're thinking."

"You're right."

"And here's your answer. Highly enriched uranium emits extremely low levels of only alpha radiation, which can easily be shielded. Unlike plutonium, the radiological hazards of handling highly enriched uranium are relatively low."

“Even though it can be used as a nuclear explosive material, making it one of the most dangerous substances on earth?” wondered Lia Ganz.

“Correct,” the professor said, letting a bird climb onto his arm. “Because exposure to HEU is not inherently dangerous, and certainly not fatal. It’s not like they can turn it into the mother of all dirty bombs.”

He began to feed the pigeon from bird snacks piled in his lapel pocket. Two more birds joined the first on his arm.

“So, assuming they intend to blow Y-Twelve up,” the professor continued, “there must be something else here we’re not considering.”

“I believe I may be able to be of service there,” said Sister Mary Alice. “Let’s start with the site’s history.

“Y-Twelve was built secretly over a two-year period as part of the Manhattan Project, and its existence wasn’t publicly acknowledged until the end of the Second World War. By then, the secret city had a population of seventy-five thousand. Few of its residents had been allowed to know what was being done at the military site, which included one of the largest buildings in the world. Y-Twelve processed the uranium used in Little Boy, the atomic bomb that destroyed Hiroshima. Seven decades later, the facility remains the only industrial complex in the United States devoted to the fabrication and storage of weapons-grade uranium. Every nuclear warhead and bomb in the American arsenal contains uranium from Y-Twelve.”

“You might also mention, Sister,” the professor picked up, “that Y-Twelve isn’t lacking in the *quantity* of security so much as the quality. There are over five hundred security officers authorized to use lethal force, five armored vehicles, miniguns that can fire up to fifty rounds per second and shoot down aircraft, video cameras, motion detectors, four perimeter fences, and rows of dragon’s teeth—low, pyramid-shaped blocks of concrete that can rip the axles off approaching vehicles and bring them to a dead stop. The Department of Energy and Nuclear Regulatory Commission have proclaimed it to be one hundred percent secure, without explaining how an eighty-year-old woman penetrated all that security with bolt cutters.”

“I was eighty-three at the time,” Sister Mary Alice noted. “And I didn’t even need those bolt cutters to penetrate all that security.”

“Then how’d you get in?” the professor asked her.

“I took the train.”

CHAPTER 66

NEW YORK CITY

And I'm not talking about Amtrak, either," Sister Mary Alice continued.

"What *are* you talking about?" Brixton asked her.

"A secret tunnel that can be accessed from a few miles away. That's how I got into the complex. The story about the bolt cutters was concocted to cover up the truth and because the powers that be had to hide the tunnel's existence at all costs."

"Why?" Lia Ganz asked her. "It's not like what they're storing at Y-Twelve is a secret."

"Unless they're storing something else there," the professor interjected.

He returned the four pigeons currently perched on his arm to their cage and collected four more in virtually the same positions in their place, turning toward Sister Mary Alice.

"That's it, isn't it, Sister?"

She nodded. "I didn't even know myself, until I spent a month watching the place. People were coming out who never went in. And I had a source who eventually told me about the existence of the tunnel."

"I didn't know nuns had sources," said the professor.

"He was a fellow activist. I didn't believe him at first, thought it was just a harebrained conspiracy theory. Until he told me what the actual freight they were bringing into Y-Twelve was, to be tucked away in five underground levels that were originally constructed to handle additional stores of highly enriched uranium, enclosed by bedrock and reinforced steel and concrete."

The professor stroked one bird's head, then the next. "Don't tell me: nuclear waste."

"A million of tons of it by now, maybe even more." Sister Mary Alice nodded. "And it appears I don't have to tell you, because you already know."

"The plan for years was to create a repository for the waste at Yucca Mountain in Nevada," the professor explained to Brixton and Lia Ganz. "When that fell through, the Department of Energy was left scrambling to find a replacement. Does that accurately sum things up, Sister?"

"Pretty much on the nose, yes," Mary Alice Rose told him, "at least according to what I was able to find out. Besides being weakly radioactive, uranium is a toxic metal likely to affect the function of the liver, kidneys, heart, and other organs. When you add a million tons of nuclear waste to the mix, you're looking at the ultimate dirty bomb. Triggering an explosion with a fraction of that size of high explosives, and you'd have your three to five million deaths, Robert. And that figure may turn out to be conservative."

"Because of the resulting radioactive cloud spreading," concluded Lia Ganz.

"Indeed," the professor noted. "And notice I didn't mention anything about the cloud dissipating. That's because highly enriched uranium has a higher atomic weight than nuclear waste product. The molecules of the waste will bond to those of the HEU, creating a toxic, deadly cloud that won't be going away anytime soon."

"No wonder they had to make you effectively disappear, Sister," Brixton managed, through the fog that had suddenly enveloped his thinking.

She nodded, unflappable as she'd been since Brixton and Lia Ganz had rescued her from her federal marshal escorts. "I interpret what I'm hearing to mean that those five million deaths, at minimum, aren't going to necessarily be immediate or even close to it. In Hiroshima and Nagasaki, more people died from the effects of the radiation than the actual blasts themselves."

Impressed, the professor grinned at her as he continued feeding the new set of pigeons roosting on his arm. "No offense meant, but that's not language normally used by a sister of the Immaculate Conception."

"No offense taken, and I have a master's degree in cellular biology from Boston College."

"You're no stranger to science, then."

"Far from it. My father was a molecular biologist. I got my first microscope for my fifth birthday, around the same time my parents became heavily involved with the Catholic Worker Movement. So activism, you might say, runs in the family."

The professor's quizzical, taut expression suggested he was studying her, trying to make sense of the aging nun who'd been arrested staging numerous protests over her life, but only one that had landed her in jail. "Now, let's get back to those five million deaths," he said, prodding Sister Mary Alice. "How big is this train?"

"A few years back, eight freight cars, to conform to the size of the underground loading platforms, both at the entrance to the tunnels and beneath the facility itself."

Brixton weighed that in his mind. "And if those cars were all loaded with drums filled with high explosives . . ."

"The bomb that was dropped on Nagasaki in World War Two," the professor picked up from there, "contained the equivalent of two hundred and seventy tons of high explosives. Eight train cars filled with C4, thermite, or one of the newer experimental explosives would at least approximate, or even exceed, that."

"Spewing a million pounds of radioactive waste into the air. 'Ultimate dirty bomb' would seem to be an understatement," said Lia Ganz, not bothering to hide the fear in her voice.

"Indeed," acknowledged the professor. "One study found that over the course of a year, one milligram of uranium oxide emits three hundred and ninety million alpha particles, seven hundred and eighty million beta particles, as well as associated gamma rays, for a total of more than one billion high-energy, ionizing, radioactive particles and rays that may produce extensive biological damage to a person's ovaries, kidneys, lungs, lymph nodes, blood, bones, breasts, and stomach, not to mention fetuses. That's *one single milligram*, mind you. And you know the most important component of all in this?"

"All that concrete," Sister Mary Alice said, even though the question had been aimed at Brixton.

The professor nodded, even more impressed with her than before. "The very concrete you chipped away at, once you penetrated the Y-Twelve facility. Every hammer strike would have produced a fissure of concrete dust into the air. Multiply that to the nth degree and you'd have—"

"A toxic dust cloud," Sister Mary Alice completed. "Utterly massive in size."

"I'd estimate a half-mile radius, though I'm tempted to revise that to as much as a mile, potentially steadily expanding from there, depending on wind and other climate factors." The professor swung back toward Brixton. "Remember all the people fleeing from that debris cloud after the Twin Towers collapsed?"

"How could I forget?"

"Multiply that effect by maybe a billion and add in deadly radiation to the mix. And since the facility is located in Tennessee . . ."

"What?" Ganz prodded, when the professor's voice tailed off.

"You may want to cover your ears for this, Robert," he advised, then continued as Brixton mocked that notion. "This time of year, the dust cloud would ride the same steering winds that drive spring storms up the East Coast. No one living in the entire so-called Acela corridor would be safe. Upon further review, I'd say the number of casualties might well be closer to ten million over time."

Brixton had to remind himself to breathe.

"And I haven't gotten to the financial costs of this, or the fact that large swaths of areas would become uninhabitable for decades due to lingering radiation, and that includes major metropolitan centers. The devastation would be incalculable. The country would never be the same, at least not in any of our lifetimes."

"That's not saying a lot, in my case," Sister Mary Alice remarked.

"If you can survive federal prison, Sister," said Brixton, "you can survive anything. And we need to get back to Washington. According to that recording Kendra Rendine got a hold of, zero hour is tomorrow, and we've got to stop it."

"They wouldn't risk carting the explosives in any sooner than necessary," the professor noted. "My guess is that they'll bring them in tomorrow morning and disperse the drums through all five underground levels to maximize the explosive effects."

"There's something else," Brixton told them all. "Tomorrow is Vice President Stephanie Davenport's funeral."

CHAPTER 67

WASHINGTON, DC

Let us pray," the Reverend Francis Tull said.

He squeezed the hands of President Corbin Talmidge and First Lady Merle Talmidge at the round table in the White House residence that was used for their weekly prayer meetings.

"Lord, give us the strength to persevere against our enemies and be strong enough to do the hard thing. For in the hardest of things we show our undying love for You, O Lord. In those moments we are Your most faithful of servants, forever devoted to keeping Your word and remaking this world in Your image. 'And walk in the way of love,'" Tull continued, squeezing the hands clutching his harder as he quoted from Ephesians, "'just as Christ loved us and gave himself up for us as a fragrant offering and sacrifice to God.'"

Both the president's and the first lady's eyes were squeezed tightly closed, Tull's too. He was the son of one of the most famous men of God, if not the most famous, of all time. A man who'd built an empire of devoted followers and worshippers long before the age of the televangelist took hold. But Francis Tull possessed none of his father's charm, conviction, or even business sense. He'd been bleeding donations since an initial spike that had followed the great man's death. His piety was threatened by scandals, he had a son who wouldn't talk to him and had fallen victim to drugs, and his lawyers were currently fighting a losing battle with the IRS over the Tull church's tax-exempt status. If the Talmidges hadn't welcomed him into their fold and into the White House, providing a much-needed lifeline to resurrect his flagging reputation, Tull hesitated to think where he'd be right now. They'd even managed to make that IRS investigation go away.

"'So Christ was sacrificed once to take away the sins of many,'" he continued, quoting the Book of Hebrews, "'and he will appear a second time, not to bear sin but to bring salvation to those who are waiting for him.'

"O Lord, hear us on this blessed day, for that salvation is what the sacrifices that are to come require. As is Your word, many must die so that more might live, and live their lives true to that word."

Tull separated his hands from the president and first lady, opening his eyes toward the heavens, as he quoted from First Kings.

"'Then the fire of the Lord fell, and consumed the burnt sacrifice, and the wood, and the stones, and the dust, and licked up the water that was in the trench.'" He waited for the first couple's open eyes to regard him before he resumed. "Now, in a coming dawn, another burnt sacrifice will be upon us, one certain to extract a terrible toll that will threaten the faith of all but the most chaste and deserving of Your faith and wisdom. They shall walk the scorched earth and the fires shall tremble under their step, only the residue of smoke left in the wake of the true lot among us who are righteous. Help us, O Lord. Guide us in this time of upheaval and sin and answer the prayers of those who've stepped forward to those who keep Your word. 'Their work will be shown for what it is, because the day will bring it to light. It will be revealed with fire, and the fire will test the quality of each person's work,'" Tull finished, quoting from First Corinthians. "Amen."

Corbin and Merle Talmidge opened their eyes.

"That was fun," said the president. "Especially the part about fire."

"Bless you, my son," Tull said, touching his shoulder.

"Are you my father? You don't look like my father."

The first lady took her husband's hand and squeezed it affectionately to distract him. He smiled at her.

"Can we pray again?" he asked both of them.

"You should pray in silence," Tull told him, "so you may hear God speak to you."

"Just me?"

"Just you."

The president squeezed his eyes closed again.

"I can be with you when the fateful hour arrives, to offer comfort," Francis Tull offered the first lady.

"Your presence would provoke suspicion, Reverend," Merle Talmidge cautioned. "Let's make it *after* the fateful hour. Your comfort will be needed for years to follow."

"'Mount Sinai was covered with smoke, because the Lord descended on it in fire,'" he said, quoting from the Book of Exodus, as he patted the back of her hand tenderly. "'The smoke billowed up from it like smoke from a furnace, and the whole mountain trembled violently.' This country is that mountain. Yours is a holy mission, undertaken to assure His word is not squandered."

"You would bless a mission certain to cost millions of lives?"

"'And He does great wonders, so that He makes fire come down from heaven on the earth in the sight of men.' From the Book of Revelation, Madam First Lady. The earth was forged and preserved in fire. That fire can take many forms, like the one that is soon to be upon us."

"You haven't warned any of your people, of course," Merle Talmidge said.

"I serve the Lord, not them. And to let that word leave this holy house with me would be to rebuke the word of God and prove myself unfit to be

His vessel. It is not my place or within my power to bless your holy mission. But I can, and have, blessed you in the time of strife and sin that requires true courage to act. Luke chapter one: 'Do not fear, for you have found favor with God.' And from Proverbs: 'Have no fear of sudden disaster or of the ruin that overtakes the wicked, for the Lord will be your confidence and will keep your foot from being snared.'"

Merle Talmidge took Tull's hand in both of hers, while the president continued to pray silently to himself, his lips moving and eyes squeezed so tightly closed that his expression looked made of patchwork skin. "You are a great comfort to both of us, Reverend."

"It's never easy to do the difficult thing, Madam First Lady." Tull glanced toward the president, who continued mouthing the silent words of prayer. "Your husband's illness is a great gift in the making, because it has sowed the seeds that will soon sprout. That could only be God's work, and you have only followed his word."

The first lady eased her hands away. "God may speak to you, Reverend, but he doesn't speak to me."

"He speaks to all, but only the most fortunate and worthy among us can hear Him. You've heard Him loud enough to put His words into action. You and your husband are His vessels. You do what you must, only to serve Him."

The president's eyes snapped open suddenly. "Can we sing again now? We haven't sung yet tonight."

A knock fell on the door and Merle Talmidge rose to answer it, while Francis Tull moved his chair closer to the president's.

"I told you we were not to be disturbed," she said to the assistant she found standing there.

Then she saw the look on his face, no words required.

"Tell them I'll be right down," the first lady told him.

CHAPTER 68

NEW YORK CITY

Robert!" exclaimed Mackensie Smith. "Where have you been? I've been worried sick. What in God's name is happening?"

"I can't tell you, not over this line."

"I still have the secure one," Brixton's best friend told him.

"Hang up. I'll call you back there."

Mac Smith picked up his secure phone before the first ring was complete. "Okay, I'm listening,"

"Me saying too much would put you in grave danger. Annabel too," Brixton added, referring to Mac's wife.

"What I don't know, I don't have to deny."

"Exactly."

"Spoken like a lawyer, Robert."

"I've been around one of the best in the last few years. Guess it rubbed off. But I don't want to involve you any more than is absolutely necessary."

"Where are you?"

"New York City. I just broke a nun out of federal prison."

"You . . . *what*?"

"Don't bother checking the news, Mac. It's not going to be reported. None of what I'm involved in will ever be reported, if we can stop them."

"Stop *who*?"

"Does your office still overlook the White House?"

"I'm the one who's moving, Robert, not the building."

"Enough said."

Mac hesitated. "You sound scared."

"Terrified."

"How can I help? What can I do? Who should I call?"

"Nobody," Brixton said, answering Mackensie Smith's final question first, "because they won't be able to do a thing to stop what's coming."

"And what exactly is coming?"

"We need to have this discussion in person, Mac."

"Where? I'll meet you. Just give me a place and time."

"That's why I'm calling. We need a place to hide out, just until tomorrow."

"*We*," Smith repeated.

"Numbering three. The names don't matter."

"But one of them is this nun, I'm assuming."

"I was thinking maybe the office," Brixton suggested, "given it'll be empty until the new tenant moves in."

"No, too much going on. People packing up, moving stuff out. What about the house Annabel and I are building on the Chesapeake?"

"I thought it was a work in progress."

"We've made a lot of progress. The place is virtually habitable now, and there's even some furniture, though not enough to make it feel like home."

"I'm not picky, Mac," Brixton told him.

Smith knew better than to push him further on that, especially under the circumstances. "Anything else I can do for you right now?"

"You could tell me if you heard from anyone asking questions about me."

"Not a peep. I would've told you as soon as I heard your voice a few minutes ago, if that were the case."

"You need to be careful, Mac. Annabel, too."

"How much of this has to do with the whole mess surrounding the Metro bombing?"

"A whole lot."

"I'm a sucker for details, you know."

"I don't want to say any more yet, for your own good."

Brixton could hear Mackensie Smith's breathing on the other end of the line as he paused. "Okay, here's what I'm going to do. I'm going to take a drive out to the new house and make sure everything's in order, no strangers lurking about and all that. Stock up the fridge and cupboards with provisions from the Food Lion in Princess Anne. One thing to remember, though, Robert. The house is located on Deal Island. Just one bridge on and off. Not sure if that makes for a great hideout."

"It's perfect, Mac, because at least we'll be able to see them coming. And I need one more favor. I'm working this with a Secret Service agent named Kendra Rendine. She's gone dark and I can't reach her. I was hoping you—"

"Robert," Smith interrupted, "it was just on the news."

"What?"

"Kendra Rendine was found dead an hour ago."

Mackensie Smith kept talking, but all Brixton heard was "Starbucks" and "slumped over a table."

"They killed her," Brixton heard himself say.

"Who?"

"Doesn't matter. I'll explain everything when I see you. You need to leave now. Use the back door. Don't take your car and don't go home. Just get somewhere safe, somewhere in public."

"You mean," Smith said, "like a Starbucks."

CHAPTER 69

WASHINGTON, DC

They met in the first lady's official office, located in the East Wing of the White House. The briefing covered the most salient points of what had become an unmitigated series of setbacks at the hands of two people who were now threatening the entire plot that she and others had so painstakingly put into motion. Covering all the bases, anticipating anything and everything. Or so they thought.

"If they broke this nun out of jail—"

"They didn't actually break her out," the director of the FBI reminded, after providing a full briefing. "She was already out when they neutralized the transport team comprised of federal marshals."

"I believe you mentioned that there were six of those marshals. Six against two."

"One of those two was this woman," the Homeland Security secretary said, placing a photograph in front of the first lady on her desk.

"Lia Ganz," Merle Talmidge noted, recognizing her from a still photo isolated off the security footage of the mosque in Baltimore. "Again."

She aimed her next words toward the secretary of state.

"You assured me this had been taken care of. You assured me the Israelis were cooperating."

"They were. They did. Something went wrong. They don't call Lia Ganz the Lioness of Judah for nothing."

"So Ganz and Brixton are now in the company of Sister Mary Alice Rose. The risk they took in absconding with her could only mean they've somehow figured out that Y-Twelve is the target."

"They're still otherwise alone, cut off, isolated," the secretary reminded her.

"That doesn't seem to bother Ganz much—or Brixton for that matter, does it?"

"Madam First Lady," began the secretary of defense, "we have poked a hornet's nest and are now dealing with what flew out."

"Do we have any idea of their whereabouts?" Merle Talmidge asked all of those assembled before her, none of whom so much as flinched. "Not even a clue?"

"We put a tracer on all transactions associated with Brixton," said the director of the FBI. "We can do that because we're privy to all his personal information. Not so with Lia Ganz. She could be ten different people and we'd never know it. Nobody does fake documents better than the Israelis, even in the digital age. We believe she most likely rented a vehicle to get the three of them out of the area and are following that up as best we can by collecting security camera footage from all rent-a-car outlets in the general and surrounding area."

"That must be hundreds."

"Dozens, anyway," said the FBI director. "It's going to take some time."

"We need to find them. Robert Brixton is not without friends in Washington, and it will only take him getting one lawmaker's ear to cause a shit storm that could land right on the White House welcome mat. Do we have *anything*?"

"We're following a few leads—contacts and that sort of thing."

"I'll take that as a no."

"We're looking into people Brixton is most likely to contact," the director of the FBI picked up. "It means marshaling a lot of forces."

"If manpower is an issue, just say so."

"I'd prefer to keep the circle small, Madam First Lady."

Merle Talmidge glared at him across her desk. "You mean 'small' as in a former State Department contractor and a retired Israeli intelligence operative? Oh, and add to the mix an eighty-five-year-old nun, for good measure."

The head of the FBI didn't respond.

"Because we can't allow these people to waylay our plans. We can't afford it and the United States can't afford it. You don't need a crystal ball to see that the future holds chaos for this country and this world. My husband's illness has cast us with this one last opportunity to make things right, to set this country on a difficult course that's the only thing that might save it. With this Sister Mary Alice Rose in their company, it's clear that Robert Brixton and Lia Ganz have figured out what's coming tomorrow."

The director of Homeland Security smiled, not finding that to be a significant source of worry. "And what chance do the three of them have in penetrating one of the most secure installations in the entire nation?"

"If I'd asked you two years ago what chance an eighty-three-year-old nun would've had in doing the same, what would have you said? What would any of you have said?"

None of them said anything at all.

"Just what I thought," noted the first lady, returning her gaze to the director of the FBI. "Find them. Whatever it takes, find them."

CHAPTER 70

DEAL ISLAND, MARYLAND

Mackensie Smith was sitting on the front porch of his new home on the shores of Chesapeake Bay when Lia Ganz pulled the SUV she'd rented in New Jersey during their drive south into the driveway.

She explained to Brixton that she was on her third and final American identity. It was a long drive, taking the bulk of the day, to the point that they had watched the light bleeding from the afternoon sky. Mac's new home was located in the fishing village of Deal Island on Tangier Sound, in a very private subdivision on its own private acre of land, just a half mile from the Deal Island Bridge and marina.

Brixton took advantage of Lia Ganz driving, and Sister Mary Alice snoozing in the backseat, to do a deeper dive into where they were headed on his phone. Both ends of Deal Island offered public boat ramps, where there were any number of local skipjack and fishing captains to cruise the miles of waterways that stretched through the thirteen thousand acres of tidal marshes. Charter fishing and cruises could be reserved with boat captains at Wenona and Deal Island harbors. Brixton made a mental note of all that, along with committing to memory the location of boat rental outlets, on the chance they needed to flee the island that way.

Mac Smith bounced up out of his chair like a boy excited to greet his parents at the end of the day. He hugged Brixton more tightly than he ever had, after which Brixton introduced him to Lia Ganz and Sister Mary Alice Rose.

"*Sister?*" Smith repeated. "That's right, you're the nun Robert here broke out of prison."

"In the flesh, Mr. Smith," Sister Mary Alice told him.

Smith looked at her with a spark of recognition flashing in his eye. "Friend of mine from another firm helped defend a nun arrested for staging a protest at a nuclear facility."

"He did the best job he could. The deck was stacked against him."

Smith looked toward Brixton. "Why do I have the feeling that same nuclear facility is a part of what's going on here?"

"Because you're a smart man, Mac."

"And this all goes back to the Metro bombing . . ."

"It goes further back than that."

Mackensie Smith's expression tightened. "You need to tell me what's going on. Everything."

"Mac—"

"I couldn't live with myself if something happened to you, Robert. As of two hours ago, Annabel left to join some friends at our house in Saint Croix. I need to know everything, on the chance I can help you by more than just putting a roof over your head. And you need me to know."

"Because if something does happen to me . . ."

"It won't, but just in case."

The house seemed to be formed of nothing but glass, letting huge swatches of light into every single room, depending on the time of day. The direct views of Chesapeake Bay were spectacular from the living room, kitchen, and front porch as well as from a pair of master bedroom suites on the second floor. Those master suites would share a six-foot whirlpool tub that hadn't been installed yet.

Lia Ganz went off to scout the area, as she put it, while Sister Mary Alice found a sun-splashed space for her prayers, leaving Brixton and Mackensie Smith to adjourn to the front porch, where the view of the bay was sprawling and magnificent in the cool, late afternoon breeze. A few sailboats and fishing craft dotted the waters, none of them appearing suspicious, although if they lingered into the night that would change.

"I can see why you chose this place," Brixton noted, as a trio of pelicans flew overhead, joining the herons, egrets, and ibis which came and went in flocks.

"Never mind that," Smith started. "Tell me exactly what that Metro bombing has to do with a nuclear facility?"

"What's the most obvious answer, Mac?"

"Terrorism."

"You're half right."

"Half?"

"The Metro bombing wasn't a terrorist attack; it was only supposed to look like one. Same thing for what's coming. You heard about the gunfight at that Baltimore mosque?"

"Details are all over the place," Smith affirmed.

"That woman you just met, the one scouting the property . . ."

"Was that accent Israeli?"

"It was."

Smith's eyes bulged. "The mosque? Don't tell me she was . . ."

"I just did," Brixton said, when his best friend's voice tailed off.

Smith accepted that at face value. "And this nun, Sister Mary whatever?"

"Sister Mary Alice, Mac. Lia Ganz and I interrupted her federal prison transfer from the Metropolitan Detention Center to parts unknown. That nuclear facility she was arrested in is called Y-Twelve."

"Never heard of it."

"You will, and for all the wrong reasons."

Brixton laid out for Mackensie Smith what was coming tomorrow, supplementing the broad strokes with just enough of the details the professor had furnished about the massive catastrophe the United States was about to face, noting that the event was virtually certain to change the narrative enough to both radically shift the agenda and to assure that the Talmidge administration remained in power, with the first lady eventually succeeding her husband as president. When he was finished, Smith sat back far enough to shrink into the wooden Adirondack chair. He remained silent for a time, as the sun fell, long enough for the descending darkness to hide his features from Brixton.

"Five million people is more than the sum total of Americans lost in every war this country has ever fought, and that includes the Civil War."

"It could be more, Mac, even millions more."

Smith visibly shuddered. "Did you know that during the Manhattan Project, more than a hundred scientists signed a petition urging the government not to use the bomb? They believed there was a very real chance that the blast would start a chain reaction that would destroy the planet."

"I didn't."

"The point being that nobody was sure of the actual effects. Everything was theoretical then, just as it is now. They may have tested all this in a lab, just like they tested those first nukes at Alamogordo, but until Y-Twelve blows, nobody's really sure of how bad it's going to get. What if this death cloud moves west? What if it moves south? What if it reaches Canada? What if it spreads directly over Washington, Philadelphia, New York, Boston, and all the densely populated places in between to land direct hits? How long would people have to stay inside?"

"I'm not sure staying inside would save them, Mac."

Smith lapsed briefly back into silence. "You've got to let me help you, Robert."

Brixton gazed about him, gesturing toward the house at their rear. "You already have."

"I'm talking in a bigger way." He took out his phone and held it up. "You have any idea how many congressmen, senators, and former government officials I have on speed dial?"

"I'm sure it's a veritable who's who of power brokers."

"Damn right." Smith brought the phone in closer. "Pick any letter in the alphabet and let's call somebody right now. Get the wheels turning with more than just you, your Israeli, and your nun behind the wheel."

"They'll crash, Mac. I thought I'd made it clear how high up all of this stretches."

"Then maybe I didn't make clear how high up my contacts go. The deep state personified, Robert. I'm talking career officials who won't take kindly to someone rewriting the Constitution and turning the East Coast into a graveyard. And, if you let me, I think I know the strategy to pursue."

"What's that?"

"Make sure word gets out, through the right sources, that the president has literally lost his mind."

"You don't think the first lady would be prepared for that?"

Smith flashed his phone again. "I've got her in my contacts list too."

"Nobody would dare touch this and you know it, Mac. Corbin Talmidge's approval rating is higher than it's ever been, and the only thing stopping him from coasting to a second term is the fact that he can't string two coherent sentences together unless they're written down before him. Even if they believed you, they'd never risk their careers on coming forward, on the chance your information it wrong or faulty. Or, this being paranoid Washington, if they think they're being set up."

Smith nodded. "You raise a good point, Robert, so let me make another of my own. Do you really think I'm going to just stand by and let you and your Israeli friend handle this alone?"

"We're not going to be alone, Mr. Smith," Lia Ganz said, seeming to have materialized out of nowhere, just to the right of the porch steps.

CHAPTER 71

CHESAPEAKE BAY

She flashed her cell phone in a manner identical to the way Mackensie Smith had just flashed his. Neither Smith nor Brixton had any idea where Ganz had come from or how long she'd been standing there.

"There are people I can reach out to," Ganz continued.

"Who? Your own government recalled you," Brixton reminded her. "That's not a strong recipe for requesting backup."

"Then I suppose I should make a phone call."

You need to come home, Colonel," Moshe Baruch said, by way of greeting, as soon as he answered the phone.

"And you need to listen to what I've got to say."

"I thought I had, prior to your ignoring my instructions and then refusing the orders of the escort team who tracked you down."

"Did they file a report?" Lia asked,

"They didn't have to. They claimed they weren't able to locate you. I can read between the lines."

"Israel already has enough widows, Commander. The country didn't need two more."

"It also doesn't need any more grandmothers turned heroes who think they know better."

"What I know is what's coming, and what's coming is bad, as bad as it gets."

"So you hinted at before."

"No more hints, Commander. Millions of Americans are going to die and the Middle East is going to be reshaped. Where we fit into that is up for argument. All bets are off."

Lia heard Baruch utter a deep sigh. "What do you want from me, Colonel?"

"Two things, starting with permission—"

"Which you know I can't give."

"Nor do I expect you to. You didn't let me finish: Permission to make some phone calls."

"To who, exactly?"

"That's the second thing I need from you."

* * *

How many men can you get?" Brixton asked Lia Ganz, after she'd explained what she was asking Moshe Baruch for.

"The commander says he'll get back to me. How many do you think we're going to need?"

"You mean, short of an army? Why don't we ask the resident expert?"

Sister Mary Alice was in the living room, seated in silence amid the falling darkness, as if waiting for them to come to her.

"We need to know everything you do about the site, Y-Twelve," Brixton said.

"That would take until my next birthday."

"We'll settle for the condensed version," interjected Mackensie Smith, as Lia Ganz looked on.

Smith's phone came complete with a projection feature that allowed them to project onto a wall a series of photos of Y-12 pulled off the internet. They chose a white, unfinished wall in the same downstairs great room. They also found a pair of thick Magic Markers to better designate areas of interest—their primary target as well as means of entry and exit marking up Mac's freshly painted wall.

"Wow, that's big," Smith commented, noting the sprawl of the fenced-in compound, which was obvious even in the projection.

An overhead shot captured the facility in all its scope. It was more like a small city, given the number of buildings and the hundreds of people working in, or responsible for securing, each. There seemed to be no rhyme or reason to the construction or relative placement. The buildings were long or squat, multiple or single storied, small or large. Parking lots were nestled amid the sprawl. In this particular shot, the cars and trucks looked tiny, but not a lot of pavement was visible.

"You can ignore all of the structures except for that one," Sister Mary Alice said, rising to point out a structure set off by itself and enclosed by heavy chain link fencing topped with barbwire.

Smith enlarged that section, the projection growing blurrier.

"That's the dedicated highly enriched uranium facility where I was arrested," Sister Mary Alice followed. "It hadn't been opened long when I broke in. They spent a billion dollars building it. This is where they relocated the reserves of HEU that had previously been divided up among five other existing structures that had fallen into disrepair. Those five underground levels were constructed secretly at the same time, the square footage at least equal to the aboveground storage capacity. The United States is, regrettably, not lacking in nuclear waste."

Lia Ganz joined the others in front of the wall, though she seemed to be seeing something entirely different in the projection. "These underground levels, that's where they'll set the charges. It'll take a dual explosion, the first with enough force to the implode the aboveground structures so they collapse downward, the second to blow the debris into one massive deadly, toxic cloud. Not a mushroom cloud, but the next best thing."

"Or worse, depending on your perspective," Brixton noted.

"I think your friend in New York was wrong about the size of the resulting cloud, Robert," Ganz told him.

"On the high end or the low?"

"The low, unfortunately. He said the cloud would stretch between a half mile and a mile in radius. But judging by what I'm seeing in this picture, the size of the facility, the resulting debris field would be closer to two miles."

"A two-mile-wide cloud promising death all the way up the East Coast," Brixton summed up. "That's what you're saying."

Ganz nodded. "And I think the casualty numbers will definitely top out closer to ten million than five over time. The question being, How do we get inside the complex in order to stop them?"

"Simple," Brixton said, joining the two of them at the wall. "The same way Sister Mary Alice did. We take the train."

"I might be able to be of service there," offered Mackensie Smith.

"You've done enough, Mac," Brixton said stridently. "I can't let you expose yourself to further risk."

"Can you let me make a phone call, Robert? Because the firm has represented the Department of Energy in a number of cases and I still have pretty high-up contacts there. I represented a few of them individually, and one has a rather large outstanding bill."

"I believe we must have stood on opposite sides a few times, Mr. Smith," said a smiling Sister Mary Alice.

"I'm sure we did, Sister, but not today. Let me make a few phone calls, Robert, and report back on what I come up with. What's the harm?"

"I assumed that about a whole bunch of things until a week ago."

Nearly an hour later, Mackensie Smith returned from another room, visibly shaking over whatever he'd just learned. He seemed excited, even fervently so.

"The call turned out to be much more productive than I thought it would. Turns out my contact has suspected something awry at Y-Twelve, particularly thanks to some new security forces that were brought in recently. The man's got three kids and a wife sick with cancer. He needs the medical, so he did he as he was told."

"But he talked to you."

Smith nodded. "He's also a patriot, and I promised to keep his name out of this, as well as erase his legal bills. I think he was waiting for the opportunity, so much so that he also came up with tickets for us."

"Tickets?" Brixton repeated.

Smith nodded. "In the form of Department of Energy inspector credentials that will get you on that train tomorrow, the same one likely to be carrying the explosives intended to re-create the Big Bang. He's going to call me to arrange pickup as soon as he has them in hand, likely in a few hours."

Lia Ganz took the floor. "These new security forces your friend mentioned will be playing the role of the Islamic terrorists who are going to be pinned with the blame for this. The first lady and the other conspirators have thought of everything, haven't they?"

"Except us," Brixton told her.

CHAPTER 72

WASHINGTON, DC

Merle Talmidge sat in a chair before her husband in the media room of the White House residence, where they'd set up a podium so he could practice the eulogy he'd be giving for Stephanie Davenport the next day. Such visuals were vital in establishing the kind of connections his failing mind could still grasp.

Corbin Talmidge could no longer read a speech off paper, because he inevitably lost his place. Nor could they use a teleprompter, since the colored stream of lit letters distracted him to the point that he'd forget where he was and what he was doing. The amazing thing about his mental decline, though, was that it had seemed to leave him with a savant-like ability to memorize what he was supposed to say. And as long as he was reciting the words from memory, he was able to stay on task and focus only on what had been stored in his mind through multiple practices.

When he finished his third try at the speech without a single flaw or slipup, the first lady burst to her feet, clapping.

"I did well?" her husband asked her.

"It was brilliant."

He was grinning now, beaming. "I did well."

Merle Talmidge hugged him tightly, felt him trembling slightly under her grasp. And when they separated, she could see his eyes were moist with tears.

"The things I'm going to say about this woman, the vice president, they were true, weren't they?"

"She was a good woman," the first lady said, leaving it there. "And she served this country well."

The president nodded at that, his mind working to make sense of what was in his mind. "Can I practice the speech again?"

"If you'd like, but you don't have to."

"I don't?"

"You're ready. We'll practice again tomorrow before we leave for the church."

"I'd like that," he said, smiling, but the smile slipped from his face as quickly as it had appeared. "I liked the vice president, too, didn't I?"

"Very much."

"I wish I could remember more about her. I remember her smile."

"She was a pleasant person, but tough when she had to be."

"Like you," her husband said. "You can be tough when you have to be. I've seen that."

"We all have to be tough right now." The first lady hesitated, ready to test the waters again on something else. "That's why you need me by your side."

"Like you are now," Corbin Talmidge said, speaking literally.

"I meant in a different way."

"What's that?"

"As your vice president, like we discussed."

"I'd like that." Her husband beamed.

"It's what's best for the country."

"We could work together."

"Yes."

"You could keep helping me do things."

"Of course."

"I'd like that," the president repeated, tensing suddenly. "Did we kill her?"

"Who?"

"The woman who died, the vice president. Stephanie Davenport—that's her name. Did we kill her?"

It was that way with the president sometimes. Out of nowhere, his mind would latch on to something he'd gleaned but couldn't always keep track of. It was like a remnant, a shadow in his mind that he couldn't stop following.

"We had to," the first lady said, surprising herself with the honesty.

"Why, if she was a good person?"

"Because she meant to do us harm. Because sometimes even good people can do bad things, the wrong things. She didn't believe in what we were doing."

"Did we have to kill her? Couldn't we have just asked her to stop?"

"She wanted to hurt you," the first lady said, also honestly.

"She did?"

"She wanted to hurt you badly."

"I don't remember wanting to hurt her."

"Because you didn't," Merle Talmidge told her husband, rubbing his shoulders in a way that comforted him.

He looked sad, almost mournful. "She must not have liked me all of a sudden."

"She didn't."

"Why? What did I do?"

"You believed things needed to happen that she didn't agree with. She didn't want you to be president anymore."

“But I’m a good president.”

“You are.”

“I’ve done good things.”

“You have,” Merle Talmidge said, hugging her husband again. “But the best one of all is still to come.”

CHAPTER 73

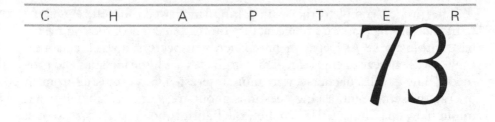

CHESAPEAKE BAY

Brixton spent much of the night working with Sister Mary Alice Rose to familiarize himself with every inch of the complex. He was no stranger to such a process—far from it, thanks to his protective work on behalf of the State Department during his tenure with SITQUAL. Site intelligence was crucial to manage when it came to planning routes and positioning detail personnel in static locations. This was little different than that, though it had been a long time since his memory had been tested to this degree. When working the field, you never had time to consult a written note. Everything had to be available on instant recall, and in this case that meant committing to memory both the available photographs of Y-12 and the details Sister Mary Alice was able to add from her own amazingly sharp recollection.

"I think time has been frozen for me these past few years," she said, by way of explanation. "I feel like I was arrested in Oak Ridge yesterday."

"Here's hoping you don't face a similar fate tomorrow, Sister," Brixton told her.

Lia Ganz was waiting outside Mackensie Smith's unfinished home when the four Israeli special operators she'd been expecting arrived in a pair of SUVs. She immediately recognized the two who emerged from the lead vehicle as the same pair who'd pulled her over on the road the night before.

"No hard feelings, Colonel?" the bigger of the two asked, smiling.

"Of course not. You're still alive, aren't you?"

Mackensie Smith returned from his rendezvous with his contact at the Department of Energy, toting proper clothing for Ganz, Brixton, and Sister Mary Alice, having been advised that the Israelis would be bringing their own. He also had the proper badges, passes, and authorizations in hand, along with actual equipment provided by his Department of Energy contact, in keeping with exactly what site inspectors would be expected to bring along with them.

They worked through the remainder of the night, hollowing out portions of the inspection equipment to create space to conceal weapons. As expected, sidearms were all that would fit, along with a number of extra magazines.

That process complete, they painstakingly reviewed the pictures and intelligence on the massive storage facility on the outskirts of the complex, a base within a base. As Department of Energy inspectors, it was crucial that they at least appear to enjoy a general familiarity with the logistics and protocols. The Israelis, of course, were more interested in the logistics from an operations standpoint, asking questions about areas of concealment, what might blow up if impacted by a bullet, the lighting, noise levels, size, scope, distance—no detail was omitted from their preparation. And when that was completed, they disappeared out into the darkness of Mac Smith's one acre of land to prep physically.

While the Israelis were off training somewhere on the property, Brixton walked to the end of the private pier, where he found Lia Ganz gazing out into the night.

"Grandparents shouldn't have to do what we're about to do," she said, without turning his way. "Such work should be left to the young."

"We were young once."

Ganz looked toward Brixton through the darkness. "I tell myself I'm doing this for my granddaughter. But I'm not. I'm doing it for myself."

Now it was Brixton staring straight ahead over the softly rippling waters of Tangier Sound. "I think I'm doing it for my daughter Janet. I think a lot of the things I've done these past five years have been about her, not all of them good."

Ganz let that remark pass. "You know what Israelis are good at more than anything? Living with the past instead of trying to change it."

"You can't change the past, Lia."

Their eyes finally met.

"Figure of speech, Robert. Maybe I should have said *relive* it."

"A comment aimed at me."

Brixton felt her take the hand that had been dangling by his side. She squeezed, and he squeezed back.

"You relive what happened every day, in the misplaced hope it will end differently. Since it can't, you find things that can, under your direction," Lia Ganz said, squeezing his hand even tighter, painful and tender at the same time. "But whatever happens tomorrow, it won't bring your daughter back. The surest way to become a ghost, Robert, is to keep chasing them. That's coming from someone who's chased more than her share."

"And yet, here you are."

"Chasing more," Lia said to him. "Just like you."

"Where do we go from here?" he asked her, after they'd finally separated.

"Oak Ridge, Tennessee, Robert."

CHAPTER 74

OAK RIDGE, TENNESSEE

Mackensie Smith had reserved a private jet for the next morning, to take the entire team to McGhee Tyson Airport, twenty-six miles from the Y-12 facility in Oak Ridge, Tennessee. From there, they crowded into an SUV that would bring them to the entrance of the train tunnel Sister Mary Alice Rose had pinpointed on a map, set amid the ridges that gave the town its name, fifty miles from the city of Knoxville.

That entrance was located five miles to the northwest of the complex, nestled in a valley abutting the shuttered American Museum of Atomic Energy, a renovated World War II cafeteria on Jefferson Circle. It was now supposedly a security holding station for Y-12, and much of the interior of the building had been hollowed out to allow access to the train tunnel constructed immediately beneath it. Trucks toting nuclear waste from across much of the country used a separate underground entrance to the tunnel, where their contents were loaded onto train cars.

Brixton rode up front with the driver, who Mac Smith insisted could be trusted without fail. Sister Mary Alice was seated directly behind him, centered between Lia Ganz and one of the four Israeli commandos. The remaining three were crammed into the rearmost seat. The pass that had come courtesy of Mac's contact in the Department of Energy got them into the parking lot without incident, after which they set about unloading their gear to walk the rest of the way to the former museum. If it bothered Sister Mary Alice to return to the scene of the crime that had cost her two years of her life, she wasn't showing it. The woman, in Brixton's mind, was unflappable. He imagined she had taken that attitude into federal prison with her, and it likely had a great deal to do with how well she had fared during her incarceration.

Which made Brixton regret even more what he had to say to her before heading across the parking lot to the former American Museum of Atomic Energy.

"Sorry, Sister," he said, easing her to the side. "This is the end of the line for you."

"I guess I shouldn't be surprised," she said, clearly disappointed.

"I don't think the Department of Energy employs many eighty-five-year-old women, and we can't risk drawing undue attention. Beyond that, there's the very real chance you might be recognized."

"Well," Sister Mary Alice said, nodding, unflappable as always, "I've heard every break room has a picture of me tacked to a wall so employees can throw darts at it."

Brixton touched her arm tenderly. "You've done your part and then some. We couldn't have come this far without you."

She shrugged his hand off, suddenly stone-faced. "Spare me the sanctimonious bullshit and just get it done, Robert. Today's as good a day to save the world as any."

WASHINGTON, DC

The president and first lady of the United States strode down the center aisle of the Washington National Cathedral after everyone else was seated. The place was packed to the gills, with nary an empty seat among the four thousand the church boasted. The cathedral had hosted four previous state funerals, for presidents Eisenhower, Reagan, Ford, and George H. W. Bush. The structure was as iconic on the outside as it was on the inside, a staid, neo-Gothic historic marvel with spires stretching for the sky, which made it look like a medieval castle.

Merle Talmidge had no idea whether Vice President Stephanie Davenport had ever set foot on the premises before her coffin was wheeled down the aisle, shortly before the Talmidges' arrival. The first lady's heart was beating a mile a minute. If her husband flubbed his eulogy speech for the vice president, the truth of his condition might become known, or at least suspected, throughout the country. Rumors would run rampant, investigations would be demanded, resignation would be called for, never mind waiting for the coming fall election.

Of course, none of that took into account what would be happening in Oak Ridge, Tennessee, as the funeral was taking place. The huge amount of explosives, packed into individual storage drums, would be strategically placed throughout the underground facility under the guise of a shipment of radioactive waste product. It wouldn't be detonated until hours after the service was completed and the president was safely back at the White House to take charge of the response. He'd rehearsed the speech he was about to give, from memory, for the final time this morning, clocking in at a powerful and moving twenty-two minutes.

It amazed Merle Talmidge no end how her husband could still command a room, in spite of his condition. He seemed to rally during occasions like this, was at his worst when they were alone or in small groups, which seemed the steal his focus, in contrast to today. A teleprompter had been set up for other speakers, but Corbin Talmidge wouldn't be using it. The pages of his prepared speech had already been placed on the lectern, though there would be no need for him to refer to them.

Again, the first lady was at a loss to explain how the president managed to present a facade of normalcy during times like this. It shouldn't have been possible, especially not with him in the midst of a steady decline. She believed, with no particular proof, that it had everything to do with the kinetic energy in the room. He'd been a powerful speaker before the disease had begun ravaging his mind, and he remained one even today. It was the one thing about Corbin Talmidge that was still *him*, and it had given rise to the first lady's conviction that the collective energy of those gathered revived her husband somehow, brought him back to the time before he began to slip mentally.

His next speech would be delivered in the aftermath of what was to come later today, only the beginning of the horrors to be visited upon America. Sometimes you have to break something to build something better. Merle Talmidge could justify her actions in any number of ways, not least of which was that it was best for the country if her husband remained in office. By the time he could no longer serve, the administration would have responded in any number of preplanned ways to the radiological terrorist attack, which was certain to kill millions. Retaliatory targets in the Middle East had already been selected and the entire region was about to be reshaped, with no quarter provided to anyone who rose in support of the attack launched on America.

And, by that time, she'd be sitting in the Oval Office in the president's stead. Here, within the walls of this magnificent cathedral, the thoughts and prayers of the Reverend Francis Tull moved to the forefront of her mind: *O Lord, hear us on this blessed day, for that salvation is what the sacrifices that are to come require. As is Your word, many must die so that more might live, and live their lives true to that word.*

Corbin Talmidge took the first lady's hand in his as they continued their slow walk up the center aisle, smiling softly to reassure her that everything would be all right. In that moment, he was again the man she had fallen in love with, in full possession of his brilliance, dreams, and ambitions.

She clung to the hope that she could say the same thing an hour from now.

OAK RIDGE, TENNESSEE

Brixton and Lia Ganz led the way toward the entrance of the former museum, a pair of guards flanking the glass doors on either side. One of the guards checked their Department of Energy IDs, then reviewed those belonging to the Israeli commandos, who were toting the heavier equipment. After being passed into the building, the group was ushered to a kind of reception desk, where they were provided with security badges that dangled from lanyards around their necks, complete with radiation detectors that another security guard insisted was strictly precautionary.

Brixton gazed about through the whole of the process, studying the former museum, which clearly had been reconstructed inside virtually from scratch to accommodate the train tunnel that now stretched beneath it. While he was no engineering expert, he could imagine the vast resources that must have been expended on secretly digging that tunnel through shale and limestone. The expense must have been mind-boggling, though well worth it to those in government responsible for the storage of spent nuclear waste, for which it had been virtually impossible to find a home. Any number of factors made Y-12 the ideal storage repository, particularly the fact that it was an existing infrastructure that only needed to be enhanced and expanded as opposed to being built from scratch.

The group was led next to a single elevator across the lobby, where all their IDs were checked yet again and their radiation detectors were confirmed to be operational. An armed guard was on duty inside the elevator as well, remaining silent when Lia, Brixton, and the Israeli commandos entered, hands looped through the handles of their Department of Energy sensor devices, which resembled old-fashioned computer towers. When the door slid open after a brief, rapid descent, another pair of guards checked their IDs yet again before a gleaming platform right out of some futuristic science fiction movie.

Brixton saw the train they'd soon be boarding, directly before him, a glistening iron monster with a rounded front and engines on both ends. Four of the eight train car cargo doors were open and personnel wearing baggy protection suits and respirators were loading the last of the steam drums on board—filled, no doubt, with high explosives, in keeping with the plan to change America forever.

WASHINGTON, DC

The first lady forced a slight, reassuring smile as the president rose from the chair next to her and approached the lectern. He took his place where the minister who'd opened Vice President Stephanie Davenport's funeral service had just been standing, hands grasping the sides of the podium as if to steady himself.

Merle Talmidge held her breath over what was coming next, a dozen possibilities rushing through her head in that singular moment, all of which portended disaster. She only relaxed when her husband began to speak, sounding exactly like the man with whom she had fallen in love and who had led this country so magnificently for three years.

"My fellow Americans, we gather today on this solemn occasion to bid farewell to a statesperson, American hero, servant of the people, and believer that our best days lie ahead of us. It was Stephanie Davenport's most fervent hope to long be a part of it that, but, sadly, life had other plans. Maya Angelou once said, 'I think a hero is any person really intent on making this a better place for all people.' I don't think I've ever heard more accurate words than that ever spoken about Stephanie Davenport. Indeed, it was Benjamin Disraeli who said, 'The legacy of heroes is the memory of a great name and the inheritance of a great example.'

"Now that Stephanie is gone, who among us will provide that great example?"

CHAPTER 75

OAK RIDGE, TENNESSEE

There was only a single track, so the trucks that had hauled the high explosives this far were stacked up three deep, farther back along the platform, after off-loading the cargo, the last of which was being loaded onto the front three cars. An earthen wall finished in shiny concrete marked the end of that part of the tunnel, and the nose of the train on that end was practically brushing up against it.

Brixton tried to picture eight train cars full of heavy explosives that, taken as a whole, were more powerful than either of the atomic bombs dropped in Japan at the close of World War II. Trying to picture the effects of the explosion, once those canisters were scattered appropriately through the underground layers of the complex, was mind-boggling, impossible.

As Brixton approached, with Lia Ganz and the Israeli special operators behind him, all toting their hollowed-out, DOE-regulation sensors, he noticed a single dark-blue shipping pallet resting atop each of the beds, perfectly conforming to their contours. Stacked two deep, he estimated, the total cargo numbered somewhere right around one hundred steel drums contained inside each of the dark cargo containers, for a total of eight hundred.

Also mind-boggling.

As their escorts led them toward the front engine, which was equipped with a passenger compartment at its rear, Brixton felt his skin prickle with cold sweat, and he glanced toward Lia Ganz. He could tell she was thinking exactly what he was, a fact that was confirmed when she met his gaze. Their escorts brought them to the passenger compartment extending back from the engine and politely gestured for them to enter. Brixton led the way, toting his DOE-regulation equipment, which, as expected, had not been passed through any electronic or other inspection. It contained a Glock 18 pistol and three spare magazines of ammunition, just like that of Lia and the four Israelis she'd summoned like a conjurer might summon demons. He considered the notion of blame for this attack being laid at the doorstep of Islamic radicals, creating a pretext for a retaliatory reprisal and subsequent response that would result in the suspension of the coming election, along with the Constitution itself, to be as utterly unprecedented as the loss of more than five million lives in an attack orchestrated by the government itself.

Once under way, the train wound its way along a curved, brightly lit tunnel, built to conform to the natural contours of the ground through which it had been erected. The whole process reminded him of those trams that connected terminals at some of the nation's busiest airports. The ride's silent, airless quality brought that experience to mind.

Brixton had turned his gaze on the guards accompanying them. One of them met his stare and in the next moment turned quickly away. There was something unsettling about that brief moment when their eyes had met. As if on cue, he felt Lia Ganz squeeze his knee, and he looked subtly toward her.

Ambush, she mouthed.

Brixton watched her flash unspoken signals to the four Israeli commandos, watched them tense, looking like predators ready to spring. None of them went for the pistols hidden in their equipment housing. Instead, Brixton watched them stretching their grasps toward the knives they'd hidden on their person, formed of a plastic composite invented and manufactured in Israel, undetectable by metal detectors.

That's all it took for these operators, little more than a simple gesture. Four of them and four security guards armed to the teeth, with three minutes to go before the train reached the station.

Brixton watched Lia Ganz twisting her body in preparation to join the action, saw the Israeli commandos lurch into motion.

The train rolled past the start of the loading platform on the lowermost underground level, bright light replacing the darkness of the tunnel to illuminate a cavernous facility that looked like a massive warehouse layered with shiny steel shelving stacked all the way to the high ceiling and a gleaming floor colored the same steel-gray shade. The train doors *whooshed* open, and a dozen guards wearing flak jackets and tactical gear indiscriminately opened fire on the figures inside. Spraying bullets everywhere to leave nothing to chance, then freezing when the targets they'd just pulverized became clear: the security guards who were supposed to deliver their targets to them.

And then those targets burst out, firing.

WASHINGTON, DC

We must listen to our better angels, because the songs they play in heaven carry the words of Stephanie Davenport. She was an angel among us, in that the concerns of others inevitably trumped concern for herself. That's why she fought for the weak and downtrodden, stood up for people no longer able to stand for themselves, especially with enemies so big and powerful they couldn't see the face glaring down at them. I once asked her why that was so important to her, why she'd dedicated her entire life to helping those who couldn't help themselves.

"'It's simple,'" she told me. "'Because I never would have gotten anywhere if people weren't there to help me. And no one ever told me I couldn't achieve my dreams if I worked hard enough. Yet there were so many without dreams, or who'd had their dreams dashed. I want to give their dreams back to them,' she said. 'I want to give them hope.'

"Somebody has to win and somebody has to lose—that's life. But it was Stephanie's mission in life to ensure it was the good that won out."

OAK RIDGE, TENNESSEE

Brixton held back reluctantly, on Lia's instructions, long enough to see the bottom level of an underground facility that looked lifted from a science fiction movie. The walls were finished in dull gray steel, from which extended rows and rows of shelving jam-packed with individual locker-like compartments fit to the precise specifications of steel drums that were virtual twins of the ones Brixton had witnessed being loaded onto the train.

The platform was peppered with space-age-looking loaders to speed the process of off-loading the latest eight-hundred-drum shipment, packed with high explosives, that would be distributed throughout all five underground levels. Robotic forklifts, meanwhile, wheeled and whirred about, prepared to deliver stores of the additional canisters to their appropriate slots. The entire process looked to be automated, the forklifts maneuvering across the floors and crisscrossing each other like far more technologically advanced versions of those automatic vacuums popular in homes these days. Then, at the appointed time, a single trigger would detonate the bulk of the batch en masse, with the remainder igniting moments later to create a chain reaction that would spew a massive amount of radioactive waste into the surrounding air, creating a toxic death cloud certain to spread up the entire East Coast. It was one thing to picture the ramifications of that; it was quite another to view the means by which the destruction would be wrought, up close and personal.

Brixton recorded all that in the moment before he lurched through the open doors with pistol in hand himself, firing at the figures garbed in dark uniforms and landing nary a shot. Figures were running, darting, firing as they went. Bullets whizzed past him in all directions. Their force was outnumbered three to one, but as Brixton watched, Lia Ganz was taking her own steps to remedy that.

Instead of aiming her fire at the enemy gunmen, she spun and dove in the direction of a phalanx of automated loaders positioning themselves to lift more of the shiny steel drums into place in their slots. She aimed at the loaders themselves, the controls made obvious by the rows of colored LED lights, and opened fire, the burst indistinguishable from the others exploding around her. Almost immediately, the machines began spinning wildly, stripped of purpose. Their memories and databases damaged, they charged wildly about, slamming into each other and upending the enemy gunmen who strayed into their paths.

The upper hand lost by the enemy gunmen when they fell for the subterfuge engineered by the Israeli commandos was further squandered, those Israelis' lithe motions timed to coincide with the chaotic paths of the loaders for cover. For his part, Brixton lunged inside one of the forklifts positioned to remove the deadly cargo from the train cars. He twirled the machine around, facing the opposite direction, while raising the fully adjustable pincer apparatus five feet in the air, steadied with the prongs flush with the floor. Then he wheeled into motion, taking out one enemy gunman, then another, and then a third before a barrage of fire forced him to lurch from the cab.

He hit the floor just as the forklift burst into flames, the coarse black smoke providing cover for what he needed to do next.

The explosives! The explosives were everything! Without them, there could be no disaster, no millions of lives lost. Without them, there could be no suspension of the election or of the Constitution itself.

The explosives.

Chancing enemy gunfire determined to thwart his efforts, Brixton ran along the side of the train, feeling bullet after bullet pinging off its steel frame. He was suddenly conscious of Lia Ganz directing her fire to cover him, tying up as many of the enemy as possible, to free him to race toward the train's front engine and spirit the deadly cargo away.

WASHINGTON, DC

The tears brimming in First Lady Merle Talmidge's eyes were genuine, not out of grief for the loss of the vice president but out of wonder and awe for her husband's performance. It was as if time had rewound nine months, back to when the first symptoms of his rapid mental decline had begun.

The first lady listened to her husband's cadence and tone, amazed by the power and forcefulness of his words, the best and strongest of him captured in one last shining moment.

"For in the darkest moments of our greatest despair, a light will shine through the darkness as our guide to avoid the abyss that lies in our path."

CHAPTER 76

OAK RIDGE, TENNESSEE

For Lia Ganz, the battle was the same as all the others she'd lived her life in, and yet different. It was the same in that firefights came with their own set of tangled emotions and twisted thoughts. It had been so long since she'd been engaged in one like this that the shattering gunfire and wild rush of bodies seemed surreal at first, until muscle memory kicked in. Then the battle became the same as all the others, with proximity, positioning, distance, and the merits of the opposition as the driving factors.

Lia quickly fell into the practiced rhythm she had known so well, through so many years, years that had left her a bit slower, a bit more laggard in her response, but still a crack shot, thanks to the regular practice to which she'd committed herself. Her initial foray of fire had achieved the desired effect of turning the automated loaders into battering rams to strip the enemy fighters of the advantage their superior numbers would otherwise have provided. She used those loaders for cover, dipping and dashing behind and then before them to steady her fire.

She'd just emptied her final magazine when one of the loaders rolled over a downed body of one of the fighters, sparing his assault rifle any damage. Lia slid across the floor, taking hold of the weapon, but the strap was still pinned beneath his frame. Unable to easily free it, she fired from the floor, her initial spray taking down more of the men clad in dark tactical gear. She noted that one of her own men was down and another was crawling aside across the slick floor, leaving a bloody trail behind him.

Lia was vaguely aware of Brixton charging away from the scene, toward the head of the train. She realized his intentions in time to train her fire on the gunmen who were concentrating theirs on him, and she breathed easier when he disappeared inside.

Brixton emptied most of his Glock into the doors at the head of the train and crashed through the remnants of the glass. The train's driver rushed toward him, Brixton turning to shoot the man—who kept right on going, with escape instead of heroism on his mind. He'd left the sliding security door leading into the cab open and Brixton surged through, facing a bevy of high-tech controls that reminded him of piloting a simulated flight on the space shuttle.

Foremost among those controls, though, was what looked like a gearshift or throttle, green light glowing over it. Brixton clutched its top knob and eased it forward. The train bucked briefly, then settled into the same easy glide with which it had come into the station. He pushed the knob gradually farther, gathering more speed before he finally shoved the throttle all the way forward.

The train jerked mightily before rapidly picking up speed with a steady electric whir, accompanied by the *whoosh* of the tunnel speeding by around him.

WASHINGTON, DC

In his famed *Lord of the Rings* trilogy, Tolkien wrote, 'The whole thing is quite hopeless, so it's no good worrying about tomorrow. It probably won't come.' But if we are to take one thing, one vital thing, from the life and work of Stephanie Davenport, it's that tomorrow *always* comes. It comes carried on the backs of faithful, selfless public servants like her, willing to put the country's needs above their own, knowing the needs of the many vastly outweigh the demands of a few.

"For if we let ourselves become prisoners of those demands and those few, we will be a lesser people for those we've forgotten and left behind. Stephanie Davenport never forgot or left anyone behind. She believed in the capacity we still hold to do something better and greater, refusing to accept that our best days were behind us and that a single person could do nothing against a system determined to best them. For Stephanie, the individual was always bigger than the system, and only in doing those better and greater things could that system be changed to better us all.

"'A bad system will beat a good person every time,' wrote W. E. Deming. But he was wrong. Because the only person a bad system can beat is someone who's already surrendered to it. Stephanie Davenport was never willing to surrender, because she believed that same good person could change a bad system and not be changed by it. She believed there was always hope, could see it shining through the despair, that no matter how long the odds, good will find a way to triumph over evil."

OAK RIDGE, TENNESSEE

In the end, the enemy force's superior numbers were too much to overcome. Ironic, thought Lia Ganz, that her final battle would be fought not on the hallowed shores of her beloved country but across the world in the morally unhinged United States. Her men were all down, dead or clinging to life, their numbers too small to overcome the onslaught. Just her now, she thought, as she scooped up an assault rifle shed by the dead Israeli who'd just been run over, and then another from the grasp of one of the fake terrorists, now dead too. Kill as many more as she could before she fell was the best she could do now.

In that moment, she had the odd feeling she was back in Caesarea, only on the beach when the drones came spitting fire instead of in the water. Protecting her granddaughter, knowing both of them were going to die.

Her granddaughter . . .

Lia wasn't going to die then and she wasn't going to die now either. Something lifted inside her, a confidence and surety that slowed her heartbeat and turned her breathing normal. One of the out-of-control loaders whirled by and she leaped upon it, feeling what it must be like for a rider atop a bucking bronco.

The loader spun and rolled. She spun and rolled with it, firing with both assault rifles, a crazed circular spray of fire that cut down everything in its path. The world sped past in a dizzying blur around her. She felt separated from herself, separated from the world, one with the machine, until her assault rifles locked up, empty in the same moment, with no targets left to shoot.

Brixton held fast to the control board of the train, which now seemed to tremble underfoot. He could feel the sensation in his gut as it continued to pick up speed through the final stretch of tunnel, the throttle engaged all the way forward.

He knew he was closing fast on the point where they'd originally boarded, nothing but the end of the concrete and steel tunnel beyond. He didn't know if the train had safeguards in place, and he wouldn't have known how to override them anyway. Nor was there any way he could jump free of the train before the looming crash against the concrete-reinforced earthen wall.

Brixton thought of his daughter Janet, thought of joining her in moments, thought he felt her presence standing alongside him, before the controls in the train cab. He was secure in the notion that there would be no dirty bomb, no ten million deaths, no radical change from which the country would never recover. It wasn't everything, but it was enough. He barreled forward instead of slowing, picking up more speed as the earthen wall finished in concrete rose before him like a vast monolith.

At first it seemed, impossibly, that he had driven straight through it, that the train had just receded into the air around him. Then he realized he was airborne, banging up against glass and then steel, a numbness spreading through him in place of the pain he expected to feel.

A blinding flash of light flared, before something jolted his very being and Brixton surrendered to darkness.

WASHINGTON, DC

First Lady Merle Talmidge didn't have to manufacture the tears that spilled freely down her cheeks. Her husband was in the midst of the greatest speech she'd ever heard him give. There had been nary a fumble, twitch, stumble, or misstep; he had risen to the occasion. For this one shining moment in time, President Corbin Talmidge was himself again, the man who had captivated America, with whom the country had fallen in love and who would have soared to a second term virtually uncontested, if his tragic condition hadn't intervened. For that one brief shining moment, he was again every bit the man with whom she had fallen in love.

Then the president's chief of staff sat down next to her, leaned closer, and whispered something in her ear. She listened, trying not to appear distracted or distraught, needing to hear the report from Oak Ridge, Tennessee, again to be certain she'd heard it right. She looked at him for confirmation and watched him nod.

"So, in closing, I ask you to remember Stephanie Davenport not for who she was but what she was. I ask you to spend every day endeavoring to live up to her example and doing something every day to make the world a better place. Go with God, Madam Vice President."

A ripple of applause spread through the cavernous hall of the National Cathedral, growing into a tremor and then an all-out ovation as the audience rose to its collective feet.

Merle Talmidge didn't approach her husband until the president had acknowledged the response humbly, as if unsure who it was for. He finally turned toward her and she hugged him tight, tighter than she ever had before. There was no need for her to tell him that their plans at Y-12 had been thwarted, that no massive explosion was going to begin the process of transforming the United States forever while securing his administration's hold on power, because he wouldn't remember anything she said anyway. He'd played his part beautifully, done everything that had been expected of him today and more, making her prouder of him than she'd ever been.

"How was I?" Corbin Talmidge asked her.

"You were brilliant."

"I was?"

"Never better."

"Then why are you crying? Did something bad happen?"

"Yes," the first lady said, her tears coming from an altogether different place now, "but it doesn't matter."

OAK RIDGE, TENNESSEE

Brixton was climbing through the darkness, climbing toward the light. Just fissures of it, cracks in the obsidian world that had encased him. Was he pulling himself through air, sky, debris?

He didn't know.

It didn't matter.

What mattered was that it was done, over, the horrific plot to murder millions finished.

He was still climbing, hand scraped raw by the steaming rubble in his path. It was like being trapped underwater, with no surface to reach, just a black void.

Then more pinpricks of light formed, widening as they joined up, seeming to burn away the darkness. Brixton pushed, stretched, imagined someone pushing from beneath him as the light grew brighter. He felt bony hands grasp him in a grip of steel, pulling and yanking. And then the light was his, shining through the refuse of the collapsed structure that had once housed the American Museum of Atomic Energy.

The small, bony hands eased him to the side, to someplace reasonably whole and flat, as his eyes cut through the light to gaze at the figure stooped over him.

"Praise God," said Sister Mary Alice Rose.

E P I L O G U E

The meeting was held in the conference room of Mackensie Smith's soon-to-be-shuttered law firm's offices. The table itself was decorated with chips and dings from the many cases that had been discussed and disseminated here, this one being the last.

"I'm going to lay things out as plain as I can and need to, on behalf of my client, Mr. Robert Brixton, who is seated to my right," Mac started. "I fully expect this to be our one and only meeting, because if we need to have another, it will not be in the interests of anyone at this table. It won't just be heads that roll but entire bodies, careers, and reputations, as I will make it my life's mission to bring down anyone who pursues this matter beyond these walls. Let's take things by the numbers, shall we?"

Three days had passed since Brixton, Lia Ganz, and company had thwarted the plot that would have changed America forever at the Y-12 facility in Oak Ridge, Tennessee. No news source, credible or otherwise, was reporting anything about the gunfight that had claimed the lives of four Israeli nationals and briefly hospitalized a fifth. Lia Ganz, it turned out, had been shot twice in the battle, but she had already been released from the hospital and was expected to make a full recovery, the role she had played in saving millions of American lives to remain forever buried beneath the very rubble from which Brixton had climbed.

After being pulled the last stretch into the light by Sister Mary Alice Rose, Brixton was treated for a number of bruises, contusions, and strains, but nothing that promised any lasting damage. He'd refused to speak to anyone in authority while being treated, referring all questions to Mackensie Smith, who again proved himself to be as good a lawyer as he was a friend. Brixton had no idea what had become of the eight hundred drums of high explosives that had never been triggered, though he suspected they had been removed from the train cars in clandestine fashion; a security perimeter had been established almost immediately around the former museum turned way station for deadly nuclear waste.

It was Mac who managed to bring together those gathered around the table. He hadn't told Brixton what he intended to say, and he spoke without benefit of notes. His gaze rotated among the others at the table, none of whom had introduced themselves and none of whom Brixton recognized. His arm was in a sling and he needed a single crutch to maneuver about, all of which went with a face that looked like a boxer's after a fight that had gone a full twelve rounds.

"Let's start with some news you haven't heard yet," Smith continued. "This evening, President Corbin Talmidge is going to step down as president and will be replaced immediately by the Speaker of the House, in the absence of a sitting vice president. Shortly thereafter, the secretaries of the departments some of you work for—State, Defense, and Homeland Security—along with the attorney general, will be stepping down as well and taken into custody by Justice Department officials, along with the first lady herself, to face multiple charges. You should know that some argued for a more discreet resolution, with the perpetrators permitted to walk away, but saner heads prevailed, rightfully convinced that the damage to the country would be far worse for concealing the truth than exposing it."

Smith waited for shocked, befuddled stares to be exchanged. No one said a word, but Brixton thought he detected at least two audible gasps.

"To tell any of the story, we have to tell all of it," Mac offered, by way of explanation, "lest we risk putting the country in front of another set of crosshairs down the line. In other words, an example must be set that this is a country of laws and procedures, both written and otherwise. We don't want to tear this country apart figuratively after so narrowly escaping having that happen literally, but at the same time, we must ensure the truth comes out on our terms instead of its own."

Mackensie Smith waited for any questions or points to be raised, resuming again only when there were none of either.

"As I said earlier, my client, Robert Brixton, is sitting to my right. As you may have noticed from the injuries he suffered, we have Mr. Brixton to thank for being the primary cog in a machine that prevented the worst disaster and crisis this country has ever seen and would likely never have recovered from. We all owe him a great debt of gratitude. He's a security professional by trade who knows how to keep a secret, which he has every intention of doing."

Smith ran his eyes around the table to let that sink in.

"In the event, however, the departments associated with the people seated at this table seek their own retribution or do Mr. Brixton any harm whatsoever, heads will roll, with all of yours being the first. As Mr. Brixton's lawyer, I can tell you I will make sure he's protected by every means available, and woe be the man or woman who decides to challenge that. That's a message you should take back to your respective departments, and it's a discussion you should plan to have as soon as you leave this office, so today may officially mark the end of this most sordid chapter in American history. So," Mackensie Smith finished, leaning forward across the table, "are we clear?"

When no one at the table responded, he resumed.

"You should also know that I've decided to reopen my law offices, with an eye toward hiring attorneys who will serve as relentless watchdogs and advocates against ever coming so close to losing control of our government again. So, to anyone who may be of a mind to repeat the same mistakes made by this lawless administration, or for a single moment believe they are above the law, I have a message for you: don't."

At the meeting's conclusion an hour later, Mackensie Smith escorted the participants through the reception area to the elevators that opened directly into the firm's offices. Brixton trailed him out of both propriety and the reality of his need to move gingerly to avoid tearing any of his stitches or exacerbating his slew of injuries.

As men and women filed into the cab, turning their phones back on, none of them seemed to notice Lia Ganz seated off to the side, a cane resting against the side of one of three metal folding chairs that had replaced the elegant office furniture.

Smith noticed her after the elevator had begun its descent, casting her a smile before turning back to Brixton.

"I've got some things to finish up in my office. Can I trust the two of you alone?"

"Thanks, Mac," Brixton said, hugging him tight with a single arm and balancing the majority of his weight on his good leg.

"Hey, what are friends for?"

Lia Ganz waited for Mackensie Smith to take his leave before she rose and hobbled toward Brixton, relying heavily on her cane. He met her halfway across the floor with his crutch, taking her hand in the one not held in a sling.

"You're looking your age," Brixton commented, wincing from the pain in his chest when he started to laugh.

"From one grandparent to another."

"We need to stop doing that," Brixton told her.

"What?"

"Reminding ourselves of our age."

Lia considered that. "It was Henry Ford who said, 'Anyone who stops learning is old. Anyone who keeps learning stays young.'"

Brixton moved a step closer to her. "And what have we learned from all this?"

"That the world still needs people to show them how it's done."

"Hopefully we'll never have to do that again, Lia."

"I've been doing it all of my life, Robert. Why should tomorrow be any different? If nothing else, it makes us appreciate the truly important things in life. Like grandchildren."

Brixton's mind was clearly elsewhere. "And more."

Flo Combes was redressing a mannequin perched in the window of her Manhattan boutique when a steady *clip-clop* of hooves meeting pavement announced the arrival of a horse-drawn carriage directly in front of her upscale boutique. Carriages had been limited to Central Park for years now, so its presence seemed entirely anomalous—until she spotted Robert Brixton stepping down from the rear, wearing full tails and a top hat, his injured leg still requiring him to move gingerly.

Mystified, Flo met him on the sidewalk, where a crowd had begun to gather even before he dropped slowly to one knee and peeled open a ring box.

"Well?" he posed.

Flo dropped down to the pavement and hugged Brixton tight, like she never intended to let go, until she finally did.

"Can I take that as a yes?" he asked her.

ACKNOWLEDGMENTS

Longtime fans of the thirty-one previous Capital Crimes books, as well as readers familiar with my work, will note that this is my first effort in Margaret Truman's fabulous series and I find myself extremely fortunate to have inherited that mantle from the great Don Bain.

Many thanks to our mutual agent, Bob Diforio, for giving me the opportunity and to Tor/Forge CEO, Tom Doherty, for trusting me with one of mystery-thriller fiction's most iconic brands. Both Tom and Forge's publisher, Linda Quinton, are dear friends who still publish books "the way they should be published," to quote my late agent, the legendary Toni Mendez. The great Bob Gleason is there for me at every turn. Editing may be a lost art, but not here thanks to him, and I think you'll enjoy all of my books, including this one, much more as a result. Thanks also to Robert Davis, Jessica Katz, Anna Merz, and my great copyeditor, Todd Manza. I'm eternally in debt to Russell Trakhtenberg, who designed the cover and created a graphic package that perfectly complements the story I told the best way I know how.

No one is more important to assuring that than Jeff Ayers—there is indeed a reason why I call him "the Wizard," and his sage advice on this book was more vital than ever. Thanks, again, to Jeff's wife, Terry Ayers, for making my scientific jargon sound much better than it did originally and for introducing me to nuclear physicist Jeremiah Ratcliff, who helped me make my impossible conjuring credible.

A final and special acknowledgment to Sister Megan Rice, the inspiration for the Sister Mary Alice Rose character you've just met in these pages. While Sister Mary Alice's exploits were the product of fiction, Sister Megan's exploits on which they are based are anything but that. She should be an inspiration not only for a character in this book but to all of us in terms of stopping at nothing to make a difference in the world. Sister Megan sacrificed her freedom and spent three years of her ninth decade in a federal penitentiary fighting the same fight waged by her fictional counterpart in this book. I find myself in awe of her fortitude and bravery, and no mention or acknowledgment this slight does her justice.

Check back at www.jonlandbooks.com for updates or to drop me a line, and please follow me on Twitter @jondland. And if we haven't met in such pages before, I hope we will again soon, perhaps in one of my Texas Ranger

Caitlin Strong thrillers I hope you'll check out online or at your favorite bookstore.

I remember the end credits of the early James Bond movies starring Sean Connery always included a teaser about the next film coming in the series. Picking up on that tradition, let me say that Robert Brixton will indeed be back in *Murder at the CDC*. So let's make a date, you and I, to meet up the same time next year.